lily@lilywhitebooks.com
http://www.facebook.com/authorlilywhite
www.lilywhitebooks.com

ILLUSIONS OF EVIL

A Dark Erotic Thriller by Lily White

LILY WHITE
BESTSELLING AUTHOR

If you are interested in reading additional books by Lily White or would like to know when new books are being released, Lily White can be found on:
Facebook, Instagram and
Twitter

Join the Mailing List!

If you are interested in receiving email updates regarding additional books by Lily White or would like to know when new books are announced or being released, join the mailing list via this link.
http://eepurl.com/Onoeb

Join the Facebook Fan Group!

If you are interested in receiving exclusive previews for upcoming novels, or to participate in giveaways, join the fan group for Lily White Books.
FAN GROUP LINK

Follow Lily on BookBub!

https://www.bookbub.com/profile/lily-white

OTHER BOOKS BY LILY WHITE

MASTERS SERIES:

Her Master's Courtesan
(Book 1 of the Masters Series)
(Available on Smashwords and lilywhitebooks.com)

Her Master's Teacher
(Book 2 of the Masters Series)

Her Master's Christmas
(Novella in the Masters Series)

Her Master's Redemption
(Book 3 of the Masters Series)

Her Master's Reckoning
(Book 4 of the Masters Series)

STANDALONE NOVELS:

Target This
Hard Roads
Asylum
Wake to Dream
Four Crows
Crazy Madly Deeply
Rules of Engagement
Wishing Well
The Five

Sin & Discipline

ILLUSIONS DUET

Illusions of Evil
(Book 1 of the Illusions Duet)

Fear the Wicked
(Book 2 of the Illusions Duet)

DARK EXCLUSIVE - Available only on LilyWhiteBooks.com:

The Director

Author Note and Disclaimer:

This book is intended for entertainment purposes solely. This novel discusses sensitive subject matters. Readers who sensitive to triggers are advised to proceed with caution.

The opinions given by the characters in this novel do not reflect those of the author. They are fictional characters with minds of their own.

Table of Contents

PROLOGUE

"Present yourself across the altar, child. Remember what I have taught you."

Tears seeped from my clenched eyes.

My pulse beat hard and fast.

A shiver chased up my spine, but I was ready regardless.

He was hovering over my body, preparing.

"Your needs are his. You are the gift that will open the gates..."

Trapping my bottom lip between my teeth, I laid my body down.

"You were born for this. You are pure."

Lying prostrate in a candlelit room, my chest was pressed to the ground, and my arms were spread out as if I were flying.

A blindfold covered my eyes stealing my sight. My forehead was pushed painfully tight to the floor. No person could question my faith. Not Elijah. Not my family. No one.

Only I knew that I wasn't the person I pretended to be.

Large, warm hands explored my ankles and calves. Reaching my knees, they tugged the hem of my dress.

Higher and higher he pulled, until frigid wind and warm breath mingled across my skin.

My shame almost exposed, I dragged in a deep breath, my body prickling from the cold. Anticipation and fear collided as a wicked, ravenous storm inside me.

Small flames illuminated the large space, large black candles that somehow stole the very light they gave off. Wind whispered through the large room despite the closed doors and sealed windows.

A crowd had gathered, a sea of faces that included my parents, my brother, and my friends. They sat as silent witnesses watching me become lost to the moment.

I lay in acceptance of the acts. I spread my body out in devotion.

My faith was the tether keeping me still.

A draft caressed my bottom, the tip of a thumb trailing up the cheeks. I shivered at the soft touch, my teeth clenched painfully tight, a sliver of anxious dread crawling along my spine. This moment would rid the sin from my body. His hand would force it to the surface, would expel it from my skin and destroy it with a blast of God's light.

Elijah's knees lowered to the floor on either side of me. His hands touched me. His fingers gripped my hips, lifting just that part of me that spoke of good girls and poisonous kisses.

2

I struggled to move from the position I'd held for over an hour.

Was it normal not to be scared? I was exposed, helpless, and being touched in a room full of people.

They could see every mark, could plainly witness my temptation.

It wasn't fear that ran through my blood at that moment. It was piety, it was trust, it was need. But *fear* was absent.

What kind of person did that make me?

Elijah's voice was deep and calm – hypnotic in the soft accent to his words. Saturating the air, it vibrated against my skin, reminiscent of a whisper as he instructed the gathering to begin their part.

Words rolled over their lips, notes softly hummed and rattled from their chests.

They watched, they participated, and they stood behind us with blind eyes opened wide.

Lowering his body over mine, Elijah's lips touched the rim of my ear. He spoke to me alone, reminded me what he would do to make me his.

I felt his knees move between mine, but I kept my toes pointed out as my legs were spread apart. My forehead pressed closer to the floor, the pain forcing tears from my eyes.

Desire was my constant companion, the phantom that would drag me away from salvation's gates.

There was no question that I would fail.

I was a sinner and he was pure. He just didn't know it yet.

Hands slid along my thighs, slowly moving over my hips. His fingers entwined with the fabric of my panties, slowly pulling, revealing me to his silver-blue eyes.

I refused the urge to push away, to move, to escape.

I refused the urge to push back, begging for more.

What I did didn't matter. Within seconds, the choice was no longer mine.

The fighting started slowly, growing louder until one familiar voice rose above the others.

There was a struggle above me and I was pulled from the floor. My feet barely held my weight when the blindfold was ripped from my head.

Opening my eyes, I saw my brother's face, his mouth open, anxiety, anger and fear rolling behind his eyes.

Time snapped into place all at once. I heard one word that woke me from my stupor, a word that made me realize what I had to do.

It was my brother's voice that screamed, a voice that I trusted above all else.

One final word breaking my faith.

One warning that rang out above all.

My brother wasn't only fighting, he was screaming for me to run.

1

SEDRA

One Week Earlier...

Now as the church submits to Christ, so also wives should submit to their husbands in everything. - Ephesians 5:24

I remember it clearly. It was a day just like any other, a moment of serenity as I swung lazily on the tire swing hanging from the branch of a stately oak. I flew back and forth, my gaze on the lake next to our home.

The sun beat down warming my tanned skin. The sky's reflection glistened off the small breaking waves. Sunlight scattered a million sparkling diamonds to float serenely over the surface, a sight so beautiful you felt alive for having witnessed it.

I was happy in that moment – ten years old and still believing in the magic that comes with childhood.

It would all end that day.

When I think back, I see my parents moving toward me, and my brother swinging beside me in slow motion. Smiles adorned their faces, their hands joined and my mother's long cream skirt billowing out around her ankles as they walked. The light caught their faces in its grasp, my father's bright blue eyes shining in promise.

Jumping from my swing, I ran to them when I saw them. They were happy. My mom had picked wildflowers and placed them in her hair and mine once I was within arm's reach. They called my brother over to tell us both about how they'd found us a new home – a new life.

A life I never wanted.

Things would be better. We'd have friends. We wouldn't be isolated in the middle of nowhere at the only house we could afford.

My parents wouldn't have to work away from where we lived. There would be other children with whom to live and play. They promised that I'd find comfort - that I'd be safe - in this new life they'd arranged.

I believed them, believed there was a better life awaiting us over several state lines. I was excited about a place more serene than the paradise we'd created in the woods by that beautiful lake.

As I've said: I remember that day. Its details remain frozen exquisitely in my mind, a single solitary moment that became nothing more than a series of still photographs in my head.

But it's not that *particular* day that hurts. It's the reason *why* I remember that day that gnaws at my heart and batters the surfaces of my thoughts.

It was the last day I would have happiness – the last day before I met Elijah.

Eleven years would pass to find me running, the muscles in my legs burning while my body was wrapped in a wet blanket of ice. The chill in the air tore through my clothes, shredding my skin to reach in and wrap possessively around my bones.

Errant branches tugged at my hair, spindly fingers reaching out to stop me in my path. A storm rolled above, its thunder matching the beat of my labored breath.

"The woods will eat you alive, Sedra."

My brother had warned me so many times when we were young. Ever my protector, he grabbed my arm or threw me over his shoulder to drag me back when I wanted to run. I was never allowed to explore beyond the barriers, never allowed to find *my* way.

That all changed when I was challenged to prove my faith.

A starving wolf chasing me down, the wind howled behind me. It carried the whispered words of the man I knew was coming for me.

Elijah was twenty-five years old when I'd first arrived to the compound. He was thirty-six now, and somehow still looked the same.

However, the eleven years I'd spent with the *family* had changed me in significant ways.

Gone were the bouncing, mouse brown pigtails. Noticeably absent was the baby fat I'd always hated around my abdomen. My chest had grown and filled out. My legs had lengthened. And my face had thinned down until I was the spitting image of the young woman my mother had once been.

Each year led me to this moment. Each day filled with the assurance that I had been born for one solitary purpose.

The only problem was that nobody who knew that purpose had bothered to tell me.

Until today.

7

I was Elijah's purity, his redemption and his grace. I was the woman who would help him realize his dream, the one who would walk beside him into the blessed arms of salvation.

Elijah himself had told me this truth about my life. His voice was soft. His authority was unquestioned. And my devotion was strong when he chased me from the compound, forcing me into the woods wearing nothing but the blue, full-length dress all the women wore.

Our leader, Elijah, was a mystery covered by fantastical deceit and beautiful lies. Every night, eloquent poison would drip from his perfect lips, words so mesmerizing that it was easy for every person who came to know him to fall for the man who would eventually guide their lives.

For my parents, devotion to him had been instantaneous.

But for me, it had been a struggle.

Attempting to appear as if I'd believed as strongly as the others, I'd worked the gardens during the day and attended the nightly meetings where Elijah would preach his gospel of *truth* – his calling for a revolution against the evil that plagued our lives. I'd listened, nodding when it was necessary, and I'd repeated back whatever phrases were expected of me.

Even that hadn't been enough for me to truly believe, at least not yet, so I ran.

My dress snagged on bushes as I pushed through the pitch black forest, sounds whispering to me from the distance. The rustling of the wind through the trees overshadowed an owl's haunting song.

I wanted to cry, wanted to curl up into a ball on the ground and cover my face to block out the nightmare of being forced out alone with no instructions but to find my path and discover my destiny.

A crack of lightning flashed above me, the responding thunder shaking the ground at my feet. Rain pounded across the canopy of the trees, the sounds I'd heard previously drowned out as it fell. I was helpless and alone, cold and afraid.

I didn't belong here. I didn't know where I was going, much less what I was supposed to be seeking. The rain poured harder, stealing what little bit of sight I had left. My heart pounded against the walls of my chest as my body shook, partially from cold, but mostly from the abject terror that paralyzed me.

Dropping to the ground, I gathered my dress around me to keep it from becoming soaked in the puddles of water. Leaning my head against a tree, I tilted my face into the deluge of wet misery that was relentless in its force. I could have drowned there and not cared. Cast out and lost, I was a woman left to the elements, her life nothing more than a game to the man who'd ordered her exile.

Tears fell from my eyes and were lost in the rain that drenched my skin. As if beaten by the fists of the people I thought loved me, my heart ached in my chest. My stomach felt like it carried the weight of a hundred heavy stones.

I'd stopped running after only a few hours. The skin on my feet was bruised by the rocks and underbrush I'd pushed through while getting lost in a world I'd never known.

"Have you given up so soon, Sedra? I thought you had more spirit than that."

My body jumped before my brain could place the voice. Opening my eyes, I was lost to the thick curtains of rain pouring down. Shaking from the cold, I was lifted by two large arms, the warmth of a man's chest pressing against my body as I was carried to a place much darker than the woods where I'd become lost.

The pace of his body was slow but steady, a gentle bouncing motion that made me curl into his warmth, lulled into a feeling of safety because I was no longer alone.

The sound of creaking wood shook me from my stupor, my eyes opening once more to see the interior of a small wooden shed. Candlelight flickered softly inside. I shivered when the door closed behind us, the wind reaching out one last time, angry that I'd been pulled from its frigid grasp.

Although my vision was still blurry from the water that dripped from my lashes, I could make out the dancing flames of a small fire. Beside the fire was a platform covered in fur blankets that stood two feet off the ground.

"I'm going to put you on your feet now. Hold on to my shoulders in case you lose your balance."

A dark whisper, his soft voice brushed across my senses. I shivered more, but not from the cold. Only Elijah had this effect on me. Simultaneously desirous and fearful, I always froze in front of him, completely losing my ability to function on any normal level.

His arm pulled out from beneath my legs, his other wrapped firmly around my body as he lowered me to my feet. Gripping my fingers over his shoulders, I wobbled on shaky knees, my body leaning forward like a moth drawn to his scorching flame.

Releasing me, he steadied me by placing his hands on my shoulders. The silence was deafening, but he broke it with a melodic voice, a deep baritone rumble that could both frighten and soothe me.

"You're soaked to the bone, beautiful girl. We need to remove your dress."

His hands released my shoulders and my knees buckled beneath me. Elijah caught me quickly, laughing softly before picking me up and carrying me to a wall.

Pressing me against the surface, his hips touched mine. Tremors ran over my bones and skin. My eyelids fluttered and my breath was stolen to feel him so hard where he touched me.

I was scared, so scared that I didn't know what was worse: the storm that awaited me in the pitch black woods, or the dangerous man who now caged me against a thin, wooden barrier.

Securing me with his massive frame, his fingers slowly moved over the button at the top of my dress, his knuckle brushing against my chin as he released the tiny bit of plastic from the eyelet. Fear knocked my teeth together. He didn't stop or slow down, didn't seem to care that I wouldn't look at him as he undressed me. My voice was stolen with every new button released.

"I'm not going to hurt you, Sedra."

Elijah stopped peeling the wet cotton dress from my body, leaving the sides pulled apart just enough that only the top swell of my breasts were exposed. Running his finger along my jaw, he brought his mouth to my ear, allowing the heat of his breath to roll over my cold skin. On a deep whisper, he confessed, "I'm going to transform you."

My knees buckled again. He caught me at the hips, steadying me before returning his attention to my dress. I opened my mouth to object, but my anxious breath left me on a rush of exhaled air with no sound. Shaking my head, I silently pled with him to stop. Attempting to speak again, I finally reclaimed my voice.

"Elijah, please stop. You can't see me without clothes. It's wrong. You've always told me it's wrong."

Broken and high-pitched, my words flew from my lips, barely loud enough to break the heavy blanket of silence in the room. He laughed in response. It was a sound so deep that it vibrated inside me, grabbing hold of me in places that were forbidden for me to explore.

A woman was to be purity and light, an object to be treasured and adored by the man who called himself her husband. It would only taint my soul to allow Elijah to see me without clothes.

"You're wet, Sedra. You'll get sick if you don't get warm. I'm not undressing you out of lust. I'm only looking after your health. There are circumstances that allow for *drastic* measures. There is no other person around who can help you."

I shook my head again, averting my eyes from his probing silver-blue gaze. His eyes were luminous tonight. Even in the flickering shadow of the candles, they glowed. I couldn't look at him. Couldn't stand to look at his face without sinning within my thoughts. He was the type of man that it hurt to look at, the kind whose smile could cause you to melt inside.

"We can walk back, pick up clothes from the compound -" I begged.

His finger pressed against my lips. I shivered at the warmth of his skin.

"You're freezing. If we go back out, it'll only make you worse."

He smiled, his voice deepening impossibly lower until I could feel his words caress my skin. "We have work to do tonight. You have something I want, something I need. You are going to be mine, Sedra. That is why you are here. Between us, and before God, we will be one. But, you had to fall so I would know you'd walk blindly into any situation I demanded. You are the key."

"No." I was shocked that I'd found the strength to interrupt him. "You're soaked as well. You can't stay in those clothes and we can't -"

Silenced again by his hand, he pressed into me, the weight of his body holding me in place while his hand held back the words I wished to speak.

"Stop talking. After tonight, it won't matter. You're here for a purpose. There is a destiny to which you are tied, a reason for your existence. Do you not believe strong enough?"

I blinked long and hard, finally allowing myself to stare up into his face with shock spread across my own. "I don't understand."

He laughed, his eyes flickering in the candlelight. "I never expected you to understand. It's not for you to understand. Hence the reason I exist. I need to right the wrong in this world. I need to reveal truth. With you, I can walk that path. You are the only woman who can walk me down that path. You can be pure, untouched in both body and mind. Don't you want to help me?"

I looked up into his blue eyes, the silver practically glowing in the candlelight. His gaze was always discerning, always able to see through me straight down to those parts I preferred stay hidden. But beyond that, he was beautiful.

13

Flawless golden skin, shadowed with stubble. Wavy, dark brown hair framed his face and square jaw. He had a straight nose, except for the crick in the middle that was his only imperfection. Full lips that when opened released a low, throaty tone, a voice that was both bold enough to freeze you in place, and soft enough to force you to tremble.

Elijah was everything a good man should be, and me? I was a shadow that would only prohibit his growth.

Questions screamed in my head, doubts that I would never admit to having. He led us. He provided for us. He walked us down a path that would grant us entry into paradise. How could I not believe in him when all he'd done is guide me? No matter how much I fought, the doubts were what haunted my thoughts. And, to him, doubt was the ultimate sin. Wasn't that what Thomas did? At least until he was shown the truth.

"I'm going to undress you, Sedra. It's not wrong when God himself has created us for each other."

Uncrossing my arms from my chest, I stared at him, desperate to find the faith I knew I should have. It felt wrong to pretend. It felt like a lie.

He made quick work of the remaining buttons to slowly pull the sodden material from my skin. My breasts felt tight when they were exposed to the air. I could feel his stare, his gaze that was heat and longing caressing my skin. It was unsettling to know that he looked at my chest now bared to him for the first time.

When his fingers slipped beneath the sides of my panties, I pulled away, my back slamming against the wall and blocking my escape. He stilled for a moment, waiting for me to resign to him once more. After I'd done so, he pulled the panties down my legs, releasing them to allow the cotton to fall across my feet.

"Kick them off."

Lifting a shaky foot, I followed his instruction, my body visibly trembling to be exposed. He moved away from me, the cold air rushing between our bodies. My skin was tight across my bones, my heart hammering so violently I feared it would tear through my chest.

I didn't know what I expected to happen next. I was in a state of opposites; juxtaposed between a foreign desire for him to touch me, and a fear so powerful it made me want to run away.

In retrospect, the cold, black rain seemed far less dangerous than the man standing in front of me.

"Lie down on the platform in front of the fire. Wrap yourself in the blankets to get warm."

Demanding was the only appropriate term for his tone of voice. There were no options left open to me but to dutifully obey.

Elijah didn't glance down at my naked body, but instead, he held my eyes transfixed in his gaze. It wasn't until he took another step away from me that I found the ability to do as he'd ordered.

My bare feet padded over the rough wood floors until I reached the platform where I could lie down. Pulling the blankets over my body, I refused to look up while he undressed. A few silent seconds ticked by before I recognized the sound of his wet shirt dropping to the floor, the thick buckle of his belt being unfastened, that same buckle hitting the floor where I'd just walked.

Heart knocking against my ribs, my blood was a roar of thunder rushing through my skull.

15

"Take the position of faith, Sedra. You need to prove your loyalty."

Bringing my forehead down to the platform on which I lay, I crawled out from beneath the blanket, spread my hands out to my sides, and brought my outstretched feet together behind me to assume the position I'd been taught since my arrival to the compound.

I was a cross. The symbol of my faith. The example of God's power on Earth.

The questions wouldn't stop whispering. What would he do next? Would he steal my purity? Would I be cast out when the others discovered what I'd allowed him to do?

With my face pressed to the platform, I couldn't see him as he moved to kneel by my right side. His large hand wrapped around my wrist, locking a soft restraint around it. I attempted to pull away, but he gripped harder, admonishing me with his words.

"I'm going to secure you, Sedra. It's for your own good."

I stilled, tears escaping my eyes as he continued trapping me in place. When he'd bound the first wrist, he moved to the left to bind the other.

My feet were next – bound together before being secured to the platform. I couldn't move as the room fell into silence.

"You're here to be taught how to serve me. Seven days that we'll use to explore each other before we make our vows before the family. Tonight we will be united before God, and you'll have seven days of training so that you'll understand what you must do."

He walked to stand at my head, his hand lightly touching my hair.

"Be honest with me, even if you think it is wrong. If your thoughts are impure, warn me what is running through your thoughts. The rite cannot be completed if I don't know what's in your heart."

Nodding, I silently agreed to what he'd asked.

"Do you want me to touch you?"

Broken apart by my tears, I forced an answer from my lips. "Yes."

Shame enveloped me to admit it. My thoughts were evil and unclean.

I heard him breath out a heavy sigh before he removed his hand from my head.

"Will you be my wife, Sedra? Will you follow me and obey me if I grant that to you?"

I was flooded with confusion so thick I could barely think around it. Why would he want me? I'd just admitted that I wasn't without sinful thoughts.

"I'm not worthy of you, Elijah. I'm not without evil."

I felt the blanket being pulled away from my skin, his hands running down my spine. He reached my lower back, and God help me, my body arched as much as it could, my bottom pushing up into the air, instinctively begging for him to move lower.

I cried harder knowing that a pure woman would never react in such a way. Evil had taken hold of me. I deserved the exile and my shame left me drowning in the pleasure given by his touch.

"Only God can determine your worth, child. But only you can answer my question."

No emotion, just darkness. He wasn't angry, despite what I'd said.

His hand swept lower until his finger pressed into the slick skin between my legs. A moan escaped my lips, my body trembling beneath the soft touch.

I was a slut – a whore – a woman who couldn't control herself when it came to the carnal pleasure we were always taught to avoid. His touch was revealing my deepest sin. He'd pulled my hidden thoughts from me with nothing more than the brush of his skin.

I realized then just how powerful our leader was.

When his finger pressed deeper, just barely penetrating my body, I cried out, feeling an odd dampness between my legs.

He pulled away almost immediately, running his hand along my back before placing it on my head.

"No, my beauty. Your reaction is what is needed. It's the sign I needed. We are meant to be together. No matter what, your body will only react like this to me." He paused, his words lingering on my skin. "I can't give you what you need until we are married. For that, I will cleanse you of all the evil and impure thoughts you've had before this moment."

I didn't respond. I was too lost in my shame – my pain.

"Are you willing, Sedra? Answer me and I will help you."

He removed his hand and I groaned at the loss of his touch.

Seconds ticked by before I found the strength to respond. If this was what he wanted, if he was sure he could make me worthy, I would give him anything he asked.

"Confess, beautiful. Tell me the evil that lurks in your thoughts."

Shaking my head, I wanted to refuse. They were my secrets. Like phantoms, they crept inside my head, stealing away the serenity of a life lived in purity and grace.

"Confess. Exorcise the evil that resides within you by spilling it from your lips. Purify yourself."

My body jumped in reaction to the strength of his voice. I could hear his steps as he moved around the platform, my naked flesh left exposed for his eyes. I didn't want to speak, didn't want to admit the desires I'd attempted to hide every day of my life.

He knelt down beside me, placing his hands on my shoulders, the heat burning into my skin. His mouth was to my ear again and I pushed my forehead against the wood of the platform until it hurt. I didn't want to say the words. I didn't want him to know.

"Confess." A whisper that spread across my nerves, my skin prickling in response to the soft quality of his voice.

After several failed attempts, after forcing my breath back into my lungs, I spoke.

"I've had impure thoughts, dark thoughts, thoughts about you that no woman should have. I have images in my head that no person should see. Even now, I want to look at you. I crave you, desire you, want you in ways that would hurt you...that would *tarnish* you."

He breathed out heavily, the force of the air rustling the hair on my head. His hands slid down my back and his chest pressed against my head. I didn't move – couldn't move – too frightened about what he would do now that he knew how I felt.

"Would you like to know a man's touch?"

"You're testing me now, Elijah. I know you're trying to tempt me. I won't fall ... I won't."

Tears streamed again as I pled with him to believe me, as I pled with myself to believe that I wouldn't succumb.

I felt him touch me intimately, the breath I'd been holding forced from my lungs.

"You are mistaken, sweet girl." He pulled away, pushing himself off me and kneeling down in front of me.

"Do you accept purification, Sedra? Will you believe me over the demons that have spread doubt in your head?"

Swallowing hard, I shed a few more tears before responding. I had to trust him, there was no other choice. I had to believe that he knew what was best. He wouldn't lead if he didn't know.

Elijah remained silent while I convinced myself of my own faith.

With fear gripping at my vocal chords, I managed to squeak out an answer. "Yes."

The tip of his finger trailed down my cheek, his touch the sign of approval that I needed. I would trust him, would believe that I could help him achieve whatever God had planned.

I believed, or at least I told myself I did.

Whispering so that his voice barely brushed across my senses, he professed, "With purification comes pain. And with pain, comes rebirth. Are you ready?"

"N-no."

He laughed. "You never lie, do you?"

"No."

Standing, he commented, "Which is why you are the one."

Seconds passed and I heard metal scrape across stone. I didn't look up, couldn't see what it was that he planned to do. The silence crushed me and the muscles tightened over my bones. When he spoke again, I jumped.

"I'm going to mark you. Once you bear that mark, you will no longer be Sedra. You will be pure, reborn in a body ready to serve me." Metal scraped again and I heard him move to stand behind me.

"Welcome to the world, my beautiful Eve."

I blinked at the odd name just as searing hot metal pressed into my shoulder, the smell of my burning skin choking me when I opened my mouth to scream.

2

EVE

Present...

Put your finger here; see my hands. Reach out your hand and put it into my side. Stop doubting and believe. – John 20:27

It was like deja-vu. Running through the gripping branches of the trees, a moonlit night that disguised the path. I ran barefoot through the underbrush, slicing and scratching my skin on the various roots and rocks that littered the ground.

The pitch black darkness of night, the sounds of the animals, the pain that came with each step I took forward, it was all the same; except this time, I wasn't alone and cast out into the wilderness with only my wits to survive.

This time, I was being followed.

Three men trailed me from what I could hear. At their heels were the dogs kept on the compound that were never allowed to socialize with the community members. We were told that they were kept separate in order to prevent disruption of their training to defend the property. I was now learning they were also kept to chase down errant members of the compound who tried to escape.

Fear shot through me, a wicked electric burst as my pulse pounded in time with my feet. I couldn't stop, couldn't look back. I was terrified of falling, of feeling the angry hands of the men who chased me touching my body, of the sharp teeth of the dogs ripping at my skin.

For once, I found myself thankful for the dark night.

The voices would dissipate every so often and I'd slow down, but like a specter that couldn't be seen, they'd reappear to my right or left, causing me to change course, leading me in directions I hadn't explored before.

Crawl toward me, Eve. Show me how you want me. Reveal the sinner inside you...

Elijah's voice whispered in my mind, the memories of my training in that small, wooden shed. Until that place, those nights, I'd never experienced fear mixed with seduction – terror weaved through need.

Good girl. Always such a devout believer...

My lungs were on fire. I could barely draw in a breath, but that's the thing with running for your life: despite your muscles screaming to slow down, despite the shock to your bones from your heavy steps – you always keep going.

Adrenaline pushed my body, panic made it possible.

I was being herded toward a particular place. I wondered if there were other buildings in these woods, places where they would trap me so that whatever punishment I deserved could be carried out without the others hearing my screams.

23

Since becoming Eve, I'd learned what Elijah was capable of. I'd been dragged into the center of his world, been made witness to the horrifying and eye-opening reality of the compound. I understood it was necessary. I knew that evil could still exist even within the safety of the gates. Elijah warned me, he told me how demons would attempt to corrupt us.

It was his job to seek them out, to convert them or destroy them if they were too deep in shadow to see the light.

God was in everything Elijah did. I'd witnessed the might of his hand when he condemned new members who would not conform and accept the grace that had been offered to them. The devil lived in every single one of us and it was Elijah's job to cast him out.

If it couldn't be done, if a person was so lost to the evil that his soul couldn't be saved, he was killed.

Belief was not an option, but a requirement. We were safe if we had faith, but only if we refused to live among the unfaithful.

Within an hour, exhaustion weighed me down. Not hearing the men or dogs any longer, I allowed myself to stop. My tears had ceased pouring from my eyes. My arms and legs shook with the exertion of what I'd just done.

Why had Joshua stopped the ceremony? Why had my brother stepped into the middle of a holy rite, one that would elevate me to the greatness Elijah knew I possessed? Didn't Joshua know I was meant for God's glory? Didn't he know I was drowning in sin?

I don't know why I ran and I'm not sure that I'll ever know. But hearing Joshua's voice tell me to go had awakened me, made me remember the years that my brother had protected me, when he'd been the safety blanket I could hide beneath. He'd always been my escape from the violence that was sometimes necessary in our lives.

Sitting down by a large tree, my thoughts shifted to my parents. They were madly in love with each other, two free spirits that always chose to shun society. They were peaceful and joyous in their lives together, but also fearful of the world.

Even before the compound, we lived separate from the various towns where we'd moved each year. My parents wouldn't stay in one place for long.

We were always running, always scared, always...

When I was seven, they found a house in the country beside a beautiful lake. I was given three good years in a place I could call home. I thought it was the end of running, the end of constantly moving to a new place.

It wasn't.

Now, because of them, I was trapped in a world I never wanted to know.

I was alone. Frightened. Lost.

So very lost.

I had to return to the compound.

There was no life without Elijah. Especially now. Especially after everything he'd taught me about myself.

My demons were still inside me.

A week wasn't enough time to exorcise them fully.

There was only sin and pain, evil and ugliness. There were monsters that would seek me out and bad men who would steal the purity that Elijah had given me with his mark. Maybe even now, I was tainted. My faith had not been strong enough. I'd not believed hard enough when I'd listened to my brother.

25

I'd failed and I feared I would be forever lost for that failure.

The pressure in my chest was unbearable. My heart struggled to beat, its rhythm heavy with grief and shame.

Burning tears fell down my cheeks as I made the decision to return. I would face punishment. I deserved it.

I *craved* it.

Pushing up from the ground, my foot stumbled on the hem of my dress. I launched forward, my head colliding with a rock and my knee scraping against the broken branches on the ground. But I didn't feel the pain of that fall, didn't cry when my skin split and blood spilled. The only pain I felt in that moment was heartache mixed with the fervent hope that Elijah would forgive me for having run.

Standing again, I spun in circles, not sure which way I'd come from or which way I should go. Like a thick curtain, the night concealed the forest around me, the moonlight above unable to penetrate the canopy of trees.

I walked forward, unsure if it was the right way. I placed my faith in God at that moment, my faith that forgiveness could exist for a wayward soul.

Praying that mercy would meet me when I returned, I knew that pain would be required to cleanse me of my indiscretion.

Pain.

That beautiful, decadent salt only he could wipe into my wounds.

I'd become addicted to it.

Taking careful steps, my feet navigated an unfriendly landscape. My skin was torn by rocks, my muscles bruised, but I kept going.

An hour could have passed, but instead of finding the chain link fence, the barbed wire and the gates, I found a small road.

Unpaved and only wide enough for one car, I didn't recognize it. Stepping out of the shadows, my eyes were met with the brilliance of moonlight and thousands of stars scattered haphazardly across the sky. I'd never seen so many stars before and I was saddened to think that the floodlights kept on our property drowned out the sheer beauty of God's world.

We needed the light to remain safe from the evil that lingered in the shadows. I understood that need. But, in that moment it occurred to me that evil was separating us from the divinity with which we should always be united.

It was the sign I needed.

Perhaps God had led me to a simpler path for my return.

"Okay, Father, lead me." I prayed into the cool night air, going with my gut as I listened, turning my body right towards what I believed would be home.

Another hour passed as I followed that lonely road. My mouth was bone dry with thirst, my dress was stained and torn, my hair was matted, but I kept going.

When the sun began to peek over the horizon, morning light crept along the ground like fog.

In the distance, something flashed and I turned thinking that, maybe, I'd found my way. Hope flooded my system and gave me the strength to push forward down a dirt driveway.

The trees cleared, opening to a large lot. In its center stood a building that was much smaller than the compound. Lights illuminated the area that surrounded it, leaving the yard dark.

It wasn't home.

The bit of strength I'd found dissolved into the ground as I sank to my knees.

I held the position, lost within a sticky soup of heartache and loss to see I'd been led astray once again.

God had abandoned me.

As the door to that building opened, I closed my eyes and let go, finally delivering myself to the darkness I knew I deserved.

3

JACOB

But you, man of God, flee from all this, and pursue righteousness, godliness, faith, love, endurance and gentleness. 1 Timothy 6:11

The road that led me to the priesthood was not straight and narrow. Rather, it was a long, winding road, one that was as convoluted as it was simple, as arrogant as it was disastrous.

Every day I dress in a black shirt with a crisp, white clerical collar snapped in place. Black slacks cover my legs and black work boots protect my feet. But even disguised in the uniform of a devout man, I carry darkness. I drown daily in the guilt of my crimes.

Seen as chaste, I am corrupted. Believed without sin, I bear the worst sins of all. Yet, I am the shepherd that leads his flock - the spectacle of God's power and love. A rural Catholic priest who guides the fallen.

My parish isn't the kind you'd find in large tourist destinations and bustling cities. Nestled in the heart of rural country, my church is tucked away in the slow moving lifestyle of the Appalachian mountains. There are no magnificent spires to glorify God's grace, no flying buttresses that signify the beauty of our devout faith. It is a simple building in a simple town with stained glass windows that filter God's light in jewel toned colors onto the rows of pews and the altar behind which I deliver a message I haven't always believed.

Although, I was born to a wealthy family in the city, raised with my brother in the strict arms of the Catholic church, I found myself in a place that was far off from the life I'd once lived, isolated enough that I believed I could escape my demons.

Scars adorn my soul and shame is woven into my very existence. I'd once rejected God and the church right along with him. But like most foolish heroes you read about in tragedies and similar stories of warning, my belief that I could turn my back on something as great as our Savior only led to my eventual downfall.

Every parishioner who attends my church believes I am a godly man. Little do they know that I am the last person they should emulate or admire.

I am no stranger to sin, just as I am no stranger to salvation. And now, donning the uniform of a holy man, I have taken the tragedy of my life and used it to give back to the only faith that could save me from the pitfalls and potholes of the road that led me to this particular morning.

Routine woke me, just like every day, in my small, humble room in the rectory near the church. I showered and dressed, and I knelt down before the crucifix hanging in plain view to whisper my prayers to the Almighty.

I prayed for good weather for the farmers and laborers that worked in the county. I prayed for enough food, shelter and clean water for my parishioners and their families. I prayed that the day would pass as peacefully as it began, that it would provide me the time and clarity of mind to tend to the duties I carried as the leader of my congregation.

As it turned out, the last prayer had been one too many.

While pouring a cup of coffee in the large kitchen that stood at the front of the church nearest my office, I caught sight of an image that was as confusing as it was unexpected, as unbelievable as it was harrowing.

A young woman was kneeling outside in the grass blanketing the front courtyard. Confused, hurt, and plainly injured, her long dress was a deep navy blue. Her dark mahogany hair, although frayed and knotted at her head, was long.

I didn't have my glasses and I couldn't make out her features, but the blood dripping from her head, the way her body wobbled over the sodden ground, made it clear she was in distress.

Like an apparition, the morning light caused her to flicker in an out of focus. I was surprised I'd noticed her through the small kitchen window. It was a quick glance, something out of the corner of my eye, but I caught her movement as she knelt down.

Running through the hall, I threw open the front door to approach the young woman. She collapsed, her frail body crumpling, her head hitting painfully against the ground because she'd failed to brace herself. My hands were on her shoulders as soon as I was within arm's reach.

"Miss?"

Patting her cheek, I attempted to wake her. There was no response.

"Father Hayle?"

One of the sisters ran up behind me, probably having noticed the way I launched myself through the interior of the church to get outside. She was immediately by my side and tending to the woman. I stepped back, lingering in close vicinity in case there was anything I could do.

"Call an ambulance, Father. This woman is alive, but she's not responsive."

Reaching down, I touched her skin and found it was cold. "Let's carry her inside first. She's already freezing and the damp weather will only make her worse."

Picking her up took little strength. Her body couldn't have weighed more than a hundred pounds. Even as dead weight, I had no difficulty carrying her inside and laying her down on a couch in the front narthex.

Sister Joyce knelt to continue tending to the woman, however as I started to pull away, the woman opened her eyes. They widened almost instantly, a dazed smile crawling across her features.

"Elijah?"

A memory tugged at my thoughts, a shadow I'd kept hidden for some time. Her eyes were the same color as...

No. I must not think of such things.

The name the woman used startled me, but I shook it off, not recognizing it. Unsure why she'd referred to me in such a way, I pulled back.

"Elijah?" she said again, her voice growing with strength and panic. "I'm sorry. Please don't leave."

Her movements became frantic. Reaching for me, tears burst from her frightened eyes. Before I could step back, she grabbed me, burying her face into my shirt, sobbing as she begged me not to leave.

I exchanged a glance with Sister Joyce before finally addressing the woman.

"Miss, my name is not Elijah. I'm afraid you have me confused with another person. My name is Father Hayle. I found you in the yard in front of my church. Are you hurt? Do you need us to call an ambulance?"

Her eyes peered up at me, stained red by her tears. She had the face of an angel – the face of a memory I was fighting to forget.

"Please," she begged, "I know I failed. I know I didn't trust God or you by running. I know I deserve to be punished, but please don't abandon me. I'll do whatever you want. I'll repent, but I can't be thrown out. I was confused. Please…"

Her voice trailed off into her tears. This girl was deeply scarred. Looking up, I motioned Sister Joyce towards the kitchen and kept my voice at a whisper.

"Do me a favor, please. Grab a glass of water and some towels."

She nodded, turning to do as I'd asked.

As an afterthought, I called out. "Also, we'll need a first aid kit."

Kneeling on the ground, I stared at the woman's face.

"What is your name, child?"

Shaking her head, she sniffled before answering, "Sedra."

"Sedra." I repeated.

She shook her head again. "No. Oh my God, no." Her tears fell harder. "My name is Eve. Please tell me my name is still Eve."

Sister Joyce returned, silently handing me the glass and towels. Unfolding one, I wrapped it around the woman's shoulders.

"Sedra..."

"No! Please let me be Eve. I want to be Eve. Please, don't leave me." Shrill and hoarse, she cried, fear shredding her words.

Inhaling deeply, I looked up to see Sister Joyce's concerned expression. "Sister, please go have a room prepared. I don't think she needs an ambulance, but she definitely needs a place where she can rest and have her wounds tended."

Placing my hands on the young woman's shoulders, I said, "I'm not leaving, but you need to rest."

Sister Joyce hadn't yet walked away and I cast her a questioning look. Her eyes widened in horror at the woman's condition, but eventually she turned to do as I'd asked.

Whispering, I continued, "God is not mad at you, Eve. You've done nothing wrong. I'm having a room prepared for you. You can stay here until you're well. When is the last time you slept?"

"The night before ... the night before our wedding. I slept the night before our wedding."

Wedding? Finally, she gave me something I could use to locate her family.

"Do you have a husband, Miss? Is there somebody I can call?"

"You are my husband, Elijah. Why are you asking me these questions?" she cried.

34

She was exhausted to the point of confusion. "Yes, of course. Come with me. You need to sleep."

Lifting the woman by her arms, I held her weight to my side, steadying her so that I could escort her to a small bedroom kept for parishioners who fell ill during Mass. We passed through the open doorway as Sister Joyce held up a blanket for me to cover the woman once she was lying on the bed.

The woman grabbed my hand before I could leave.

"Please stay with me until I fall asleep."

Not knowing who the poor woman was, I took pity on her and nodded my head.

Searching the room, I spotted a chair in the right corner. "Sister, could you please hand me that chair? I'm going to stay as she's asked, tend her wounds and pray over her until she's sleeping."

"Of course, Father. Can I assist in any other way?" Grabbing the chair, she quickly crossed the space to place it by the bed.

"No. I'll call for you if I require anything further."

Silently, she exited the room.

Using clean towels and antiseptic from the first aid kit, I cleaned the blood from her head, and tended the cuts on her arms. There was no swelling or other sign of injury beyond superficial scrapes.

Once she was bandaged, I grabbed a rosary and Bible from the side table. Leaning forward in my chair, I bowed my head and prayed over the confused and frightened young woman.

She shivered beneath the blanket each time I lifted my eyes to look at her. Lying still, her breathing evened out.

"Miss? Are you still awake?"

There was no response.

I didn't leave immediately, instead choosing to look at the woman who'd crumpled over herself in the yard. She had thick mahogany hair, the deep brown woven through with strands of red. Even matted and dirty, it was beautiful. Images played in my head. Nightmares reminding me of a mistake for which I would never be granted forgiveness.

Jacob...

The voice dragged me to the past.

Blinking away the images – the voice that called to me still - I focused on the face in front of me.

Sedra or Eve - I wasn't sure of her true name - appeared angelic. Her round cheeks were still full with youth, but her body was another story entirely. The bones of her arms and legs were clearly visible and the pallor to her skin spoke of dehydration or malnutrition.

She stirred, causing me to jump in my seat. I'd been studying her too closely and after watching her a second longer to ensure she was asleep, I left the room as quietly as possible, shutting the door but not so much that it latched.

Sister Joyce waited at the end of the hall, her hands wringing nervously over themselves. "Is that poor woman going to be okay? Maybe we should call an ambulance."

I considered her suggestion, wanting nothing more than to alleviate myself of the puzzle the woman presented. However, she had no severe injuries other than obvious emotional trauma. I thought that, perhaps, sleep would cure that particular ailment.

"I'd hate to incur the cost of medical treatment if it's not required. The people in this area are not in the best of financial circumstances. Maybe it will be best to wait and see if she is calm and better able to tell us her name and where she lives when she wakes. We could then contact her relatives and let them to make the decision as to whether she should seek treatment."

"That's wise, Father."

Friendly eyes, the color of leaded glass stared out from Sister Joyce's aged face. Besides the faint pink on her cheeks and the paleness of her skin that shone out against the black of her habit, I didn't know much else about what she looked like. I didn't care much either, but every so often the passing curiosity crossed my thoughts.

Walking back into the kitchen I poured the cup of coffee I'd been after earlier when I'd first spotted Eve ... or Sedra. My thoughts returned to everything she'd said to me, but even as I digested it, I still couldn't wrap my mind around it. She was scared, that much was obvious, but why did she insist I was someone else?

There was only one possibility for such confusion, a possibility that was an *impossibility* as well.

I'd been charged to this parish for twelve years now, but my life hadn't always been in the Church. It started there with my father who was a devout Catholic. My brother, Jericho, and I were both raised with strict rules regarding our lives and beliefs. Every Sunday we were at Mass, but the other six days of the week also revolved around our faith. It was in everything we did: our schooling, our entertainment, our meals.

However, my devotion to the faith was never deep-seated or pure. I preferred science to religion, tangible properties that I could test and weigh, to the things I had to blindly accept were true.

By the time I graduated high school, I'd left the faith entirely, my family as well. Choosing to go away for college, I studied psychology and pre-medicine in hopes of becoming a psychiatrist. The human mind always fascinated me, and maybe, in truth, it was as a result of my father and brother's devout faith.

I never made it back home to my father and brother, but I learned that Jericho had left only a few years after me. He'd fallen out of favor with the Church and had disappeared when my father chose his faith over his own son.

If Eve had known my brother, Jericho, that would be the only way she could confuse me with someone else so adamantly. However, it was impossible. The chances of Jericho ending up in the same remote part of the Appalachian mountains as me were slim to none.

Maybe she was drugged, whether administered herself or by another person, she could have been hallucinating. Except for a racing heart rate due to her distress, her other vitals appeared fine. Her eyes dilated with light, she was breathing regularly by the time she fell to sleep. Her skin had warmed almost immediately after she'd been brought inside.

Once my coffee was poured and I pulled myself from my thoughts, I walked the length of the modest church to my office.

A simple room, there was nothing more than a wood desk, a chair and the standard crucifix and degrees on my wall. I'd graduated college with my Bachelor's Degree in psychology, but attended seminary school immediately after. For all intents and purposes, I was a bona fide priest, trained and ordained in my calling and devotion to God.

However, the weight of the true reason I was here always sat heavy on my shoulders, a burden and mistake I wore like a second skin.

I fell into work heavily, nothing occurring that dragged me from the depths of my thoughts. I had several requests for financial assistance that I had to negotiate with the Diocese. I served a poor area in the Appalachians, most people having low to moderate incomes as a result of chain grocery stores and malls that eventually led to the loss of the mom and pop shops that most of the residents owned.

Small farms and pastures were being foreclosed on daily, and big industry removed the means of these people to survive. Most only had a high school education, if that, and their struggles were my biggest concern.

Just as I picked up the phone to call a larger parish regarding the needs of mine, Sister Joyce stepped into my office.

"Father Hayle, I apologize for disrupting you, but the young lady has woken and I've been unable to calm her."

Looking up, I noticed the worried expression on her face. "How long has she been awake?" Glancing toward the clock, I realized that I'd been lost in my work for several hours.

"She woke only a few moments ago. She has been demanding to see you, however..."

She paused and I circled my hand in the air to hurry her along.

"She keeps referring to you as Elijah, Father. She's adamant that she knows who you are."

4

EVE

A wife of noble character is her husband's crown, but a disgraceful wife is like decay in his bones. Proverbs 12:4

Surprised to wake in an unfamiliar room, I must have cried out without realizing it. Almost as soon as I opened my eyes, a nervous woman entered. She was dressed strangely, a long black robe with some type of headpiece that concealed all of her features except for her face. Around her neck hung a large wooden cross, dangling back and forth over her body from her hurried movement.

"Miss, are you okay? I've been waiting nearby so that you wouldn't be scared to wake up alone."

Instantly on guard, I was unsure of the woman. Memories crept into my thoughts in vaporous waves, not quite solid enough for me to understand them, but portentous enough to warn me I was no longer where I wanted to be.

"Where am I? Where's Elijah?" Not even my own voice sounded familiar.

"You're at Our Lady of Serenity. Father Hayle and I found you in the front yard. You were inconsolable, so we brought you inside to allow you to sleep. We're hoping you can help us contact your family so they can pick you up. Are you hurt? Do you need medical attention?"

"I need Elijah. Bring him to me." Agitated and afraid, I practically screamed the words at her.

Bits and pieces surfacing, I remembered running, but I'd found my way home. Hadn't I?

Who was this woman and why was she dressed so strangely?

"I'm sorry, Miss, but there is nobody by the name of Elijah in the parish."

Attempting to stand from the bed, I stumbled on legs that were weak and sore.

"Elijah is here. He carried me inside. I bear his mark and he'll be angry if you don't let me see him. He'll have you punished if you don't find him immediately."

The concern on her face was replaced by shock. She nodded before quietly backing out of the room.

I wasn't sure what came over me. In Elijah's presence, I was a child, shaking and trembling from fear and reverence. But at that moment I felt stronger. My destiny called to me, not on a scream, but a whisper. It told me I was on the right path, that as Elijah's wife, I wielded a small part of his power.

Elijah wouldn't want that woman to hide me. She was only a person interfering with my absolution – my forgiveness for having strayed. To bow to her would be to bow to the Devil, and I wouldn't allow that to happen.

I couldn't.

Not again.

Events came back to me in the silence of the room: the ceremony, my brother's voice, my weakness for having listened and fled the compound.

How Elijah found me in this strange building, I wasn't sure. I remembered the shed in the woods, wondered if this was just another place he'd set out from the compound for his use.

The compound where we lived was a large building that was as decrepit as it was strong. With thick cement walls and floors, it was also silent and cold. It wasn't the first place I'd lived with Elijah's family, but it was where we'd moved when space became an issue as the family grew.

I hated the compound when we first lived there, hated that Elijah knew the structure so well he could use the maze of halls and well placed doors to appear and disappear when he wanted. It made him seem more ethereal in his existence, more spirit than flesh and blood.

Even in the years I'd spent with him, I'd never fully grasped that he was watching me. Perhaps it was his ever-observant eyes that sent chills across my skin when I thought I was alone. Or maybe it was simply his proximity.

The trembling of my body that had once been fear became something more honest and mature as I grew older around him. Thoughts of hiding away were lost to thoughts of pressing my body to his. The sin of yearning replacing the chastity I'd been sworn to maintain.

Elijah was everywhere and he was everything. And I was just a girl becoming a woman, a girl who was too blind to see the power that lived with me since the day I'd met him.

When he entered the room, relief swept in to steal the breath from my lungs. Questions flooded me - his odd clothes, this strange room - but I ignored them, my eyes transfixed by the beauty of his face. His hair, his eyes, the strength of his hands when they clutched my body to his.

It was all so wrong. So terribly impure.

My thoughts led to foolish actions, but he was my husband, maybe not in the eyes of the family, but in the eyes of God. How could I not think about what his touch has done to me?

His stride was powerful and sure. His body moved fluidly across the space, an air of fortitude and strength surrounding him. Dropping to my knees, I bowed so low that my forehead scraped the floor.

"Forgive me," I begged.

The fall of his heavy steps stopped just before I felt his hands on my shoulders. I jumped at the contact, my breath stolen from me yet again.

"I have nothing to forgive you for, Miss. You've done nothing wrong." His voice was soft, the hint of whispered power hypnotic. There were nights that listening to his voice, his sermon, had been enough to put me in a euphoric state, lost in my absolute reverence and faith.

"I was weak. Forgive me. I returned. Please."

Precariously balanced on a precipice between pure relief and devastation, I wouldn't let myself fail him. Doing so would only push me from my ledge to fall to the side where I would be torn apart by the wolves.

"Miss, I don't understand. Please, let me help you up off the floor." Strong hands grasped my arms and pulled me to my feet. I stood in front of him, refusing to open my eyes, too afraid to see an answer that I prayed he wouldn't give.

Was he testing me now as I bowed before him?

When alone, we were free to explore the flames burning between us. He had been the one to tell me that. It was only while in view of the family that we had to remain separate, had to deny ourselves the closeness we so desperately needed, at least until the official ceremony could be performed – the ceremony I'd foolishly run from when my brother screamed.

"Elijah, please..."

"My name is Father Jacob Hayle. Not Elijah."

My eyes opened.

Why was he refusing to admit who he was? It didn't make sense. Terror touched my spine to remember I was being tested. Would I fail again?

"Please, sit." Leading me to the wooden chair, he helped me down. Kneeling in front of me, his blue eyes were piercing. "What is your name?"

"Eve," I whispered, confusion thick in my response.

He didn't blink, didn't give me any indication that this wasn't normal. "Fine, Eve. Where have you come from? Where do you live?"

"With you." Leaving my tongue on a whisper, my words sounded more like a question than a response. I feared he was telling me I could no longer live on the compound. I'd be shunned, left with nowhere to go and no person who could help me.

"No, Eve," he answered slowly, his tone that of a parent speaking to a confused child. "You do not live here."

"Please!" Sliding from the chair, I fell to my knees once again.

My hands found his and refused to let go.

It was stupid to keep falling down so easily, but it was the only place where I belonged. On my knees, begging him to forgive me.

Tucked inside some strange reality that was the opposite of the routine I'd followed for so many years, I felt like I was alone within the eye of a storm. To the left and right of me, above and below, I was surrounded by battering winds and slashing rain, but with him standing next to me, the storm could not close in.

Evil existed on the outside, the hearts of men turned away from God until they became filled with a vicious hunger. Money, sex, drugs, fame and greed – they were always ravenous, always wanting, always willing to tear at the bodies of the pure just to satisfy their needs.

If Elijah left me, I would be left to those men. And after time, I knew I would die by those men.

"Please don't make me leave, please don't." Tears broke free of my eyes, my thoughts giving in to the horror of being exiled. The trembling of my body betrayed my fright, my fingers squeezing his, aching from how hard I held on. "Please. I'll do anything, Elijah."

Pulling his hands free, he inched back to place distance between us. His eyes locked to mine, narrowing in rejection and doubt. I was flayed open by that rejection, rendered useless and tossed aside.

"Eve. I need to contact your family. Do you know where they live?"

"Here! They live here. Why are you doing this to me? I don't understand." My words were broken apart by my tears, my throat shredded by the volume of my voice. I couldn't turn away, couldn't allow him to shun me so easily. Life was not worth living if I was cast aside, the moment of my weakness would become an eternal cross to bear.

A thought came to me, an explanation for what he was doing.

I'd been the one to leave. I'd been the one to run so easily away. How could I expect him to welcome me back with open arms?

I'd rejected *him* by not believing, Joshua's voice the catalyst that spurred me on.

Elijah wanted to know I knew better. That's why he kept asking me these questions, that's why he made me repeat myself over and over again.

He needed assurance that I knew my place was by his side.

"Please, Elijah. I'll do anything."

Crumpled on the floor like a child, I begged as he watched me.

"I bear your mark," I reminded him. "I took on the pain of your stamp, and I was transformed by your love. You watched me change. You saw *everything*. I want you. I want this. I'm not afraid anymore. How can you brush me aside? Is there no mercy inside you?"

Silence was a heavy blanket between us. Stifling and hot, I trembled beneath its weight.

With a quiet voice he attempted to appease me. "I'm not making you leave. I just need to know how to help you."

A soft hand touched my shoulder, his body heat seeping through my clothes to warm my skin. My body trembled more, large waves of fear and terror crashing over me as reality took hold.

"Please, Elijah. Please."

Could he hear my hushed voice? Did he understand how his words had crippled me, crushing me into a fine dust that could be swept so easily from the room? I was nothing without him. Not anymore.

Strong hands lifted me again. I glanced down to see that my knees were red from where they'd hit the floor. I couldn't scream, so I whispered as I pled with him to forgive me. "Please. I'm faithful. I'm only loyal to you."

Reaching up, the palms of my hands met with the strong muscle of his chest. Sliding them higher, I wrapped my arms around his neck. Desperation not to be cast aside tightened my grip. I wouldn't let go – couldn't. My life was in the compound. The outside world was too frightening to walk alone.

Weakness overtook my knees. The room was spinning. Parched and on fire, my throat refused to work. How could I convince him to keep me? How could I prove my faith? How could I prove I was sorry for running away?

"Elijah..." My voice trailed off when my mouth brushed the warmth of his neck. Salt from his skin stung the fissures where my lips had cracked from lack of water.

Every muscle of his body stiffened as soon as my lips touched him.

"Miss..." His hands moved to push me away, but I clung to him tighter, unwilling to release my hold until he promised to take me back.

"Finish the ceremony, Elijah," I begged.

He was too strong.

I was pushed aside, my arms jerked from around his neck. I fell helplessly to the floor. Crying out, I lunged forward, crawling towards him as he stepped back.

The door slammed shut before I could reach him, a metal lock slamming into place. Broken apart, I remained huddled over my shaking body, my entire world fracturing before my eyes.

My heart – my soul - was left to splinter into small, repentant shards.

5

JACOB

A friend loves at all times, and a brother is born for adversity. Proverbs 17:17

Her cries were audible through the thick wood of the door. Standing in witness, I listened to her pleading still. My body was tight with anxiety, my mind grasping to understand how she could confuse me with another.

"What is wrong with her, Father? Should we call for an ambulance now?"

A long sigh escaped, evidence of my own confusion. "Yes. I think we should. She's delusional, Sister Joyce. At least, I believe she is. I don't want to burden her family with the price of her treatment."

"Perhaps the church can fund her convalescence."

Darkness ran across my thoughts, carrying with it the frustration and anger that I held towards the organization of which I was part. What good was the parish if it could not assist its own members? Fighting against cursing the church itself, I bit my tongue hoping not to distress Sister Joyce with my struggle.

"I'll go make the call."

Stepping away from her, I was followed by the echo of my steps through the seemingly abandoned building. My breathing was heavy for reasons that were unfitting of a celibate priest. I wanted to deny to myself that her touch had affected me, to deny that for a split second I'd wanted to pull her into me rather than force her away.

Shaking myself of the thought, I remembered the reverence in her expression when she looked at me, the way her green eyes had danced beneath the low light of the room. Her hair hung heavy down her back, dark and thick, a reminder of a past I'd left behind.

"Father Hayle? Will you be able to look at the gardens to approve my work? I won't get paid until the Church hears from you."

Pulled from my thoughts, I turned, my eyes searching over the haggard appearance of George Whitaker. An elderly man, his clothes hung from his emaciated body, the years of manual labor worn like a shadow over his frame. "Yes. Of course, George. I need to make a phone call and then I'll be out to approve."

When I stepped away, he called out, "Is that young lady okay? The one from the cult?"

Frozen in step, I spun back to where he was standing. "What did you just say?"

He looked sheepish to have intruded, but still, he couldn't refrain from pressing for more information. "The woman who collapsed in the yard this morning. I was outside getting an early start before the afternoon storms and I saw her fall. I was going to help, but you and the Sister got to her so quickly. I decided my help wasn't needed. I just wanted to know if she's okay."

Shaking my head, I specified what I meant by my question. "Yes, she's fine, George, but what did you mean by cult? What do you know about her?"

Shrugging his thin shoulder, he answered, "She was wearing one of those weird blue dresses all the women wear. We see them in the neighboring town from time to time. Every other week, I drive out there to sell vegetables and fruit at the Farmer's Market. I think they stay at the old abandoned crazy farm little ways down the road from the market. Don't know how they stay in that place. It gives me the creeps just driving by it. Used to be an old tuberculosis hospital before it was a mental place. Seems to me, they risk getting sick living inside there."

The hospital wasn't familiar, but that wasn't surprising. I barely left the parish except to go into town. I'd never traveled farther, or to the neighboring town.

"How do you know they are a cult?"

He shrugged again. "Don't know for sure, but I see them carrying around Bibles, and the main guy is always telling the ladies to mind their eyes and keep them directed to the ground. He says sin and temptation is all around them. He especially stays on the poor girl that collapsed in the yard."

His eyes narrowed as he scrutinized my face. "Come to think of it, you look a lot like that guy. In fact, you're his spitting image if my old eyes aren't deceiving me now. I'm surprised I never noticed before."

My curiosity was piqued, a thought brushing my mind that couldn't possibly be true.

"Thank you, George. I'll go take a look at the gardens now."

51

Walking away, I changed my mind about calling the police about Eve. I was more interested in finding out about the supposed cult that was in the town neighboring mine.

. . .

Just as Mr. Whitaker had said, the abandoned hospital was only a few miles inside the neighboring town.

Slowing down, I approached and studied the razor wire running along the large cement walls that blocked my view of the property. The road leading up to the entrance gate was unpaved. Dirt and dust rose up from where my tires crossed, casting an ominous haze over the dwindling, afternoon sun.

The entrance gates were tall and poorly maintained. White sheets were woven through the bars, obscuring my view. Stopping my truck on the road outside the main drive, I stepped out to walk the remainder of the distance.

An odd silence hung over the land, the wind blowing through the trees the only source of noise. With heavy, cautious steps I approached, dust kicking up around me only to settle back down as if it had never been disturbed in the first place.

With only feet between where I stood and the softly blowing sheets over the gates, I heard metal slide against metal.

Pulled from the center, I stood motionless as the gates opened.

Nothing could have prepared me for what I faced.

Staring into my own reflection, I almost fell to my knees.

The wind from an approaching storm whipped through the now opened gates; black clouds racing in to steal the light of the dying sun. The canopies of the trees cracked and groaned, their boughs bent forward by the violent weather that encroached.

"Jericho," I whispered, too far in denial to put strength to my voice.

I hadn't seen my twin brother in almost eighteen years.

He smirked, his expression far more placid than mine. "Brother. I was wondering when you'd find me. I'm surprised it took this long."

When I found my voice again, I spoke. "You don't sound as surprised as you claim to be."

Tension hung between us, as thick as the stirring of my memories of our youth.

Lightning cracked in the distance followed by thunder that mimicked a rumbling train. I found the timing of nature's display to be prophetic, a warning that trickled along my spine as the static shock spread across my skin.

Jericho stepped forward, the soft thud of his shoes carried over the distance by the turbulent wind. Three men stepped up behind him, each man wearing dark blue pants and a white collared shirt. Jericho stood out among them. Dressed all in black, the gleam of his silver buttons flashed in the scant sunlight still breaching the clouds.

"Is that any way to greet your brother? And here I thought you'd be happier to see me." The corner of his lip twitched with humor.

"How long have you been here?" I asked. "What is this place?"

He shook his head, tsking as he stepped forward. "So many questions. You never were one to simply accept that God has a plan. We're twins, Jacob. We came into the world together. It only seems natural that once split, we would find our way back to each other. Blood calls to blood."

Studying me, his sharp gaze traveled over my clothes, pausing on my clerical collar. "I guess your faith isn't as weak as I thought." His eyes met mine. "What happened that could have sent you running back into the open arms of the Church?"

"How long have you been here?" My patience was running thin. Even as a younger man, Jericho would never answer a simple question. He always turned the inquiry around on the asker with another question.

Jericho smiled, finally stepping close enough that he could reach out and place his hand on my shoulder. "Why don't you come inside?" Glancing skyward, he made a point to remind me of the impending storm. "Unless, of course, you prefer standing in the rain."

We stared at each other for a few seconds before he finally relented and answered, "I've been here for ten years, Jacob. However, my family..." Waving his arm, he motioned to the men behind him. "...we've been together since I left our childhood home."

He circled behind me, allowing a better view of the property within the gates. I knew Jericho better than to believe the movement wasn't intentional. He was attempting to intimidate me, throw me off guard so that I would be more receptive to his manipulation.

"Why are there rumors that you're running a cult? What is this place?" Refusing to be intimidated, I turned and stared him directly in the eye. "Why did one of your *family* collapse in the front of my parish this morning?"

His eyebrows rose with the strength of my voice. Another small grin played over his mouth before he answered, "Eve is alive. That's good to hear. I was wondering where she'd run off to in the middle of the night. A small woman like her wouldn't survive long in the woods by herself."

"Why was she running?"

He leaned in my direction, his mouth close to my ear when he whispered, "You should come inside and look."

Backing away, he raised his voice to ask, "Why do you seem so nervous, Jacob? Aren't you excited to see your long lost twin? If I didn't know you better, I'd swear that you're upset to see me. But that can't be true, can it? It makes no sense. Blood is blood, after all."

"It might have something to do with the condition of the woman I found this morning. She was freezing, emaciated, so fucking exhausted that she passed out in my yard. Any man who could allow a member of his *family* to end up like her is one that concerns me. I came here after I was told about your group. I wanted to see for myself what, exactly, was going on."

Chuckling, he said, "It's unbecoming of a priest to swear. It appears you're not as clean-cut as you present yourself to be. Does your flock know?"

He turned, looking over his shoulder when he walked away and called out, "I've invited you inside, Jacob. Come and see for yourself."

Swiveling around, Jericho kept his eyes trained forward as I watched him walk onto the property.

The looming clouds obscured the sunlight. I looked up to see lightning brighten the dark sky. Doubting that he would harm me, I accepted the invitation, silently following him through the gates.

Once we were safely tucked within the entry room of the hospital, large wooden doors slammed closed, the sound rolling in waves through the empty space. Jericho moved to the center of the room, turning to look at me.

"What would you like to know, Jacob? Ask me and I'll gladly tell you."

"I want to know why a young woman collapsed on the front lawn of my parish." It wasn't my intent to yell, but I was sick of his dramatic gestures. "Cut the crap, Jericho, and tell me what is going on."

"It's Elijah now," he murmured, his voice as dark as it was soft.

No longer confused as to Eve's insistence on the name when she saw me, I stood in silent shock.

"Did anybody call you or find you when I left home?" he asked, an eyebrow arching over his blue eye.

"Yes. Aunt Rose called to tell me that you'd fallen out of favor with the Church and our father."

"Did you wonder what happened? Why I was excommunicated and cast aside as if I were diseased?"

His admission stunned me. Gathering my thoughts, I finally choked out, "I didn't know you'd been excommunicated. I was told that they asked you to leave. I assumed you would go to another parish."

He chuckled, his eyes flicking up to catch mine. "You know what they say about assumptions, right?"

People flooded into the room from doors on every side. Within seconds, the space was filled with men on the left, women and children on the right. It appeared that they all wore the same clothes, each person only distinguished by the color of their hair or the features of their face. There must have been at least a hundred in total, each person appearing healthy and calm.

I glanced from face to face as Jericho spoke again. "Do you see the condition of my family? We're not *exhausted*. We're not *emaciated*. We're not freezing or trembling or hurt in any way."

I looked at him.

He smiled. "We're not afraid, either."

They might not have been frightened, but I was certainly less than thrilled. Completely surrounded, I was at the mercy of my brother. "What do you have to be afraid of?"

He didn't answer, instead lifting his hand to snap his fingers. It was an apparent dismissal of the others, only a few men remaining behind to stand in front of the entrance doors.

With a detached voice, he said, "You have Eve. I want you to return her to me. She became lost, that's all. We were out for a walk and somehow, she wandered away from the group. We searched for her. However, with the lack of light, we were unable to find her and decided to resume our search when sunlight returned."

His words didn't make sense. "How many men do you have out looking for her now?"

Smiling, he shrugged his shoulder. "You always were the smart one." Stepping forward, he stopped inches from my body. I didn't back down as he'd expected.

"I tell you what. Why don't you keep Eve for a period of time? When that time is up, I'll come collect her."

Anger slithered across my skin, my muscles painfully tight over my spine. "She's not a possession to be traded back and forth. She's a human being."

A black eyebrow arched inquisitively over his eye. "She was. Yes. Sedra was a boisterous child when she was brought to the compound. So beautiful, passionate, energetic ... full of innocent youth."

Ratcheting higher, my anger was barely containable. "What did you do to her, Jericho?"

"It's Elijah. I'll not respond to any other name."

Choosing not to respond, I awaited his answer.

"Nothing happened to her. I helped raise her. I enlightened her and led her down the path of a righteous woman. She is extraordinary, Jacob, a woman who knows nothing in this world except God. There is no one else like her."

I scoffed. "And from what I learned by talking to her, she doesn't even know her own name."

Taking a step forward, I grinned when he took one back. My voice dripped with ice. "Does she know Elijah is not your actual name? Do any of your *family* know?"

Pacing, he mocked me. "Who? What? When? Where? Why?" He spoke slowly, stressing each word by pausing in between. "So many questions, Jacob. Always the scientist."

His steps stopped. "You never were one to just blindly believe in the way things worked without the need to discover the reasons."

I glared at him, a sardonic grin pulling at my lips. "And neither were you. We're twins, remember?" He sneered when I threw his words back at him. "There are some common traits we share. Tell me, *Elijah*, was it your incessant questions that caused you to fall out of favor with the Church? Or was it your deviant behavior?"

His eyes burned into mine, cruelty and disgust rolling behind the clear blue color. "You'll have your answers, Jacob. Just not today."

Footsteps echoed through the silent room as he walked in the direction of a side door. Looking back once more, he smiled. "Enjoy Eve. Keep in mind that your time with her is limited."

His exit from the room was punctuated by the loud creak of the entrance doors as the men who'd remained behind opened them.

The storm having passed, sunlight rolled into the room, bits of dust and debris swirling within the beams.

There was nothing I could say or do to change the situation with Jericho, but there was something I could do to save the poor lost soul who'd collapsed in front of my parish earlier that morning.

Stepping out, I didn't bother looking at the men standing by the entrance. The slap of wood as they closed the doors was the only sound I heard as I walked away.

6

EVE

Do not fear, for I have redeemed you; I have summoned you by name; you are mine. Isaiah 43:1

My skin prickled from the cold air of the room contrasted against the wood floor beneath me that was warm from the heat of my naked body.

Feet pointed out, arms spread wide, my forehead pressed to the ground: that was the position I took to earn his approval.

I remained perfectly still, prostrated and serving, in hopes that my servitude would gain his forgiveness.

He liked to touch me. It made his eyes soften, his anger subside.

It made me feel wrong, something dark inside me surfacing with my sin.

Still, my body yearned for his touch, my heart knowing I'd fallen prey to temptation.

His temptation.

Temptation that would lead me down a path of reckless abandon, spiraling out of favor with God.

But it was too late.

I'd fallen. I'd weakened. And I would give him whatever he desired because he said it was right.

Hours passed, the only sound to keep me company was my heavy breath against the ground. In and out, the air moved through my lungs. My muscles burned and my heart pounded, but I would not move, would not risk failing him again.

This is what he wanted.

It's what he always wanted.

Ever since I'd become his Eve.

7

JACOB

You are not your own, you were bought at a price. 1 Corinthians 6:19-20

My mind raced the entire drive home. What could be done with a woman who didn't even know her own identity? How could I cure years of brainwashing or torment, abuse or restrictions? What had he done to her to break her so completely?

I knew well the games Jericho – *Elijah* – could play. I'd played them all myself in a time long past.

Pulling up into the driveway, I found Sister Joyce walking out the back door in an apparent hurry. Her robe flew out behind her from the speed of her pace. Climbing out of my car, I called out, "Sister? Is something wrong?"

Flustered by my sudden interruption, she tripped over her own feet when she turned, catching herself before falling down. Placing her hand over her chest, she replied, "Oh, Father Hayle. You scared me."

"Has something happened with the woman...with Eve?"

"No, Father. I'm scheduled to read to a children's group at the hospital today. However, I've been concerned about leaving the woman unattended. I waited as long as I could, but..."

Her anxiety was clearly written over her expression and movements.

I raised a hand to silence her. "It's okay, Sister. I didn't expect you to keep watch over her all afternoon. Is she still in the bedroom?"

"Yes. She's been in the room since you've left. I've knocked on the door but she hasn't responded. Did you discover who she is? What's been done to her?" Whispering her last question, she hugged her Bible tighter to her chest.

There was no point in upsetting her further with the details. The less she knew, the better at this point.

Deciding to keep Sister Joyce separate from Eve until a time came when I could fully evaluate her, I said, "Take your time at the hospital, Sister. I'll tend to Eve. You can also return to the convent for a few days. I won't be needing you again until Saturday to prepare for Sunday Mass."

She looked confused, her eyebrows furrowing from a question she chose not to voice. Nodding her head, she answered, "Anything you say, Father. You are always wise."

I nodded in response and left her to her task.

Walking inside the parish, I was haunted by my own footsteps. Death could not have been more silent than the halls and rooms of the building. Every slight noise echoed through the empty space as I made my way to Eve.

Pulling a key from my pocket, I unlocked the door, hesitating as I turned the handle.

The old wood creaked in complaint to the movement of the door, but the sound of shock on my breath was louder.

My eyes moved over her milk white skin, the vertebrae of her spine just barely showing along her back. Her dark hair was pulled to the side, hanging down like a curtain to shield her.

I trust you, Jacob. Always you. Only you...

My memory whispered to me of my sins, warning me away from the young woman lying on the ground in front of me.

Eve didn't look up as I entered. I took three steps and knelt down to lay my hands on her outstretched arms.

"Eve."

Cold and dry, her skin felt like silk beneath my fingertips. She was dirty from her venture in the woods, still marked and bruised from whatever had happened to her. Other than that, I could see no marks or other imperfections, except for the red and raw burn on her shoulder.

Worry flooded me, spinning me in place until I wasn't sure what direction I was facing.

"Eve, look at me."

Pushing my hand beneath the fall of her hair, I cupped her cheek and lifted her face from the floor. A red mark ran over her forehead, her eyes stained the same red. She must have been crying for hours.

"I need you to get up, Eve."

It had been my intent to only use her real name, but at that moment she was so lost in her fear that I went along with whatever she believed.

She was Eve and I was Elijah.

My heart was heavy with dishonesty, but I lied with the hope that once she was functional again, she would be able to learn the truth without it sending her back into a panicked state. I had no choice but to play out the fantasy in order to help her understand how she'd been deceived.

Keeping my voice soft, I said, "You need to follow me. You need a bath and you need to eat."

She hesitated, her lashes fluttering over her swollen eyes. Moonlight poured in from the window, glowing against the hair that framed her face. Her expression was grief stricken, but when I spoke, her eyes flickered with the hope she carried.

"Will it please you?" Rough from not having been used in hours, her voice still rang out like that of an angel. The pitch wasn't too high or low. I closed my eyes against the way it vibrated across my skin.

A twinge of lust whispered into my thoughts, guilt following closely in its wake. What kind of monster was I to have any attraction to this woman? She was exposed and vulnerable, naïve and alone.

Clearing my throat, I took a deep breath and answered, "Your health pleases me. Your health and cleanliness pleases God."

On a whisper, she said, "My body is his temple."

My eyes closed again, the lids falling down heavily at her words. "Yes."

"I was bought for a price."

Anger touched my mind, feathering across my thoughts at how Elijah had perverted the faith to hurt her. She was quoting scripture while surrendering herself to the man she thought I was.

Unable to disguise how I felt, my voice was firm when I said, "Not by me. You weren't bought by me.

Stand up. There's a bath in the rectory. You can use that for now."

She jumped at the harshness in my voice, her eyes opening wide in fear. "I'm sorry. I was only repeating what you've taught me, I..."

Placing my finger over her lips, I quieted her.

"You have nothing be sorry for." I held my finger to her lips for too long, caught in the spell of the heat of her breath over my palm.

Pulling away, I stood up and stepped back, unable to pull my eyes from her. When she moved, the muscles of her body were fluid beneath her skin. Long hair fell down from across her shoulder and my eyes settled on the mark I'd seen previously. She moved again so that I was no longer able to look closely at it, but I lost my ability to care when she was finally on her feet.

It was due to my own mistakes that I'd sworn my life to the Church ... to God. Still, there was something left over, a stirring of tastes and desires I'd had in my youth, and it wasn't until now that I realized I still had the capacity to feel.

Swallowed by my slow heat, a rush of blood hissed beneath my skin. Sweat broke out over my body and I turned away when she was standing before me.

But not soon enough.

Before I could avert my eyes, I'd already caught sight of the swell of her breasts, the perfect curve of her full hips. I turned completely, not able to hide my reaction to her skin. My body tightened in memory of the pleasures of flesh. Wicked thoughts seeped in, dark and disturbing, reminding me of a time when sex had been the ultimate power.

Who owns you?

You do, Jacob….forever…

My fists clenched at the memory, my head falling back in response to the nightmare I would never be able to escape.

Forever…

Her eyes dull with the loss of life, her trust broken by a man who didn't know when to stop. *Forever* was a truth she never had the chance to understand.

I forced myself back to the present.

"You'll need clothes. I believe there are some baptismal robes you can use until I can get into town and buy you something else."

"If that is what you want. I don't mind being exposed to you. I'm not ashamed anymore."

Breathing with slow pulls of air, I tempered my resolve. Her voice, the reverence and absolute adoration, she would do anything I asked.

You can't understand the feeling of control until you've held it, until you've heard your name roll off a woman's lips with no will of her own. Almost as if the name belonged there, a necessary part of her existence.

"It's what I want."

I was a priest for Christ's sake, yet none of the thoughts I had about this woman were proper or pure.

"Then it's what I'll do."

No hesitation, no question, nothing. She was certain in her resolve to follow me blindly, to do everything I said, exactly as I told her to do it.

My heart hurt for Eve even though something far darker was awakening inside. For a split second, I regretted my decision to send Sister Joyce back to the convent. She could have tended to Eve: clothed her, fed her, bathed her. But she would have also been a witness to Eve's mental instability. She would have called the authorities while I was away, would have called for an ambulance if Eve's health had concerned her.

I couldn't allow Eve to be taken away. They'd only return her to the man who had *created* her in the first place.

"I want you to be clothed in my presence. It doesn't please me to see your skin. God is watching. Always remember that."

She flinched at the censure in my tone.

Moving through the doorway into the hall, I ignored the sound of her grief. My thoughts returned to Jericho, to what he'd obviously done so that my rejection of her naked body could reduce her to tears.

Our steps weren't hurried as we wound through the halls and common areas in route to the rectory. She sniffled as she walked, but I refused to look back or attempt to console her.

Wearing temptation like a cloak, Eve was dangerous to a man like me.

My life before this moment had been dark.

Jericho knew that both he and I had secrets, habits that we never spoke about except to each other. I'd carried those secrets and tastes with me to college. I'd reveled in the freedom to sin.

My unhindered corruption came to a crashing halt on one drunken evening. I'd lost control and I'd lost the woman I loved.

I gave myself back to God after that night, both in surrender and as restitution for having taken a young woman's life.

8

EVE

Be sober-minded; be watchful. Your adversary the devil
prowls around like a roaring lion, seeking someone to devour.
1 Peter 5:8

I couldn't help my tears, couldn't help but feel his rejection roll through me like a violent storm. My skin prickled when he denied me, the loss of absolution setting every nerve on fire. It was the type of pain that creeps through you, catching you off guard and striking so deep that your breath is knocked from your lungs.

I refused to scream, and I didn't fall to my knees begging. He hadn't shunned me. Not yet.

There was still a roof over my head.

I hadn't been cast out into the night that would consume me.

Rounding a corner, we came to a doorway. Unlocking it, Elijah moved through, leading me into a dark room.

The click of a switch and the room lit up, the light diffused and softened by the shades of the bedside lamps. This room, like the other, was utilitarian in its lack of decoration. All it contained was a simple bed, two bedside tables and a desk set off to the other side. The walls were bare except for a single crucifix hanging alone.

Elijah continued walking until we were both inside a small bathroom, also bare except for the standard features: sink, toilet and tub. Nothing else.

I watched him kneel down by the tub to start the water, but I felt faint once steam rolled off the surface.

My vision tunneled, my knees weakened and the next thing I knew I was lying on the cold, stone tile floor with Elijah hovering above me.

"Eve, are you okay?"

The back of my head throbbed, the skin burning. Blinking open my eyes, I looked at him in confusion. "What happened?"

"You fell. Are you okay? Does your head hurt?"

Pushing myself up, my hip brushed his hand.

He placed distance between us and looked away. "Will you be able to bathe yourself?"

Still lightheaded from whatever spell had hit me, I sat on the floor, barely able to hold up my weight. "I'm not sure. I'm so dizzy. The heat in the room is only making it worse."

I hated that he refused to look at me.

"It's probably your blood sugar. When did you last eat?"

"I'm not sure."

I wasn't sure of anything at that moment. All I knew was that I was in a strange place with Elijah. It was all so confusing, so frustrating that I wanted to scream. Was I being tested? Had I been forgiven?

He bit out a word under his breath. I didn't recognize it.

Voice pained, he said, "Get in the water, Eve. I'll help you."

Standing from the ground, I almost fell again. My legs were weak and my abdomen felt like it couldn't possibly hold the weight of my upper body. Elijah's hands gripped over my right arm and left hip. He was walking closely behind me, his body brushing against mine.

I shuddered when the soft linen of his shirt touched my back, when the stiff cotton of his pants grazed my bottom. His nearness was a tease, and I was desperate to push back against him.

Controlling my actions, I remembered he was the only person who could lead.

We reached the bath, his hand releasing my hip to allow me to step in. My breath hissed over my lips at the heat of the water, my muscles relaxing as I sank beneath the surface. Once lowered completely, I looked up and saw that Elijah still refused to fully glance in my direction.

Reaching for a sponge and soap, his arms moved over me, his chest appearing rock solid beneath the crisp black of his shirt. He handed me the items and asked, "Are you strong enough to wash yourself?"

Nodding, I spoke shyly. "I think so. I'm not sure what's wrong."

With the soap in one hand and the sponge in the other, I leaned as far forward as I could, dragging the soap along my leg with only the sound of moving water echoing through the room. Elijah knelt on the ground beside me, supporting my back.

His fingers against my skin were sweet poison, his breath a whisper of sound over parted lips.

Is it pain you seek tonight, sweet child? Is it pain that will cleanse you of your sins?

The memories of our nights together tormented me still.

I wanted to be clean for him. I was desperate to be pure. Our union was made in the eyes of God, our passion forged in fire.

The soap slipped from my hands, splashing down to the bottom of the tub. There was no reason for my weakness, but even a bar of soap was too heavy for my trembling fingers to firmly grasp.

Elijah pulled his hand from my back, still averting his eyes as he unbuttoned the cuff of each sleeve. Rolling them up, he revealed the taut and toned muscles of his forearm.

I watched in absolute wonder.

My breath came harder, memories seeping in of the week we'd shared while preparing for our wedding ceremony. The heat of his breath on my skin, the strength of his hands brushing across my body - the sting of pain that always accompanied everything he did.

As tears threatened my eyes, Elijah's hand disappeared beneath the water in search of the soap. My head fell back against the tub. His arm slid over my inner thigh.

Slippery and wet, his skin was temptation against mine, hotter than the water that billowed with steam.

My breath rushed from my lungs.

Opening my eyes, I was met with the molten heat of his stare.

72

"Can you sit forward?" he asked, a whisper of sound in the silence of the room.

Nodding, I couldn't speak around the lump in my throat.

"I'll wash the dirt off your back."

Time slowed while I savored the feel of his touch.

I breathed in.

He breathed out.

Water splashed in the tub.

Every small sound echoed through the room.

His fingertips brushed against the side my breast as he brought the soap down along my arms. A tremulous breath rattled out of me, the sound so loud that his eyes locked to mine, heat stirring beneath the hypnotic blue.

The single light bulb that illuminated the room flickered softly, light playing off the water in strobes. When his hand swept down just above my bottom, my back stiffened, my breasts tightening in desperation for his touch. His hand shook as he brought the soap down lower and when he brushed over the cheeks, I couldn't contain my soft moan.

I was lost in that moment; lost to a man that cared for me despite my having run from him only hours before.

Was this what forgiveness felt like?

My head was dizzy, my eyes blinking slowly. I sat in absolute adoration. I was swimming in the torment of his soft touch, unable to stop the trembling of my body within the gossamer curtain of steam that enshrouded us.

Moving so that he could cleanse my legs, the tip of his tongue moved over the fullness of his bottom lip. Soft, yet strong, his movements revealed the tension in his body, the restraint he used to keep from touching me in ways he'd allowed while we lived at the compound. I couldn't help my need, the desire filling me to a point of agony.

"Please…"

The word escaped on a whisper.

Glancing up from beneath the fan of my lashes, I saw his eyes flash with something I couldn't recognize. Need, desire, thirst…or anger; every emotion I was desperate to see inside him, there one minute and gone the next.

Dropping the soap back into the water, his hand gripped my ankle, pulling my leg to the side and spreading me open before him. His body shook again, his eyes trailing across me, heating as he looked over my breasts. As fast as he'd grabbed me, he let go and jumped away from the tub.

I wasn't a viper waiting to strike him, but he moved as if I were.

His eyes closed and I watched him gain control over something I couldn't understand. Why did he refuse me when only days ago he'd granted me pure freedom?

"You're done. I'll go get you something to wear." Rough with tension, his words came out on a pained whisper.

Pushing himself off the floor, he moved fluidly from the room, his steps heavy as he left. I listened as they grew silent, minutes passing before I could hear them approaching again.

Entering the room, he held a white robe. The material slipped from his hand to the counter where he placed it. Once again, he kept his eyes directed anywhere but towards me. "Are you feeling well enough to get out of the bath by yourself?"

I wanted to cry, but nodded my head in response despite the fact that he couldn't see it. Finally forcing the painful words from my lungs, I answered, "Yes. I think I can manage."

"Good." He nodded before walking from the room, leaving the door cracked open when he faded into the soft light of the bedroom.

With the lack of emotion in that one simple word, he left me broken. I wanted to slip beneath the water, let air escape from my lungs in bubbles above me as liquid death flowed in to replace it.

But what good would that do? Even death couldn't save me from the emptiness I felt inside at his newfound rejection.

Climbing out of the water, my skin tightened to meet the rush of cold air. Goosebumps erupted over my arms and I shivered as I stepped out of the tub.

My breasts were firm, the nipples beading as I walked to the counter. My hands were on the robe when I turned my head in response to a noise.

We locked stares for only a split second before Elijah was gone again.

9

JACOB

For since He Himself was tempted in that which He has suffered, He is able to come to the aid of those who are tempted. Hebrews 2:18

Dark and malevolent, a sickness was coming over me that I'd left in the past at the moment I gave my life to the Church.

I'd vowed to remain celibate. I'd promised to repay God for my sins through my service.

Why now was temptation being danced in front of me, a siren leading me back to the dark?

Every time my eyes glanced in Eve's direction, I was haunted by another voice I would have given anything to hear again. Soft and innocent, she'd trusted me, believed in me, only to ultimately be destroyed by me.

What I'd done could not be forgiven if I broke my promises to God and repeated the act.

I was supposed to be helping this poor woman, not ogling her with thoughts of the many ways I could use her. She was flawless both in body and mind, an empty vessel that could be filled with light or darkness.

Years before, there would have been no question of what I would do. But now? Now, I was charged to set her at God's side, not shield her from the truth of good versus evil.

The door creaked open and I wrenched my neck turning to watch her step out from the bathroom. With her body covered, I was more comfortable looking in her direction, better able to control that part of me that whispered within my thoughts.

Even knowing what I *must* do, I couldn't help my gaze from tracing along the line of her legs the robe was too short to cover.

"You need to eat."

She blinked in response, the full pout of her mouth turned down in disappointment. What had she been hoping for, this innocent child of God?

"If that's what you want."

"It is."

Turning away from her, my hands curled into fists, the tension along my spine unbearable. The air in the room was stifling despite the frigid temperature. "You should do what pleases you, Eve. It is not your place to abide my every desire."

"But that is what you taught me."

Turning back, I couldn't help the sharp edge to my voice. "Then it's something you need to forget."

She cowered at the sound, dropping to her knees on the floor and pressing her forehead to the ground. I was surprised she didn't have permanent marks on her head for as often as it met the floor.

"Please. I'm sorry. I don't know what to do anymore. I'm loyal to you, Elijah. I'm yours."

You own me, Jacob...

Images flashed through my head: her hands tied to a bedpost, her lips spread on a seductive moan ... her eyes, dull and lifeless, the shock still written into the last expression she ever wore. I shook away the nightmares, the memories that I'd absolved when I'd sworn my loyalty to God.

"Eve, stand up. If you want to please me then stand up. The only being you should bow before is God. And I can promise you I'm not him." My words shook with my rage. Rage at how twisted this poor woman's head had become. Rage at my brother for having been the one to twist her thoughts into this chaotic, sordid mess.

"Stand up and follow me into the kitchen. You need food. You need water. You need -"

My words cut off, the last bit of patience inside me wearing thin. My first instinct was to grab her arm and force her up, but that wasn't what she needed. Her only hope of breaking through the fog created by Jericho's actions was for her to learn the truth about her life, about God.

She needed to think for herself. It was imperative that she understood her decisions were her own, not another person's.

Trusting your life to another person was not only foolish, but dangerous. I knew first hand the tragic mistakes that could happen with too much trust in another.

Cassandra had died by my hands.

Only because she'd trusted me too much.

Slowly, Eve pulled herself from the floor, her robe swishing around her legs giving hints of the flesh below. Keeping control over my gaze, I forced myself to look away. I had nothing to say to her, nothing that would help her. Despite the belief that I'd been saved, I was being reminded that I still was weak, as weak as I'd always been.

Without speaking, I led Eve out of my bedroom, through the church and to the large kitchen where I'd first spotted her through the window that morning. Passing by the small breakfast nook, I motioned to the chairs. "Sit down. I'll make us something to eat."

"I can cook."

I turned to look at her, my eyes drifting to where her robe hung open revealing the upper swell of her breasts. Beneath the white satin, I could see that her nipples were hard and I groaned at the sight.

Lust tingled within my veins, sending blood to areas that would be dangerous for us both.

Shaking away the sudden need, I returned my attention to the stove, flicking on the gas burners. I wanted to hold my hand over the flame, to punish myself for seeing this girl in the same light as I'd seen all the others before giving myself to God.

My voice came out strained. "As faint as you are, I don't believe standing over an open flame would be in your best interests."

"I'm feeling better. I'm not sure what happened earlier, but I can manage cooking something for us to eat."

Standing from her chair, she crossed the room and attempted to pull the spoon from my hand. Refusing to release it, I turned to face her, my heart racing to see how close she stood. Her neck was arched so that her face was angled up, her full lips slightly parted.

I stepped back, pulling the spoon from her weak grip, ignoring the brush of her fingers against mine.

"No, Eve. You'll sit down at the table."
Strengthening the tone of my voice, I ordered, "Do as I say."

Her eyes widened and I inwardly scolded myself for taking advantage of her condition - hated myself for enjoying the submission she gave.

Telling myself that commanding her worked, that it was for her own good, I only slightly eased the guilt I felt inside.

I had to get Eve to a point where she was thinking for herself, but in order to do that, I needed her to stop freaking out over every perceived rejection.

"I'm sorry."

"Stop apologizing, Eve."

"I'm..."

I looked at her and saw that her face was red from how hard she struggled to hold back tears. Breathing out my frustration, and remembering that it was my place to lead her to the light, I moved to her side, kneeling down so I could take her hand and look her in the eye.

"I appreciate your obedience. However, your attempts at second-guessing my judgment are frustrating. You've done nothing wrong. I'm not mad at you. I'm not sending you away and you're not going to be punished for anything. Do you understand?"

Whispering on broken breath, she answered, "Yes."

"Good."

Standing without speaking more than that one word, I returned to the stove, stirring the beef stew I was preparing for our meal. We remained in silence even as I placed the bowls on the table and sat down. After grabbing her spoon, she hissed out a breath, pushing at the stew in her bowl. The color drained from her face at the sight of the food.

"What's wrong?" The metallic clang of my spoon dropping to the table accented my question. Reaching across the table, I touched her arm, attempting to determine what had scared her so violently.

She looked up at me with accusation in her eyes, the fear in her expression so obvious that I looked behind myself to see if some threat lurked nearby.

Not seeing anything, I looked back at her, noticing how she stared directly at me.

"Why are you giving this to me? What are you trying to do?"

She didn't scream the words or even speak them loudly. Her voice was barely a whisper when she asked her questions. There was no emotion to them. Only pain.

"Because you need to eat."

I thought it was a simple answer, but based on her continued behavior, there was obviously something much deeper that was occurring. "Tell me what's wrong, Eve. I don't know what the problem is."

"Meat." Dropping her spoon so that it clattered loudly against the bowl, she continued, "You're serving me something that is unclean. Why are you doing this to me, Elijah?"

It all clicked.

Understanding and comprehension collided like thunder in my head, the realization of what my brother had done.

"How long has it been since you've eaten meat?" Waving off my own question, I asked, "What do you normally eat?"

She looked at me like I'd grown a third head, but finally swallowed down whatever it was she was feeling. "The same as the rest of the family. The vegetables we grow, the bread we bake. I'm free of the flesh of animals, of the blood of anything but what God has created within me. You were the one that taught me that."

That wasn't biblical, not even something written into dogma. That was classic conditioning used by a predator.

I'd learned in college that there are many ways to control a mass populace. Cult leaders, prisons, the armed forces and other groups have used these tactics in the past and continue to use them to make those they want to control more malleable. Take away protein and B-12 by taking away meats, nuts and other foods necessary for the proper function of the brain.

After enough time they have people who are not only physically tired, but mentally as well. It's an element of brainwashing that makes a person more open to suggestion, more willing to believe the lies they are being told.

Breathing out heavily, I released her arm and sat back in my chair. I needed to make changes for her and I wasn't sure how much time I had before Jericho arrived to collect her.

If I could convince her before that time, she stood a chance of escaping the sick community he'd created. But if he arrived beforehand, I was afraid there was nothing I could do to keep her from returning to him.

"I want to establish some new rules, Eve, and I want to start with you. You can be an example. I want to teach you these new rules away from the others. It's why I'm keeping you here."

It was a horrendous lie, one for which I would pray for forgiveness later. But it was necessary and that fact was obvious when she smiled shyly, the glow of hope peeking out from behind her eyes.

"What are the new rules?"

I stared at her for a few seconds wondering how quickly she would be able to integrate herself to a new way of life, to a non-jaded system of beliefs. "The first rule is that I want you to refer to me as Jacob. I'm not Elijah any longer, and that's not how I want you to address me."

Her eyes blinked slowly and she appeared as if she would resist. Rather than arguing, she simply opened her full lips and said, "I can do that. Will my name change as well?"

Remembering when she first spoke to me, I reminded her of her former name. "I want to call you Sedra again, not because you've done anything wrong, but because I was wrong."

"No." She shook her head, reaching out to grab my hand. "You can't be wrong."

She was so loyal, she would *do* anything, or *be* anything, I wanted.

Twelve years earlier, she would have been the perfect woman. One who looked to me for direction, who trusted blindly and would hand over every part of herself if that's what I asked her to do.

The faint brush of memory trickled along my spine. Images of the woman who would never say no to me, who allowed me to take her to places that most women would never see in their lifetime.

It was complete surrender, absolute submission; a woman placing her life into the hands of a man she believed she could trust.

And I failed that woman.

I wouldn't make the same mistake again.

"I can be wrong. Everybody but God himself can be wrong."

"Not you..."

Standing up from my chair, I rounded the small table, placing my finger against her trembling lip. "Yes, Sedra, even me. Man is fallible. All men. Even me."

She attempted to speak again, the soft brush of her lip against the pad of my finger stealing the breath from my lungs. It was erotic, that one small movement that sent chills across my skin, my muscles tightening until they felt like steel.

Her eyes were hypnotic, both of us becoming lost to a moment that was wrong, facing an eventuality that could never be. I'd sworn a vow. I would not break it for any woman, especially one that was the perfect example of innocence.

Clearing my throat, I attempted to speak again, but was unable to force my voice any louder than a whisper. "I want you to become strong, to understand the truth of not only good, but also evil. There is an entire world you don't know and I've been wrong for keeping you from that."

I was also wrong for lying to her, but I'd convinced myself that the possible result could be worth the sin I was committing.

"You need to eat. There is nothing written that says meat will hurt you. God gave us animals to use as we see fit. Some are for companionship, others for sustenance. Your body needs the protein, the iron, the vitamins and the minerals that come from all forms of food. You need to eat regularly. You need to be strong in both body..." Stroking my hand up her arm, I raised it to tap my finger against the side of her head. "...And mind."

Hesitantly, she smiled, the expression sad despite the acceptance I could see in her eyes. "I'll eat whatever you give me."

"Thank you."

I wanted to correct her behavior, to tell her that she could think for herself, but at that point, getting her to comply and strengthen her body was enough to satisfy me.

Stepping away, I sat in my chair watching as she took a bite of the stew. She didn't seem sure at first, but she moaned as if it were the best thing she'd tasted in years. Hunger took over and her spoon moved quickly to shovel down the food.

When she finished, she pushed the bowl aside, drinking from her glass of water to wash it down. A small burp escaped her stomach, her face turning bright red with embarrassment.

I couldn't help myself. I laughed.

"You liked it. That's good. Would you like more?"

She shook her head *no* before picking up her napkin and wiping her mouth. "Excuse me for burping." Another flash of color flared across her cheeks.

While finishing my own bowl, I heard her yawn from across the table. Looking up, I asked, "Are you tired? I'm almost finished and it would be best for both of us to retire for the night. I have work to do tomorrow, but you are welcome to assist me if you'd like."

"I'll be up before daybreak."

Shaking my head in disbelief, I redirected her thinking. "No. There's no need for that. You need to rest. Sleep as long as you like, Sedra."

Her response further verified what Jericho had done to control the people beneath him.

When a person was denied fuel, denied sleep, denied the basic requirements necessary for energizing their bodies, their minds became more susceptible to suggestion. It was classic psychology mixed with the knowledge of biology, a method used by monsters to confuse and corral the people they hoped to disadvantage.

Standing, I held my hand out to her, ignoring the spark that shot along my arm when she accepted and our palms met.

Leading her through the building back to her bedroom, I cherished the silence between us. Her presence was chaos in my head. Her voice - the reverence and loyalty that it denoted - only made that chaos more powerful.

Reaching her door, I opened it, allowing her to step through before I looked her over one more time.

"Sleep, Sedra. Tomorrow we'll go over your new way of life. It will be better for you in the long run."

She nodded her agreement even though there was still the touch of suspicion and confusion in her expression. Silently, I nodded back, closing the door until the snick of the handle was the only thing I heard echoing down the hall.

Walking back through the church, I ensured that all the doors and windows were locked, eventually retiring to my own room in the adjacent rectory. After stripping down and hanging up my clothes, I showered, dragging the towel through my damp hair as I walked into my room to put on a pair of pajama bottoms.

Dead silence surrounded me when I knelt beside my bed to pray. Thoughts raced through my head of Sedra, of her body and of her mind. She was the perfect temptation, my body reacting painfully to the strain of not touching her, of not reverting back to the mistakes I'd made as a younger man.

Thinking of my vows, I found myself whispering them aloud, strengthening them somehow by repeating them into the silence of the room.

Those prayers slowly faded into memories - into thoughts of the present.

I didn't notice my hand moving down until I was palming myself over my pants. I didn't stop myself when I gave into the temptation of pulling myself free of the restrictive material.

Swollen from lust and sensitive to touch, my hips bucked as soon as my palm wrapped around the tight skin.

Stroking myself, I couldn't help the memories: Candlelight sliding along slick leather, light flashing off the silver rings and pulls. The perfect curve of her breast as her back arched, the tips meeting my lips.

Cassandra would always beg, small whimpers and moans meant to seduce me into action.

Now, the memories that had been locked away reemerged with vicious speed. My hand moved forcefully. My guilt threatening to drown me where I knelt by the bed.

Even more than those past phantoms were the images in my head of another body - of Sedra's body - wet in the tub as I bathed her. The knowledge that she was so close didn't help silence the powerful need that forced its way violently through my veins.

My lips drifted apart on a moan, but I opened my eyes to the cross that hung on my wall.

What I was doing was wrong. Apprehension filled me, fear that I'd take another life with the desires that fueled my darkness. I was losing control of myself and I pulled my hand away, my breath hissing over my lips at the pain the lack of a release had caused.

My eyes trained on the cross, I gripped the blankets in front of me to keep my hand from finishing myself off.

Pleading into the silence, I begged.

"God help me."

10

EVE

*But she who is self-indulgent is dead even while she lives. 1
Timothy 5:6*

**Dreams became nightmares on my first night in
this new place.** Sleep crept out of my reach at least
once an hour, my eyes peeking open each time to find
the dimly lit room where Jacob had left me.

One small light worked hard to illuminate the
space, but only served to cast shadows over the desk
and chair to its right. The cross above the light was the
only thing truly visible and I wondered if its placement
had been deliberate or merely another *coincidence* that
proved the existence of divinity. The rest of the room
was bathed in shadow so dark that where the light was
able to touch, it seemed like a portal between two very
different realities.

Tossing and turning on my bed, sticky sweat
covered my skin. I kicked the blankets away from me. I
was too hot. Too...*needy?*

Even the soft cloth of the robe Jacob had given me
was too warm to bear.

Untying the sash, I allowed the two sides to drift open and away from my body.

"Now *that* is a beautiful sight."

I jumped, my heart leaping into my throat, my breath catching so suddenly it hurt.

His words were not spoken loudly. They broke the silence on a whisper. I strained to see him, but there was nothing except the outline of a desk and chair - the brightly lit cross on the wall.

"Jacob?"

"Is that what you call me now?"

Spoken slowly, the deep, rolling lilt of his voice placed emphasis on each word.

Shaking my head, I was so puzzled by names that I thought I'd lost touch with my own identity somehow; transformed into his destiny only to be reverted back to who I'd been before.

Who was he?

Why was I being tormented with the constant shift in rules and facts about everything I thought I'd known?

"You told me to call you that."

My fear had subsided to recognize his voice, but anxiety raced in to fill the places left vacant.

"I know." He didn't move into the light, didn't make another sound to let me find where he stood. I couldn't gauge a general direction from his voice. When he spoke, he was everywhere at once.

"I'm just in awe of how quickly you've changed already. Is there nothing you won't do for me?"

I didn't know from what direction it came, but a cool breeze drifted across my body, reminding me of my nudity. Sitting up, I continued to peer into the darkness searching for Jacob while cinching the robe around me.

"Leave it open."

A command, his voice was stronger, more robust, than how he'd spoken before. I released the robe, desperate to please him and give him anything he asked. A strange joy filled me, his desire to look at me showing me the connection between us had returned. He wasn't angry anymore.

"Let me see you."

My hands shook as I pulled them from my body, my chest tightening because I knew that his eyes could see every part of me.

The silence was suffocating. He didn't move, didn't speak, didn't give me any sign of his approval. I sat completely still, closing my eyes against the heat that raced along my skin.

One footstep and then two, the sound of them crept through the small space.

He came into view just barely, the shadows cast by the low light lending a cutting edge to his cheeks and jaw. His clothes were black, blending seamlessly into the darkness of the room.

"Climb onto your knees and turn around. Place your hands against the wall. Look at nothing but the pillow beneath you."

My body jumped at the raw heat in his voice. I had to obey. Had to...

To upset him would be to destroy myself.

Denying him would be the same as denying God.

Faith filled me as I took the position he'd asked of me. His footsteps warning me he was near. I jumped at the single fingertip sliding softly over the skin of my calf.

91

The pressure of his finger softened at the bend in my knee, but that touch soon spread open to the full width of his hand, his grip painful yet enticing in the way it moved over the back of my thigh.

When he neared the apex of my thighs, I quivered, the skin between my legs becoming slick with anticipation of his caress. But he pulled away before he granted me his touch. And I was reduced to ashes.

I turned my head to look back at him, not thinking about how it was a violation of his command.

His hand was on me, his fingertips digging into my skin as he gripped the back of my neck. Crying out, I felt a tear slip free, my muscles beneath his fingers burning from how tightly he held me.

He said nothing as he leaned down, his breath hot against my ear while he held me in position. Pain screamed along my shoulders from his hand, but I refused to complain. Trembling, I waited anxiously for him to speak, for there to be any sound besides the rhythmic inhale and exhale of his breath.

It felt like hours before he finally asked, "Do you know how badly I want you?"

"I'm yours."

No hesitation.

No doubt.

There was nothing inside me but need.

I was desperate for him to understand that I was sorry I'd run. I would never leave his side again.

"Please..."

His hand released my neck to fist in my hair.

Keeping my eyes trained to the mattress beneath me, I swallowed the whimper of pain that tried to force its way up my throat. Pain was cleansing. Pain brought me closer to the light.

Pain was what propelled me into the ecstasy of God.

Adjusting to his hold, I relaxed, remaining quiet and waiting for him to speak again.

His other hand swept up the back of my thigh, pulling with it the robe that hung loose from my body. My bare bottom was exposed to the air, the muscles of my core rippled inside me. I was desperate for his touch.

Jacob's palm brushed over the cheek of my bottom, pulling the robe higher until the material gathered over my upper back. I was completely open to him as he stood above me silently.

Heart pounding, my blood was thunder in my head.

Wickedness coursed through me. My sin was being brought to the surface to be purged by his hand.

His mouth was next to my ear. His breath hot.

So hot.

Too hot.

"Make one sound, and I'll stop. If I stop, you've failed."

Fear struck my heart with each beat, my teeth sinking into my lip to keep from speaking, from reacting in any way to what was to come.

Jacob's fingers traced the line of my hip, tickling the skin of my waist and reaching to graze across the tips of my breasts. My body jerked in response, my lip feeling like it would split from how hard I bit down.

Trembling beneath the strain of my position, the muscles in my arms shook as if they would give out. I forced myself to remain strong, to hold my body exactly as he'd directed, the terror that I would fail crippling my ability to think clearly.

His fingertips moved over my bottom, stopping just before touching the slickened skin between my legs. I writhed, my hips pushing up into his touch.

But it only served to push him away.

I couldn't complain at the loss of his heat, couldn't whimper or moan. I'd been silenced by his demands and there was nothing I could do but breathe through the rejection.

He stood above me, not moving or speaking.

I could feel him watching me, the hair on the back of my neck standing on end. I was frightened while turned on, terrified while completely and wholly surrendered.

Minutes passed, one after the other, my anxiety building as I wondered what he would do. Would he hurt me? His anger always led to pain, but it drove away my sin – it cleansed me.

I deserved the pain, cherished it because it would leave me pure.

Breaking apart the thick silence, he asked, "Does it hurt when I refuse you?"

"Yes." Spoken on a broken voice, the one word came out on my tremulous breath.

His hand was on me again, his skin sweeping across mine with slow, precise movement.

Deep and on a soft tone, he spoke to me.

"You need to seduce me, my love. No matter what I say, what I do, you must show me how loyal you can be."

Despite the hushed manner in which he spoke, his words reverberated through the room, along my skin until I swore my heart beat loud enough for him to hear it.

Reaching down, his finger slipped along the flesh that was swollen with my need for him. He never pushed inside, simply moving his hand back and forth, touching places that made my entire body quiver and squirm.

With his other hand, he pulled on my hair, lifting my head from where it had been positioned. Looking down, he said, "I'll challenge you. I'll enjoy refusing you. But you can still seduce me. You *must* have faith in me, Eve. No matter what, you *must* seduce me when I test you."

His teeth nipped the bend of my neck and shoulder. His finger pushed inside my body.

I was lost.

I was found.

I was damned.

I was forgiven.

Biting my tongue, I held in the pleasure that fought to escape on a scream.

Split apart I wanted to beg him for more. I wanted him moving inside me, to take my body with his.

I wanted the pain to end, for my cleansing to be complete even though I knew this was just the beginning.

Releasing my neck with his teeth, his free hand ran down my right arm, the tips of his fingers digging into my muscles that were already sore and burning from the position I held. My own hands trembled against the wall where they were still firmly pressed, a tear escaping my eye at the terrible pain his touch elicited.

He worked his finger inside me, waves of a building euphoria crashing through me.

Pushing in.

Pulling out.

Slow.

So damn slow.

I held my breath to keep from crying out, my mind spinning from the lack of oxygen. My lip was swollen and bleeding where I'd bitten down.

He pulled his finger free to rub over my clit. My body bucked against him, the release small, not enough...never enough.

I couldn't hold the position. I crumpled to the mattress. His touch was too much.

Fear shot through me that I'd failed.

Pleasure isn't really pleasure, not when the feelings raging through you battle against the terror overwhelming your mind.

I curled into a ball on the mattress.

Jacob didn't touch me, didn't speak, didn't move to let me know if he was above me or if he'd left the room.

I was disgrace.

I was shame.

I was desire and need, fire and brimstone.

Had I tarnished him?

Not him...

Minutes felt like hours. My body wouldn't stop shaking. I couldn't move my arms and I felt unclean between my legs.

I was a whore.

I was his.

Jacob's hands were on me, grasping my leg and arm. A startled cry broke free of my lips as he flipped me onto my back.

My robe fell open, exposing every part to him.

I could feel the heat of his breath wash over me. His hand wrapped around my throat, squeezing to a point where I couldn't breathe. I wanted to reach up to stop him, but even if I could use my arms, it would only make things worse.

Why did I always fail?

Why did he think I was the *one* when I did nothing but disappoint him?

Picking me up by my throat, he held me so that my arms dangled uselessly by my side. The waiting was unbearable.

Would he?

Wouldn't he?

My body convulsed in his hold, my lungs screaming for the air they were desperate to draw in.

He laughed.

Soft, sensuous and deep, he laughed.

"Why can you never follow directions, Eve? Why must you always be so disobedient? Accept your place."

Jacob's voice was soft, so damn dark. "Confess."

His hand released, my body falling against the bed while my lungs filled with air. I couldn't help my tears, couldn't move to save myself for fear that it would only make the punishment last longer.

"Turn over."

I tried to obey, but my arms still burned, still refused to move the way I needed them to move. I tried to flop over, but it was useless, I was too terrified.

He grabbed me, flipping me over before I could do as I'd been told.

The slap of his hand against my bottom echoed through the room.

It was followed by another.

And another.

He was relentless, dominant, cruel.

Oh God, he was beautiful.

"Assume the position, Eve. Try again. *Never* stop trying."

Crying, I pushed myself up. I forced my arms to support my weight so that I could sit on my knees before placing my hands on the wall.

My face was directed towards the mattress. My body presented for his use.

I waited breathlessly for what he would do.

His fingers played through the skin between my legs and he growled, the sound low and menacing, but still forcing heat to blossom inside me. I wanted to please him, was desperate to please him. I would do anything he asked.

"You're so ready, so needy, so swollen. If only you could learn to behave. When will you stop fighting?"

His fingers were inside me, stroking me, forcing pleasure along my nerves and through my core.

My body moved of its own volition, my muscles gripping at his fingers greedily. I'd only known a man's touch from him, but that touch had shown me true divinity. Every time he'd granted me his pleasure, I drifted on clouds that I never knew a person could reach. I wasn't good enough, wasn't strong enough or pure enough, and I couldn't understand why he didn't see it.

The mattress dipped with his weight.

His hips and legs moved between mine.

I could feel his pants brush my skin.

His mouth was by my ear, my body writhing against his hand. My breath was frantic, the bed below shaking from the way I moved.

"P-please…"

I was almost there, almost in that place that only he had been able to show me.

His fingers pulled away.

A buckle unlatched.

Thick and hard, he pushed against my body.

Teeth sunk into my shoulder. Fingers wrapped around my neck. He pulled his mouth from my skin when he told me to *confess*.

He pushed inside my body.

Stretched taut, my muscles gripped around him.

My body came alive as my lips parted, as I told him all the ways I had sinned.

"I didn't believe," I whispered, "I didn't try hard enough."

It was all I could say.

He was moving inside me and I was lost to everything but him.

In and out, back and forth. My sin beaded over my skin.

Temptation had found me.

Trapped to sensation, a slave to his breath against the back of my neck, I pushed my hands against the wall, bit my tongue harder, soared to that place where I could finally let go.

The storm was building. It was teeming. It was a rush of lightning and honey inside me. A burst of shockwaves, lingering until I was drowning.

My muscles pulsed over him.

He pushed impossibly deeper.

I couldn't breathe.

I couldn't think.

I couldn't...

His body stilled, the head of his cock buried so deep it was the only thing I could feel.

Like a hopeless addict, I cried out when he pulled away.

Tears slipped down my cheeks to fall to the mattress, my arms burning from the position I refused to release again.

The grit in his voice was my undoing. "Seduce me at all times, Eve. Show me you can behave. Show me how loyal you are. I'll resist you. I'll refuse you. I'll tell you things that can't possibly be true. You must believe. You must show me that you still hold faith in everything I've taught you." His forehead pressed against the back of my head. "Do you understand me?"

"Yes," I breathed.

"Show me the way to forgive you. Show me that I am your only light."

Nodding my head, I squeaked out, "I'll do it. No matter what, I won't give up."

"Good girl."

The mattress moved, cold air rushing in to fill in the areas where he'd been pressed to my skin.

"I have something for you. Never take it off."

Cold metal slipped around my neck, a large pendant hanging now, swinging against my breasts.

I heard his steps moving away from me, but they stopped before he could step out of the room. "Stay as I've left you. Do not move until I return."

The door opened and closed, the room left in silence and darkness as if he'd never been there in the first place.

I was too afraid to move, to glance back to see if he'd truly left or if this was just another one of his tests.

Despite the pain I was in, I held the position.

I swore I wouldn't move again. It was time for me to prove to him just how loyal I was.

100

11

JACOB

So I find this law at work; Although I want to do good, evil is right there with me. Romans 7:21

I was exhausted when I woke.

The haunting dreams that taunted me were ceaseless. Crawling from beneath my blankets, I threw my legs over the side of the bed, scrubbing my face with my hands before looking up at the crucifix on my wall.

He stared down at me, the image and symbol of the only being that could grant me salvation from my sins. The only being that could grant me absolution from my past.

After showering and donning my clothes, I fastened the white clerical collar in place, believing that what I carried inside was the worst of the nightmares I would face. Sedra was fresh in my mind, her plight taking up the majority of my thoughts.

How would I avoid her while helping her at the same time?

There were no answers and on this subject, God, as usual, was silent.

I was a priest, a man who was supposed to know exactly how our creator had intended for us to live, but with this situation – this puzzle – all the archaic knowledge written in His book was useless in answering the questions I had.

Battling my own demons while trying to exorcise Eve's was too much for a man like me. I whispered my vows again as I fell to my knees, hoping in earnest that giving them voice would give them weight. Would give them meaning and the power to mean something when I was faced with temptation.

Finally stepping out of my room, a scream sounded from the sanctuary. My head spun in its direction, my feet carrying me through the empty hall.

Entering the nave, I looked up toward the altar, freezing in place to find a young nun dressed in the white habit of a woman who had not yet taken her vows.

She was slumped down in front of the statue of Mary that stood to the left of the altar, her hands working in the sign of the cross over her shoulders, head and heart.

Horror was written into the nun's expression when she looked up again.

I, too, was silently lost to the desecration that stood before me.

The normally pure white statue had been mutilated - drawn upon in what appeared to be a dark red color.

Tears streamed from her eyes like blood, her lips were painted to resemble lipstick. Nipples had been drawn over her breasts and the base of robe had been covered to appear as if she'd walked through a slaughter. *Whore* was written across her forehead, the babe she held had been drawn upon to appear gutted and crushed.

Liquid pooled on the floor where the statue stood. I assumed it was paint despite the noticeable absence of the smell.

Finally pushing myself up, I ran to where the young nun had crumpled. Kneeling down, I prayed beside her.

Unable to close my eyes, I watched her fingers work over the rosary beads, tears streaming down her forlorn face, her lips moving and releasing her prayers on a fast paced whisper.

Turning, I touched the paint at the base of the statue, bringing my hand up to realize that it wasn't what I'd hoped it would be.

Blood covered my hands, sticky and cool to the touch, the red color only barely shining forth from the damp black it had become in its thickness across the floor.

Sedra...

My heart lodged in my throat, my pulse so heavy and hard that it beat noticeably against my skin.

Running out of the sanctuary, I turned down another hall without even thinking about what I was doing.

I threw open the door to Sedra's room, stopping suddenly at the sight before me.

She was spread across her bed, face down on the mattress, her arms stretched out above her head, the palms of her hands pressed against the wall.

Her body was exposed from where her robe had been opened and bunched up across her shoulders. The glimmer of moisture dripping down her legs.

Without thinking, I rushed to her side and grabbed her. She screamed when I touched her arms.

Fear and relief, guilt and desire, they met in a perfect storm inside me, splitting me apart at the seams.

"Sedra..."

"I'm sorry. I'm so sorry..." She interrupted my whispered words with her own.

Sedra could barely talk, her mouth opening and her body trembling. I couldn't help but see her body bared to me, her robe lying open at her sides, Pulling it from where it had gathered, I covered her quickly, the act only causing her to cry harder.

Looking her over for any injuries, I was relieved to find none. The blood in the sanctuary couldn't possibly have come from her.

My eyes locked on the black and blue bruising around her throat.

Created by large hands, it was if whoever had grabbed her still held on, refusing her peace despite having left her alone in the room.

"Sedra..." I spoke softly, slowly in an effort to keep from upsetting her more than she already was. "Who did this to you?"

"I'm sorry. I'm sorry. I'm ..."

On and on, she apologized, but when I moved to console her she cried out at my touch.

Bags hung heavily beneath green eyes that stared at nothing. She wasn't completely with me in the room, her mind disjointed and fractured to a point where whatever reality she existed in at that moment was far beyond my reach.

Pulling the blankets from beneath her, I winced each time she whimpered from the pain it caused.

Covering her, I placed my lips on her forehead, reaching to close her eyes with my hand.

Softly, I begged, "Sleep, Sedra."

She stilled beneath me, the shock of my words causing her entire body to flinch, but within seconds I could feel her relax against the mattress, her tired body finally giving into the rest she'd been denied.

Quietly creeping from the room, I closed the door, turning to find the young nun standing in front of me in the hall. Her rosary was clutched to her chest, the blood from the sanctuary staining the bottom hem of her clothes.

"Evil has been here, Father. Evil unlike anything I've seen before." Tears continued to stream from her eyes, damp rivulets sliding down her cheeks to drop to the floor.

Touching her chin, I angled her face to look at me. She opened her eyes and I jumped to see they bore no color except for the black of her pupils.

"Why are you here, Sister? I've not called for assistance today."

Her hands shook where they were cradled to her chest, the crucifix that hung from her rosary swinging in choppy motion at her breast. "I've been sent by Mother. Sister Joyce did not return last night. I'm here to check on her whereabouts."

Shock tore through me. Shock and the bitter anger I felt towards a man I knew was the cause of this.

Frozen solid in my own disbelief, I looked towards the hall that led to the gruesome scene laid out in the sanctuary. Without answering, I asked, "Was anything else misplaced, vandalized or destroyed in the sanctuary besides the statue?"

She sobbed, her face falling to look at the floor beneath her feet.

"The holy water contained in the stoup has been contaminated. I'm not sure with what, but it looked like rust when I dipped my fingers inside. I'd completely forgotten about it when I stepped into the sanctuary and found our Lady had been..."

Her words segued into a heartbreaking sob, her fingers sliding over the beads of her rosary in time with her tears.

Placing my hands on her shoulders, I led her out of the hall and into the kitchen, sitting her in the same chair that Eve had occupied the night before.

"Sit here, Sister. I need to explore my parish. We don't yet know what has been done. Please do not let your fear consume you. Evil cannot reside inside God's house."

Her eyes shot up, the white and black magnified by her tears. "We need to call the police...report this."

My heart clenched at her words.

I didn't want the police involved. Not until I had all the details of what had gone on while I slept.

"I'll call them, Sister. Please. Make yourself some tea when you feel strong enough. Allow me some time to check for all the damage. I'm sure it's nothing. Probably young vandals who thought desecrating a church would be a fun time."

She nodded, still clutching her beads. Before I could leave the room, she called out to me. "Father? Have you seen Sister Joyce or heard from her? Mother will want to know."

"I'm sure Sister Joyce is fine, but no. I haven't heard from her since last night. It's doubtful that her absence and the vandalism of the parish are related."

Lies and more lies.

Untruths stacking up into a pile of immorality that I would have to atone for when the time came.

I left the young Sister sitting in the kitchen while I inspected the rest of the parish. Nothing was out of order except for a window cracked open in my office.

It hadn't been open the night before. I remembered locking it.

A breeze blew through the room, still carrying with it the smell of the night-blooming flowers that had closed when the sun rose in the sky this morning.

Shutting the window, I jumped when the wood frame slammed against the sill. Jericho had to be responsible for the damage to the statue...to Sedra.

Finally allowing my eyes to scan over the yard in the front of the parish, I saw a man dressed all in black.

Anger was a drum beneath my skin, my stride long and hurried as I made my way out to him.

He was leaning against a tree as I approached.

Carefree. Casual. Untouched.

His head lifted, his eyes finding mine.

"Are you enjoying her, Jacob?"

"Why were you in my parish last night?"

He pushed away from the tree and stepped forward, the dim morning sun highlighting the features of his face. Smiling, something wicked and dark flashed in the exaggerated expression.

"What have you done with Sister Joyce?" I asked.

His head cocked to one side, a gleam flashing behind the silver-blue as he examined me. Feigning confusion, he shrugged a shoulder and remarked, "I have no idea what you're talking about."

"I'm sure." Disbelief saturated my voice. "I don't know what you're doing, Jericho, but it stops. Here and

107

now, this is over. Where is Sister Joyce? Where did you get the blood used to destroy my sanctuary?"

Lifting his hands, he held them out to me, palms up.

"I see no blood on my hands. I'm not sure what you mean."

He smiled again, stepping forward so that a beam of direct light shifted over his body, a gleaming halo covering him. "Will you give her back to me now?"

"Not after what you've done to her. It wasn't enough to warp her mind, but you couldn't even give her one night's reprieve?"

He laughed, his sick grin revealing the malevolence that so obviously existed inside him.

"She's mine, Jacob. I've taught her, raised her, trained her to be everything a woman should be. She is one of a kind. And she will be mine again."

Stepping forward, I refused to back down, my anger fueling something deep inside that I'd tried to forget existed in the years I'd hidden behind the cloak of a cloistered man.

"She is nothing as any person should be. Not man and not woman. What has happened to you, Jericho? When I left home, you were a devout man. You believed in the faith and the Church, and now? Now you are doing everything you can to spread whatever evil it is that has consumed you. Are you that angry with what the Church has done?"

My comment didn't faze him visibly, but I knew my twin well enough to know that his momentary silence was spurred by the cutting words I'd spoken.

I expected him to explode with his retort, for him to curse the very ground I walked on, but instead, he simply shrugged his shoulder again, brushing off everything I'd said.

"You'll learn."

Looking up at me, the blue in his eyes resembled cold fire in the light of the sun. "You stand there pretending to be something you're not. Something you can never be." Taking another measured step forward, he asked, "How long do you think you'll be able to hide from your past...to keep history from repeating itself?"

My spine straightened, every muscle tightening over my body. What could he possibly know of my past? "I don't know what you're talking about..."

"In fact, you do." Holding up a finger he silenced me, sinister knowledge sneaking out from behind the placating expression he wore. "I would even bet on the fact that your past has been catching up with you in the last few days. I'm sure Eve is quite the catalyst."

"What do you know?"

"Everything, Jacob. I know...everything."

He paced the lawn, turning his back to me every so often without the slightest concern that I would attack him from behind.

"I followed you, brother. Tracked all of your accomplishments. What you did in college, the papers you published, every single one of your life events..." Stopping in his tracks, he didn't turn back to me when he added, "Including the death of that poor, innocent woman."

My teeth ground together. "Her death was not an accomplishment."

"I'm sure."

Returning his attention to me he flashed a genial grin. "However, I'm not sure her death was an accident as you told the police either. At least, not in the manner you described it happening."

The light flashed in his eyes once again. "I know you, Jacob. I know your likes, your dislikes, your darkness..."

"Those were earlier times, Jericho. We were young...stupid..."

"We are still the same creatures. You can deny it all you want, but you know as well as I that there are inherent qualities inside each of us. Denying them will only drive you mad."

"Is that what happened to you?"

He grinned at my question, but was unable to respond before we both heard the door of the parish open.

Glancing back, I noticed the young nun walking out from the doorway, the pure white of her habit stained with blood.

"Innocent youth draped in the shroud of a whore."

Jericho's voice was a murmur carried on the wind.

Anger rolled through me at the words, memories of his desecration of the statue of Mary, his words eliciting a reborn concern for Sister Joyce.

Turning back to him, my hands balled into fists. "What have you done with Sister Joyce?"

The corner of his mouth quirked. "It's my turn now to claim that I have no idea what you're talking about."

"I'll call the police..."

His eyes locked to mine. "Call them. There's nothing for them to discover. Except for a childish prank played on your church. Well..." He smiled, his teeth gleaming in the light of the rising sun. "...that and the confused girl you have tucked away that does not belong to you. The one who I assume is very frightened at the moment. Used, bruised and terribly confused about who's holding her."

His satisfaction at cornering me was tangible in the early morning air.

How the hell would I explain any of this?

The young nun approached us. Unaware of the situation at first, her expression changed when she looked between us. Her surprise came out on a loud gasp, the hand that flew to her mouth still clutching the rosary. "You two are..."

In her surprise, she'd been unable to finish the statement. I needed to force her inside the church, to protect her from Jericho.

Reaching out, I grabbed her shoulder, turning her back towards the building and taking a few steps to goad her forward.

"Sister. That's a beautiful veil you wear." Jericho's low voice rolled across the expanse, seemingly taking over the large, open space in which we were standing.

The young nun turned around, not able to resist her curiosity to look at the man who was identical to me.

Although I gently tugged at the nun's arm to gain her attention, she couldn't look away from Jericho. She was too entranced.

I heard him chuckle as he approached. Stepping away, I watched as he took her trembling hand. She jumped, something deep inside sensing the malevolence of the man in front of her.

On a hushed breath, he spoke. "Before you take your vows, please think about who it is you'll be serving. Is it truly God to whom you give yourself, or is it something different that presents itself in sheep's clothing?"

She attempted to jerk her hand from his, but he held tighter.

I don't know why I didn't act to stop him, didn't move to remove him from the innocent woman he was attempting to manipulate. I was too focused on discovering what he would say, too hopeful that he would make a mistake and clue me in to the reason he'd warped Sedra so thoroughly.

"Look at me." His voice was stern and for the first time I witnessed a glimpse of the madness I knew existed inside him.

The young nun looked up, her body held so still that I knew she was scared of him, intimidated by his presence and the confusion it created within her.

Jericho's voice was a bare whisper. "You're making yourself a whore to the Devil himself, giving up your purity and your light for a body of liars and thieves."

She tugged her hand away, stepping back with a look of raw fear written into her expression. Jericho smiled, stepping forward into her space. "What is your name?"

Her feet moved quickly to place more distance between them, her voice trembled when she answered, "Eunice."

"What a lovely name." Delighted by her responses, he continued. "Tell me, Eunice, have you been touched? Perhaps a ruler across the knuckles excited you, or maybe an overly friendly priest who helped you atone for your lifelong sins."

Reaching out, he brushed his hand across her cheek and she shuddered, the trembling of her body visible even across the distance where I stood and watched.

Jericho's fortitude slipped slightly, the persona he carried washing away slowly to reveal his malevolent thoughts. "But you haven't always been like this have you?" His mouth puckered, his tongue tsking against his cheek before he grinned again. "Oh, come now, beautiful, don't feel ashamed. Who was the little boy you let touch you? Tell me all about how he made you feel."

Slipping his hand down along her neck, he smiled when she flinched but didn't move to break free. She appeared hypnotized by his voice, her eyes opened wide in both longing and horror; the air of authority that he carried having seduced her almost fully.

"I could touch you even deeper, Eunice. My hands are not bound to mistruths and greed, my hands are freed."

His hand slipped along her body further, brushing across her breast and down along her abdomen. She shivered where she stood.

Frozen in her own fear, she was unable to break away, her eyes flicking to me silently, begging for me to intervene.

I couldn't.

Not because I was entranced by my own twin. Not because I didn't feel sorry for the young girl who stood cowering before him. It was because I was reminded of my own dirty secrets. Ones that I'd been fighting ever since another one of his *family* collapsed on the lawn in front of my parish.

Jericho was as charismatic and charming now as he had been in our youth. Able to voice bullshit and have it fall on willing and attentive ears because of the tone he used.

This woman knew he was wrong in what he said. She knew she should move away from him, that she should run if given the chance, but she stayed. It was

113

the same story repeated again almost twenty years later.

We'd both been given everything we asked, no woman refusing our advances or forgetting us once we'd finished toying with her. How many women had we abused in our youth? How many had he continued to abuse since I last saw him?

His hand slipped between her legs, the material of her robe bunching where he touched her. With wide-opened eyes, fear now strangled her where she stood. I sat in silent witness of her terror.

She was unable to pull away, possibly feeling for the first time the touch of a man's hand.

It was against everything she'd been taught in her faith. A moan – or was it plea? – escaped her lips. Jericho smiled knowing well that he'd gained the upper hand.

"You like that, don't you?" Soft laughter broke free of his lungs, his foot moving forward so that he could be closer to her, towering over her small frame.

"How would it feel if my fingers move just a little bit farther?" he asked, seduction rolling across his tongue. "How would it feel if they slipped inside your Bible banging cunt?"

Jericho's next move was so fast my eyes couldn't track it.

Within a split second, the hand that had been tormenting her between her legs was now wrapped fully around her neck. She was lifted from the ground, her kicking feet barely making contact with the dirt beneath. Dropping her rosary to reach up in an attempt to pry his hands free, her face turned blue, her mouth open on a silent scream.

His expression was impassive. Staring at her with the eyes of a man who was not new to the torture he inflicted on her.

Clearly, he articulated every word he spoke next.

"I felt you grow wet at my touch; the *fear and trembling* of your body is not a road to your own salvation but a response to the whore that exists inside you. Wearing the purity of a virgin, you mock God by giving yourself blindly to the greatest manifestation of evil that exists. Do you know how disgusting you are?"

She cried out when her body hit the ground. Dropped like nothing more than a tattered doll, she crumpled over herself, her body shaking on the choked sobs that poured from her throat. The physical violence broke my fascination. Leaping quickly to her aid, I pulled her from the ground, steadying her on shaky legs. Anger filled my body when I felt the fear coursing through hers.

My words rattled from my tight chest, my spine solid along my back. Every muscle twitched with the fury I barely contained.

"Leave this property now, Jericho. Do not let me see you here again, or so help me God, I'll…"

"You'll what? Call the cops? Send them to my property? It's your word against over a hundred others that I was even here this morning."

He smiled. "I welcome you to make that call. I'll be sure to let them know that their beloved, parish priest is holding a young woman against her will, committing untold atrocities against her in the room where he has her locked away. They'll interview her, you know."

Pausing, he gave me a second to process his words. Tilting his head, he asked, "What do you think she'll tell the police about what happened during the night she spent in your church?"

"Leave."

I had nothing to say to him and I refused to take part in the cat and mouse game he was playing. There was no room in me for patience, not with him, not any longer.

Laughing, he turned, nonchalantly walking back towards the woods before shouting at me from over his shoulder.

"Enjoy her, Jacob. You don't have much longer."

12

EVE

Do not let sin reign in your mortal body so that you obey its evil desires. Romans 6:12

Soft light touched my face. My closed eyelids turned a warm, creamy pink. Warmth caressed my face.

I was still locked inside my head, sleeping in bursts, but never really falling deeply. Not wanting to open my eyes to see the room, I refused to move. Pain radiated along my body.

The sting of my bottom was still there, my arms like jelly from having been held in one position for so long.

I remembered cringing when Jacob entered the room. I was so sure he would punish me for having moved.

Cowering down against the sheets, I waited for the strike that never came. His behavior, as usual, confused me.

Always changing his skin, it was a dance of opposition: sweetly caring for me in one minute before turning around to abuse me once again. I couldn't hold his behavior against him. I only wondered how long it would take him to realize what I've known all along:

I'm not worthy of him. No amount of pain would cleanse the deep-seated lust I had for him.

Yes, I was loyal. So loyal that I was willing to undergo any transformation he demanded of me.

My name, my image, the very essence of my being was in his control...but I hated him still for having chosen me.

I was not worthy.

And I would never be worthy.

I would endure the abuse until I ultimately failed. I would leave him when I died. I sold my soul to his image. Gave up my freedom just so he would draw near.

I ached and I cried.

And still...I wanted him.

A door opened in the room, but I refused to look at him. I was too ashamed.

Turning my head toward the wall, I wished I could curl my body over itself in protection of the pain or desire he chose to deliver.

His instructions were firmly planted in my head. I knew that I should open my robe to entice him.

But, I couldn't.

I was drowning slowly in suffocating disgrace.

Bracing myself for his attention, I was caught off guard by the sound of the chair legs scraping across the floor, the scream of wood against wood followed by a heavy thud and the susurration of skin.

Curiosity bested me and I allowed my eyes to crack open, squinting against the minimal light that bathed the room.

He sat in the chair, his elbows resting on his knees as he scrubbed his hands over his face. Shoulders slumped as if weighted by some unseen force, he neither looked at me nor attempted to speak. Stress radiated off him in obtrusive waves, light appearing to bend in refusal to touch him or brighten the dark shadows that concealed his features.

Minutes passed while I stared at him, anxiety building inside until I was in pain.

He was sad, scared or upset in a manner that somehow broke him. But I knew that couldn't be true. Not Elijah – or Jacob – or whatever he wanted to be called.

Never before had he made himself vulnerable; not to me or to any other person in our group. It simply wasn't something he was capable of doing.

He was too strong, too perfect in any way to allow evil to defeat him. He was too close to God to lose.

That was the type of person he embodied, not this hunched over man, hiding his face from me and sitting so still that I wondered if he was breathing.

"Jacob?"

I couldn't take it any longer. The quiet in the room was deafening. It wrapped around me like a thick blanket threatening to cut off the air from my lungs.

"I need to send you away."

Spoken so low that I could barely hear, his words echoed in the space, haunting by the way he'd whispered.

"What do you mean?"

Fear and terror, my ever-present companions, thrummed through my veins, chipping away at my resolve with each beat of my heart. I could feel them crippling me inside, my lungs no longer working to pull in large amounts of air, my brain no longer functioning because of the thick emotional soup his words had caused.

"You need to go back to my brother."

There was no remorse to his voice, no sadness or anger. Almost spoken without any hint of intonation, his words were intended for nothing more than information, and yet, somehow, they cut me deeper than if he'd struck out at me physically.

Shaking my head, I opened my mouth to argue, but I was frozen in place when he pulled his hands from his face to look at me.

His eyes were empty and haunted, evil peeking out at me as if I'd dared to look at it first.

I never looked at evil, never broke a rule he'd established so many years before. My eyes were always trained to the ground. The only thing I'd allowed my eyes to see was him. But when I looked at him now, I didn't see love or forgiveness. I saw hatred mixed with lust, the shiver of violence mixed with a dangerous threat.

"You have to leave tonight. I'll take you back to the compound and all of this will be over. I'm sorry, Sedra. It's the only way."

No.

I didn't understand him and I shook my head again to tell him so. Nothing he'd said over the past couple of days had made sense.

I was failing his test.

Anger coursed through me. Anger at him for having chosen me when I wasn't strong enough for whatever purpose he had. Anger with myself for loving him still.

There were no words I knew that were strong enough to describe what I felt when I looked at him. But there were words that could describe what his threat to send me away felt like:

Complete and utter devastation.

There was nothing left inside me, no hope that I'd recover and lead a life away from him. Except for a few memories of my past, I knew nothing but *him*.

He was my world...my salvation.

"Are we returning to the compound together?"

"No."

Confusion rattled my thoughts even further, but then I remembered.

He warned me that he wouldn't make sense; that he would attempt to confuse me in a bid to test my loyalty.

I wouldn't fail him, not now when it was so easy to obey what he'd ordered.

Jacob never moved from the chair, never bothered to look up at me when he fell back into a deep silence.

I had to move before my own fear froze me in place, rendering me useless in my loyalty and faith.

Taking a steadying breath, I blew it out while watching his unmoving form in the chair. He couldn't see me, not with his hands covering his face once again.

I crept quietly from the mattress, ignoring the pain in my body that intensified with every contraction of muscle across bone.

On hands and knees, I crawled to him, slowly creeping across the wooden floor until I was at his feet. I pressed my cheek against the warmth of his leg. He jumped at the contact, never pulling his hands from his face.

He was hurting and I didn't know what to do or what to say. I'd never seen him show weakness before. What was so bad that it could render him so silent and still?

I was his Eve…the woman who would lead him into the destiny he deserved. That's what he always told me. His voice echoed in my head like the haunting words of a distant phantom.

I was his Eve.

I was his hope.

I was his beginning and his end.

Because he'd told me that's who I was.

With shaky hands, I touched his legs, slowly allowing my palms to travel up his pants, never going past the knees, but simply letting him know I was at his feet awaiting anything he needed me to do.

He didn't move in response - not a twitch.

I moved higher.

Pushing up on my knees, I ran my hands over the tops of his thighs, delighting in the feel of his muscles pulsing with tension. The small reaction was enough to encourage me to go farther.

His face was still buried in his hands, anxiety rolling off him in waves of suffocating heat. He didn't need to speak in order for me to know he wanted me at this moment.

We would always be connected that way.

"I am yours." I whispered softly, putting all the strength I could gather into my words.

He didn't respond, didn't pull his hands away so he could see the faith and conviction in my expression. I breathed out heavily, gathering even more strength I didn't have.

With shaky hands, I reached for his shirt, slowly pulling it from where it was tucked neatly into his pants.

"I am faithful. I am loyal. I am yours."

Words spoken so many times over the past few weeks, I'd said them enough that I believed them. Through pain I'd been reborn to him.

No longer a daughter or a sister - I was his alone.

Releasing one button and then two, I peeled the material of his shirt from his body, revealing the heated skin of his abdomen to my eyes. My breath blew out from my lips to brush across his body. Smiling, I ran the tip of my finger over the sculpted muscles, delighting in the way they moved in response to my touch.

I looked up as he pulled his hands from his face. Jacob stared down at me, unmoving and silent, but yet communicating everything he was thinking by the way he stared.

"Let me heal you," I begged softly.

Two more buttons and another, his strong chest now exposed to my eyes. I ran my palms over his skin, lost to the feel of the masculine strength in his body.

Reaching for his collar, I pulled at the white tab to remove it from his shirt, but his hands moved so fast I wasn't able to pull it away.

Grabbing my wrists, he squeezed and my hands opened, a startled cry escaping my lips from the pain of his hold. I looked up at him, seeing lethal anger and seductive rage behind his eyes.

"Do you have any idea what I'm capable of? Do you know what I've done?" He spoke on a breathless whisper.

My body trembled in response, but I was his faithful bride, one who would walk with him through the gates of Hell if he asked.

"Do you?" He yelled and I tried to jump away, but he gripped my wrists tight. I was unable to distance myself from him.

"Do you?"

I screamed in response to the volume of his voice, to the anger that was evident in his words. Tears erupted from my eyes and I thought the bones of my wrists would snap under the force of his hands.

"Please Elijah..." I shook my head remembering what he'd told me. "...Jacob. I'm sorry. Please... I want to help you. I have to help you. I have no choice."

Begging and pleading: they were what I did my entire life.

Suffering silently while he held my fate in his hands, I was destined for him and his beliefs, terrified by him as well as in love with him. I could be bound and gagged, whipped and beaten to the point of imminent death and I would still crawl to him if it meant I could seek comfort in his arms.

That is how I felt about him.

I refused to let myself fail.

"I don't care what you did. I don't care what you will do."

He lifted me by my arms, setting me on my feet so that I stood shivering in front of him. Finally releasing one wrist, he reached up to pull my head down to him, placing my hand that he still held against his chest.

His heart beat was steady and strong beneath his skin, my body shaking just for being allowed to touch him.

With his palm against my cheek, he studied my face, his once heavy breath now slowing to match the speed of mine.

Our mouths were inches apart. Our breath mingling in wicked temptation.

He held me in awe. Like an idol, he personified everything that I thought was pure and good. He was my guide and protector, my life and salvation.

His eyes narrowed, confusion wrinkling his brow. "Do you not understand any of what's been done to you? You should care what I would do, Sedra. You should want to protect yourself."

Sighing heavily, he pushed me back to stand from his chair. I jumped when he reached for me, unable to control the anxiety thrumming through my veins. The movement was made on instinct, but I forced myself to still, to allow him every part of me that he desired.

His hands closed around the open sides of my robe. Parting the material, he stared down at my body with heat behind his eyes. And just when I thought, I'd drawn him in, he closed his eyes and closed the robe around me.

"If I tell you something, do you promise not to cry or scream?"

I didn't move except to nod my head in response. His fingers brushed up against my abdomen, the contact enough to comfort me in my confusion.

"Sit down on the bed, Sedra."

There was no hesitancy in my obedience. Stepping back until my legs met the side of the bed, I sat and waited for him to speak.

"I'm not who you think I am. I'm not the man you married."

I shook my head, denial manifesting in the movement of my body. He told me he would lie. He told me it would be confusing. By faith alone, I would see through the mistruths. "No..."

Stepping forward, he knelt down in front of me, reaching up to grasp my chin in his hand. Forcing me to face him, he said, "Yes, Sedra. Yes. What I'm telling you is the truth. For once in your life, you are hearing the truth."

Jerking my head away was useless. Each time I tried, he gripped tighter, finally becoming angry and gripping the sides of my head with both of his hands to keep me looking in his direction.

I was tired of the lies, of the puzzles and torment. Everything inside me was spinning with the thick sludge of confusion that he created.

It was too much, all of it: The lies, my fate, his destiny. I wasn't strong enough for the pressure or the pain. I wasn't pure enough to walk in grace and lead him where he wanted to go.

"Stop!" I screamed, but instead of releasing me, he pushed me down on the mattress, hovering over me with the anger I was so used to seeing in his eyes.

My mistake was quickly realized, but it was too late to take it back. I'd awoken the monster inside him that I'd somehow forgotten existed.

His chest moved with heavy breath, his eyes wide, the cords in his neck sticking out with barely contained rage.

Fear flooded my system, paralyzing me where I lay. I knew not to fight, not to look away from him. To do so would bring only punishment.

How easily one could forget previous pain when a kind hand is there to soothe it. Black and white, night and day; he was two people, both tucked away into one body, one heart, one soul that was so much greater than me.

He lied.

He always lied.

Yet, I was left to believe those lies because they were the only truths I knew.

"Never..." He spit out his words while struggling against his rage. "...ever speak to me like that again. Ever."

I shook my head and felt my growing panic tremble across my body. When he was angry like this, he was violent. So painfully violent.

"I'm sorry." I breathed out, hoping, *praying*, that my submission would calm him.

He liked it when I submitted to him. He enjoyed the infusion of erotic power domination gave him. It was as if by controlling me, he was able to siphon the strength from body, further building his own.

Jacob let me go as quickly as he'd touched me, stepping back and shaking his head of the confusion so obvious inside him.

Sitting in the chair with a heavy thud, he immediately resumed his former position: head in hands with his elbows propped on his knees.

"You have to go."

I shook my head, silently refusing his continued lies. He wouldn't send me away. I wouldn't let him.

Pushing up from the bed, I bit my bottom lip to stop it from trembling. My body shook with the apprehension I felt, but I had to be strong.

I had to seduce him.

Slipping the robe from my shoulders, I allowed it to fall and puddle at my feet. I straightened my spine and stepped closer to him, using my knees to push his legs apart. Standing completely still, I waited for what I knew would happen.

He leaned back in the chair, his face tipped up to look at my body. I didn't look down at him, didn't acknowledge the fact that I shook violently with the need for his warmth.

I wasn't a person. I wasn't an opinion or something separate from him. I was what he needed, an object, a desire, a cloak that would shelter him from whatever pain existed inside.

I was a distraction.

I was his light.

I was the woman who belonged beneath his steady hand.

My eyes were trained to the wall behind him, my body still...waiting.

Fingertips touched the sides of my legs and I breathed out the air I'd been holding.

Slowly, softly, dangerously, they dragged up, not a caress, but a tease.

Refusing to move, I let him explore me, let him look and touch, lead and command. Words weren't necessary in this. I knew what he needed from me.

By the time his fingers reached my hips, his hands were shaking.

He gripped me, those same fingers pressing down until the nerves beneath my skin came alive.

The chair creaked as he leaned forward, my feet moving only when he tugged me to him.

Leaning toward me, his breath was a fan of heat across my abdomen, his lips just inches from my skin, teasing me – toying with me.

I was coming undone.

He was letting go.

Only God knows what would have happened if somebody hadn't knocked on my door.

13

JACOB

And do not lead us into temptation, but deliver us from evil.
Matthew 6:13

It was as if God himself were knocking on the door, the might of His hand pulling me away from the temptation that stood naked and trembling before me.

Yanking my hands from the heat of Sedra's skin, I pushed back in my chair, wincing at the sound of the feet scraping over the scuffed wooden floors.

"Father Hayle? Are you in there? Your confessional hours begin in a few minutes. You have one person waiting already."

It wasn't God's voice that spoke through the door. It was Gabriel Hart.

My mouth opened to speak, but the words lodged in my throat. Guilt, I assumed, clogged the flesh, left it swollen and teeming, sitting there festering until I cleared it after several attempts. Even then my voice didn't come out much stronger than a gritty whisper.

"I'll be out in a second."

The lack of footsteps clued me in that Gabriel hadn't walked far away and his presence alone was enough to push me out of my chair. Sedra stood still in the same place. Her body didn't move, her eyes didn't stare at me accusingly. She just stood there...waiting.

What had I been doing with my fingers on her skin? What had I been thinking to allow myself even that small contact? The girl was sick, not physically but emotionally, and there I was falling prey to the *ease* of her...to her unwillingness to say no.

I deserved to be struck down. I deserved a fate worse than Hell. But yet, I still found myself staring at her, *wanting* her as no priest should want a woman. Knowing little about the young woman, it wasn't love or even fondness that drew me like a moth to her ever-burning flame. It was much more insidious than that, a part of me that I'd thought dead, that I'd thought the faith had forced away.

Without speaking, I moved past her, noticing that when my shoulder brushed hers, knocking her back a step, she immediately moved to where she'd stood before, her eyes still trained to the wall, her body still presented like it wasn't a temple shielding her soul, but a cage.

Not just a cage.

Her body was a weapon.

One aimed directly at the parts of me that were more dangerous than my head, my heart or my soul.

Not only was she perfectly compliant, frustratingly obedient, and so ready for whatever I wanted to give her that she'd crawl for it, she was also a picture from my past. Her face, her skin, her hair and eyes, they all reminded me of another woman just as compliant, just as obedient and trusting. Jericho couldn't have chosen a woman who looked more like Cassandra if he'd tried, and I had to wonder at the likeness.

Was it merely a coincidence, two twins who have similar tastes in women, or had Sedra's appearance been intentional? Had he trained this woman for his own deviant tastes, or had he intended her for something more?

I wasn't sure, but what I did know was that I needed to stay away from Sedra, needed to stay as far away as I could.

Grabbing the robe she'd dropped to the floor, I wrapped it over her shoulders, my hands gripping over the bones to pull her away from the spot she held like a well-trained soldier. She tried to resist, but her strength, her size, her will wasn't enough to keep me from directing her to the bed.

Sitting down on the mattress, she looked up at me with pain blazing behind her eyes. I felt that pain, absorbed it, sipped on it until the taste was acrid across my tongue, blending and mingling with the guilt already choking me.

"I have to go," I explained, hating the regret clearly etched in my voice. Regret shouldn't have been allowed. I should have *wanted* to go. "Once I finish my work for today, I'll come get you. We'll find you more clothes and then I can take you back to the compound."

"Jacob..."

I held my hand up to silence her. "You're unwell, Sedra...confused. You don't know up from down at the moment and I can't - I *won't* - take advantage of that."

The pleading look on her face nearly broke me, memories creeping in to weave through the present, pain slicing deep to remind me of all the horrible things I'd once been. Monsters didn't deserve salvation, and yet God had given it to me anyway. You don't throw something like that away.

My resolve wavered when I looked at her. Her sad eyes, her hunched shoulders, the defeat and heartache that was plain to see. I took *joy* in that heartache. I felt powerful for that defeat. And I would gladly burn in Hell for acting on those feelings.

Where Sedra was confused, I could see clearly. And while she thought she walked down the path of a righteous woman, I knew that she walked down a terrible road, one filled with all the same traps and potholes that had almost destroyed me.

I wanted to rip her from that road, wanted to grab her and never let go. I wanted to show her that the God to which Elijah had her pray was not God at all. But the life I'd so carefully constructed was falling apart with her around, and I had no choice but to let her go. I couldn't help her. Couldn't offer her salvation because I was too damn tempted by her to remember my place.

"Father Hayle?" A voice called through the door.

Thankful for the voice, I turned toward the door. I had to fight not to look back as I walked through it.

Gabriel leaned up against a wall, his thick arms crossed over his chest, his beard neatly trimmed for the first time that I'd seen. He'd worked as a handy man for as long as I'd known him, not only for the parish, but for odd jobs people in town needed done. That work had given him a strong body and keen eyes, eyes that were now staring directly at me.

"I couldn't let her into the sanctuary. She would have seen..." His voice trailed off, anger a vibration over his skin. The muscles in his forearms were clenched where he'd crossed them. "I can clean up the statue, but when that girl came in for confession, I

133

hadn't started yet. I don't want her to see that. She's too young."

Pushing off the wall, he moved to leave, but I called out to him. "How did you know about the statue, Gabe? Did somebody call you?"

The only other person who knew about the vandalism was the young nun, but she'd left almost as soon as Jericho.

"I came about some repair work I knew needed to be done in the atrium. When I didn't find you in the rectory I came here. Still couldn't find you but then I heard a noise, so I knocked on the door as I passed it."

The last thing I wanted to do was sit there and listen while somebody confessed their sins, but I couldn't turn them away. In truth, it was a blessing in disguise, because it kept me away from Sedra. "Thanks, Gabriel. I'll take care of the young woman outside while you repair the damage. You can finish whatever you need in the atrium as well."

Inclining his head, he grumbled, "Damn vandals," before walking away.

Weaving through the halls, I crossed the narthex and opened the large front door to find Annabelle Prete sitting lonely on a front bench. She reached up to push her glasses farther up her nose as she read a book in her lap.

With striking red hair always kept in a braid, she had light skin that revealed the dusting of freckles across the bridge of her nose. A young woman, she'd just turned eighteen and graduated high school. I'd watched her grow up during my tenure at this parish. She and her parents both dutifully showed up for Sunday Mass, they took the Eucharist whenever it was offered and Annabelle always took a role in the nativity play we put on every Christmas.

She was heading off to college, from what I'd been told, on a full scholarship she'd earned for her perfect grades and dedication to learning. She was a good girl in every way, probably one of the purest I'd known.

"Annabelle," I called, stepping out into the sunlight, shielding the glare from my eyes with one hand. "Why don't we use the reconciliation room instead of the confessional today? There's some work being performed in the sanctuary."

Over the years, the Church had been trying to modernize itself and dispense with antiquated practices. However, this particular parish, and the convent down the road, still held on to certain traditions shunned by others. It's why the Sisters still wore their habits, why we still kept a confessional when a less restrictive option was in hand.

Many of the younger parishioners turned up their noses to the dark traditions of what the Church had been. The confessional was musty and dark, full of regret and flagellation, where the reconciliation room was simply a place where I could talk with those who wanted a lighter feeling when they confessed. It wasn't small and condemning. It didn't trap you within its iron grip. It was simply a room where they could approach me with their problems, where they could ask for forgiveness for even the smallest sin.

The reconciliation room wasn't appropriate for many older members. They still preferred the small, sheltered closet that kept them private while they voiced their innermost problems. They preferred what they believed was anonymity thanks to the screen between us that concealed their faces.

Annabelle's head shot up at the sound of my voice, a broad smile spreading across her lips as she closed her book over a torn piece of brightly colored paper she'd used to mark her place.

Color spread across her cheeks, the hint of a youthful crush on me so clearly written into her features. The blush had occurred since she turned sixteen, since her childhood was being left behind and womanhood was fast approaching. I found it adorable more than anything, she would never act on the attraction, she was too good for something like that.

Running up, she gave me a hug before pulling away with a darker red spreading across her cheeks. "Sorry, Father," she said, embarrassment coating her words. "I'm just really happy to see you."

Poor thing must have thought that even touching a priest with desire in your heart was somehow wrong enough to step on God's toes.

I didn't blame her. Many woman found me attractive even though I wear the clothes of a devout man. In fact, if Annabelle wanted to practice flirting, I'd rather her do it with me than a young man who would take advantage.

"You can hug me, Annabelle," I teased. "There's nothing wrong with that."

She flushed, her hands waving around her at a dizzying speed as if she didn't know what to do with them. "I know, it's just that you're a priest and I-"

Her words cut off, her blush deepening. "I'm, well, whatever...the reconciliation room is fine." An awkward smile spread across her face, forced so that I wouldn't notice she was flustered.

My shoulders shook with silent laughter. Wrapping an arm over her shoulders, I led her inside and down a hall towards the room. "Why are you so happy to see me?"

I couldn't help the grin that slid across my face to see the color on her cheeks deepen more.

"Well," she explained, happily walking ahead of me into the room and selecting a seat on the brown, overstuffed couch. I took a seat in the stuffed chair that faced her.

"As you know, I'm heading off to college. And I think in an effort to be right with God, I need to make a confession before I leave."

Instructed by her parents to only make confessions in that dark box in the sanctuary, Annabelle seemed lost to be out in the open. She couldn't look at me, her hands wringing over her lap, her book tucked demurely beneath them. "Is it done the same way in here?"

"We can skip the formality if you'd like. It's giving voice to your sins that matters to God, not the routine we use to do so."

"I have a crush on *someone*," she blurted out, her blush spreading down her arms and legs where I could see them.

Not surprised by the outburst, I almost wished for the confessional just so I could hide my expression. Thankfully she didn't want to look at me as much as I didn't want her to see my reaction, so I was able to hide the smile without her knowing I 'd found her confession amusing.

Leaning forward, I rested my elbows on my knees and locked my hands together. "There's nothing wrong with having a crush on someone."

Her head shook. "Oh yes there is. Especially if it's a someone I shouldn't have a crush on."

Breath poured over my lips. I was thankful for this one *normal* moment after the past few days I'd had. This was my element, this room, this space, this innocent moment where I could explain to a member of my faith that their perceived sin wasn't as bad as they thought. Having this break helped pull me back into place, helped remind me why I'd sought shelter in this life in the first place.

It also cemented the fact that I needed to push Sedra away. She was too tempting, too painfully sexual that if I'd been sleeping I could call her a succubus. Like the demon who supposedly haunted men in their dreams, who stole their ability to refuse while sucking away everything decent and good about them, Sedra was the ultimate tease.

She was a bridge back to my former life, a bridge I thought I'd burned when I became a priest.

"I'm going to go out on a limb here and tell you that it's not a sin to have a crush on a priest."

Her eyes widened where she stared out the window. "You know? Oh, of course you know. You're a priest. You can see sin."

The squeak in her voice during the last sentence she'd spoken had me biting my cheek not to laugh. "I can't see sin, Annabelle, it doesn't work like that. But I am a man who had a life before becoming a priest, and I recognize the signs of an innocent crush. Most men do, and some will prey on that, which is why you should always be careful."

I neglected to add that I had once been one of those predatory men, the kind who took innocence and crushed it beneath my fingers.

Annabelle's face lost its color. "Yeah, but maybe it's not just an innocent crush," she admitted. "I've

138

had...dreams...and those dreams became thoughts, and those thoughts led to fantasies-" She sighed, her eyes clenching tight enough to force lines at her temples. "I've thought about you in a sexual way," she blurt out. "There I've said it."

Peeking an eye open, she looked at me. "Am I going to Hell?"

Resisting the temptation to laugh at Annabelle's innocence was almost as difficult as resisting the temptation that was sitting in another room.

Somehow, I refrained...on both.

"Sexual thoughts are natural. As long as you're not acting on them with somebody who isn't your husband."

"But the Bible says to sin in thought is the same as sinning in act. So if I think it -"

Cutting her off, I asked, "Did you follow through on it?"

"No."

"And did you regret thinking it afterward?"

"Yes."

"Then you've done nothing wrong."

The same couldn't be said for me. Each moment alone with a woman who didn't even know my name was pushing me closer and closer to acting on the very thing I was warning Annabelle away from. My fingertips came alive with the memory of her skin beneath them. My entire body froze at the thought of how close I'd been to tasting her just once.

Forcing that thought away, I focused on Annabelle. "You can't always control the way you feel. Just like you can't always control who you're feeling it for. But what you can control is whether or not you act on it." It was almost like I was trying to convince myself of that fact more than her.

Damn it, focus...

"Just remember that when you head off to college, Annabelle. Just because you feel something doesn't mean you've failed your faith. It means you're human. Make good choices. Do good things, and do them in a way that pleases God. That's all that's asked of you."

Nodding her head, she reached up to push the tail of her braid over her shoulder. "Do you hate me now that you know how I feel?"

"No," I breathed out. "And I'm glad you felt the need to confess it and be honest. It might be the weight you needed lifted from your shoulders so you can go off to school with a blank slate."

"I wish I could erase my embarrassment," she said on a laugh.

Smiling, I asked, "When do you leave for school?"

Her face lit up, pride a joyous glow behind her brown eyes. "I leave in two months. I wanted to go right now, but the dorms aren't open and I should probably stay on the farm with my parents. I'll miss them when I'm gone, but I'm just so excited. Only three people in my class got full scholarships to college and I thank God that he took that worry away from mom and dad. They had no idea how they were going to pay for me."

"God works in wonderful ways," I agreed. "Do you feel better now that we've talked?"

"Yes," she answered, shrugging a shoulder. "It was the only secret I've kept for a while and I'm glad to have it off my chest."

Standing, I offered a hand to help her from her seat. "Well, then I'm glad we've talked as well. I'll walk with you outside."

Silently, we made our way back to the front of the church, every step building the anxiety in me that I would be left alone with Sedra. I couldn't take her out until it was dark because I didn't want anybody to see her. Which meant I had several hours of knowing she was lying in the room...just waiting. Scrounging my thoughts for any idea of what I could go do to keep me away from the church, I drew a blank. There was no escape from her while I rode out the agony of my desirous storm.

Sunlight poured in when Annabelle opened the front door. We both stepped out and my attention was drawn to another parishioner, Michael Grinnis, where he stood waiting.

Annabelle waved her hand in goodbye, but my eyes were directed at Michael, my focus on greeting him as Annabelle walked away.

I failed to notice the man following her.

14

SEDRA

But he knows the way I take; When He has tried me, I shall come forth as gold.
Job 23:10

Second after second.
Minute after minute.
Hour after hour.

I waited.

I didn't close my eyes or think of sleep. I didn't pace the room or move off the bed. I sat while the hall outside remained empty and I sat when I heard footsteps approach only to turn around and walk away.

My bottom grew numb after a while, my legs like pins and needles, but I wouldn't move, wouldn't budge, wouldn't even consider leaving the spot where Jacob had left me.

It's ridiculous, isn't it? The obedience, the love, the hatred and fear. Every emotion, every action, every possible facet of my world revolved around him, leaving me waiting. It made me wonder when the last time had been that I could call myself my own person.

Sick of the tears that kept falling, I struggled to fight them hours ago. Eventually they stopped, the burning and swelling of my eyes the only evidence remaining that I'd cried at all. It didn't make sense for me to cry this much, didn't make me feel good about myself or more at home, but yet I kept doing it. I kept begging and pleading and putting myself aside just to dutifully follow behind him, just to say that, in instances when I was what he wanted, I became his entire world.

And those moments, when he was with me and I was everything he needed, they were the only thing I wanted. They are real and they were raw, they were primal, wicked and devout. They were the moments when he showed me the sun still lingering inside, expelling my evil until I felt free.

He had that power.

I'd doubted it before, but I lived for it now.

Footsteps approached my room, slow, punctuated thuds that were as hesitant as they were loud. I turned my head toward the door, waiting.

Unlike the other times when those steps had reached my room and then disappeared again on a quickened beat, the handle turned, the hinges of the door creaking as the wood was slowly pushed forward.

Jacob stood in the doorway, his broad shoulders filling the frame, his face masked in shadow.

In his arms were a set of clothes, and he dropped them on the bed as soon as he was within reach.

"I'm not sure how well those will fit, but I went to town and bought them for you."

Pulling the clothes from the bed, I couldn't understand why he'd want me to wear them. Men and women were not the same. Not in body, mind or heart. Those differences should be celebrated in the way they cover themselves, distinguished so that women don't overstep, so that they know their role and are reminded of it by the clothes they wear on their body.

"These are pants. I can't wear them."

My eyes met his, my expression a mask of confusion while he appeared frustrated. His brows pulled together as he stepped back, thick arms crossing over his chest as his gaze locked on my chest. "What is that?"

I glanced down, my fingers moving to the cross pendent that hung between my breasts. "You gave it to me. Last night. Don't you remember?"

Words hissed over his lips, curt and angry, they were spoken too low for me to hear what he'd said. Jacob paced the room, tension running across his shoulders, before he slammed a wall with the sides of his fists. His back was to me as he pressed his forehead against the plaster. "Get dressed in the pants, Sedra. You're going home."

"You are my home," I reminded him.

"No," he yelled, his body spinning until I could clearly see the angry color of his face. "I'm not. I'm not even who you think I am. I'm not Elijah. The man who is your *home* is my twin brother. It's almost impossible to tell us apart."

I wanted to laugh in his face. After everything he told me last night, after his insistence I seduce him and have faith in him no matter what name he used or what lies he told me, did he really think I'd so easily fall for this lie?

144

No. He wouldn't fool me. He wouldn't cause me to fall without a fight. I knew better now. He'd told me exactly what he wanted from me.

"I don't believe you. I know better. I know who you are. There's nothing you can say or do that will make me run from you again."

"Damn it, Sedra." His voice echoed through the room, a booming sound that would make any person tremble. But not me. Not now. Not when I knew beyond a doubt what he needed from me.

Running had been my mistake, and if this game was the punishment I had to endure, then I'd take it. I'd take anything, as long as it meant I could still walk by his side. I'd prove myself to him, even if it meant being beaten down by the family's fists. Even if it meant giving up my life.

This game, I didn't understand it, but he must have a purpose for playing it and that's what mattered. He knew how to lead me to the light, and if the only way to get there was by suffering, then I'd play whatever game he wanted.

Jacob stormed toward me, the tension of his body so pure it was an energy that saturated the air in the room. My muscles tightened over bone, my throat went dry as I held still in my place on the bed, ready for whatever he had planned for me.

Stopping just before he reached me, his hands curled into fists. Instinct told me to cower, to block my head with my arms to prevent his blows, but I fought the need to ball over myself, and instead I faced him down.

His lips pulled into a thin line, his eyes locking me in place. Sweat broke out along my spine, but I wouldn't give in to it.

I wouldn't.

It had been weak of me to run from the ceremony. No matter what he did, I wouldn't run now.

Where he expected me to cry, I smiled instead. And where he expected me to back away, I moved forward to climb to my feet. I had to crane my neck to look up at him, had to balance on weak legs to remain in place as I stripped off my robe.

"I'm yours," I said, clear in my intent not to run away. "I am your purity. I am your light. I am the woman who can lead you to destiny. I am Eve."

"You're Sedra," he bellowed, his hands coming up to lock on the sides of my head. Forcing my face to stay angled up toward his, he squeezed so hard that pain shot across my scalp. His arms trembled with the exertion, his chest heaving with breath. I cried out at the pain I felt, but I didn't fight back, didn't care if he crushed my skull over my shoulders because at least I was with him when I died.

His voice was strained when he spoke again, barely under control. "What in the hell did my brother do to you?"

He released me with such fury that I fell back on the mattress as he paced away. Pain was a pulse across my head, but I ignored it and pushed to my feet again. By the time he reached the farthest wall, he spun back to me, his face even redder than it had been before.

"You need to wake up, Sedra! You need to realize that you've been lied to and deceived."

"You're lying to me right now," I argued. "There's nothing you can say to make me believe you. Nothing you can do and -"

He crossed the room on a powerful stride and his hand was at my throat. The bruises that were still an angry purple throbbed beneath his hold. He could squeeze the life out of me for all I cared. I would not fall to doubt.

Speaking slowly, darkness was a shadow to his voice. "Twelve years ago and I would have eaten you alive. I would have taken this *present* my brother has given me and used you until there was nothing left."

He let go to pace away again. Stopping just before hitting the wall, he kept his back to me and said, "I'm not that man anymore."

When he turned to face me, there was genuine pain in his eyes. "You need to get dressed in the clothes I've given you, and when you're done doing that, you can meet me in the hall."

Trembling in place, I barely managed remaining on my feet. "Is that a command?"

His fist hit the wall beside him before he marched toward the door. "Yes," he yelled and walked through. The wood shook with how hard he slammed it.

It didn't take me long to get dressed and do exactly as he'd demanded. When I walked out into the hall, still barefoot, but dressed, I found him leaning up against a wall, his head cradled in his hands.

"I'm taking you home, Sedra. And when I do, I want you to take a long look at my brother. I want you to see how he's playing some screwed up game against you and leading you in the opposite direction of the God you think you're praying to."

Pulling his hands from his face, he looked at me. "Where you are now is God's house. I'm a priest for his Church, a shepherd for his flock, and I promise you that the man Elijah has made himself out to be is not the type of *godly* man you should be following."

I pressed my lips together to keep silent, blinked my eyes to chase away the tears that threatened to fall. "Say what you want, Jacob. I know what's expected of me."

Pushing away from the wall, he approached on measured steps. Within feet of me, he reached out to tuck his finger beneath my chin and raise my face to his.

His voice returned to a whisper. "You are beautiful, Sedra. And I'm sure somewhere in that head of yours, you're intelligent and faithful as well. But what's being done to you is not healthy. It's not good. It's not anything God would have wanted for you."

I didn't bother to respond. I wasn't playing his games. There was nothing he could say to change that.

It wasn't clear how he'd interpreted my silence, but his shoulders relaxed, his expression falling as he pulled his hand away. "I'm sorry I can't help you, Sedra. But I know that wherever I take you, whatever I do to protect you from that man, you'll just return to him. So I'm protecting my parish and myself by taking you back. I hope, someday, if you ever escape him, you'll understand."

Still silent, I blinked, my lashes fanning over my cheeks before I redirected my eyes to his.

Jacob sighed. "Come on. I can take you in my truck."

Leading me through the building, Jacob turned the mazelike halls until we reached an exterior door. Shoving it open, he held it while I stepped outside, closing it and locking it after I passed. We didn't speak again as we climbed into his truck, didn't even look at each other as we drove through the night back to the compound. I still wasn't sure of the point of this game, but I wasn't giving up.

The night crept further into darkness, not even the light of the moon could brighten our path. But within an hour, a glow lit the distant horizon, and I knew it was the floodlights of the compound. As the truck weaved its way along more streets, turning right and then left, I kept my eyes trained to those lights, wondering what would happen when I had to face the family again.

It didn't take much longer for us to pull up to the gates, and Jacob climbed out of the truck faster than I could find the handle to open my door. By the time I was stepping down from my seat, he was banging on the metal gates, yelling for Elijah to come outside.

For the first time since he'd taken me in that strange building where I'd been kept, doubt crept insidiously in my head, its icy fingers tracing my thoughts, making me question everything, including myself.

"Get out here, Jericho! Be a man and show your damn face!"

His breath disturbed the sheen of mist that hung in the air, the moisture illuminated by the lights beaming down on us. I stood by the truck, not sure what to do with myself while he played out his games.

The gates opened from the center and Jacob stepped back. Richard Cross and Charley Dempsey stepped through wearing the white shirts and blue trousers typical of the men. The gates slammed shut behind them.

"Where's Elijah?" Jacob asked.

Richard was a tall man. He was broad shouldered and pot bellied despite the constant work he did around the compound. Still slightly shorter than Jacob,

149

he had a balding head and a long beard, his brows so overgrown they resembled fuzzy caterpillars above his eyes. In response to Jacob's question, those brows pulled together to become one.

"She believe you yet?" Richards lip curled with humor before he glanced in my direction. Inclining his head in hello, he returned his attention to Jacob. "We're out here like you asked, Elijah. Now what would you like us to do?"

Jacob's expression tightened with anger. "I'm not Elijah. And I'm sick as hell of people calling me that." Stepping forward, he didn't care that he was nose to nose with Richard. "Bring me my brother."

"I don't know who you're talking about."

To Richard's side, Charley laughed, the sound carrying across the distance on the wind. Jacob turned to look at him, his expression dark, empty of patience or humor.

Charley had never been the smartest family member. Unlike Richard, he was short and skinny. It didn't matter how much he ate, he never put on a single pound. Probably the smartest thing I'd ever seen him do is stop laughing when Jacob stared him down. Still, he couldn't keep his mouth shut.

Nodding his head in Jacob's direction, Charley asked, "What's with the priest clothes?"

Jacob didn't bother to respond, he just turned back to Richard, his eyes narrowing in rage. "Bring me my brother. You can tell him I've brought *Eve* back. I don't want her."

Even though the words hadn't been directed at me, and even though they were all part of whatever it was he was doing, they still stung. How could he not want

150

me? Except for running, I'd done everything he'd asked. Maybe hurting me was part of this punishment.

"Play your games with her all you want, Elijah. She's the one who failed. But she's not coming through these gates. I promised you that when you told me you'd show up, and I won't disobey like she did. I don't want to have to prove my faith."

Both men stepped back, their bodies turning in unison to walk inside the gates. Jacob called out before they could walk through them.

"I'm leaving her here. If Elijah wants her, he can have her, but she's not coming back to the parish with me."

Richard barked out a laugh, twisting in place to side-eye Jacob. "What parish? Your church is right here."

His name wasn't Jacob. That much had been proven with this little stunt. If he were anyone other than the man who led this family, Richard would have dragged him inside to make him face Elijah. But Richard couldn't do that now. You can't drag a man to himself.

Before turning back, Richard said, "You can leave her all you want. She's not coming inside."

The gates closed and the men were gone. Elijah was on me before I could climb into the truck. I'd put one foot inside the cabin before he was dragging me away, almost pushing me into the fence with how far he forced me.

"You stay here."

He stepped and I followed, but jumped back again when he turned and lunged at me. I'd seen him this mad before. He'd terrified me then, even if his anger hadn't been directed at me. Elijah killed a man right in front of my eyes, and I'd learned then just how powerful he was.

"I'm done, Sedra, or Eve, or whatever your name is. Stay here. I'm not taking you with me."

Ice shot through my veins, the cold seeping out to freeze my muscles in place, to slow my heart until it felt like I was being crushed from the inside out. Pure pain, *genuine, overwhelming* fear, coursed through me. This was worse than the woods at night. This was worse than being chased by dogs. This was the first time he'd openly rejected me.

"You can't mean that," I breathed out, disbelief and agony edging my words. "You can't do that to me. I gave you everything."

Regret flashed behind his eyes. "They'll let you in once I'm gone. I'm sure of it." He paused before saying, "Good luck, Sedra. I hope you find your way out of this place."

Breath rushed from my lungs, my eyes wide and unblinking as he walked off. The door slammed, the engine started, and dust was kicked up in my direction as Elijah drove away.

This wasn't happening to me. He wouldn't actually leave me. God wouldn't -

"Hey Sedra!" A shotgun went off behind me, birdshot spattering the ground at my feet just inches from hitting me.

I jumped back, fell down on my butt, and crawled as far I could. Richard stared down at me from one of the wooden perches, shotgun in hand, a smile across his face.

Tears streamed down my cheeks to drop off as muddy splotches, the dust just now settling from

152

where the bird shot had hit the road. I was frozen in place, terrified and out of my mind with grief.

"Get moving. We'll give you a head start before we release the dogs."

I could hear Charley's laughter from behind the gate. I heard a dog bark in the distance a second or two later.

"I mean it, Sedra. You failed him by running. Nobody here wants you around. Only true believers can live on this side of the gate."

I wasn't sure what came over me, but before I could think about what I was doing, I was on my feet, screaming at the top of my lungs. It was a pressure release, a way to escape the fury that swallowed me.

"I am a true believer. I'm Eve! I'm Elijah's wife."

"You aren't Eve anymore. And Elijah will take a new wife. One who can be what he needs her to be. There's no reason for you to be here, girl. Get moving."

He shot at me again, one pellet grazing my toe enough to make it bleed. Dust and rocks were kicked up against me, but the pants Elijah gave me prevented it from breaking my skin.

The pants...

Had Elijah given them to me because he'd known I'd need them?

Was this all still part of his game?

With tears streaming down my face and my toe bleeding, I ran off. Richard had made it clear I wasn't welcome at the compound anymore. My heart broke as the lights faded behind me. With every step I took, the velvet darkness of night consumed me. But I found a road and followed it, making my way back to the only place I knew I could find Elijah.

153

Perhaps I was meant to find him. Perhaps not. But he was the only hope I had left, even if he'd claimed he didn't want me.

Slipping deeper within shadow, and just barely managing to find the road I remembered would lead back to him, I whispered to myself to bind my faith, to ask God to ensure that I made it home.

Our Father, who art in heaven, hallowed be thy name...

15

JACOB

Submit therefore to God. Resist the devil and he will flee from you. James 4:7

Why did she have to get under my skin so easily? What was it about Sedra that was driving a spear through my gut as I drove away? Glancing in the rearview mirror, I'd watched as she'd stared at the back of the truck. I saw every emotion flash across her face. Surprise. Fear. Sorrow and shame.

It was the last expression that hurt me the most. The girl had nothing to be ashamed of. It wasn't her fault she'd believed Jericho's lies.

He was an expert at telling them. I should know. I was an expert all the same.

But I'd given up the games of our youth. I'd taken a life - not intentionally, but does intention ever matter to the dead? Because of *me*, Cassandra was no longer breathing. She was dust in the wind, cremated by her family and scattered over the ocean she'd loved as a child.

It's you Jacob, only you, forever...

My fingers gripped over the steering wheel as her voice whispered in my head, the red needle of the speedometer pushing higher as my foot sunk down of the pedal. The shadow of trees became a blur, the road rushing beneath me faster than was safe. And as the memories came crashing back, no longer still pictures, but film with action and sound, I slammed my foot on the brake, and held on as the truck fishtailed while the rocks and dust beneath it were scattered.

The truck groaned as I pulled off onto a side road, the body lurched when I finally brought it to a stop. And as my forehead fell down to press against the steering wheel, I witnessed a memory that I would have given anything to forget.

Before Cassandra, I was never loyal to any one girl. Jericho and I had started our games at sixteen, two boys just coming into adulthood, who learned quickly that girls found them desirable.

It had been a break from our strict upbringing, a secret shared between twins. But, God, how those girls could play.

The first time we cornered one, the first time we discovered what a succulent drug temptation could be, we fell easily into its rapturous hold, emerging from that room as tarnished and changed men.

But that first taste had been so sweet.

Little Ellen Baker, a devout Catholic like us, had grown up in the same church. She attended catholic school and wore the uniform, her knee socks and the hem of her pleated skirt leaving just enough skin exposed in between for us to imagine what it would feel like between our teeth.

Her blond pigtails had disappeared as she'd grown, becoming a wave of long hair that flowed down her

156

back with the sheen of finely spun silk. Big blue eyes that only saw God when she'd been a child, were opening onto her adulthood, being exposed to the handsome faces of the boys she'd known since they were children.

We didn't do it on purpose, but intent doesn't always speak for action. And in a moment when we were left alone together, the three of us preparing for a charity dinner being hosted by the Diocese where we lived, we learned how addictive sin could taste as we explored the gifts of our bodies.

Deep down in that dusty basement, Jericho had been the one to start the game.

It had been a joke at first - a tease. Jericho's fingers slipping up her skirt, the flip of the hem giving us just a peek of what she wore beneath. Pink panties with turquoise ribbons at the side, innocent, pure and inviting. Ellen swatted at his hand but still smiled brightly. She liked being teased. She liked having both our attention.

Another flip of her skirt, a soft brush of a hand across the swell of her breast over her shirt. A kiss planted lightly on her cheek as the warmth of our breath rolled down her neck. I don't remember which one of us had been the person to lock the door, but once that lock was thrown, Ellen's clothes had come off.

Jericho bent her over a folding table, one of the ones that would be used to serve the parishioners their charity meal. Her small breasts pressed against the wood as he stood behind her, his hands exploring as I circled in front. Squatting down so I could watch every expression that flashed across her face as my brother stuck his fingers inside, I was hard beneath my hand, desperate to know what wet heat felt like.

She'd purred when he touched her in forbidden places, guilt a simmering flame behind her eyes. But she never said no, never told us that we weren't exactly what she wanted.

We took advantage of a childhood crush. Ellen had always followed us around like an adorable puppy that was looking for someone to pet her just right.

In that moment, hidden down in a basement full of tables and chairs, the nativity scene for Christmas and the white, glitter edged wings of the angels who would raise their voices in chorus, we obliged her the attention she sought, and we took our first taste as well.

Jericho hadn't yet penetrated that sacred space before her lips wrapped around me. And fuck, for days after I thanked God for her mouth. I praised it. I worshipped it. I could think of nothing better.

I wasn't the one to take her purity, my brother had that honor. And when virginal blood ran down her legs, she sang in the pain and pleasure he gave her.

It had been innocent at first, but things never seem to remain that way. Not love. Not forgiveness. Not tranquility or passion. Not my life after I'd left for college and before becoming a priest.

Jericho and I had worked our way through so many girls before I left to start my adult life. And every seed had been planted, every sin had been explored, every devious, dark and dirty cruelty had been brought to life inside me. I carried those tastes with me when I left, still clutching to them like the only island within a sea of lies and promises when I met Cassandra on Halloween night.

Ironically, I was dressed as a priest, she was a nun wearing a white habit. We'd met because of those costumes, but they hadn't stayed on our bodies long.

Divine sexuality, a woman born for sin. Her body was so beautiful that even time and God must have mourned its destruction. With long, dark hair and green eyes that were the color of fresh leaves in spring, Cassandra was everything I could have asked for. Her submission was absolute, her love of pain exquisite. She craved the sting of clamps and collars. She worshipped my body when I undressed in front of her.

She wasn't religious, but she found God when her arms and legs were bound. She didn't sing in a choir full of innocent youth, but she sang my name when her body came to life beneath mine. She didn't pray, but she praised Heaven when I pushed her over the edge of temptation into the deep waters of ecstasy that stole her breath away.

Through it all, I became just as addicted to her as she was to me. She didn't know it. I would never admit it. But I loved her after that first night I found her.

If one person can be made for another, Cassandra had been made for me. And I was ultimately the one to destroy her.

The coroner's report said it had been a blood clot. They blamed her veins, they blamed her health, they blamed the bruises on her skin that showed she was clumsy and often hurt. But most of the bruises had been from me.

I was the one who'd used clamps on her body, and I'd been the one to deliver pain with the palm of my hand. I'd been the one with my hand wrapped around her throat at the moment her climax forced her heart to pump harder making it possible for that clot to reach her brain.

Although her death had been peaceful - sex sending her into the open arms of eternity - it had been my hands that put her there, no matter what the medical examiner had to say.

I watched the color drain from her face as I shook her and screamed her name. I held her hand as the warmth seeped from her skin and the ambulance sirens blared as they tore down the road. I walked behind the gurney as they escorted her body away, and I cried alone that night begging God to forgive me for my sins.

It was the moment I chose to return to the Church, the moment I decided to give myself to God and never have sex again.

Yet, here I was, a celibate priest, sitting on the side of a deserted dirt road wanting to race back to that compound and steal away a woman who looked and behaved so much like the one I'd killed.

Where God had created Cassandra for my use, Jericho had created Sedra. I had to wonder if both the Almighty and the twin who understood my darkness hadn't known I'd be destined to fail.

I hadn't been able to save Cassandra, but everything inside me told me I still had the chance to save Sedra.

My palms banged against the wheel, every curse word I'd avoided saying for twelve years rolling effortlessly off my tongue. And when I put the truck in drive and turned it around to head back to the main road, I didn't make a right towards my parish like I should have, I turned left toward Sedra instead.

160

16

EVE

*Yea, though I walk through the valley of the shadow of death,
I will fear no evil. Psalms 23:4*

You haven't known loneliness until you've walked down a dirt road in the dead of night. You haven't known fear until you've been abandoned to the wolves.

My bare feet ached, the rocks and pebbles over the ground digging into the bottoms without mercy or apology. It was becoming normal for me to feel this pain - penance, I assumed for my sins - and for as often as I'd run over broken twigs and jagged stone, I could probably walk over hot coals at this point and not feel a thing.

I couldn't feel anything really. But I could see and I could hear. That's how I knew a car was careening toward me, its headlights blinding my eyes and music blasting away the silence of the forest that surrounded me.

The car fishtailed this way and that, dust kicking up from its tires until the road looked like the gateway

161

to Hell. But it slowed when it approached me, when its lights caught me in their beam and illuminated my entire body.

"Damn, baby! What's a beautiful girl like you doing walking all alone on a night like this?"

I didn't like the smell that emanated from the car when he rolled the window fully down, I didn't like the music that was blasting or the way his bloodshot eyes looked me over. He was one of the wolves that would tear me apart with sharp teeth if I let him. But still, despite my fear, despite everything, he was the only living, breathing soul that was near me. And his car would be a faster way to Elijah than my feet.

Maybe God had sent this man to help me along in the direction I traveled. I'd been praying to him for help, after all.

"I'm walking to church," I answered, my voice not strong enough to be heard over the blaring music.

The man turned the music down and leaned low to look at me through the passenger window. "What was that, baby? I couldn't quite hear you."

A tremor of fear shot through me, but I put my faith in God. The only problem being that I was too focused on what I'd prayed for Him to send me to hear Him whispering in my thoughts to run.

"I'm going to church," I said again, adding what strength I could find to my voice.

The man smiled, his lips crooked and sloppy, his eyes bloodshot and studying me with sharp focus. "Church?" He laughed. "What would make a woman like you need a church at this time of night?"

"I'm a sinner," I answered, figuring the explanation Elijah had always preached in his sermons would resonate with any person who knew why God was needed in our lives.

His grin widened. "Aren't we all?" he murmured.

The response he gave made me feel a little better. He understood that we were all damned without the grace of God's light. He must have been sent in answer to my prayers.

"Well, let me help you out, beautiful. Ain't nothing good that can come from being so alone in the dark like this." His hand hit the handle to the door, pulling it quick so that he could step out of the car that sat idling with its headlights casting a bright glow over the landscape around us.

Rounding the front end of the car, those headlights caught his face, brightening it until I could see the scruff over his cheeks and the greasiness of his brown hair where it dusted his shoulders. He wore a pair of baggy blue jeans and no shirt, dark hair dusting his chest and running a line down his center. That trail disappeared beneath those jeans and I couldn't help but follow it with my eyes.

The only man I'd ever seen without clothes was Elijah. This man didn't hold a candle to him.

"What's your name, beautiful?"

His voice lowered to a deep baritone as he approached me and continued talking. I stepped back without realizing it, my arms coming up to cross over my body as if that would stop the trembling.

"Eve," I said on a shaky breath.

"Eve," he repeated back, his tongue peeking out to roll along his bottom lip. "That's a good Christian name."

"Hebrew," I blurted out. "They wrote the Old Testament."

163

He shrugged a shoulder. "It don't matter. We're all the same in the eyes of God."

Elijah wasn't. He was blessed with the strength of God's hand. But I didn't tell him that.

"The biblical Eve, huh?" He scrubbed his hand against his jaw. "Guess that makes you responsible for the fall of man."

"I haven't made anybody fall."

"Oh, what a sweet thing you are. Don't worry, Darlin', I fell a long time ago."

He lunged forward faster than a snake to wrap his large hand around my bicep and pull me close. I didn't like the smell wafting off him. I knew it was alcohol that rolled off his breath. Never having tasted a drop of it myself, I recognized the smell from some of the men in the family. They'd been indoctrinated with that stink on their skin, but Elijah had wiped it away as he'd eradicated them of sin.

"Why are you fighting me, Eve? I'm just trying to talk to you."

I wasn't fighting, not like he claimed I was. All I wanted was to pull away from him, but every time I tried, his hand gripped tighter and his smile pulled wider apart.

Realizing I wouldn't get away from him, I settled down. But instead of letting me go, he pulled me even closer, his chest brushing up against my arms where they were crossed over my chest.

"There you go, baby. Just calm down a little. Daddy wants to take care of you. It's not safe for a girl to be alone." His gaze scanned down my body. "Not safe for you to be barefoot on a dark, deserted road either."

"He didn't give me shoes," I explained, not liking the fear that cut through my words.

"I don't know who he is, but it sounds like he's not the kind of man to take care of a woman. Not like she needs anyway."

Although he'd turned down the music in his car when he first pulled up to talk to me, it was still a soft beat across the wind. There was still a voice crooning a song that crawled across the surface of my skin.

"Dance with me, baby girl. I'll even let you step on my boots so you don't hurt your feet."

Frightened to the point of losing the ability to think, I clenched my teeth together and tightened my arms over my body. "I don't dance," I finally said, hoping the confession would make him go away.

His hips swayed against me, his large arms wrapping around my shoulders as I was pulled flat against his chest. "There's nothing wrong with dancing, Eve. God wouldn't give us music if he didn't want us to move to it. You know what I mean? Now step up on my boots so you don't hurt yourself. Let me take care of you for a change."

An owl called out in the distance, lending his voice to the music that softly played. Beyond the glow of the headlights beaming from the car, I couldn't see the road, the forest, or anything that would help me. This man was the only person who knew where I was. The only person who could help me escape the thick darkness of night.

Slowly placing my feet on his boots, I let him crush me to his chest.

"There you go, Eve. Now doesn't that feel better?"

We swayed left and right, my stomach pressed up against his jeans, his excitement hard and bulging. A shiver coursed through me at the feel of him. I didn't like this man, but I didn't know what else to do. I had to play along. Had to hope that a simple dance would be enough for him to open the car door, tuck me inside, and take me where I needed to go.

Elijah wouldn't be happy to know I'd let another man touch me. He would reject me if he knew I was no longer pure. But Elijah wasn't here to save me from the man who had his rough, strong hands wrapped over my hips. He wasn't there to keep those hands from traveling farther south.

I flinched when his fingers massaged over the cheeks of my butt. I bit my lip when he rested his cheek against my head and moaned.

"Damn, baby. You certainly are a sinner, aren't you? You definitely have the body of one."

His voice was gritty and low, his hands working over me as his excitement pressed into me more. "Tell you what, baby girl. You need a ride and I need something else. And there ain't nobody here to know what you've done. Why don't you let me take a little look at you? It'll be a secret between us."

Tears welled in my eyes, my arms shaking from how hard I held them against my chest. "You can't keep secrets from God," I argued, my voice shaking and weak.

"God never said there's anything wrong with looking. I give you a ride. You let me take a peek at what the Good Lord gave you, and we can call it a fair trade."

The tears welled harder and the man tsked to see them stream down my face. "Don't cry, baby girl. You just found a man who's willing to save you. You should be celebrating."

I was so confused. So lost and terrified. It was pitch black in every direction and if you listened hard enough you could hear the animals moving around in the woods. It was only a matter of time before one of them got curious and walked out to see if I could be a snack.

What could I do? If I ran, he'd catch me. And that was only if I was strong enough to break free of his grasp.

"Just a look? That's all? You promise?"

"Shit, beautiful. I'd promise you anything just to have a chance to see what's under these baggy clothes."

"And you'll take me where I need to go after?"

He laughed, his chest shaking against me. "Baby, you just tell me what direction and I'll take you anywhere you want to go."

Just a look. How big a sin was that? I wondered if Elijah would understand. If he would know that I didn't have a way to escape. It was just a look. Just a peek so that he would save me from the dark that threatened to enshroud me in its cold fingers until I forgot how to breathe.

"Okay," I mumbled. "Just a look."

"That'a girl. I like a woman who knows how to make a deal."

He let me go and I turned to stare down the road, hoping and praying for another set of headlights to light the path. But we were alone in the middle of nowhere. Not a single soul around to know my shame.

"I'll take a step back if that makes you feel more comfortable. You can lean up against the car and keep warm by the engine. That way, when you show me what you have, you don't shiver from the cold."

The man stepped back like he said he would and I considered running. But he was bigger than me and

167

most likely faster. There wasn't anywhere I could go that he wouldn't find me.

Moving to the car, I leaned up against the hood and refused to look at the man as I uncrossed my arms. "What do you want to see?"

"All of it, baby. Take it all off real nice and slow."

My hands shook when I reached for the buttons of my shirt, images flashing in my head of the wooden shed where Elijah had first seen me without clothes. He'd married me that night in the eyes of God. He'd marked me and he'd taken my body like a husband does a wife. For six more nights he'd shown me just how a woman acts for a man. He'd shown me what it felt like to bask in his light.

Maybe if I pretended it was him standing in front of me, this would all be a lot easier.

My fingers moved over the buttons, unhooking one before moving to the next. My bottom lip trembled harder with each button that came undone. When I reached the bottom and pulled my shirt apart, I flinched at the soft hiss of breath over the man's lips. I cried to feel my nipples beading tight in response to the cold air that slipped in with greedy fingers to dance across my skin.

"Damn, baby. Your momma named you right. You definitely are the reason for the fall of man."

A zipper lowered, the soft susurration of metal against metal grabbing my attention where it carried across the wind. "I hope you don't mind if I touch myself while looking at you."

Pressing my lips together, I tried to stop the trembling, but it spread like fire over my body instead.

"The pants, baby girl. Take them off too."

I reached for the button and hesitated. When I peeked over at him, his hand was working back and forth over his length. He nodded his head in my direction. "Go on, baby. There's no need to be shy. I'll show you mine if you show me yours."

His grin widened showing me all his teeth. I bit the inside of my lip and pulled the button loose on my pants, my hands too shaky to work the zipper.

For as loose as the pants were, the zipper wasn't necessary. The material slipped down my legs regardless. By the time they puddled at my feet, the man was jerking himself harder, his own bottom lip caught between his teeth as his eyes widened and his chest beat with heavy breath.

"Kick them off," he demanded, the fake sweetness in his voice he'd used until then completely absent.

My voice wavered when I argued, "But you've seen me. Can't we just leave now?"

He laughed, the sound carrying over the way his hand slapped between his legs. "I haven't seen your ankles. And you haven't turned around to let me see your ass."

Tears were dropping steadily off my chin, but I nodded and kicked the pants away.

"I haven't seen your shoulders either. Take it off, all the way."

Closing my eyes, I did as he said and pulled the shirt from my shoulders. It slipped down my arms to fall to the ground, bunched and useless lying over the dirt.

He practically growled when he said, "Now turn around and spread your legs. Bend over the hood so I can get a real good look. I'm almost done and then we can go wherever you want."

169

"I don't want to," I cried.

"We made a deal, baby girl," he answered, his voice strained as his hand continuing pumping.

I'd already come this far. I was already naked and trembling on the side of the road, and there was nobody who would know what I'd done. Nobody but God. He had to forgive me. He had to know it was the only choice I had.

Turning slowly, I ignored the way he moaned to see my bottom. Spreading my legs, I bent over the hood like he said, the heat of the engine pressing against my chest sending goosebumps down my legs.

He was on me within a second, his excitement pressing against me as his hands reached between my breasts and the hood of the car. I bucked back, desperate to get him away, but he made a hushing sound at my ear as his fingers found the tight nipples of my chest.

"Shhhhh, baby. Calm down."

"You said look only!" I cried.

"I know. I know," he answered, his voice as soft as satin once again. "But baby, how can you blame me with the way you look? You were born to tempt men. I just want to touch you. Nothing more. Just a touch."

His hand massaged my breast, his excitement pressing against the split in my cheeks. When he forced a hand between our bodies he slipped that hard part of *him* between my legs. I closed my legs together, but it was still there, taunting me.

My body responded despite what my mind and heart were saying. This damn body full of sin and everything wicked. Crying harder I whispered to myself what Elijah had told me about myself, the words coming fast and growing in strength as I repeated them over and over.

"What's that, baby? I can't hear you."

His hips pushed closer, my legs pressing painfully into the side of the car.

"Your body is your temple? Is that what you're saying over and over again?"

Nodding my head, a sob broke free of my lungs.

"Oh, sweetheart, don't you worry. Your body is my temple, too, and I want to walk on inside to worship it properly."

I hated that I was wet between my legs, hated that my sin couldn't be contained without Elijah there to take it from me. I hated myself at that moment and just wanted this man to go away.

"It's not going to hurt, sweetheart. I promise. I'll make sure I make you feel right."

He reached between us again and pulled his hips away. When he pressed forward, he was against the opening of my body, threatening the sanctity that had only been Elijah's.

I screamed, but he released my breast to cover my mouth and muffle the sound.

And just as he was about to force himself in, something hit the back of his car hard enough to send us both flying.

17

JACOB

And you will know my name is the Lord when I lay my vengeance upon thee. Ezekiel 25:17

I was so angry when I pulled up on the scene that I didn't give a damn about damaging my truck just to get that son of a bitch off her. I sent a prayer to God that she wasn't hurt and that he'd forgive my rash behavior.

Feeling better after asking forgiveness *before* committing the sin, I jumped out of my truck and raced to where they'd landed, taking only a second to look over Sedra and make sure she wasn't injured before turning my attention on the asshole who had his disgusting hands all over her.

My fingers fisted into his greasy hair as I dragged him back. He could kick and scream all he wanted, but there was no seeing past the red haze of anger consuming me.

Eve sat up in the dirt to our side, sobs tearing through her body as she crawled toward where her clothes lay in a pile. Knowing she was physically okay made it easier for me to keep my attention on the bastard struggling beneath me.

"What the fuck? You hit my car! Let me the fuck go, asshole!"

He screamed up at me as I continued dragging him off the road. Slamming my fist into his face, I laughed when he spit out a tooth. I didn't give him a chance to yell again before my fist struck him four more times.

"You like to force yourself on crying women, you sick son of a bitch? Is that what you do for kicks?"

"She wanted it!" he screamed, blood gurgling in his throat from where his mouth was busted open.

Still holding him by his hair, I lifted my head to look at Sedra. "Did you want this guy shoving himself on you?"

She shook her head, tears spilling from her eyes as she clutched her shirt to her chest. "No," she answered, the one word cracked and broken from how hard she cried.

My gaze locked to the guy's face. "She just told me you're a liar." My fist hit his nose. "It's a sin to lie." Another punch. "You want to tell me the truth now?"

"Fuck man! Stop!" he cried out, opening his eyes to look at me. "What the fuck? Are you a priest?"

My fist caught his jaw and his head snapped back. I'd completely forgotten I was wearing my clerical collar. I hoped nobody happened to drive along to see a priest beating a man down along the side the road.

"Yes," I said, my voice eerily calm. "I am a priest and I'm here to tell you that you should have gone to church-" I hit him again before dropping him down to punt my boot into his side." "-a little more often-" Another kick, his body curling over itself as I hit him again. "-because it's a son of a bitch like you that needs to learn that raping women on the side of the road is not something God wants." Another punt. Another punch.

He was whimpering at that point, struggling to push himself up while I kept beating him back down. Every ounce of the violence I'd restrained inside myself was pouring out. Every drop raining down on him as a punch to the head or a kick to the spine. I knew I should stop. I knew I should leave him to wallow in his own blood now that Sedra was safe, but I lost control.

Just like every time this girl was around, I slipped away from the life I'd built for myself and found myself sliding towards temptation.

"Stop! You're a priest, please stop!"

Standing over him, my chest heaved with labored breath, my hand stung where I'd split my knuckles open on his teeth. And all I wanted to do was beat him down again.

"Elijah! Please! Stop!"

Sedra screamed from where she was seated by his car, her eyes locked to me, wide open to my violence. She was terrified not only because of what this asshole had done, but because of the violence she could plainly see bleeding out of me.

Huffing out a few more breaths just to force myself to speak evenly, I stared down at the pathetic excuse for a human being and struggled to remember my place. I was a priest, not some insane vigilante whose job it was to eradicate evil. I was supposed to spread love and the word of God, not brawl on the side of deserted roads.

I glanced over at Sedra one more time and remembered I was supposed to be the shepherd for my flock and not one of the wolves salivating to take down the weakest among them.

Shit!

This wasn't supposed to be my life.

My eyes focused on the man bleeding and crying at my feet. "The next time you want to think about God, you should remember what was written in His Holy Book. My God is a vengeful God toward all those who would dare destroy the righteous."

The weak, beaten man kept crying as I marched to my truck. He was still crying when I opened the door and slammed open the glove box to grab a Bible I kept for distribution. He was just pushing himself up to his hands and knees when I marched back to him, kicked him beneath the ribs until he was flat on the ground again, and slammed the Bible down on his head.

"Here's the Lord's book you pathetic piece of shit. I suggest you read it!"

I wanted to kick him one more time - just *one* more time - but I didn't. I fought to gain control of myself in that moment no matter how badly I wanted to end this guy and toss him out to whatever animals would eat him.

But I didn't.

Instead, I stormed over to where Sedra was sitting and helped her to her feet. She hadn't bothered to put her clothes back on, she only clutched them to her chest. She was trembling so hard she couldn't walk and I picked her up to carry her to my truck. Once I had her tucked into the passenger seat, I rounded the back to climb in the other side. Casting one glance at the man still struggling over the dirt where I'd left him, I reversed my truck and peeled off down the road.

Sedra sobbed beside me as I drove silently along the dark road. I willed myself to calm down and help the woman who had made a mess of my life.

What I did to that man wasn't my best work, it wasn't even a proper sermon, but it felt so good to strike down the type of person that embodied the very thing I was working against in my calling. He was the demon wallowing in corruption. He was the wolf that would see a stranded woman on the side of the road and rape her just to make his life better.

He was exactly what I was supposed to be fighting against, but actually *fighting* him hadn't been the right answer. The ultimate judge is God. It was his vengeance that mankind had to fear. It wasn't our place to throw stones or condemn our brothers, but I was struggling with the forgiveness and love I was supposed to portray in my life as a devout man.

I didn't regret hurting that man so badly, but I still felt guilty about it. And there wasn't a confessional within a hundred miles for *me* to crawl into and admit all my recent sins.

Resisting the urge to reach out in comfort to touch Sedra's shoulder, I kept my eyes trained on the road, driving without speaking the entire ride back to the church.

I pulled up behind the rectory, happy for the cover of dark night and moved around the truck to open Sedra's door. She flinched in her seat when I touched her to help her down.

"Hey, it's fine. It's just me. I won't hurt you."

She didn't respond, just balled up tighter over the bench seat.

"Sedra-"

"It's Eve," she whispered, her voice growing louder when she spoke again. "Not Sedra. You named me Eve and that's my name."

At that point I was willing to call her whatever she wanted just to get her out of the truck and into a bath. She was filthy, she was freezing, and she was trembling so hard, the edge of the truck was knocking against my knees.

"Okay, Eve. I'm going to carry you inside and get you into a bath. You need to wash the dirt off and get clean-"

"I'd be clean if you hadn't left me outside the compound. I wouldn't have been forced to do the things I did with that man, if you hadn't-"

Her voice cut off abruptly, violent sobs racking the poor woman's body until it seemed like she couldn't breathe.

"Eve," I whispered, "Come on, let me help you."

Slipping my arms behind her back and under her knees, I pulled her out of the seat and cradled her against my chest. I didn't even bother closing the door to my truck. She was too fractured, too in need of warmth and peace that the details didn't matter.

I was responsible for this. Not Jericho. Not Sedra. Not the two men at the compound who refused to let her inside.

Me.

I'm the one who decided to take her back knowing all the horrible things my brother was doing to her. I was the one who left her on the side of the road when they refused to accept her back.

It might as well have been me on the road forcing my body on her, because if it hadn't been for my selfishness, my cowardice and my disregard for what it

177

truly meant to be a priest, she wouldn't have been in that situation in the first place.

Even though I was the person responsible for every horrible thing that happened to her tonight, it didn't mean I couldn't remember who I was, who I'd been for the past twelve years, and give everything I had just to put her back together.

Watching her break down in my arms was my flagellation. Suffering to refuse temptation while I put her back together would be my penance.

Entering the rectory, I took her straight back to my room, kicked the door open and walked her through into the bathroom. I sat her down on the floor while I hurried to fill the tub. Steam billowed off the surface of the water, a gossamer shroud that would conceal us in the nightmare she needed to wash away.

Sedra was so splintered, so regretfully innocent that she had neither the knowledge nor the ability to protect herself in the world around us. She was the perfect prey, the bait that tastes the sweetest because she only wants to see the good in people.

She only wanted to be good herself.

Giving everything to a man she believed loved her. Sacrificing her own identity to fulfill whatever sick delusions he had of her. They were all symptoms of the good inside her.

When she first appeared in my life, I couldn't move fast enough to get away from her. Her body was the perfect temptation, her submission the poison that could drag a godly man into Hell itself. She was everything evil we're warned about in the world just by merely existing.

But yet, she wasn't evil.

She was the illusion of evil.

178

Purity wrapped in the sinful cage of a woman who didn't know any better.

Tempting me had never been her intention. That was a problem with me, with my weaknesses and my deviant darkness.

Sedra had the essence of a fallen angel, and when she opened her eyes to look up at me from the floor, all I saw behind them was tragedy.

Swallowing down the acrid taste of guilt that coated my tongue, I spoke softly. "Do you need help getting in the bath?"

Her eyes darted from my face down to my collar and back up again, a shiver coursing down her spine immediately after.

Turning to look in the mirror, I saw the blood splatter that had stained my white clerical collar black. Ripping it off my neck, I tossed in the trash next to the sink and sunk down onto my knees to look Sedra in the eye.

"Can I help you, Eve? Please."

She shook her head, opening and closing her mouth several times before finally saying what was on her mind.

"You shouldn't say please. It's beneath you, Elijah. You're stronger than that."

On a softer voice, she added, "Stronger than me."

If she'd used a knife to slice at my soul, it would have been less painful than her words. All her life, this woman had been led astray, misguided, made to believe that her entire existence was meant for one man. She'd been cast out into the woods in the dead of night. Made to run miles just to land at the doorstep of a priest who should have helped her.

And what did I do? I threw her back to the monsters who'd used her, who'd abused her, who'd stripped her of her entire identity and replaced it with everything *they* wanted her to be.

All because I couldn't handle my own desires. All because I didn't want to deal with whatever games my brother had in store for me.

Sedra shouldn't call *me* the strong one, at least not the man I'd been up until this moment.

It wasn't until I'd had it shoved in my face in the last few days that I realized I hadn't become a priest out of some desperation to know and love God. I'd become a priest to hide from life, to seclude myself in an existence that kept me safe from the mistakes of my past, and especially a life that kept people safe from me.

If I wasn't strong enough to control myself, who was I to believe I could save another person's soul?

"I'm not stronger than you."

She laughed, the sound sad and distressed. "You have the might of God at your hand, and I have nothing. Not now that you've abandoned me."

Picking her up, I pushed to my feet and crossed the room to lower her into the water. She hissed as the heat met her skin, but within minutes she stopped shaking. Her head fell back against the tub and she released a sigh full of every terrible emotion. Water splashed around her, the sound soothing in the silence of the small room.

Settling down next to her, I handed her a bar of soap and a washrag. She took them from my hands, but her attempt at bathing herself was shaky at best. Sedra wasn't with me in the room. She was still stuck out there on that deserted road.

180

"Why did you walk away from the compound?" I asked. "I told you to stay there, that they'd let you in."

Lifting her foot out of the water, she jut her chin at a large cut on her big toe. "They shot at me. If I stayed there, they would have killed me."

Her head twisted to the right until her green eyes locked with mine. "But you already know that, don't you? It's why you made me wear pants. So the rocks and birdshot wouldn't cut my skin when it sprayed up."

My head shook in denial. "No, Eve. That's not why I gave you the pants."

A tear slipped from her eye, her lips pulling tightly together as she struggled not to cry. "So, all of this wasn't part of your test? Part of my punishment for having run?"

"This isn't punishment, Eve."

There was no excuse for me continuing the charade that I was Elijah, but I feared telling her that this wasn't a game - at least on my part - would only upset her more.

When it came to Eve, there was only one reality. There was the cult she called her family, and there was Elijah. Her existence was intended for him only. She became Eve on the night he warped her mind and showed her the pleasure that comes from pain.

There wasn't a world outside the walls of the compound. There was nothing in this life for her but the man she believed she'd married.

To her, I was that man, and there was nothing I could say or do to prove otherwise. My brother and I were identical. In appearance, in DNA, in blood and all that mattered. The only thing that told us apart was our fingerprints.

I highly doubted Eve would take what I could offer as proof, without accusing me of lying again.

She was that far gone.

"I'm sorry I left you. It was a bad decision, and everything that happened to you was my fault. I won't do that to you again."

The corner of her lip curled; shy, resolute, and so full of sorrow that her expression was a palpable pulse across my bones.

"It's my fault for running in the first place," she finally said, her eyes averted as if she couldn't look at me and admit what she believed was the truth. "And what happened on the road is my fault as well." Her eyes met mine. "You know that."

"I don't know that."

She laughed, a short burst of sound that shook her shoulders once. Water splashed in the tub at her feet, and then everything went so quiet you could hear the small drops of water slide off her chin to fall to the bath below.

"I'm full of sin, Elijah. You told me that in the cabin by the compound. You showed me how-" Her lips pulled together, her eyes blinking once before she looked away. "You showed me how bad I want it. How easy it is for me to give in. How my body craves it. That makes what happened out there tonight my fault. I am temptation. It's why we keep our eyes down. It's why the only man I'm willing to truly look at is you."

Her eyes lifted, the green dull with uncertainty. "I didn't want that man tonight. He was disgusting and evil and not you, but-"

It drove me to the edge of madness each time her voice trailed off. Somewhere inside that head of hers, there was Sedra, the girl she'd been before my brother groomed her. Before he'd twisted her thoughts so thoroughly that she couldn't see beyond what he'd taught her.

I knew members of cults, and other individuals who had been brainwashed or deceived for years, needed help beyond what I could provide Sedra. I knew they needed therapy and rehabilitation, and that sometimes it took years for them to finally open their eyes and *see* the truth staring them directly in the face. I also knew that forcing that help on them was practically impossible, especially if they were adults and weren't in obvious danger.

As far as I knew, Jericho hadn't done anything that was a verifiable crime. And if I knew my twin well enough, he would have covered his tracks if he had.

Taking Sedra some place for the help she needed would be the same as what I did tonight. It would be handing her back over to her manipulator because she would always return to him and there was nobody who could stop her.

Even now, even after being abandoned on the side of the road and almost raped as a result of it, she still looked at me like I was her world. She looked at me exactly as she would look at Jericho.

To her, my brother and I were one in the same. He wanted her to believe I was him. It's why he had ordered she not be allowed back in the compound and refused to show his face next to mine. But what I didn't know was whether the men who came to the gate were in on Jericho's schemes, or if they also believed I was him.

The worst of the problem, for me at least, wasn't the game being played against Sedra, it was the fact that I hated the way she looked at me, only because there was a part of me that wanted to take full advantage.

There was still darkness inside me that not even God's light had been able to touch.

"But," I prodded softly in an effort to continue pulling out the thoughts she kept secret, if for nothing more than to piece together the puzzle and find a way to break her of Jericho's hold, to find a way to rid myself of the situation before I was ensnared in temptation's web to become a fallen man.

"I need to confess," she breathed out, the words barely loud enough to cross the little distance between us.

Remaining silent, I thought she'd speak her confession once she'd found the strength to do so. Instead, she looked to me for help.

"What do you need to confess?"

"Pain," she whispered. "Just like in the cabin. Just like what you taught me."

A tremor coursed across my bones, my skin prickling with warning. I couldn't be the person who gave her that pain, only because I worried I would lose control.

"Haven't you had enough pain tonight?"

Tears burst from her eyes, a sound escaping her chest that was so full of mourning it hurt just to hear it.

"Please. I need the pain that purifies when I speak my confession. It's the only way to purge the sin."

Damn it, Jericho. You son of a bitch.

The more I was learning of what he'd taught Sedra, the more I wanted to end him simply to wipe his type of insanity from existence.

"That's not how confession works, Eve."

184

"I need it," she whispered between clenched teeth. "Please, Elijah, please don't make me carry this. I'm not strong enough, I'm not-"

She panicked as she spoke, her anxiety building until water was splashing out of the tub, her body moving in my direction to grab on to me while I moved back. When her hand landed on my arm, her fingers gripped down, devastation building behind her eyes until I thought she'd break under the pressure.

"I need this," she breathed out, her tears a steady stream from eyes swollen and red. "I can't get rid of this myself."

There was no doubt she *truly* needed what she asked for. Instinct told me to get away from her as quickly as possible, but compassion told me to give her what she thought she needed.

It wasn't entirely without reason that she believed pain would purify her of the emotions teeming inside her. For many - even those who haven't been warped by a manipulator like Jericho - physical pain was their only escape from the storm of emotional pain inside. Some people become self-harmers. They cut themselves or seek solace in substances that destroy their minds and bodies. Some seek the release through violence against others. And some seek release through sex. The physical pain, the exertion of their body, is a means to an end, a valve through which they can relieve the pressure threatening them on the inside.

Jericho had found Sedra's means of relief, and he'd apparently twisted it and groomed it, until it was the only means for her to cope and survive.

Had I not felt so guilty for what happened to her on the road, I may have been strong enough to deny her what she thought she needed, but there was a small voice inside me that told me the emotional pain she suffered now was entirely my fault.

I owed this to her.

Didn't I?

"Okay, Eve. I'll help you."

Her body relaxed, a breath of pure relief flowing over her parted lips that drew my eye. So full, those lips were the gateway to my brand of sin, the rounded, soft perfection that reminded me of the man I'd once been - of the woman who had been my undoing.

My eyes closed as I threw up a silent prayer, as I begged and pleaded for the strength only God could give me to remain true to the vows I'd made to him in atonement for my crimes.

"Let's get you out of the bath," I said, opening my eyes to find her looking at me in a way that no woman had looked at me since Cassandra.

A shiver coursed through my body, a thread of darkness coming alive to weave itself around my self-control.

Happy to stand up from the side of the tub and move away from her into the bedroom, I pulled a towel from the closet, shut the door, and pressed my forehead against the cool surface of the wood.

Could I do this without losing myself to it? Was I strong enough to find a way to help her that didn't drag me back down into the depths of ultimate sin?

I didn't know, and that lack of *knowing* is what terrified me the most.

By the time I forced myself back into the bathroom, Eve was standing up in the water, the drops slipping over her naked body begging to be chased by my tongue. But remembering what I'd seen done to her tonight, remembering the way that beast of a human

186

being had hurt her, was enough to snap me out of the desire I didn't want to admit or face.

I needed to confess, but given everything that kept happening, I didn't think God was listening. Either that or this wasn't Eve's test of faith. It was mine.

Approaching her, I wrapped the towel around her and pulled her from the tub. After helping her dry off completely, I was filled with dread for what was about to occur. I didn't speak because I couldn't trust my voice not to crack under the strain of my internal battle, so I just motioned with my hand for her to walk into my bedroom.

So *perfectly* obedient, she dutifully crossed into the next room, planted herself against the wall and waited for me to punish her for whatever it was she felt she did wrong.

My jaw ached from how hard I clenched my teeth, but I walked over to her regardless. I felt my body responding to temptation. That part of me filling and lengthening until my pants were uncomfortable and I wanted them off. The collar of my shirt was too tight, the pressure only relieved when I pulled the top two buttons loose.

Sedra's eyes immediately tracked down to the small amount of skin those open buttons revealed. But it wasn't the direction of her gaze that killed me, it was the absolute need I saw behind it.

Taking a steadying breath, I reached out to take her wrists in my hands, pull them above her head, and hold them to the wall. Her body quivered, forcing a pang of bitter torment through mine. I stepped forward and pressed myself to her. Moving so that her wrists were trapped beneath only one of my hands, I trailed my fingertips down her arm, along her side, finally placing it on her hip as my forehead pressed to hers.

"What is your confession, child?"

My question came out breathless, revealing the pain she was causing me.

The warmth of her breath fanned over my face, my eyes closing against a sensation I hadn't felt since the day I promised God I would never give in to my desires again.

"I asked for it," she whispered. "For that man to scare me. For him to want me."

If Sedra had been a sex addict, or some other person who just needed the act regardless of who they committed it with, I would have worried that I'd beaten down an innocent man. But I knew that couldn't be possible. Sedra was fully devoted to only one man.

Her eyes only saw Elijah, even when it was me staring back at her.

I despised how much that blatant truth hurt.

Whereas I was trapped in her web without her even realizing it, she would never see *me*.

18

EVE

Keep me from deceitful ways; be gracious to me and teach me your law.
Psalm 119:29

"Tell me how you asked for it."

His voice was strained and I worried that he was angry with me, that what he'd witnessed tonight on the side of the road had been the final strike, the spear that was driven into his side.

Or more accurately – the spear that was driven into *my* side.

"I should never have stopped walking. I shouldn't have talked to him. I shouldn't have tempted him by looking him in the eyes. My eyes weren't trained to the ground as you've always told me they should be. Evil is all around us, Elijah, and I fell prey to it."

His lips pulled tight, his breathing so steady that it was a beat against my chest. I watched the shadows dance over his face, followed the stray rays of light that reached in to highlight the dark stubble along his tan skin, the twitch of his jaw from clenching his teeth.

He breathed out, long and hard. It didn't make his voice any stronger. "You are forgiven."

"There's more," I admitted, my eyes wide open while his remained closed. "Something much worse."

His fingers tightened over my wrists and hip and the first delicious rush of pain crept through my body. I needed more.

I *craved* it.

"I let him touch me. Not like, you know, *that*. Not at first. But I let him dance with me. I tried to fight, but he wouldn't let me go. So I gave in."

His hands tightened more, another decadent tendril of pain wrapping over my bones.

Seduce me, Eve... No matter what I say, what I do, you must show me how loyal you can be.

I was giving him all of myself, even those parts that I didn't want to show myself.

"I opened my clothes for him. He promised me he'd help me for just one look. I knew he lusted for me. He touched himself when my breasts were exposed."

Elijah's body shuddered against mine, his hands wrapping even tighter. I breathed out the pleasure his teasing torment caused and it felt like his breath stopped for just a split second in response.

Time moved so slowly between us at that moment, I wasn't sure the world outside our bodies still existed at all.

"I liked watching him touch himself," I breathed out.

I thought my bones would snap beneath his fingers and I cried out, his grip releasing slowly as his body went completely still.

190

"What happened next?" he asked with so much tension in his voice that my breath hitched in my lungs to hear it.

"He asked me to take off my pants. To spread my legs and turn around so I could bend over the car. He wanted to see every part. He said he needed to so he could finish what he was doing."

Elijah's eyes opened and pinned me with their intensity. Slowly his gaze trailed down between our bodies, pausing on my breasts, on the painfully tight tips, before climbing back to my face.

His mouth was dangerously close. It was so tempting just to push forward that small amount of space to lick my tongue against the soft flesh. He must have noticed my gaze locked on that part of him. His teeth bit down on the pillow of his bottom lip, his hands holding me against the wall until I couldn't move.

"And you did as he asked?"

"*Exactly* as he asked. Even when I knew I shouldn't. I was so scared. So -" My words cut off. I couldn't admit that part, I was too afraid of his anger for knowing how I'd felt.

"When I turned, when I was no longer watching him working his hand over, well, over *that* part of him, he was on me, against me, it felt like he surrounded me."

Tears streamed from my eyes, my guilt building until even the pain of his hands wasn't enough to assuage the turmoil consuming me. I took a steadying breath, knowing that I had to tell him everything. That he wouldn't accept not knowing the full truth.

"I'm sorry, Elijah, for what I have to tell you next."

"Confess," he breathed out, his eyes closing so slowly that I could follow his sooty dark eyelashes down, could see them fan out over his skin.

"When I thought he would take me over the hood of that car, when I felt the heat of his body pressed to mine..."

Oh, God, I'm so sorry...

"...I liked it. I need to be controlled. It's what brings me to life."

His body shuddered again, his hands so tight that tears sprang from my eyes, euphoria spreading over me until I was weak beneath him.

If his weight hadn't been pressed to mine, I would have melted to the ground, a puddle of shameful need that could only be reshaped by the strength of his hands.

His lips parted, heavy breath blowing through to caress my face. Our chests beat together, our mouths so dangerously close. Elijah moved, and when I thought he would kiss me, his head angled just slightly, the warmth of his lips trailing along my jaw, down my neck, until stopping on my shoulder.

The scent of his hair overwhelmed me, the excitement of his body pressing against my stomach, stealing every bit of my focus.

When his teeth bit down into my skin, my mouth parted on a cry of pleasure, my mind spinning in so many directions I didn't know up from down, right from wrong, or where my body ended and his began.

Releasing the bite, he spoke against my skin. "I forgive you."

"Show me," I whispered.

A sound emanated from his throat, a growl, or something I couldn't quite name, but it wasn't the sound that pinned me to the wall, that broke me down piece by agonizing piece – it was his hands.

Still holding my wrists against the wall, he released my hip to slide his palm down, his fingers moving between my legs until just one tip found the spot that had me crying out from the pleasure versus the pain, from the rush of sensation that was so intoxicating it was a delicious poison seeping beneath my skin.

Slowly, his hand moved, my legs spreading apart on their own. Rubbing back and forth, he teased me, he worked me, his hand trapped me with its movement. I was unable to escape, unable to breathe past the need that consumed me.

A tip pressed against the entrance, circling ever so slow over the sensitive rim that my heart raced, my eyes closed and opened again.

He was staring at me, the intensity in his gaze as frightening as it was seductive. I could feel my sin coming to the surface, could feel the temptation exploding inside me.

His finger slipped inside my body and my muscles gripped him, refusing to let go.

Driving his hand slowly in and out, he watched me without blinking, his eyes locked to mine. I feared to look away, feared not letting him see me, see the devotion I had for him alone.

But I couldn't hold my eyes open as his hand moved faster, as his other hand gripped tighter over my wrists. The force of him between my legs pushed me onto my tiptoes, the back of my head falling against the wall, my hair tugged from my scalp where it was trapped behind my shoulders.

My hips moved with the thrust of his hand, my bottom banging against the wall with each punishing blow.

Lowering his head, his teeth locked over the taut peak of my breast, and when he bit down, sinking the edges into my flesh, I cried out and lost all control.

Pain and pleasure.

Sin and forgiveness.

Master and slave.

God and the Devil combined.

We were all of those things, and I was the helpless addict, a woman who had no course in life but to seek his staggering warmth.

Another finger pushed in, followed by another. Stretched so tight, I didn't know how I would keep from being pushed over the edge of madness.

My body wouldn't stop hitting against the wall, the strength and power of his hand relentless. The sin was drawing closer, pulsing against my skin, fighting to be released as I was shoved into God's light, knocked from the precipice of hatred and doubt, and catapulted into pure forgiveness.

I was his Eve again.

His one.

His only.

The woman who was born to walk beside him.

Something crashed to the floor beside us, but I couldn't look to see what clattered against the ground. There were too many stars in my eyes, too much toxic desire that I was lost to everything but the man who continued tormenting me with his hand.

I knew it wouldn't last. I somehow understood that he wouldn't give me a part of himself.

When my body relaxed against his, when my lips parted on the final force of breath that was expelled by the release he gave me, he pulled away from me, but still held me up with his hands gripped over my hip and wrists.

I could feel the slickness of my release against my skin.

And it only made me want him more.

I wondered if he would ever fully exorcise the sexual demon that lived inside me.

"You've confessed," he finally said, his voice broken and gritty, his jaw so tense I worried his teeth would shatter beneath the pressure.

He released my wrists and made sure I was steady on my feet before releasing my hip. Cold air rushed in to caress my skin where his warmth no longer existed.

On shaky legs, I followed behind him as we left the room, but something called for me to look back.

I almost wished I'd resisted.

Only feet from where we'd been standing, the crucifix that had hung on the wall above our heads was now embedded upside down in the wooden floor.

. . .

I fell asleep to Elijah's hands playing through my hair, and I woke up that way as well.

It was still dark outside, the morning sun not yet high enough to breach the horizon with the warmth of its light. From outside the window, the night birds sang their chorus, the land was quiet except for the nocturnal creatures that still hadn't found it necessary to crawl to their beds.

"You've done well, Eve."

Soft, soothing, and utterly hypnotic, his voice was alive inside me, all around me, swallowing me within its endless depth. I slid my gaze to where he sat beside me, the mattress dipping beneath his weight.

As usual, he was draped in deep shadow, his black clothes lost to the velvet darkness of the room.

But there was nothing dark enough, no shadows deep enough, that could prevent me from seeing the clear focus of his eyes, the penetrating stare that haunted my sleep and chased me through the endless hours of night.

"Elijah," his name fell off my lips as a reverent prayer. "You stayed with me."

His fingers stroked through my hair, sweeping it back from my face.

"How can I leave a woman who was made for me? How can I deny myself your perfect obedience?"

Light filled my heart, spilling over into my body until all I could feel was the heat of it beneath my skin. He'd forgiven me. I was his again.

Leaning down, he pressed his lips to my forehead, his fist tightening in my hair. A moan crawled up my throat, tears welling in my eyes in response to his seductive violence.

"I'm yours, Elijah. My body is yours. My soul –"

Pulling his mouth from my skin, he jerked my upper body from the mattress by my hair, his fingers fisting into the thick silk even more. I shook beneath the force of his hold, but I didn't cry, I didn't scream or refuse him in any way.

Why was he angry? I'd confessed to everything. He'd forgiven me. He wouldn't have tucked me into bed so tenderly if I were still exiled on the perimeter staring in at the grace he could offer me.

His mouth pressed against my ear, his breath whispering against my skin. "I may have forgiven you, Eve, I may have touched you in ways I know you'll always crave, but how can I trust you? You ran from me. You left me standing there while you listened to another man tell you what to do. How can I believe that your devotion is what it needs to be?"

"Please," I breathed out, the pain of his grasp leaking out of my voice.

"Please, what?"

"I can't live without you. I'll do anything, Elijah. Anything you could possibly want or need. Just, please, don't leave me. I'll die without you."

His chest shook with soft laughter. I wasn't sure if this was a nightmare brought on by the terror of the night, or if he really held me, if he was really laughing at the pain so obvious in my voice.

Trailing his lips along my cheek, he found my bottom lip and bit down, his teeth pulling away fast enough for his mouth to cover mine, for him to swallow the moans that escaped me.

Fingertips trailed down my body, between my breasts, over my stomach, down farther until they nestled between my legs. I was wet for him, soaking – always so ready.

He was my greatest sin.

I doubted that God himself was powerful enough to force the fire of need from my body.

Only Elijah could tamp down the flames.

Only him.

His fingers loosened through my hair, his hand cupping the back of my head as he kissed me while laying me down.

Breaking the kiss, he left me breathless, his face hovering inches above mine. I didn't mind the loss of his mouth, but when he pulled his hand from between my legs after having set me on fire with his touch, I wanted to scream out my frustration.

Why was he refusing me still?

Didn't he know that I would give up my life for him if that's what he wanted?

"I have a task for you, Eve. A way you can prove to me that nothing will keep you from pleasing me. Follow through with this one act, and I can promise you I'll never let you go again."

His palm smoothed over my scalp, ice to soothe the fire, a salve to ease the pain.

I nodded my head, my eyes locked to the glimmer in his. "Anything."

"There's my Eve, right there. You were always the purest and most devoted of the good little girls."

19

JACOB

Therefore, my dear friends, as you have always obeyed – not only in my presence, but now much more in my absence – continue to work out your salvation with fear and trembling.
Philippians 2:12

I woke the next morning by throwing myself out of bed. At first I thought it was guilt for what I'd done that abruptly pushed me from deep sleep into a seated position, but then a sound outside drew my attention, a light tapping that forced my bleary eyes to the window to peer out into the haze of the first light of morning sun.

Rubbing the sleep from my eyes, I squinted against the darkness still fighting the dawn, but with sleep weary eyes, seeing that clearly in the distance was impossible.

Throwing the blankets off, I pushed my legs over the side of the bed, shuffling just enough to press my bare feet to the cold wood floor. I scrubbed my hands over my face, pulling my palms down for my eyes to catch sight of the crucifix I'd never bothered to pick up from the floor when I'd returned from Eve's room to go to bed.

A deep breath rushed out of me.

What more did I need as a sign of what I'd done wrong than an inverted cross planted firmly in the ground next to where I'd broken my vow to God?

The tapping sound from outside happened again, a little farther in the distance than it had been before. I wondered it was a bird or some other animal attempting to break into the bark of a tree to get at what little food could be found there.

Standing from the mattress, I padded barefoot across the floor, pulling the threadbare curtain aside to take a look.

I didn't see an animal, but what I did find was my truck in its usual parking space, the passenger door wide open.

"Crap," I muttered. I'd neglected to remember to run back outside and shut it after bringing Eve into the rectory. My battery was most likely dead from the interior light staying on all night. Another sign perhaps. One that signified that I was slipping quickly into the past where I was a man wrapped securely in blankets of sin.

I would have left the truck for later and gone back to bed if I hadn't heard the tapping sound again. Concerned that an animal was rummaging through what little I had in the interior, I didn't bother grabbing a shirt to cover my bare chest. I didn't grab shoes or anything else, just walked the short halls to the door and threw it open in nothing but the black pajama pants I'd worn when I finally laid down to sleep.

My throat hurt from screaming at the bastard I left on the side of the road – or was it from praying last night until I'd run out of breath? I ignored the pain to stumble over twigs and rocks in the dirt driveway. Instantly regretting the decision not to grab shoes, I'd almost reached my truck when a particularly sharp rock caught me in the dead center of my foot.

I cursed under my breath and lifted my foot to inspect the damage.

"That looks like it hurt. I thought dad had taught you better than to wander outside without the proper clothes."

Spinning in place, I almost lost my balance. Jericho leaned back against the trunk of a large tree, his arms crossed at his chest, his body covered in black pants and a black shirt.

"You ever wear anything other than black?" I asked, not sure why that was the first question out of my mouth. Even though I was surprised to find him standing there, I wasn't shocked. After the events over the past few days it wasn't hard to figure out that he'd been watching me longer than I'd known he was living close to my town.

"Do you?" he asked, a smirk pulling at his lips.

"I have a reason," I reminded him.

That smirk broadened into a smile. "As do I, brother. As do I."

Pausing, he said, "I hear you attempted to return Eve to me last night."

"Yeah," I bit out, "And I hear you had your *family* shoot at her until she had no choice but to run to save her life."

He shrugged a negligible shoulder. "I'm not sure I know what you're talking about."

"You're never sure about anything."

He laughed. "When can a man be sure about anything?"

"Why are you here, Jericho?"

Smiling just enough for the expression to be a threat, but not quite enough to reach his eyes, he didn't move from where he leaned against the tree. The sun still hadn't climbed over the horizon and he'd intentionally settled himself where he'd be concealed in shadow. Even if someone happened to walk by and look up the drive, it was doubtful they'd see him where he stood.

"I came by to deliver a gift."

I reached up to run my hand through my hair, the anger and frustration I was feeling making it impossible not to move in some way. "Did you destroy the sanctuary again like some random teenager?"

"Not quite."

Tired of his games, and tired of the non-answers he always gave, I turned as if I were walking back in the direction of the rectory. "Goodbye, Jericho. Do me a favor and stay the hell off parish property and out of my life."

He allowed me to walk a few steps before calling out again. "Do you remember Ellen Baker?"

Stopped in my tracks by a name from my past, I didn't bother turning back to him. "Of course, I remember her." I'd been thinking about her the night before, but I didn't tell him that. "Why?"

"I was thinking about her last night. Thinking about what we did to her down in that dusty basement beneath the church while preparing for a charity dinner."

My curiosity got the better of me. I turned to lock my eyes with his. It was like looking in a mirror.

Thirty-six years, eighteen of which were spent apart, and we still looked identical. He even had the same haircut as me.

"Okay. What's your point?"

He grinned, his eyes darting out into the distance before they were directed back to mine. "Innocence always tastes so sweet, don't you remember? How many virgins did we have notched on our bedposts by the time you left for college? Seventeen? Or was it eighteen? That number doesn't even come close to the whores, but none of them really mattered. It was the innocent that we always focused on during the worst of our games."

"I'm not that man anymore, Jericho. I don't care what you've done with your life. I can't help the people you're still preying on. I have my own parish to run. And a woman sleeping inside that is so fucked up she doesn't know her own name. But you wouldn't know anything about that, would you?"

Uncrossing his arms, he slipped his hands into his pockets, his face cast down so that he was looking at the ground beneath his feet. Regardless of where he looked, his voice still carried. "Have you enjoyed her yet? I seem to think you have."

My thoughts rushed back to what I'd done to Eve against my bedroom wall, my guilt sweeping in to drown me for having enjoyed doing it. I didn't sink so low as to use her to pleasure my own body, but watching the expressions of her face, knowing that the sounds crawling up her throat were because of me, it was a feeling I'd long forgotten in the years I'd been a priest.

Jericho's gaze lifted to mine. "Have you yet supped on her sweet divinity? I can promise you there's nothing else like it."

"No," I growled, anger a jagged pulse in my veins. "And I have no plans to take part in screwing her up anymore than you've already done."

He tsked, a smile spreading across his face. "I think you're lying, Jacob. You can tell me that all day long while you attempt to convince yourself, but the truth is obvious behind your eyes."

I didn't respond – couldn't respond due the lump of rage threatening to choke me.

"Tell me, do you look at her and see all the little choir boys you've played with in your role as priest?"

My hands curled into fists. "I haven't touched anybody."

"Lying is a sin, you know?"

At that point, lying was the least of my sins. I'd convinced myself that touching Eve like I had was for her own good. It was only a means to an end. She needed relief after the night she had, and since I was responsible for the events of that night, I'd gone against my own beliefs to give her what she believed she needed.

After escorting her back to bed, I'd sat with her and run my fingers through her hair until I was sure she slept peacefully. Yes, I'd enjoyed what I'd done to her, and that was my cross to bear. But it wouldn't happen again. I would make sure of it.

"I haven't touched her," I said again, adding strength to my voice now that I was fully awake and the fury I felt toward my brother was spreading its wings inside me and coming back to life. "And I haven't touched any choir boys."

He shrugged again before reaching up to scrub his hand over the back of his neck. Tilting his head to the left and right to relieve the muscles of his shoulders, he looked back at me, a smile pulling across his face. "How about your young parishioners? I can think of one that looked awfully happy to see you yesterday. The dear, sweet thing ran up to give you a hug just outside the church doors."

My breath caught in my lungs to remember exactly who he was talking about.

"What have you done, Jericho?"

Laughing, he stared me directly in the face. "I've done nothing. I just thought it was sweet, the deep color of the blush that ran across her cheeks. From where I was standing, I would even venture to guess that the girl was in love. With a priest, no less."

"There's nothing wrong with the way she feels. She's an innocent girl. Leave her alone."

I couldn't read his expression, but there was something in it I didn't like. A shadow, or mockery of my calling, I wasn't sure, but I wanted nothing more than to slap the look from his face.

"Tell me you haven't wondered, brother. That you haven't looked at the innocent girls sitting there listening to you preach about God, the ones kneeling before you to accept the body of Christ into their bodies, their lush little mouths sliding over your fingers, and remembered what it was like to *show* them what it meant to see the divine."

Fear traced up my spine. Not for myself, but for the innocent people who were being dragged into the crosshairs of a man who was obviously lost to his insanity. "Why are you doing this?"

"Why not?" he asked, raising his hands up as if what he'd done to Eve meant nothing. As if his cryptic threat against Annabelle was just a simple joke between brothers. Pushing away from the tree, he took measured steps toward me, but stopped when he was still ten feet away.

"Try as much as you like, Jacob, hide behind your clerical collar, drop to your knees to beg forgiveness and pray to a God who isn't listening. None of that will rid you of the man you really are deep down inside. We started our games together, but it was always you who played harder, who bit deeper into the hearts of the sweet women who invited us to their beds."

He paused, his breath even while mine was a storm within my chest.

"Tell me, brother, are your prayers helping you? And who will God listen to when you pray for the strength to avoid Eve while I pray for your weakness so that you give in and remember exactly who you are?"

I couldn't listen to him anymore. Just like the asshole I'd left bleeding on the side of the road, I wanted to rage against Jericho, wanted to slam my fist into his face so many times he would no longer look like my twin.

"Stay away from my parish. Stay away from my parishioners. And if you know what's good for you, you'll stay away from Eve and from me."

Soft laughter shook his shoulders. "Now, that I can't help you with. Eve is only on loan. And time is moving quickly toward the moment I'll be taking her back. Tick tock, Jacob."

Stepping forward, I stopped myself before getting so close I'd be tempted to act on the violence churning inside me.

"You may have convinced Eve that I'm you. Hell, you may have convinced your entire *family*, but there are people who know I have a twin brother. There are people who can tell the police or whoever I end up dragging into this that you've been lurking around this church."

"Are there?" he asked, the corner of his lips pulling up. "I guess that means I should be on my way then. I would hate for all of this to be for nothing."

Turning away from me, he waved from over his shoulder as he casually strolled towards the woods that lined the property. "Take care, Jacob. I'm sure we'll run into each other again soon."

"No, we won't," I yelled back.

Stopping in place, he glanced at me from over his shoulder. "I won't stop until you give in to the fear and trembling, brother. Fear," he repeated, "and trembling. You'll understand what I mean by that soon enough. The gift I left you is in Eve's bedroom, by the way. You may want to get to it before she does. I don't think she'll appreciate it very much."

With that, he walked off, becoming lost in shadow before disappearing into the woods entirely.

"Fuck," I hissed, hating that I'd lost the ability to have anything more intelligent to say. Kicking at the rock that had pierced my foot when I first walked outside, I crossed the driveway to slam the door to my truck, and turned to walk back inside.

I didn't appreciate hearing he'd been in Eve's bedroom again, and I feared I'd find her in pain and struggling just like the last time. She couldn't stay alone in her room any longer, which meant she'd have to stay in my room with me.

207

Eve being within easy reach wouldn't make my life any easier.

Racing into the rectory, I grabbed a shirt and wound through the halls into the church, around the sanctuary and down the hall leading to Eve's door. Fear was a tension over my bones, but I threw open the door, expecting...

Hell, I didn't know what I was expecting, but it wasn't what I found.

Eve slept peacefully in her bed, the first rays of morning light shining in through the window to illuminate her face. There were no new bruises that I could see and the blankets were pulled up snug to her chin.

Jericho must have left her alone for once.

Which meant there was something else in this room that he'd tucked away, a *gift* he intended for me to find before anybody else had the opportunity.

Moving quietly into the room, I was glad for my lack of shoes. It made it easier for me to creep around without making a sound, without waking up the young woman sleeping on the bed. Quickly scanning my eyes over the room, I didn't see anything that was out of place, but while running my eyes past the small desk positioned beneath the crucifix on the wall, I caught sight of just the corner of a white envelope where it had been tucked inside a large Bible.

I glanced at Eve to ensure she was still sleeping before padding slowly over the floor. A board creaked beneath my foot. I stopped and waited to see if it was enough to wake her up. She didn't stir in response to the sound so I kept going.

Reaching the desk, I slipped the envelope from the Bible, refusing to open it until I was out of the room and away from prying eyes. I closed the door behind me without letting it latch and walked at a brisk pace down the hall toward the rectory. Before I could make it through the sanctuary I was stopped in my path.

"Father Hayle? Do you have a minute to talk?"

I spun in place to lock eyes with Sister Agnes, one of the senior nuns that lived at the convent a few streets away. As soon as I saw the black of her habit, I remembered that I'd never heard what happened to Sister Joyce.

"Sister," I said, inclining my head and stuffing the envelope discreetly into my pocket. "Can I help you with something?"

Her gaze trailed down my body and back up to my face. "Why are you running around in pajamas and no shoes, Father?" Her face turned toward the hall from where I'd just emerged. The last thing I needed was for her curiosity to lead her down that direction to find Eve sleeping naked in the recovery room.

Quickly, I marched forward and took her by the hand. "I'm sorry, Sister, I know it's not proper for me to be running around half dressed. I'd rushed inside to make some coffee, but before I could walk into the kitchen, I thought I heard a noise. I was just checking that all the windows and doors to the church are locked."

Her expression fell, her hand reaching up to clutch the rosary that hung from her neck. "Oh, yes. I heard about what happened to the statue of Mary. It's horrible business, I tell you. Darn kids think it's funny nowadays, but they have no idea how mean spirited their pranks are. Sister Eunice returned to the convent very much in distress for having seen it."

I patted her hand. "It's been taken care of. We were able to clean the statue," I turned to show her, "and as you can see, it's good as new."

A small smile spread over her lips, but she was still upset. "Well, I'm glad to see that, Father, but I need to talk to you about other matters. Is there somewhere private we can talk?"

Glancing around the sanctuary, I noticed there was nobody else in the room. How much more private did she need it to be? Still, she was obviously concerned about something and I needed to get this conversation over with as quickly as possible before Eve woke up and came looking for me.

"We can talk in my office, if you like."

"Yes, Father. That will work."

I motioned with my arm. "Ladies first."

She blushed, but tried to turn her head in time for me to miss it. I didn't.

Sister Agnes did the sign of the cross as soon as she entered my office. Her eyes had gone straight to the crucifix on the wall opposite my desk. She kissed her rosary and walked to take a seat facing me.

Seated behind the desk, I could feel the edge of the envelope pressing against my leg, and the sharp corner of whatever was inside. I needed to get the Sister out of here. "What would you like to talk to me about?"

"Two things," she announced, her lips pulling into an apologetic line. "The first is about Sister Joyce. We contacted the hospital to see if she showed up to read to the children, and they told us she did. But nobody has seen her since that time. Do you know if she came back to the parish?"

"I don't think she did," I answered honestly, happy that, for once, I could say something without it being a lie. I was racking up the minor sins so fast that a few Hail Marys wasn't going to be enough to make up for them.

Plus, there was that slightly major one I still had to atone for, not to mention the inverted cross in the floor of my bedroom. Twelve years of my life were being washed away.

"Well, we've called the police so they can start looking for her. But we're asking around ourselves as well. Didn't the issue with the statue happen the morning after you saw her last?"

"It happened that night." My eyes blinked slowly as the reminder of that particular nightmare was slapped in my face. Through all the other chaos with Eve, I'd neglected to remember there was a missing nun and puddles of blood in the sanctuary.

Reaching up, I pinched the bridge of my nose.

"Are you okay, Father Hayle?"

"Yes," I groaned, pulling my hand from my face. "I'm just exhausted," I explained, glad that it wasn't a lie.

"Where were you the night Sister Joyce disappeared and the statue was violated?"

"Here," I answered honestly, even if I was leaving out the part where I was busy tending to a brainwashed naked woman. Technically it was a lie of omission, but I tried not to think about that.

"And what happened the following morning? When the desecrated statue was found?"

"I heard a scream coming from the sanctuary, so I ran in to investigate. It was the young initiate. I led her into the kitchen and then went outside-"

"I mean, what happened with Sister Eunice?"

My thoughts were immediately back in the front courtyard where my brother had scared that poor woman to the point of tears. In my rush to go tell Eve that I was taking her back to the compound, I hadn't given Eunice the time to calm down. I hadn't been the shepherd I should have been for all members of the church. "She saw the statue, which I assumed is what upset her so much."

I hadn't yet mentioned my brother because I didn't want the cops involved with Eve still in such a fragile state. The Diocese would discover she was staying at the church and demand she be taken to a hospital or a home for people in her less than healthy mental condition. Although, if the time came when I needed to involve the police, the young nun would be a witness to the fact that I have an identical twin who's been lurking around church property.

Sister Agnes frowned. "That sounds like very little for her to have reacted so poorly."

My eyebrows arched up my head. "What do you mean?"

"She's left God's service, Father. We're unsure where she's gone, but she left a note in her room explaining she'd changed her mind about taking her formal vows."

Crap. That only left the gardener, Mr. Whitaker as an eyewitness regarding my brother.

"I'm sorry to hear that, Sister. Perhaps there were other factors playing into her decision."

"Our life is not for everyone, Father. You know that as much as I."

Inclining my head in agreement, I moved my leg in an effort to get whatever was poking me from the envelope to shift. I only succeeded in making it press tighter against my leg. "Is there anything else, Sister?"

Her frown deepened. "Well, yes. There is the upsetting business of what occurred late yesterday afternoon."

Folding my hands over each other on the surface of my desk, I waited patiently for her to reveal whatever that upsetting business was.

"Where were you last night, Father? Not late, but around sunset?"

"Here." Another lie.

"Are you sure? You see, George Whitaker was in an unfortunate accident on his property."

My eyes widened. "What happened? Is he okay?"

"He's dead, Father."

My heart dropped into my stomach. George was the only man who could verify Jericho's existence beyond Eunice. Without either of them, I had no other person who could tell the police that Jericho was on church property.

"How did he die?"

"He was tending to his lawn and there was apparently an accident involving his lawn mower. Horrible business, really. When he was found, he was on the brink of death. Someone was sent to fetch you from the parish so you could pray over him, but nobody could find you."

"I was here," I lied, swallowing down the lump it left in my throat.

"Your truck wasn't, Father."

No. No it wasn't. But I couldn't tell her I was dropping a brainwashed woman off to the cult my twin brother was running only to find her getting raped on the side of the road where I proceeded to beat down her attacker.

"Oh, you know? That's right. I had a few errands to run. I'm sorry. I forgot that."

As if God himself were sitting in the room testing me for each lie that was easily falling from my lips, Sister Agnes' gaze dropped to my hands, her eyes widening instantly. "What happened to your hand? You're injured."

I followed her gaze to the bandage I'd quickly wrapped over my busted knuckles before going to bed. Blood had seeped through the white cotton.

"Um, I -" Another lie was coming. Another festering knot clogging my throat. "That was the errand. I'm having battery issues with my truck and cut my hand working on it."

Only a partial lie. I really was having battery issues, as in the battery was most likely dead from having left the door open all night.

"You really must be more careful, Father."

Nodding in agreement, I had nothing to say. I was simply biding my time for her to leave so I could open the envelope and find out what other *unfortunate* surprises my brother had in store for me. As it appeared now, each person who could have confirmed he was around or near the church was missing or dead. My blood pressure was steadily rising and I needed this meeting to end.

I was also finally aware of why Jericho had grinned when I told him there were people who could attest to what he was doing. At the time I made the statement, he must have known for a fact those people weren't around any longer.

"Well, I've taken enough of your time, Father. I'm sure you're busy today preparing the homily for Sunday Mass tomorrow."

I groaned. No matter what occurred today, I had no choice but to prepare the homily. My absence at Sunday Mass couldn't be explained away by a dead truck battery. People would notice, which meant people would start asking questions.

"The police will be stopping by at some point to talk to you about the vandalism to the sanctuary. I just wanted to let you know."

My brows shot up again. "Is that really necessary? The statue is fine and -"

"They also want to talk to you about Sister Joyce's disappearance. It's all normal procedure when a missing persons report is filed."

Drawing in a deep breath, I forced a small smile. "Of course, Sister."

She stood and I stood along with her to walk her to my office door. Taking her hands in mine, I said, "May God bless you and walk beside you in your day."

Her smile was unsure. "You too, Father."

She left immediately after and I watched through the window to verify when she was off parish property. Once she was happily on her way down the sidewalk, I ran back to my desk, pulled the envelope from my pocket and sat down in my chair. Staring at the non-descript white paper, I whispered a quick prayer before opening it to discover what was inside.

Three Polaroid pictures were tucked neatly within the envelope, and were upside down as I pulled them out. When I turned them over, the shock was so sudden that I pushed back my chair, grabbed my wastebasket and dry heaved over it.

This wasn't happening. This couldn't possibly be happening.

Sweat broke out over my forehead to drip along the side of my face, and the rage inside me was ratcheting so high that I feared there was no other way to release it without punching walls.

That sick son of a bitch.

Flipping the pictures over to lie side by side on the surface of my desk, my eyes blinked in disbelief and heartache.

The first image was innocent. Annabelle Prete was hugging me in the front courtyard of the church on the day she'd come to confess her crush on me. The picture was taken from a distance, as if someone happened to be walking by and snapped the shot.

But the other two photos were what drove my heart rate to the point of pain - to the point where my hands were clutching into fists and dread was a steady stream trickling down my spine.

The first was taken from a vantage point above the young woman's partially naked body. Her arms were spread out above her head on a bed, her breasts were exposed where her shirt had been unbuttoned and her skirt was pooling around her hips. Below, her legs were spread and the shot captured the moment a cock was being pushed inside her body. A mixture of pain and pleasure was in her facial expression - joy, love, doubt and guilt obvious in her eyes.

But it was the next picture that worried me, only because it was the next picture that showed me exactly what Jericho had done.

Annabelle was still naked in the shot, her mouth open on the cry of a young woman having sex for the first time. And in the mirror that was also included in the frame, was a clear reflection of my brother's - *my* - face, below which was a black shirt like I always wore, together with the stark white strip of a clerical collar.

20

EVE

Do not worship any other gods or bow down to them, serve them, or sacrifice to them. 2 Kings 17:35

An hour is a long time to wait when you have to go to the bathroom.

I'd woken peacefully that morning, tucked in and warm beneath soft blankets. I felt light and easy, relieved of some horrible pressure that for the past few days had been squeezing the life out of me.

Sitting up on the mattress, I felt a smile pull at my lips, the corners creeping up slowly. It was if my mouth had forgotten how to form the expression, probably because it had been so long since I remembered making it.

Full sun beamed through the window and I narrowed my eyes against it. God's warmth met my face, the glow filling my body until I was light as air.

Not wanting to upset Elijah after the promise he made me, I waited for him to come get me like he has every morning since I've been here. But seconds turned to minutes. Minutes turned to an hour. And my bladder was screaming for me to rush to the bathroom.

I couldn't wait any longer, not without making a mess of the floor.

Elijah never demanded I stay in my room in the mornings. He'd never given any instructions for how to behave when in this place other than the efforts I had to go through to prove to him I wouldn't run again.

Throwing the blanket off me, I stood from the bed and grabbed the robe Elijah had given me the first night I was here. I slipped in and walked to the door.

The door wasn't fully closed, so I pulled it open slowly to peek my head into the hall. Elijah wasn't in sight, and the building was as quiet as a tomb. Slowly padding barefoot down the dark, narrow hall, I pushed doors open as I passed, but couldn't find a bathroom close by. I also didn't remember the way Elijah had led me the two times we'd walked between his bedroom and mine.

Wondering if I'd remember the turns if I saw them, I kept wandering hallways, turning left and right. When I walked by one particular door, his voice called out.

"Eve."

My head spun right to find him seated behind a desk, pen in hand and papers spread out over the surface of the desk. A pair of thin rimmed glasses were perched on his nose, but I couldn't remember ever seeing him wear them before.

"What are you doing?"

Dropping the pen and taking off the glasses, Elijah stood up. Rather than the button down shirt with the odd white collar he normally wore with black pants, he was in a short sleeve black t-shirt and loose black pants.

Although the color hadn't changed, I'd never seen him in informal clothes before.

I stepped into the office and cinched the robe over my body. "Looking for a bathroom," I said softly, worry still coursing through me about whether he'd be mad that I left the room.

He shook his head and moved around the desk toward me. "Yes, of course, I apologize. I didn't know you were awake. There's one a little ways down the hall. I'll show you."

Throwing his arm around my shoulder, he led me out. We walked silently past two doors before he reached around me to push open another door on my left. It wasn't the same as where he'd taken me to bathe, just a small room with a toilet and sink.

"Take all the time you need. I'll wait in the hall to escort you to the kitchen for breakfast."

I moved to walk inside, but turned back. There was no telling what came over me, but I stepped up toward Elijah until we were chest to chest. With his height, I had to push up on tiptoes to barely look him in the eye. My mouth hovered inches from his as his silver-blue eyes studied mine. His breath beat against my face, quickening as I leaned even closer. But at the moment my lips would have brushed his, he turned his head.

"I can't kiss you, Eve," he whispered. "Not because of something you've done, but because I'm a devout man."

"It hasn't stopped you before," I said against his cheek.

"It should have."

He stepped back, his gaze lifting to catch mine. "We should talk, but let's do so over food, okay?"

220

I nodded my head, my heart shattering into a million pieces as I lowered my heels to the floor. "Okay."

It didn't take long for me to use the bathroom and just as silently as he'd walked me there from his office, he walked me to the kitchen. Pulling a seat from the table, he indicated for me to sit down.

He didn't say a word as he pulled food from a refrigerator and pans from a cabinet. Flame jumped over the burner on the stove and he placed a heavy iron skillet over it before spooning in butter. Even while waiting for the pan to heat, he didn't look at me, didn't speak to me, he simply kept his eyes trained on that pan as if it were the most interesting thing in this room.

Unable to endure the silence, I broke it with the first question that came to mind. "What were you writing?"

His gaze flicked to mine, torment dancing behind the clear, blue color. It was a moment of connection that made my heart burst open, but he turned back within a second, the warming pan more important than me.

"I was writing the homily for Sunday Mass tomorrow."

The word *homily* was foreign to me, but not Mass. I'd been told about that, the process described to me in detail. Hope was a hint of light fracturing through me. "Mass is tomorrow?"

Another glance.

Another rejection.

"Yes," he answered while breaking eggs into the pan.

"What's a homily?"

"It's a discussion of scripture, a message to the weak and weary."

My eyes widened just a bit, my heart daring to beat faster. "Like a sermon?"

His eyes darted in my direction. "You've heard a sermon before?"

He must have been testing me before the last act he'd instructed me to perform. There was no other reason for the odd question, or the soul shattering distance he was placing between us. "Yes. I've listened to every sermon you've given."

He bit out a harsh word under his breath, picked up a spatula and flipped the eggs in the pan. Time passed as that overwhelming silence drifted back in. Only the frying eggs could be heard.

Without looking at me, Elijah said, "Tell me about the sermons you've heard me give."

"I can't speak them word for word-"

"A summary is fine."

Pulling my hands into my lap, I stared down at them, pressing the tips of my fingers together until they turned white from the blood rushing out.

I didn't want to discuss sermons, or anything else for that matter. I just wanted to know what happened between last night and now to make him so distant and morose.

"Is something wrong? Have I done something wrong?"

The spatula slapped against the pan, greasy butter splashing up that made him jump back and curse beneath his breath. Grabbing a napkin from the counter, he moved to clean it up, his voice angry and impatient when he said, "Just tell me about the sermons, Eve."

Flinching in response to the bite in his voice, I folded my hands together, wringing them so hard the skin burned.

"God created the Earth for man," I began, trying to remember the important parts, the instructions the family lived by in order to avoid falling into evil. "But man was sinful and disobeyed God. Every man and woman disobeys."

Even me, I thought. No matter how hard I try to please Elijah, to do everything he asks of me, I still forget. I still disobey. And only I could be blamed for the way he treated me now.

Elijah lifted the pan to slide the eggs onto plates. Placing it back on the stove, he threw in strips of meat, a sizzle and pop rising up with a smell that was heavenly. "Go on."

"So the Devil gained dominion of the Earth because he'd tricked man into sinning. He tempted man with woman, because women are the most sinful of all. We're weak and we need men to cast out the sin inside us. We are man's greatest temptation. Our bodies are built for sin."

His jaw ticked in response to what I said, but it was his only response, the only indication he was listening.

"So, God sent Christ down to help man, but Christ chose the Kingdom of Heaven as his home. He abandoned mankind when he died. He left us in the Devil's dominion."

Whatever he was cooking sizzled more. Hot grease splattered out of the pan onto his hand leaving red marks where it hit. He didn't even bother moving his hand away from where the grease kept popping and burning him. "Keep going," he demanded, sharp anger edging his voice.

223

"So, God sent another Christ. And that Christ will eradicate sin and teach us to fight it. To destroy it if we believe in him."

Elijah's eyes met mine, his lips pulling into a thin line, rage wrinkling his brow. "Eli-" He stopped, his hand curling into a fist over the counter. "I told you that?"

I nodded my head, too scared to speak because of the way he looked at me.

"And who is the new Christ?"

"You," I whispered.

His fist slammed down onto the counter. "That son of a bitch," he mumbled as he turned his back to me.

A tendril of smoke weaved up from the pan, growing thicker as a bitter smell spread through the kitchen. Elijah turned to look at the food inside it, another curse word barked softly over his lips. Grabbing the handle he threw the pan - food and all - into the sink. Steam rose up from the heat as soon as the pan clattered against the metal.

Picking up one of the plates he'd prepared, he dropped it on the table and walked toward the door.

My heart sank into my stomach, filling it so full I didn't want the food sitting in front of me. "Aren't you going to eat?" I called out.

He didn't bother stopping. "I have work to do and I'm not hungry."

Elijah made a right into the hall, but the sound of retreating footsteps stopped suddenly. When they approached again, he only came in as far as the doorway. We stared at each other for a few seconds, not a word being said while I looked to him for comfort and he could barely stand to look at me at all.

"You're going to stay in my room with me tonight."

There it was, the comfort I needed, the reminder that whatever he was doing now had nothing to do with the promises he made the night before.

"I'll sleep on the floor so you can have the bed. I won't share the bed with you, Eve. And you can't sleep on the floor with me. If you try, I'll have to ask you to leave entirely. What happened between us last night can't happen again."

As quickly as that, the comfort was gone. Confusion slid in to take its seat on the throne, kicking its legs up to relax back because it had no intention of leaving.

"Okay," I answered on a tremulous breath.

"Once you're done eating, I'll take you to find some clothes that will fit, and then you can sit in my office for the rest of the day while I work."

Nodding, I blinked to chase off the tears that threatened.

He nodded back before turning to walk away.

His tests would be the end of me, I was sure of it. So close one second, just to force me away, I felt like a rubber ball being bounced by a bored child, the loud thumps it made counting down until the moment he found another toy that would amuse him.

The pain of that thought sliced through me, only to twist and turn so it could shred me from the inside out.

My hope sank into a turbulent sea, clinging desperately to the island Elijah had given me with the last promise he made. I had one last task to perform, and he had warned me that it would be a bitter road to that task. I would doubt, he'd promised. I would struggle in my faith. But if I held on, if I clung hard enough, he would reward me in the end.

21

JACOB

For a righteous man falls seven times and rises up again; but the wicked are overthrown by calamity. Proverbs 24:16

Sedra sat in my office silent as a mouse for the remainder of the day. Hours passed as I finished the homily. When done, I turned my attention to other matters that would keep my attention off the woman seated facing me, and the pictures tucked away in my desk that were still very much in mind despite being out of sight.

Every so often, I'd lift my gaze to look at Sedra to find her curled up in a seat, her hands playing over the cross necklace dangling down over the large t-shirt I'd given her to wear. My sweatpants had been too big for her, so I'd given her a pair of my boxers to wear beneath the shirt. It left her legs exposed for my wandering eye, the shirt so thin I could easily see the fullness of her breasts.

I had to rip my eyes away from her each and every time I dared look up. She was so beautiful, so easily available, and so dangerous to me that it was as if the serpent itself sat in front of me, the forbidden fruit held snugly between its jaws.

Just a taste, Jacob.

You own me, Jacob...
I need to confess...

The present was leaking into the past, setting me on a collision course with tragedy, and with the man I'd been before surrendering myself to God.

I knew well how that serpent was laughing. While I was trying to deny the sinner inside me, I'd walked blindly into his trap.

Jericho's game was making sense to me for once because, in the time I'd taken to sit and stare of the photographs on my desk, in the hours I'd spent watching Sedra sit quietly and obediently before me, the pieces fell together to show me a picture that gave me no chance to escape.

I assumed that Jericho knew I'd attempt to give Sedra back. He must have known that I'd try to force temptation away from me in an effort to save my soul. Had he waited and watched, he would have seen me drive off with her, he would have known it would take two hours at least for me to arrive back to the church. And while I'd been gone, he'd most likely staged the death of Mr. Whitaker, must have grinned as they sent someone to fetch me for prayer.

And where was I? Missing from my station, with no verifiable explanation as to where I'd been.

Except for one possibility, one that could be reported by a girl who thought she'd made love to the priest she'd had a crush on since the day she turned sixteen.

I didn't worry that Jericho had injured or killed Annabelle. That would be too convenient. No. I had every expectation that he intended for her to live, for her to walk into my parish and look at me with accusation behind her eyes.

Even though I hadn't been the one to take her virginity, I still carried the blame for what I knew was to come.

If Annabelle's own guilt wore her down enough, she would go to her parents to admit what she'd done. Those parents would come to me, and what alibi did I have to give them? Only a brainwashed woman who would tell them I left her on the side of the road for a few hours, beat down a man who tried to hurt her, only to bring her home and fingerfuck her against a wall.

That crucifix was still lying on my bedroom floor where it fell, and the serpent had wrapped itself languorously around it.

The only question still remaining was why?

For that answer, I needed to speak to my brother.

Outside my window the sun was setting, ribbons of red, orange and gold painting the sky with God's promise to man. I stared at it wishing the promise could have also been made to me.

"It's getting late," I said, my voice gritty from lack of use. "I'm going to make you something to eat and help you get settled into bed."

Sedra startled at the sound of my voice, her neck wrenched to the left for her eyes to find mine. I looked down at the papers on my desk, still too much of a coward to face what was standing right in front of me.

Her voice filtered across the room regardless, a siren's song meant to draw a man in. "If that's what you want."

228

It wasn't what I wanted.

No. What I wanted was to spread Sedra across my desk, push her legs apart and taste the sweet nectar of her body just so I could feel powerful in the way she writhed beneath me.

Just so I could listen to the sounds that fell from her lips and know that she would *never* deny me.

But I was a celibate priest. One who was in danger of crashing down to Earth with the rest of the tormented and damned.

"It's what I want," I ground out behind clenched teeth.

The serpent laughed again.

Pushing to my feet, I didn't bother looking at her when I left the room. I knew she would follow behind me, a playful puppy looking for the one person who would pet it just right. She was the obedient woman that would give without expecting anything in return, that would take whatever beating I wanted to give her because even the pain was better than living without my touch.

I made her a quick meal and waited patiently as she cleaned her plate. Still unable to stomach anything more filling than water, I chose to lean up against a wall in order to avoid sitting across from her. The temptation to reach beneath the table and pull her foot into my lap just so I could grind up against that small part of her was too much to take.

What I'd done to her the night before had been the spark to ignite a blazing inferno, a fire so hot that not even all of the heavenly angels' combined tears could douse its flames.

I just wondered how many more days I could take of this before I had to admit to myself that Jericho had succeeded in his games.

Her fork clamored against her plate when she dropped it down, her lips wrapping over the rim of a glass of water, the soft pink of her tongue visible against the glass. Setting it down, she turned to me with expectant eyes.

"You ready for bed now?" I asked, trying with everything inside me not to blame the innocent for the weaknesses of the flesh.

Nodding, she stood from her seat and followed me to my bedroom in the rectory. The bed was still a mess from when I'd woken that morning. I hadn't taken to the time to make it, pick up the crucifix or fall to my knees in prayer. The tidy, safe routine I'd made for myself over the years was falling apart at the tattered seams, revealing to me all the stuffing inside filled with my darkness and deceit.

It had always been so easy to make women believe they were exactly what I wanted. And in the end I'd made myself believe the lies that rolled off the silky tongue of a man who should have known better than to think he could deny himself his deviant violence.

"Go ahead and crawl in bed," I said, grabbing the keys to my truck from my desk wondering if the vehicle would even start.

"Where are you going?"

"I have an errand to run."

I didn't give her a chance to respond, just grabbed my shoes and walked outside, waiting until I was alone in the cab to slip them on. Forcing the key in the ignition, I didn't even bother praying the battery wasn't dead. There was no point. God wasn't listening.

It turned over without a problem, the engine roaring within the dying sunlight, the door slamming shut, as I threw it into reverse and peeled out of the dirt driveway. The one hour drive to Jericho's compound wasn't near enough time for me to calm myself down, the passing miles and silent minutes only serving to build the tension inside me until it felt like I would burst beneath the pressure.

Three days ago, I'd pulled up in front of the looming iron gates with no clue of who'd I'd find behind them. But now? Now I was marching toward the gates of Hell knowing full well the demon who would be happy to step through. I wasn't even within reach of them before they parted at the center and Jericho walked out, a broad smile stretching his face.

"Jacob," he mocked, the roll of laughter adding levity to that one word. "And here I thought we'd never see each other again. At least, that's what you told me this morning."

"Save it, Jericho. I'm done with your stupid, fucking games."

He cocked his head to the side. "That's funny because I haven't even started playing yet."

Anger beat its steady drum inside me. "Why are you doing this?"

He grinned and slid his hand up to his ear like I'd whispered the words. "I'm sorry, I didn't quite hear you, brother. Why don't you step closer to my web, little fly, and perhaps we can communicate better."

"Tell me why, Jericho!"

I could feel every vein pulsing beneath my skin, could recognize the violence inside me rearing its ugly head to roar out its might. There was a man in there somewhere that I once had been, and this son of a bitch was slowly pulling him out of me. The entire time grinning.

"Why? Why? Why?" He smirked. "Always with the questions. But instead of asking me something you know damn well I won't answer, you should tell me something instead. How does it feel to know you never shed the sins of your past? To realize you'd only hidden them behind the veil of a religious life?"

"My life has nothing to do with you." I stepped toward him, but he lifted a finger, the sound of at least three separate guns being readied above our heads. I looked up to stare down the barrels of the guns pointed in my direction. Three men stood on wooden platforms that rose just above the tops of the wall surrounding the property.

"I wouldn't come any closer if I were you. I'd hate for your handsome face to be no longer."

Breath burst from my lungs, my body frozen within the rising tide of my fury. Turning to look at Jericho, I grinned. "You always were a fucking coward."

He laughed. "No. What I've always been is one step ahead. You just never knew it."

Kicking at a stone by the toe of his boot, he casually tucked his hands into his pockets, his black hair shining beneath the floodlights of the compound. When he glanced up again, I saw the man I used to be, the bastard that wasn't trapped behind the stark white of his clerical collar.

"Ah, now don't be so mad, Jacob. I haven't done anything to you that you wouldn't have done to me before you found God. We always knew when we started playing our games as kids that at some point we'd turn them against each other. It was only natural that siblings would form a rivalry. One that I assume you thought you'd won when you left for college."

He stepped forward, his eyes directed back to his shoes, his feet careful to move with the heel of one boot placed directly in front of the toe of the other.

Stopping just outside of my reach, he was a man with no concerns because of the guns his men had aimed at me.

"So, let me tell you how the rest of this is going to go." His gaze met mine. The silver-blue color a feature we'd used to lure in all the good little girls we'd destroyed in our lives.

"You're going to go back to your parish, and you're going to enjoy the present I gave you for as long as I let you have her. You're going to stop showing up at my compound because the next time you do, I won't come outside to warn you before my men take you down to your knees. And when I decide it's time for the game to end, I'll show up at your parish and I'll let you know."

"I don't understand, Jericho. What have I-"

"It's not for you to understand. That's what you're not getting in all this," he said, cutting me off.

"And maybe that's been your problem all along, Jacob. You always wanted to understand something. You were never the type to blindly believe, and that's exactly why I know that the collar you wear is a disguise. You're not a godly man, you never have been and yet you sit as the shepherd of your flock, the symbol of God and the might of his hand. Your church is so full of bullshit I can smell the stink of it from here."

Fuck the guns. Fuck the threat. Fuck every word that falls from my brother's mouth. I stepped toward him, my hands fisted at my sides, my pulse so wicked and strong that it was thunder inside my head.

"My choices in life are my own. They shouldn't concern you."

"I never said they did," he answered, his expression unchanging, unworried and full off satisfied pride. "But there you go again looking for a reason."

We were two brothers facing each other down beneath the lights of a madhouse. Two twins that had once been united now suffering the fruits of the evil we'd allowed into our lives. And where I was balanced on a precipice between pitch dark and blinding light, my brother had not only accepted the evil that lurked inside him, he'd embraced it.

"I'll explain this to you in a way you might understand given your new *profession*," he said, his voice low, calculating, and without emotion. "Christ died for our sins, brother. At least that's what's been stuffed down our throats each and every day since we left our mother's womb to come into this shithole we call a world."

He paused, his head tilting left and right to ease the muscles of his shoulders.

"But yet," he continued, his voice softer, a whisper against the cool night wind, "after the third day that son of a bitch rose again to show us all his glory and his might."

A grin tugged at his lips. "It's the third day now, Jacob. And just look at you. Still righteous and pure. Still a man who looks to his God and the Church that serves that God as a means to escape the sinner inside you."

Holding up three fingers, he repeated, "Day three, Jacob. Do you remember what happened after that? I assume you do given you're a priest, so why don't you tell me."

When I didn't answer, he screamed, "Tell me!"

The bastard was right in one thing: I couldn't look at any situation without stumbling over the question of why. Even at that moment I was mentally mapping every word he said, every expression he made, every crime he committed and every life destroyed in the game he was playing. And there was no rhyme or reason to it.

"Christ ascended to Heaven," I finally spit out. "Body and soul."

Jericho laughed, a short burst of sound that carried no humor. "He left us to fend for ourselves against everything wrong in this world, and what happened after that?"

I shook my head in disbelief. My twin brother was stone cold mad. "Are you telling me you're doing this because you're pissed that Christ died? What is wrong with you?"

His eyes clenched tight, his hand reaching up to pinch the bridge of his nose. "I'm not telling you a damn thing, Jacob. I'm asking you to answer a simple question."

As if on cue, one of his family standing with gun at the ready shot at the ground behind me, I assumed to prod me along in answering the bullshit he was asking me. My gaze lifted to look at the bastard holding the smoking gun just so I could remember who to kill when I finally lost my damn mind.

Leveling my gaze back on Jericho, I said, "I don't know what part about *after* you want to hear. It's been two thousand years."

Jerking his hand from his face, he opened his eyes. "Man was left to fall again after Christ left this Earth. He took his toys and he went back to his heavenly playground, and just like how man was ditched after those three days we waited, you'll fall, Jacob. You had your three days and now they're over. And I'll enjoy watching you fall, because you were never a devout man to begin with."

Insane. My brother was certifiably insane.

"Get off my *lawn*, brother. I'm tired of seeing you around here."

Another gun shot rang out, the dust and stones kicking up around me close enough to hit my legs. Jericho turned without saying another word, slowly strolling to the gate that was opening as he approached.

I couldn't help it when I called out, "Do you want me to quit the priesthood? Is that what this is about?"

He stopped but didn't bother to look back at me. "Again, you're searching for the *why*. Just enjoy the ride, Jacob, and stop asking useless questions."

He took another step before stopping again, this time glancing over his shoulder toward me.

"Tick tock, brother. Tick. Tock."

He was gone two seconds later, the gates closing to hide him from my sight.

Hidden just behind the bars with white sheets woven through them, his voice rang out. "If you don't want to get shot, Jacob, I suggest you move along pretty quickly. My family will only give you a few seconds head start."

The men made a show of pointing their guns in my direction and I ran back to my truck. By the time I was speeding around a corner to turn onto the main road, I could hear shots hitting the bed of the truck behind me.

22

EVE

For you need endurance so that, having done the will of God, you may receive the promise. Hebrews 10:36

Tomorrow.

I'd find salvation in only a few hours.

His guidance, his fire, his light.

With this one last task I have to complete for him.

I will be the gates to the holiest of temples.

And he will become the sole worshipper at my heavenly altar.

That is what he promised me.

23

JACOB

Keep watching and praying that you may not come into temptation; the spirit is willing, but the flesh is weak.
Matthew 26:41

I'd tossed and turned all night. Partly because of the insane bullshit my brother had spewed the night before and partly because of the wood floor I had the honor of calling a bed.

My eyes cracked open to a dimly lit room, soft, rhythmic breathing above me a quiet sound counting down time as it passed by.

Eve hadn't stirred when I returned from Jericho's compound, hadn't noticed when my weight sank down onto the side of the bed and I stared down at her wanting to peel off the uniform of a priest and reveal the man below.

Based on her breathing, she was still up there sleeping comfortably while I lay on a pile of blankets, my head supported by a lumpy pillow that provided me with absolutely no sleep.

There were too many shitty factors colliding in my life, too much I couldn't explain that I felt like I was drowning beneath whatever madness my brother could inflict.

Yet, here it was, on God's holy day, and I had a duty to lead a service I wasn't sure I believed any longer.

Although, the majority of what Jericho had said was maniacal nonsense, there was one point he made that I couldn't see past no matter how hard I tried not to think about it:

I was a fallen man.

Maybe not at the moment of birth, but when I grew older and I learned why God had created women for men. Once I had that first taste, it was over. Jacob the doubtful believer became Jacob the hopelessly lost.

I was no longer part of the flock to which my father had indoctrinated me, and all I wanted was another taste of the divine, that moment where I became God himself, setting myself up in his golden throne above the body of whatever woman I was corrupting.

At that moment, there was nobody more vulnerable than the woman sleeping soundly beside me. Everything inside me screamed to shuck the cloth, to rebel against the vows the religion had forced on me and give in to the man I was inside.

Guilt and more guilt, it's all I'd ever been taught. And even though I knew the games I'd played would eventually lead me straight to Hell, I thought that Hell had grown impatient and risen up to greet me on the night Cassandra died.

Maybe I'd been too rough? Maybe I hadn't seen the signs she was in distress? Maybe I didn't care enough to see them.

Maybe it was God's punishment for the sins I knew I'd keep committing, and I got scared.

Fuck! How I got scared.

I ran back to the only thing I knew that could shelter me, a life without sin, a calling without remorse, and a mentality that kept me sequestered and alone, free of the temptations that were all around me.

Only I had to be shouldered again with the unbearable weight of a lifetime of guilt for my crimes.

I was sick and tired of the guilt.

And it took a sick fuck to make me see it – which made me not want to see it at all.

In truth, the only thing the Church had done in my life was draw boundaries. They'd boxed me in with scripture, bound my hands with expectations, and drove a knife in my gut, twisting it each time I stepped just outside of those lines to explore who I *really was* inside. There were parts of me that were messy and without shape, parts that didn't fit within those neat little lines that all devout people are supposed to respect. When I stepped outside those lines, I was whipped and beaten, dragged over the floor by a father who didn't agree that life itself was just as messy as me, the abuse witnessed by a mother who believed the husband is the ruler of the house.

Maybe that's where the darkness started: on those late nights and early mornings where Jericho and I both were beaten and flogged. Simple mistakes we made were somehow the same as us spitting in the face of God, and my father – a devout yet sinful man himself – made sure to brand us with our own sin, instilling in us a craving for the kind of pain that showed us we were alive.

It was only natural we'd follow in his footsteps. Once that door was opened, it was damn near impossible to close. Rather than shaping up and learning how to stay within those boundaries, we took that pain, that guilt, and all the horrible feelings that came with it and we turned it around on the good little *brats* who would drop their panties and let us invade and abuse them until they cried.

We didn't just tempt them outside those boundaries, we forced them out, their eyes opening to the world around them once they were no longer sheltered in the strict ideas of what a good little girl should be.

What scared me even more than Jericho's insistence that I'd never actually changed was his reminder that it had been *me* who always played the hardest, because, in that, he wasn't wrong.

In the beginning, Jericho and I had just been looking for a good time. We were the normal teenage boys, horny as all hell, but still respectful of the *boundaries* set for us. But our first venture outside those lines set a fire in our bodies, a ravenous hunger to go further, push harder, until we could explore in intimate detail all the sexual deviances open to us if we only learned how to ask right.

A handsome man is enough to turn many a young woman's eye, but two identical twins made attracting attention like child's play.

A coordinated team, we learned to lure them in. Jericho was only there for the sexual release, at least, at first he was. But eventually I got bored with taking a woman's virginity and I began exploring outward, seeing how far we could push them until they broke.

As it turned out, we could push very far.

Most women shied away at first, not trusting two men who wanted her bound and helpless. A little petting, a small stroke to awaken the fire inside her, and that woman was placing her wrists together, ready and willing to make herself victim to whatever pleasures we had in mind.

Fast forward a little bit later and bondage wasn't enough. I wanted to hurt those women. I wanted them to know what it meant to be like us.

I'd had pain delivered on my body all my life, and I returned that pain with the gratification of a starving man receiving a slice of bread to ease his discomfort.

Jericho went along with it, like he always had, but then I pushed the boundary too far and scared a woman half to death.

He retreated back into the life safe within religion's boundaries, and I pushed forward, packing my things and leaving for college – a free man unrestrained by the guilt I'd always carried.

Cassandra died because of me. I was as sure of that as I was the sun rising in the east and setting in the west. I never saw the autopsy photos, I never read the reports, but her mother came to see me one day, and she told me.

Almost every inch of her skin hidden beneath her clothes was bruised. Her breasts, her hips, the insides of her thighs, everywhere that my teeth, or fingers, or the palm of my hand had decided to play. Perhaps it was a symptom of whatever blood condition she had, but it was like artwork to me. I loved to sit and admire those marks only because she'd worn them in remembrance of *me*.

I put them there on all the women I took to my bed, and I wanted to put them on the woman sleeping above me now.

I needed a sign.
But for some reason, I didn't think God cared.
Or maybe his silence was the sign after all.

Pushing up from the floor, I darted my eyes to the bed to see Sedra sleeping soundly. The blanket had slipped down to her waist and the t-shirt she wore had slipped up to reveal the bottom swell of her breasts. Lush and full, they called to me to taste them, to bite them, lick them and claim them with my greedy hands.

Taking a few steps in her direction, I balled my hands into fists. It would be so easy to wake her, so easy to tell her every dirty thing I wanted to do to her, and so *easy* to follow through with it.

But it was Sunday. God's day. The church would soon start filling with the parishioners from town. They'd look for me if I ran late, and the things I wanted to do to Sedra would take hours.

I forced myself away, just to turn and see the inverted cross on the ground. Just like that I was forced back within those boundaries. Snatching the cross from the floor, I hung it on the nail in the wall and muttered, "Not today, Satan."

The serpent must have laughed his head off.

It took me a half hour to shower and get as ready as possible for the day to come. Dreading having to get up in front of the congregation and spread a message of hope and love, I sat on the edge of the bed in my room, fixing my clerical collar into place and staring down at Sedra.

243

She was so sweet. So innocent. And so off limits if I had any hope of not going insane. Every day it was getting harder. Every day I struggled with the question of whether I could go against my vows. Would I be willing to take advantage of a woman who doesn't know who I am?

To her, I was Elijah, and no matter how I tried to convince her otherwise, she would only see my brother when she looked at me.

It wasn't like we hadn't played that trick before with other women, but back then I hadn't cared.

Not that I should care now.

Touching her shoulder, I shook her softly, waiting and watching as her green eyes cracked open, a sleepy smile slipping across her face as she looked at me.

"Morning," I said, smiling back when I should have been stepping away.

"Hey," she whispered, her voice still groggy from lack of use. Pushing herself into a seated position, she tugged the t-shirt down to her waist.

Ignoring how disappointed I was by her body being fully covered, I cleared my throat. "I have Sunday Mass today. I'll be in the sanctuary for most of the late morning and early afternoon. Can you do me a favor and stay out of sight?"

"I already told you I would."

Nodding my head, I stood up from the bed just to place some distance between us. Spinning back, I stared at her. "Wait? What?"

"For Mass."

Had I already mentioned that to her? I couldn't remember with all the chaos erupting in my life. I must have.

Glancing at the clock, I realized I'd lost the time to worry about it. I needed to get dressed, gather the homily I'd prepared and be ready for the procession into the sanctuary.

"Okay. The bathroom is through there, which I'm sure you know, and I'll bring you some food once Mass has concluded."

I didn't give her time to respond, the sleepy look on her face was not making it easy to walk away.

Hurrying to my office, I waved at a few parishioners who'd already made their way into the church. I weaved the halls, grabbed the notes I'd made for today's service and then used back halls to enter the sacristy, the room where I dressed in my vestments and awaited the procession that would lead me into the sanctuary. Several of the processional members were already dressed and in place.

I quickly clothed myself in the cassock robe worn by most priests during services, hung the alb around my neck to hang down the front of my body and tied it in place with the cincture. The robe had always been a little big for me and was roomy enough that I often worried about tripping over it while making my way around the altar towards the pulpit.

Although most parishes had an elaborate set up behind the pulpit where the priest gives his sermon, mine only had the stained glass windows, and not many people to lead me in the procession.

We were a small town, after all, and this was a small building that didn't have the room for all the pomp and circumstance you'd find at a larger parish. The small size was fine by me because I'd never been one who saw the absolute need of all the decorations, glitz and glamor some felt was necessary to glorify God.

I'd always told my congregation that as long as they were in the Lord's house, he was happy to see them. Many of my colleagues scoffed at my dressed down attitude, but I didn't care much about those colleagues to give a damn.

Music softly played from the sanctuary and I walked slowly at the back of the processional, eventually weaving up around the altar to take my place at the pulpit.

The items needed for the Eucharist were set up on the altar and I inwardly groaned at being the man who would administer it. I was feeling anything but holy at that moment and wasn't even sure I believed the message I would be giving today.

Spreading my papers out on the surface of the large pulpit, I took a steadying breath before peering out at the congregation. Dread crawled along my spine, and when I reached the center pews, the reason for that dread stared back at me.

Her hair was down for the first time I'd seen since I'd known her. Gone was the messy braid she always wore over her shoulder, absent were the thick framed glasses that always slipped down the bridge of her nose, and in their place was a face full of makeup, a shirt that hung low enough to show the top swells of her small breasts, and a smile intended just for me with sensual secrets hiding behind it.

Annabelle Prete had been shown a life outside the boundaries, and she had no idea that the man she'd slept with hadn't been me. I wouldn't say she was a changed girl, not yet anyway. I had hope that she'd simply let this all go and be successful in college and the rest of her life.

The come hither stare, however, made it hard to hold on to that hope.

Darting my gaze down to my papers, I waited while the five person chorus sang, I gathered my thoughts while the routine ran its course, and following the scripture reading about God's promise of salvation, I launched into the homily, keeping my eyes pinned anywhere than on Annabelle.

It didn't matter that I wouldn't look directly at her. I could feel her eyes burning into me. More guilt poured in and I was so fucking tired of it.

My mouth was preaching to the congregation about sin and forgiveness, but all I could think about was the woman sitting in my bedroom, most likely on my bed, that looked at me the same way Annabelle was doing now - like she would cut open all her veins for me just so I could enjoy tasting the blood.

That's the thing with certain women: It doesn't matter if you ask them to give up their life, they're just happy for the attention you give them. A pure submissive personality - so deliciously dutiful and obedient - is not a person with differences and opinions. They are a lump of clay waiting for you to form them while they snuggle up to the warmth of your strong hand.

Regardless of what I was really feeling and thinking, I continued talking to the parishioners, filling their lives with hope and light while I stood behind the pulpit wondering just how fast my train would be to Hell. Would it be a long and languorous trip on a coal-powered locomotive that gave you time to think of your sins? Or would it be a high-speed rail where I blinked and found myself kneeling obediently at Lucifer's feet?

I didn't know, and for the things that I kept thinking about doing to a woman who wouldn't say no, I didn't care much either. That scared me. So, while I preached about God to a congregation that looked to me for life's answers, I silently begged for a sign that He was there watching over me, that I hadn't fallen, and that Jericho wasn't right about me all along.

He sent me that sign, but it wasn't the answer I was expecting.

My lips kept preaching, my mind lost to the torment of the past few days, and beneath my legs, something brushed against my robe. The pulpit that encased me was large and dark wood, covering me completely in front and around both sides. It was bulky and dreary, needed a good polish, and the surface where I set my papers was scarred from years of use.

Wondering if a rat or some other animal had run in from the woods and taken this as a home, I stepped back just a touch to look down at my feet and see nothing but the hem of my cassock dusting lazily over the ground. My concern bled away to relief and I kept talking about the purity of the Divine, about the seat in Heaven we'd all receive if we did our best to fight against sin and ask for redemption.

I talked about how God, in his Kingdom, watched down on us, granting us blessings for our servitude and strife. And just as I raised my voice to remind the good people of this rural town that by acting in faith, by remembering our place and conducting our lives in a manner that God would deem fitting, a set of delicate fingers traced up my leg to wrap around my calf.

Shock tore through me, striking deep into every cell of my body, my muscles bunched over bone and I glanced down again while still trying to keep my voice as even as possible.

Eve sat below me, naked as the day she was born, her full breasts exposed to what light could breach the space between my body and the interior of the pulpit. She flashed me a wicked grin, the look in her eyes almost identical to the one Annabelle Prete kept giving me each and every time my gaze quickly drifted past her in the pews where the parishioners sat.

Lifting a finger, Eve placed it against her lips, reminding me that, for this, I needed to stay silent.

Stay out of sight...
I already told you I would...

My thoughts returned to the conversation we had in my room before I left for Mass. I hated that I didn't take the time to focus more on what she'd said to me on my way out the door. This wasn't exactly what I'd meant by staying out of sight, but in her messed up head, she wasn't doing anything wrong.

Shaking my head just enough that she would see, but the congregation wouldn't notice, I tried to make her understand that she needed to stop. Eve wasn't listening. Her lips pulled apart on a slinky little grin and before I could stop her, she flipped the hem of the cassock over her head and ran both hands up the backs of my legs.

My eyes closed for a second, panic overtaking me as I inched closer to the pulpit to ensure nobody would notice the naked woman beneath. There was nothing I could do but keep talking to the parishioners staring

249

back at me, my voice still strong and steady despite the woman exploring up my legs with her hands.

It wasn't long before her hands cupped my ass, her small frame shimmying beneath the oversized Cassock that should have been tight to my body had it been the right size. As soon as her fingers squeezed over the muscles and I felt her breasts brush the front of my thighs, my hands moved from the surface of the pulpit to grip the raised ledges on the sides.

My voice wavered as my body responded and I fought to focus my attention on the homily and the congregation to whom I was speaking. A shiver coursed through me, my eyes closing and opening once more, my gaze accidentally catching sight of Annabelle's face where she sat in rapt attention watching me like I'd been the one to fulfill her most secret of fantasies.

Fuck... I thought silently while still struggling to speak with an even voice.

My erection was tight against my pants, the cotton of my underwear like sandpaper against skin that hadn't been touched by a foreign hand in twelve long years. Eve slid her fingers across the sides of my thighs, moving her grip from my ass to the front of my pants, a small tug letting me know she'd found the button that would open the front and expose me to whatever actions she had in mind.

There was no way out from between the rock and the hard place I now found myself. Moving aside or making a scene would only display to the entire congregation what I'd been hiding in the church for the last few days. I had no choice but to stand there, to let the serpent laugh as Eve freed the button of my pants and pulled down the tab of the zipper.

The relief was as instantaneous as the burden. The tight black pants of a priest no longer confined my erection. The burden was keeping my voice straight and continuing to preach God's holy light while my cock was gripped in Eve's warm hands and pulled free of my underwear.

My voice stumbled as soon as her fingers squeezed over the sensitive flesh, my eyes closed again as a hush fell over the congregation, each person looking up at me wondering why I'd stopped for that one small second and when I'd begin speaking again.

Clearing my throat, I ignored the bead of sweat dripping from my temple down the line of my jaw, and opened my eyes to keep fighting the need my body had to moan in absolute pleasure.

"Excuse me," I said out loud, finding my place in the homily to begin preaching again. "I got a little caught up in the Word of God is all."

The parishioners smiled in response to the blatant lie, their small hand fans working harder to expel the heat that tended to fill the nave and sanctuary when it was packed full of human bodies sucking up all the oxygen. I could barely breath myself, but it wasn't the crush of body heat that gripped my lungs, it was the firm grip of a hand that stroked me from head to balls, slowly moving until I knew that if I didn't start thrusting, I would die.

And there I stood like Sir Percival himself, being tempted by the devil while I sought the Holy Grail. However, unlike him, I wasn't able to deny the serpent's persuasion, wasn't able to forbid myself the freedom of my body's yearnings because, deep down inside, the serpent's darkness was the same as mine.

We are all simple men, our souls battered and striving to achieve greatness in a world that is anything but great. Nothing about me was better than the sinners staring back at me, the clothes I wore, the clerical collar. The years I'd spent denying myself were only a tattered and thin veil that had hidden away and concealed the truth of my sins from myself.

And to make matters worse, my eyes caught sight of Annabelle Prete, the shiny pink of her tongue flicking out to run provocatively across her bottom lip while down below the pulpit, Eve's hands pulled away so that she could wrap the wet heat of her mouth around the head my cock.

She suckled the tip and I sold my soul in full view of the flock I was supposed to lead. My hands gripped the sides of the pulpit threatening to shatter the thick, dark wood beneath my fingers. My legs locked to keep my hips from thrusting, the entire time my lips kept moving to deliver a message I knew at that moment I no longer believed.

The thought crossed my mind that I'd never believed it at all, that my entire existence after taking my vows had been one big lie I'd told, a farce engineered to deny myself the feeling of empowerment that came from sullying the good little girls and making them cry.

The beast that had settled silently inside me while I kneeled and prayed and pretended like I could deny my very nature came to life as Eve's mouth slid farther down the shaft, the tip of her dainty tongue flicking over the thick vein as my eyes continued to track the changing expressions on Annabelle's face, the finger that reached up to run along the deep V of her sweater.

I was a fallen man, damned and doomed, and waiting for the hour when I could shed the cloth of the devout to unfurl my dark, razor edged wings and take what should have been mine from the fucking start.

Somehow, my mouth kept speaking a message of hope and salvation, my voice much grittier now, strained with the effort not to growl as I reached down to force Eve's mouth so far that I could thrust into the back of her throat.

Of course, young Annabelle would pick up the need in my tone, the desperation bleeding out of me as fire, brimstone, and the wet heat of Hell's lava flowed over my dick, the sharp edges of teeth scraping the skin just enough to make me want to punish Eve with my hand fisted in her thick, soft hair.

My balls were tightening beneath me, dancing in delight for the storm of a climax they were readying. How bored they must have been hanging down between my legs, unused and useless, after I'd taken a vow to be celibate.

Gripping my fingers harder, I heard the faint crack of wood under the pressure, Eve's head bobbing now as she reached up to stroke the shaft with her hand in time with her mouth.

Annabelle shifted in her seat, her lips parting just barely to realize I was now staring her down.

As my climax roared through me, as my fingers tightened harder on the wood of the pulpit, and as I came so violently in Eve's mouth that it made her cough just slightly to quickly swallow it down, I finished the homily with so much passion and fury, it forced the parishioners to their feet at the moment I spilled my last drop just so they could scream, "Amen!"

A-fucking-men was right.

My eyes closed. My chest beat with labored breath and I cursed inwardly to realize I still had to administer Eucharist. The chorus began their communion songs, giving me a minute to wonder if Eve planned on tucking me back in my pants, or if I would perform the consecration of the Eucharist with my spit cleaned cock hanging out beneath my cassock.

It was definitely going to be the high speed rail that dragged me down to Hell itself, and I wondered if I wasn't already on it.

Eve did me the favor of tucking me back into my pants and refastening the buttons. Quickly wiggling her way out from beneath my robe, she stopped when the low light hit her eyes. I saw the devil himself dancing within the deep green, and I was the sadistic beast calling out to him.

Moving away from the pulpit, I stepped to the altar and went through the motions of changing wine and the wafers into the blood and body of Christ. Two altar servers stepped up to assist me and when we took our places, Annabelle made sure to step into my line.

Twenty minutes ago and I would have hated seeing her waiting so patiently, but now, freed of the ability to give a single fuck anymore, I simply looked at her and smirked.

Yes, it was wrong and yes, I should have realized I'd just snapped the leash of sanity that had held tight to my clerical collar for years, but I was sick and fucking tired of caging who I was inside, holding it within the boundaries laid out by a religion that always told me I'd be damned.

It didn't matter that I struggled and fought. It didn't matter that I confessed, and preached and lived a celibate life to escape eternal damnation. Because in this moment, during a Mass to the God who was apparently ignoring me, I realized that no matter what I did to avoid it, I would be knocking on Hell's gates regardless.

My smile widened as Annabelle inched closer, the parishioners kneeling down with their hands held out to accept the body of Christ within them. And when young Annabelle Prete stepped up, you couldn't miss the slight tremor in her body, the adoration in her eyes, and the fire of need raging inside her.

She knelt down slowly in front of me, her tongue flicking out to lick her lip, her gaze locking on mine as she didn't offer her hands for the Eucharist, but instead opened her mouth.

Taking a wafer to slip on her tongue, I shivered when her lips closed around my finger, when the tip of her tongue slid over the pad with the tempting promise of what it would feel like on another part of my body.

"The body of Christ," I murmured as she suckled on my finger, her tongue and lips sliding off as she let go and answered, "Amen."

The devil danced in her eyes just the same as mine.

Once the last parishioner had come before me to take the body and blood into their bodies, I returned to the altar to close communion with a prayer and drink what was left of the wine with greedy, ravenous gulps.

The parishioners made the sign of the cross over their bodies before filing slowly outside, and as they walked off to their early afternoon suppers, their chores around the house, or whatever it was they were going to do, I hovered by the pulpit waiting for the moment Eve and I would be alone. The exit procession had snaked off without me, but I didn't care about breaking Tradition, I simply wanted them all to be gone.

Annabelle was the last person to leave, her body aimlessly stalling, hoping for what, exactly, I wasn't sure. Eventually her mom called out to her, waving her on, and I locked my eyes to hers as her sweet smile turned into a frown and she exited through the front doors.

My hand landed on the ledge of the pulpit, my eyes studying the striation of the wood where it had cracked beneath my fingers, and when I was sure that the only two people left in the building were Eve and me, I let out a tremulous breath.

"Eve," I ordered with a barely controlled voice. "Get your ass out here."

The sound of shuffling whispered out from beneath the pulpit, a naked body being exposed with red marks on her knees from where she'd kneeled for over an hour.

Slowly, she crept toward me on hands and knees like any good girl should. When she reached my feet, she sat in wait, her bottom planted on her crossed feet and her hands folded demurely in her lap.

Damn it, Jericho. You trained her just right.

Jutting my chin in the direction of the rectory, I said, "Go to my room and wait for me."

Not able to trust myself where I was standing, I stepped back to keep our bodies from brushing together as she pushed up to her feet. I watched the beauty of her figure march away in route to my bedroom, my mind drowning in the ideas of what I'd do to her next.

24

EVE

Therefore, just as through one man sin entered into the world, and death through sin, and so death spread to all men, because all sinned... Romans 5:12

The Elijah I'd known for eleven years - the one who'd stood by patiently while I'd grown, who'd preached to me and taught me the evils of the world, the one who promised to relieve me of all the sin I had teeming inside me - was not the same man I saw staring down at me in the sanctuary.

I'd completed the last task he'd asked of me. I'd shown him exactly how fearless and dedicated I was, yet his eyes were narrowed into jagged lines, the silver-blue stained with a shadow that kept the light from hitting it directly. I was sliced open by that stare - frightened within an inch of my life.

Still, I stumbled on shaky legs back to his room. I worried and I trembled because I didn't know the man who was coming back for me.

Stepping into the room, I crept on hesitant feet to the center, turning so I'd face the door as he came in.

Minutes ticked by, the pressure building until I thought I'd be crushed beneath the weight of not knowing.

A door opened in the distance, slowly creaking before slamming shut. Footsteps followed, heavy punctuated beats leading straight to where I stood waiting. With each one that drew closer, I shivered more, my mouth going dry as the color drained from my face.

It felt like evil was coming toward me, its darkness reaching out to tickle my skin, a soft brush in sensitive places that had me squirming in place. For the fear of it alone, the breath caught in my lungs, my breasts were painfully tight and a noticeable slickness was between my legs telling me that, despite my fear, my body was ready.

What was wrong with me that I craved the Devil's touch?

How did I know that it wasn't the same man walking toward me?

I hadn't noticed until he looked down at me when I crawled on hand and foot. But now, to see him marching forward, to watch the way he held his shoulders and the bloodthirsty expression on his face, I just knew this wasn't Elijah.

He didn't have the light of God; he was enshrouded in darkness.

He wasn't a gateway to salvation; he was the temptation that would drag me down into the bowels of all that was unholy.

And I stood there frozen, my body responding with overwhelming anticipation.

What demon had been strong enough to take my Elijah over? And why wasn't I running away for fear that demon would invade me, too?

He stepped through the doorway.

I lowered myself to my knees.

Elijah's eyes weren't just cold they were *glacial*, the frost whipping over to run icy fingers across my body, the terror frozen inside every bone, every tendon and every cell.

"Do you have any idea what you've done?" His head cocked to the side just slightly, his voice a dark whisper. "Any idea at all?"

There was no intonation in his voice, no emotion or warmth, just a question posed that promised sensual torment and hedonistic sin. When I didn't answer him immediately, the corners of his lips kicked up into a knowing smirk.

"Allow me to show you."

He didn't give me the chance to respond.

Between one second and the next he was looking at me from the doorway and wrapping his hand around my neck. I was lifted from my knees to the tips of my toes, my feet kicking from panic as he dragged me back to hold me against a wall. My lungs were struggling to pull in air, my hands were reaching up to grip onto his, but he was too strong for me to free myself.

He watched as I struggled, a mischievous child discovering what it was like to rip the wings off butterflies, and when my vision began to tunnel, when I thought he would strangle me with one bare hand, he released me enough that I could stand on my feet, but still kept me pinned by the neck to the wall.

I opened my mouth to drag in a breath, but he dipped his head faster than I could fill my lungs to steal that air right back as his mouth covered mine.

It wasn't clear if the euphoria that overwhelmed me was from the lack of oxygen or the danger behind that kiss. Either way, I was floating off into the ether, my body shaking with unbearable fear as he explored my mouth with a vengeful tongue and teeth that clamped down on my bottom lip as he broke the kiss. Pulling just enough away that he could level me beneath the intensity of his stare, he pulled my lip out where it was still clamped between his teeth.

Elijah bit harder and I cried out in pain. He let go and smiled in response.

Lowering his head again, he released more pressure from my neck, but still not enough that I could hope to move away from him. Warm lips met the shell of my ear, his breath like steam against my skin as he whispered, "I like that sound, Eve. I like it so fucking much that I want to hear it again and again."

His free hand clamped onto my upper thigh just shy of the swollen and needy parts of me, and I cried out again as his fingers squeezed down.

Laughter shook his shoulders, the color of his eyes deepening until they were almost black, and before I could recover from the way he'd already hurt me, I was dragged from the wall and tossed like a broken doll onto the bed.

The springs screamed beneath me, and I tried to crawl back, to escape, but my body wasn't cooperating. Elijah just stood there watching, his chest beating with breath, his hand reaching up to tear the white collar from around his neck. Tossing it to the ground, he dragged his gaze down my body, his hands curling into fists before he dragged it back up again to meet my eyes.

"You couldn't just leave it alone, could you?"

He took a step toward me, his fingers working to open the buttons of his shirt.

"You couldn't stay in my room or stay the fuck away from me. Instead you found it cute or funny to tease a starving man with the sweetness you could offer him on a silver fucking platter."

Pulling the shirt from his body, his muscles flexed and contracted, shadows crossing over the bulges in his arms, the broad planes of his chest and an abdomen rippled with pure masculine strength.

"I'm awake now, beautiful. I'm paying attention and I'm so damn hungry, there might be nothing left of you by the time I'm done."

A wave of heat crested over me, a burning fire like nothing I'd experienced before. By the time he was pulling up his pants, the muscles in his thighs bunching and strained, I was stuck in indecision of whether I would try to run or surrender entirely.

He kicked his pants off and stood staring at me with his erection pressed so incredibly tight against his boxers that I knew running wouldn't help me.

I was his. Thoroughly and completely, and there wasn't a force on this Earth or in the Heavens strong enough to rescue me.

On a voice dripping with promises of passionate pain and tantalizing torment, he said, "You have me now, Eve. All of me. I hope you can handle what you asked for."

As if lured by his voice, my sin rose to the surface waiting and pulsing with the need for him to rip it out, to rid the burden I feared would always be a thread woven within my bones.

Even the small bit of hope that he could drive out whatever evil infected me wasn't enough to brighten the shadow of fear that consumed me as he approached.

Within seconds, he was on top of me, all around me, a heavy weight that pinned me to the mattress while his hand cupped the apex of my thighs. A deep, satisfied growl was a vibration over his chest to find I was practically dripping in my need for him. It's how I knew I was evil:

Despite the terror flooding my veins, and despite the certain threat of his raw, primal state, I craved the violence he would give me, so much so that I would gladly bleed just to be near him.

Two fingers pushed inside me, his palm still cupping me, and with every thrust of his hand, I was inched up the bed, my chest arching and my head pulling back from where he had his hand fisted in my hair. If not for his weight holding me down, he would have pushed me off the side with the sheer amount of force he was using.

I opened my mouth to cry out in both pain and pleasure, but his lips covered mine, his tongue rushing in to lick at the violence of my cries. Only when it was necessary to breath did he pull away, his mouth trailing down my cheek to rest at my ear, his voice so dark and deep it chased shivers up my spine.

"Is that what you wanted my sinful little slut, to feel my fingers inside you again?"

Shifting his leg, he closed mine tighter together which just made my muscles bunch around his fingers, sent me over an edge I always feared tumbling across as the sin pushed higher and higher, a storm threatening to unleash its full, unbridled fury.

"Answer me," he growled, not caring that I couldn't think at that point, much less talk.

Opening my mouth, I tried - God, how I tried - to say anything that might appease him, but nothing came out more than the moans crawling up my throat, his soft laughter shaking against my chest as he dipped his head again and locked his teeth over the point where my neck met my shoulder.

The storm inside me exploded. Shards of cleansing pain and toxic pleasure fracturing out beneath my skin until every muscle was cut, every tendon was severed and every bone ached with the force of the climax.

He laughed again, the sound so dark and low that I knew this was just the beginning of his vicious assault against me.

Rubbing the tip of his nose slowly along my jaw, his voice was the softest satin. "Will you answer me now?"

I'd almost forgotten the question.

"Yes," I breathed out. "I *needed* you to touch me."

"And what else do you need, Eve? What other filthy ideas do you have in that head? Tell me all the dirty little thoughts you have of me."

His erection was solid against my stomach, his fingers crawling up my chest to grip my chin. Turning my face to his, he locked me in his stare. "Do you want me to do more than just fuck you with my fingers?"

A tear slipped down my cheek full of all the agony and promise, fear and ecstasy, joy and deepest anguish. It was all there, swirling around into an intoxicating poison inside me.

"Confess," he whispered, "my beautiful, *innocent* Eve."

He chased my tear with the tip of his tongue, smiling as it were the finest ambrosia.

Breath rattled from my lungs, the fear subsiding now that something so familiar had finally happened between us. Elijah always wanted me to confess, always wanted to know my deepest secrets so that he could take from the dark parts of my soul and extinguish them in *His* brilliant light.

This wasn't about God above or the Devil below; this was about the salvation that stared at me now, the man who would make all the wicked feelings go away. Because every time he hurt my body with the force of his own, he left me floating in the safety and ecstasy of my own private paradise.

"I have thoughts about you all the time. Day and night. Hour by hour. Whether I'm awake or asleep, you're with me."

His forehead pressed down against mine, our mouths a teasing inch apart.

My voice was breathless. "I imagine your hands on me, your teeth, your tongue. I want to crawl to you if that's what you ask. I only exist to feel the sting of your hand. I live to corrupt you and ruin you and tempt you until all you know is me. I am yours. In body. In heart. And in soul."

Elijah's eyes closed, slowly opening again so the sooty black lashes pulled apart to reveal a silver-blue color that brought more tears to my eyes. The anger was gone, but not the flame of desire. Never that scorching flame.

"That's unfortunate," he crooned. "I could have sworn you were a much *nicer* girl than that." A pause, a pull at the corner of his lips. "I think I'll have to teach you what happens to women who think depraved and disgusting thoughts."

Rolling off me, he stood from the mattress. I moved to follow him, but he pressed the tips of his fingers against my forehead to direct me to lie on the bed. I stared up at him in question.

"Stay," he said.

He commanded me like a man would a dog. And I obeyed that command not because I was weak, but because I was strong.

When I was with him, I could conquer whatever evil consumed me. In his light I was free of the shadows that surrounded us all. With his guidance, I would become what God had preordained for me.

Together, we will build God's army and stand united against the demons that have infected this world.

25

ELIJAH

God is dead. God remains dead. And we have killed him. - Neitzsche

The hand of God has not touched this Earth in a long time. Don't let the Church lie to you, not the Catholics nor the Protestants, and all the dominations in between.

Christ wasn't sent here to save us, but to call us to action. He said it himself: He didn't come here to bring peace, but the sword.

History didn't hear that call, the faithful didn't hear that call, the politicians, liars and thieves didn't here that call, but I did.

Standing behind the altar that I have prepared in His name, I stare out at a sea of anxious faces, at men and women. At the children who are ready to begin again.

All were trained. All could seek shelter here. There is safety in this place.

In my voice, they hear the might of God's words speaking to them. And behind their bodies hang the bearers of evil, the demons awaiting eradication.

The game is beginning.

"It's time, my children. War is upon us. Satan's gates have opened wide and we stand here, the only ones basking in God's light."

Whimpers sound from the back of the large room, metal creaking over wood.

"Are you ready for what will be asked of you?"

Murmurs erupt across the room, my children nodding their heads and lifting their hands in praise for what they'd been taught to do.

Whimpers turn into peals of pain and grief. My children turn their heads to stare at the damned.

I lift my eyes like my children to look upon the faces of the whores where they hang from their wooden crosses.

26

JACOB

You have not resisted to the point of shedding blood in your striving against sin. Hebrews 12:4

A sense of calm came over me that I hadn't felt at any time in my life. It was the feeling of being *right* within your self. Of being whole. Of no longer hiding the *shadow* that lingers just beneath the surface of the light.

No matter how resolutely I tried, there was no denying it. Not to God. Not to myself.

But maybe, just maybe, that's the way it should have been all along.

All my life, I'd been taught to deny the parts of myself not upheld within the vestiges of the Catholic religion. I'd been taught to mourn my existence, to apologize for my darkness, to bow and beg forgiveness, not from God, but from the people who stand between us.

At times, it felt like the Bible was telling me one thing and the Church another, and there was no connecting the dots. Power wasn't seated in Heaven. It was seated in a city where Saint Peter laid beneath the ground, where man stepped over the bodies of the Holy in order to make their mighty decrees.

You would think that if the Faith were bound to the book written about it, the rules and laws shoved down our throats wouldn't change so often. But they do, and with those changes come doubt or blind obedience, guilt or undying submission.

All my life, I'd struggled with the Church into which I was born. The same Church to which I ran after committing a crime against God. And the more time I spent with it - the deeper I crawled along to learn the secrets hidden by those who run it - the more I leaned toward the side of that thin precipice that would separate me from God.

Or, at least, that's what they wanted me to believe about that particular side.

However, at this moment, with this sense of *right* that pulsed through me, I was beginning to believe the side they always warned me about was closer to God than they wanted to admit.

We are all God's creatures, the saints and the sinners, the saved and the damned. We were created in his image, we were given life through his vision, and if that is true, then the parts of me I was told should be hidden and ignored were parts God had wanted there all along.

Perhaps His intent wasn't for us to shun those parts, but instead we were to take them for what they were and glorify Him through the differences they created in us.

Because if God is part of everything, then God can be found in the shadow as much as the light.

I wouldn't feel guilty for seeking him in the pitfalls the Church had steered me away from all my life. I would feel justified in the anger that has been slowly simmering inside me about a powerful and wealthy organization that had turned a blind eye to the rural communities they deemed unworthy of their *full* support.

While my congregation scraped by on what crumbs of food they could afford, while they watched their farms taken by banks, their livelihoods destroyed by a changing world, the Cardinals and the Bishops sit in their beautiful mansions, gluttons to the measly tithes these poor farmers still gave every Sunday.

By shedding my resolute obedience to the Church that told me how to speak to my creator, I let go to the whispering voice that had always been in my mind telling me that I am *exactly* as the Lord had intended me to be.

Why hide what has been created in his image? Perhaps by doing so, I'd been dishonoring Him all along.

A supply closet was hidden behind a triangular shaped door in the back of the hall of the rectory. Angled so that it allowed for the deep slope of the roof, the closet must have been empty space at one time, a room some intelligent builder decided to turn into storage. And in that storage I knew there were old frayed ropes once used to hang the star of Bethlehem above the Nativity scene. I didn't give much of a damn about the old star itself, but those ropes could come out to play.

Pulling them from where they lay bunched and useless, I gave them new life, new purpose, and a function in direct opposition to what they'd been used for before.

I didn't feel guilty about it either.

There was no hurry in what I was doing. No rush to the finish line or desperation to seek the highest peak when half the fun was the climb.

Stepping into my bedroom, I was met with a breathtaking sight.

Eve lay still over the mattress, her dark hair fanning over the white sheets, her expression a picture of serene obedience.

"I am yours. In body. In heart. And in soul."

Words spoken in the present that dragged me back to the past.

"I'm yours, Jacob..."

Eve had grounded me in the simple phrase she'd spoken, rendering me as the man who at one time had learned to love rather than the beast who had devoured the chaste and good when I was young.

I hadn't scared her with the violence inside me, just like I never scared Cassandra. Only because Eve had dared look me in the eye, she pulled me back to the threshold, to the point where I could think clearly and beyond the primal urge that existed in all of us.

Some were better at resisting the instinct to possess – most, if I had to be accurate. Few gave in to it, luxuriated in it, *lived* solely because it existed in them at all.

I was one of those rare few.

Fear crept back inside me that I would hurt this delicate treasure by the force of the darkness I carried.

"Stand up," I said, my voice a placid tone, the calm that always preceded the storm.

She did as she was told.

Placing the ropes on the surface of the small desk where I'd once penned my letters to God, I stepped closer to the woman who'd awakened every part of me.

271

Eve craned her next to look up and I reached for the cross pendent between her bare breasts, my thumb rubbing over the large jewel that sat in the center. I wanted to rip the fucking thing from her neck.

Dragging my eyes up to hers, I asked, "Would you die for me?"

I would never do anything to purposely endanger her life, would never scar her or cause permanent damage, but as I'd learned in my past, there were mistakes that happened, passions that ran so deep you became lost to them and forgot your own strength.

"Yes," she answered without hesitation.

Arching an eyebrow, I dragged in a breath. "It can happen. I can go too far. I can strangle the life out of you without even realizing what I'm doing."

Perhaps it was fear that kept me from rushing this moment, fear that the past would sneak up to remind me why I'd run to the Church in the first place.

She didn't respond to what I'd said, just looked up at me with pure adoration in her green eyes.

Releasing the pendent, I ran the tips of my fingers up the center of her chest, along the line of her neck to grip her chin.

Asking a question that was more important to me than fearing the destruction I could cause, I requested the one thing from her that even Cassandra could not give.

"Will you live for me?"

Eve's lips parted in response, a shudder running down her skin that made me want to chase the prickled flesh with my tongue.

"I've always lived for you, Elijah. Since the day I was born."

The sound of my brother's assumed name drove a spike of anger down my spine. At least, she wasn't calling me Jericho. I wasn't sure I could stand hearing my brother's true name fall off her lips with such reverence and love.

My hand released her chin to trail down her body, my palm cupping the weight of her breast in a possessive hold. It was wrong of me to take advantage, but isn't that exactly what she had done while I'd been talking to my congregation?

I understood now that we were both pawns in whatever game it was Jericho was playing, and if this is what he wanted, who was I to deny him?

He would only play harder if I didn't give in.

At least, that's the excuse I told myself.

"On your knees," I ordered, my voice rough with the anticipation locking me in place between its fiery fingers.

Eve had a hesitant smile and slowly lowered herself down.

Within the silence of a room where I had prayed for more nights than I could count that I would learn what it meant to be pious, I let go to the *human* inside me, to the shadows and the light, so that Eve would know the danger that lurked beneath my skin.

"You know what to do," I breathed out.

My fingers curled into fists, my fingernails digging crescent shaped channels into my skin, and where my body trembled with the restraint I continued to hold over the violence inside me, an angel looked up with the steadfast belief that I wasn't the danger she should fear.

Reaching up, she curled her fingers over the waistband of my boxers, pulling them slowly over my hips, her nails dragging over the skin. I didn't bother kicking them off when they dropped down my legs to pool over my feet, couldn't allow myself to move even an inch without fear that I could lose control.

Was this the fear my brother wanted to force through me? Did he somehow know that I'd chosen a celibate life to avoid killing again?

Eve's eyes peeked up at me, her hands lifting to explore the length of my cock, her tongue rubbing over her lip before she leaned forward to take the head into her mouth. At the moment the wet heat of her tongue flicked out to lick across, her eyes closed as she opened wide to take me deeper.

A shudder coursed across my skin, my fingers tightening even more until I lost what little control I had left. I reached to fist both hands into her hair. A startled cry escaped her throat, tears shimmering at the crest of her lashes fanning across her skin because I held her head in place while my hips thrust forward.

This was what I wanted to do to her when she'd been in this exact position beneath the pulpit. This was the violence she lured out of me with the mouth she had wrapped around my cock. And although I wanted to close my eyes and luxuriate in the feel of lips working over the thick shaft, I watched in fascinated wonder as she took every thrust inside her while those tears slipped down her cheeks.

I wasn't being kind. I was giving in to the beast, and I felt a stirring in me for something far darker.

Eve sputtered as the head hit her throat, her teeth dragged over the skin and still, I kept fucking her like I wasn't choking off her airway.

"Fuck..." I growled, knowing that my climax was building and not wanting to come so quickly. When I

274

knew that another thrust would send me over the edge of pure ecstasy, I pushed her off with such force, she fell back against the floor, her glistening eyes opening to stare up at me.

"Get on the bed. On your knees. Face the bedposts."

At the head of the bed were two carved, wooden posts. They were the only ornamental touch within the room, a place I often hung my rosary at night so that I would be watched over in my sleep. The rosary still hung there now, with black, obsidian beads and a silver and gold crucifix.

As Eve climbed onto the bed, her movement shaking the frame beneath, I watched the rosary slap against the wood, eventually dropping from its high perch to fall to the floor. My eyes followed its track, my foot stepping around it as I followed after Eve.

"Grab the tops of the posts with your hands. Stay there until I say otherwise."

She didn't respond, just lifted her hands and wrapped her delicate fingers around the posts. Her body was a work of art. Arms outstretched, the line of her spine indented in, the curves of her body becoming more pronounced as she seated herself over her feet.

Rounding the bed, I stood at the end staring at a goddess. Her skin was pale and unmarked, a canvas upon which I could paint every bit of the possessive violence I felt.

Eve had been a present delivered to my door as a way for my brother to antagonize me, test me, tempt me and torture me. He expected her back after accomplishing whatever goal he had against me.

What he didn't know was that he wouldn't be getting her back.

I was the darker half of the twins. I was the stronger half. I was the half that helped drag him into madness. Tragedy had been a temporary event that forced me into the light. And while I'd lied to myself as I bowed and prayed, my brother had lost his mind.

It wasn't readily apparent whether I would eventually lose mine, but I wanted to think that I had the ability to balance both the shadow and the light.

Like every priest, I would honor God on my knees, but I would honor him as a man with two sides, rather than one who denied the *human* side of him.

Standing in place for what felt like hours, I studied every inch of the woman before me. I admired the form of her body and her perfect obedience. Only when she started to shake from holding her position for so long did I finally walk to the desk and pull the ropes from its surface.

"I can hurt you, Eve. I can lose my mind and steal your ability to breathe."

Her head bowed lower, the trembling of her arms reaching into her shoulders as they, too, grew tired.

"My marks will be all over your skin. I won't care if you cry. There will be no stopping me once I get started."

Her fingers tightened around the posts.

"I'm throwing you a life rope, Eve. A chance at escaping everything I want to - and *will* - do to you." I paused and refused to take a step farther. "You still have the chance to say no."

Silence fell heavy between us, time moving slowly as I waited for her to save herself – to save me.

The voice of a siren sang to me when she finally answered, "I am yours wholly. My body belongs to you."

We'd reached the point of no return. My fingers tightened over the ropes and my cock was granite begging for a release.

In three long strides, I closed the distance to the bed, my knees pressing down hard into the mattress as I knelt behind Eve's shaking body. Careful not to touch any part of her, I tied her right wrist to one post, and her left to the other. It only gave her a tiny bit of relief from the exertion of holding her position. She shivered beneath the heat of me and the promise of seductive sin.

The smell of her hair wafted past my nose. The sound of her ragged breathing was music to my ears. I sat back and admired the blank canvas of her body that I would paint with pleasure and pain before softly tracing my fingertip down her spine.

My breath caught to feel her trembling at my touch, to recognize her struggle in remaining just how I'd instructed her to be.

Trailing lower, my right hand fanned over the curve of her ass, my left coming up to cup the other cheek. Sliding my touch over the curve of her hips, I just barely brushed my palms up the sides of her body to reach around and take her full breasts in a possessive grip. She cried out as my fingers clamped down, bruises most likely forming beneath the skin from how hard I squeezed.

I knew the hold hurt her, but I watched how it also turned her on. Whimpers fell from her full, soft lips, her hips squirming in place, her skin turning a lovely pink in response to the sensual torment.

Without releasing the pressure, I ran my lips down the line of her neck, planting a soft kiss over her spine at the point where it curved down into her back. My cock throbbed between our bodies, but I wouldn't rush this moment, wouldn't give in to the feral beast inside me.

My lips moved against her skin. "Show me how to forgive you, Eve, for all the sinful thoughts you have about my body."

Her hips lifted from her feet, an invitation for my taking, her body shaking as she held the position long enough for me to slip beneath.

Inching forward until my chest pressed against her, I moved my head so that my lips could whisper against her ear. My cock was positioned at her swollen, wet entrance, my hand releasing one breast to trail up her chest and wrap around her neck.

My voice was breathless when I whispered, "And I hope you'll find a way someday to forgive me."

Squeezing my fingers around her throat, I forced her body down over my cock. Her mouth opened on a silent scream.

It was my turn to shake as I held on to my last thread of restraint, but once her muscles tightened around me, once I controlled her small body with mine, there was no holding back the beast any longer. Inside her cunt, I broke my vows, and once the leash had snapped from the clerical collar, I was free to devour every inch of her.

Pushing up to my knees, I forced her hips higher. Head bowed and arms extended above and behind her, Eve cried out when I pulled out to the tip, turned my eyes down to the point where our bodies met and thrust myself back in. My balls slapped against her, my hand around her neck letting go just enough for her to pull in a breath.

I hated to let go of the swell of her breast, but I needed to pump harder, faster, and more violently than I'd ever needed before. She was the perfect mold, a tight, wet space that fit around my cock like it had been designed for only me. Dragging my fingertips down her body, I folded them over the curve of her hip, gripped down, and moved inside her.

The ropes binding her wrists creaked above us, her fingers releasing the posts to grip over them. My hand tightened over her throat as my lips trailed along her shoulder to bite down against the flesh. Not hard enough to break the skin, but hard enough to bruise, I marked her body with my kiss, moving slowly across her shoulder to do it again and again.

It was difficult to control my own thoughts, at least enough to remember the danger in which I'd put her, but I remembered to let her breath every once in a while, enough that she would know she was owned, that she would float within the euphoria of deprived oxygen, but could still draw air into her body with passing out.

To know I held her life in my hands as I fucked her brutally, to know she would bear the bruises and marks, only fueled the fire sparking inside me until I was rendered nothing more than teeth and hands, a tongue and the rage of my cock.

The ropes continued to creak above our head, the mattress screaming below us, as my hips met hers over and over again, my cock driving deeper each time.

I was no longer a cognizant creature that knew what he was doing. I was that primal, feral beast within myself devouring the prey bound before him. Her cries of pain seduced me closer, her moans of pleasure driving my body harder and faster. And when the sounds of flesh meeting flesh had driven me to the point of insanity, I pulled out of her without warning, delighting in her cry of torment for being left balancing on the precipice of her orgasm.

If I was going to break my vows to God himself - if I was going to surrender to the darkness inside me - I wanted to watch the face of a fallen angel, to lock eyes with the woman who existed for no other reason than to torment me.

Moving around, I lifted her hips to straddle over my lap. I tucked my finger beneath her chin, lifted her head to direct her to look at me.

"Keep your eyes open and don't look away from me. If you do for even a second, I'll enjoy punishing you."

Eve's arms were still bound above and behind her, the angle only slightly relieved when I moved her hips down so I could thrust myself inside again. Her lips parted on a moan and her eyes closed in response. I bit her breast in warning.

She cried out at the sharp pain, but relaxed as my tongue licked over it.

Forcing her face back to mine, I reminded her, "That was just a warning, pretty girl. Just a taste of my violence. Open your eyes. Do not hide from me."

Her eyes opened, her body moving over mine in languorous circles, meeting my body for every thrust, begging for more.

Laying my head back against the wall, I watched her full breasts bounce, the cross I wished wasn't there moving between them. Determined to keep her eyes locked to mine, she winced as the ropes tugged at her wrists and bit her lip against the pain I knew they caused her. She'd carry the marks of those ropes for at least a day and I didn't feel an ounce of guilt for it.

Gripping both hands over her hips, I couldn't stand not driving myself harder, the slap of flesh a rhythmic crack of sound between us, my climax building so steadily that I lost every sense of self control.

I took her breast in my mouth, my cock thrusting in and out of her while cries of torment and pleasure erupted from her throat. My hands were everywhere, my teeth were everywhere, and my tongue dragged over the marks I left to taste the salt of her skin.

I knew she was just at that peak of ecstasy when her muscles tightened over my cock, when she molded to me like a second skin, and I listened to the sound of her orgasm as it fell in bursts of sweet, seductive sound from her lips.

Her skin was marked red where I knew my fingers had left the blooming bruises, her eyes closing again as her orgasm roared again, and knowing that I wouldn't last much longer, I grabbed her thighs to force them apart and lock my eyes on my cock pushing into her tight cunt.

My thumbs would mark those thighs just as they marked her back, her arms, her sides, and just as my teeth had marked her perfect breasts.

I lost myself in that moment, in that second when my balls tightened with the force of my release, when I came inside her without regard for pregnancy or the consequences. Pulling out wasn't an option for me once I was gripped within the wet heat, and I shuddered beneath the power of feasting on her greatest sin.

My hips thrust up one last time as I reached behind to wrap my hands over her shoulders and pull her down on top. And as the wave of power washed through me, as it seeped from my skin and my muscles could relax with its absence, I dragged my nails down her back and cupped her ass with my hands.

Staring at her, I noticed the exhaustion in her arms, the way her eyes closed following the force of her climax, the way her body hung forward from the ropes that bound her wrists above my head.

I was a devout man, one falling into the depths of Hell happily staring up into the face of what had been my last temptation.

27

ELIJAH

Religion is the sigh of the oppressed creature, the heart of a heartless world, and the soul of soulless conditions. It is the opium of the people – Karl Marx

"I'll ask that the women and young children leave the room. Their hearts and minds are too fragile to witness the exorcism we must perform tonight."

Staring out at my family, I waited as the women gathered the small bundles of hope that dotted the room, the youth born into our hearts and home to lead the next generation - the next army - when the current soldiers become frail. They walked past me whispering thanks for the ugly task only I could take on and told me they'd pray for me until that task was done.

I didn't need prayers. What I needed was their unwavering faith.

Only the men - the soldiers - from the ages of fifteen up remained standing in place, their focus on the altar where I stood. So loyal, they remained quiet while awaiting their next command.

Steadfast and loyal to the one true God the world had forgotten, they rounded their shoulders back, always fierce and prepared for whatever battle we encountered in our fight against the powers of evil.

I almost laughed at the absurdity of it.

Stepping out from behind the altar, I set my eyes on the two whores hanging from the wooden crosses, my steps soft as I wandered up the center aisle, my soldiers turning to watch me as I passed.

The two whores mumbled from behind their gags, tears erupting from their eyes as their bodies shook with sorrow beneath the metal cuffs that held them in place.

With silence falling over us, only my steps and their sobs could be heard in the room. Each step a beat that counted down the time drawing them closer to their fate.

While one hid behind a garment of black, the other wore white, the difference being that one had blindly accepted her Master, had made her vows to a false prophet, while the other was just beginning her journey.

Stopping several feet from them, I glanced up at their frightened faces, my lips pulling into a sardonic grin to see them trembling before me now.

"I gave you both the chance to deny your Master. I gave you the opportunity to denounce your prophet in favor of the one true God. You refused me then. Is that still your decision?"

Their feet kicked beneath them, trickles of blood dripping along their arms from where the cuffs were cutting into their skin. The older whore had already bled for us, but she'd still refused to bow.

Two of my men climbed up to rip the gags from the women's mouths. The screams started almost instantly.

I let them grieve and wail for a minute or two, my hands folded together behind my back, my expression as serene as a sunlit summer day.

When their voices quieted, I smiled. "Are you done yet? Or did you want to cry some more?"

More screams erupted. I sighed and rolled my shoulders back. I was nothing if not patient.

The room grew quiet once again.

Sliding my gaze to the women in her black habit, the whore for the prophet that leads the ignorant with lies, I stared at her wrinkled skin wondering if her knees were shot from the amount of time she'd spent on them. "Bring her down."

My soldiers rushed to follow the command, unlocking the cuffs and not giving a damn when the woman fell to the ground. She cried on impact, her body lost within the habit she wore, the sickening crunch of a bone being snapped a whisper beneath the pain emanating from her mouth.

I didn't regret the damage, she was useless to me. But still, I was a kind man, a true believer in the Almighty - in the eyes and minds of the family, at least. I would give her the chance to repent her sins and beg my forgiveness. Even if it was just for show.

Squatting down beside her crumpled body, I rested my forearms on my knees and looked down on her in pity.

"You were lied to, Sister. Deceived and lured in by the liar with a silver tongue. You were sold much like Christ was by Judas."

My voice softened just a touch when her clear grey eyes looked at me. "You can't help your sin because you are woman, but hasn't your heart felt hollow since you put on your veil?"

She tried to move, a small cry of pain bursting from her lungs when she discovered her leg was useless.

Leaning forward, I whispered, "I think you broke a bone. It's probably best you stay still."

I was on my feet a second later, my measured steps slowly pacing in front of her.

"I'd like to offer you redemption, Sister. It's only fair. You can't help that you were deceived. The question now is whether you can admit you were led astray."

The crows-feet at the side of her face deepened, the ridges digging angry channels across her temples. With her eyes narrowed in hatred and fear, she watched me as a mouse would a hawk, staring up at the endless circling of the predator taking its time for the kill.

I'm not sure whether she was brave or stupid, but it didn't really matter. Her decision was her fate.

Squatting again, my knees cracked to take the position. I didn't mind lowering myself to stare into the face of the fallen because below me was the only place they could exist.

"Will you take the Salvation being offered?"

Her head shook only slightly, her fear a vitriolic poison within her veins. "I found my salvation twenty-five years ago when I made my vows to God."

The corner of my lips tipped up, my voice a bare whisper. "You only thought those vows were to God."

A resolute spirit shone out from behind the clear grey of her eyes, a spirit I would have admired if not for what she said next.

"You're a sadistic tyrant. I'd call you the Devil himself, but I think even he is too good for you."

I tsked my tongue against the roof of my mouth, shaking my head with the sympathy I felt for the fallen.

"That's too bad. I will grieve for your soul when the time comes."

Pushing up to my full height, I stepped around the broken woman and walked toward the one still hanging. She'd become quiet while I spoke to the other, her attention rapt, her body still trembling where she hanged.

"Bring her down, gently this time." My eyes locked with hers and within them, I saw light shining through, acceptance and the possibility that she could be *saved*.

My men ensured she remained unharmed as they lowered her to the floor, their hands only touching her to balance her on her feet. Through touch they believed they could be tainted, at least until she was purified beneath me.

The brave, young woman held my stare as I approached her. Barely able to stand, she wobbled in place, but didn't scream or cry, beg or plead. Her resilience was inspiring.

Stopping within inches of her, I could feel the pulse of her heated breath on my face. "What is your name again?"

Her full lips parted several times before she could find any strength in her voice. Even then, it was barely loud enough for me to hear it. "Sister Eunice."

I studied her for several seconds before responding, "That's right. I remember now. How are you feeling? Have my family hurt you since you've been brought to see me?"

Holding out her wrists, she showed me the marks left by the cuffs.

My eyes lifted to hers. "Is that all?"

The white veil she wore shifted over her shoulders as she nodded. She was such a pretty little thing.

"How old are you, Eunice?"

"Nineteen."

My lips puckered at the sound of innocent youth. She reminded me so much of Eve. "We've met before, haven't we?"

"Y - You're Father Hayle."

"Don't talk to him, Eunice! You're staring at Satan! Resist him-"

The older hag's warnings cut off when one of my family struck her. Eunice jumped in place in reaction to the violence, her head turning to look upon the fallen, but I reached out to touch her cheek and lead her eyes back to mine. Genuine fear sparkled behind the blue color.

Using a soothing voice, I said, "Don't worry about that, Eunice. You need only concern yourself with me."

She was so sweet, this innocent, frightened little thing. Nodding her head, she kept her gaze trained to mine despite the pained cries echoing through the room.

"There you are," I cooed when her breathing had evened out and the trembling of her shoulders no longer looked like she would snap in two. "That's right. You can calm down, Eunice. You haven't been threatened here. There's still a chance for you."

Her lips parted, her breath growing heavy with worry. The poor girl would give herself a heart attack if she didn't stop careening back and forth between peace and panic.

My voice was deceptively soft, a comforting sound that could lead the terrified into the light. "I'm not Father Hayle, beautiful girl. My name is Elijah. And I've brought you here to make you an offer."

She didn't respond, but her gaze still held mine. There was a thread of boldness in this girl that I had to admire. "Do you remember what I told you outside of the parish a few days ago?"

Nodding her head, she blinked away the tears that had welled in her eyes. "Y- yes."

"Good," I said through a smile. "Because what I said is very important. My hands are free, sweet girl, they're untarnished by lies and greed, a history of needless death and slaughter. I can heal you with those hands if you'll let me. Do you seek salvation, Eunice?"

"Don't listen to h-"

Eunice flinched when the fallen whore was kicked again. A sigh blew over my lips for the interruption, my head craning to the right. "Do me a favor, Richard, and replace that woman's gag. Her outbursts are annoying."

The gag wouldn't mute her cries entirely, but it would prevent her from speaking. That's all I could ask.

Refocusing my attention on Eunice, I reached out to trace the tip of my finger along her jaw. "God has a plan for you. A plan that will raise you higher than you ever imagined you could go. You won't have to hide behind the clothes of the wicked, won't have to deny yourself the truth of what it means to be human. There is freedom in the light, a freedom not corrupted by the threat of shadow. Would you like to know that freedom?"

Her nod was hesitant, but it was a start. She'd need to be purified for her role in my destiny, but there was still time for that.

"Good," I said, "that's real good, Eunice. There's hope for you yet. I tell you what: You look like you've had a hard time and I want to show you there is safety and comfort here for you. I want you to go with one of my family so that he can introduce you to the other ladies. They'll feed you. They'll tend your wounds. And when I'm done here, we'll talk again. Does that sound better than the cross?"

Swallowing hard, she darted her eyes to where the fallen whore sat, her gaze tracking back to me before she nodded again.

I smiled and snapped my fingers in the air for one of my men to step forward. Without releasing her gaze, I commanded, "Show her to the women's dorm. Make sure to tell them to treat Eunice with the same love and compassion they give each other."

"Yes, sir," he answered back, his hand softly touching her shoulder to lead her out of the room. She jumped in response, but eventually turned in the direction he wanted her to go. I waited until she was led into a hall and the large wooden door slammed closed.

The room was blanketed in silence, at least until I turned my attention to the whore huddled on the floor. Only when I looked at her did she start crying and sputtering again.

She was older than most would prefer, but only because she'd been lost to the beast for so damn long. Still, there was a use for her.

Stepping over until I was looming above her, I stared down with pity. "Last chance."

I didn't need to hear what she said behind the gag to know she was rejecting my offer.

"Richard, it seems this one refuses to release the evil inside her."

"What do you want us to do, Elijah?"

A smile stretched my lips. "Use her to train the boys in the room. They haven't had a chance to learn what it feels like to drive the sin from a woman's body."

The young men around me straightened their postures to hear what would be asked of them. Excitement was woven into their expressions, their bodies becoming hard in anticipation.

I retrained my gaze on the woman after looking at each and every youth who would have his turn.

"And when you're done with that, use what's left to train the dogs."

Richard paused, a question wrinkling his brow as he looked between the woman and me. "She won't be able to run, Elijah. Her leg is broken."

Laughter shook my shoulders. "The dogs already know how to run, Richard. I'm not worried about that. It's what they do with the prey they've caught that concerns me."

The family's soft laughter joined mine.

Reaching out, I touched the woman's cheek, my fingers becoming wet from her tears. "Good luck to you, Sister. I sincerely hope we can strip away the evil you carry before you face your maker."

28

JACOB

Now the deeds of the flesh are evident, which are: immorality, impurity, sensuality... Galatians 5:19

Is there a stern line that divides the shadow from the light, the good from the evil, or the righteous from the damned?

I wasn't sure, but it was the repetitive question running through my head in the hour I'd sat on the edge of my bed staring down at a woman who bore my marks.

My head was a chaos of questions, of doubts and puzzles. What do you do when you had to choose between your faith and your heart? On one end, everything I'd just done to this woman was evil, tainted and impure. And on the other, I'd done what I could to help ease the burden she believed she carried.

It's wrong to lie down with a woman who's not your wife, and in my case, it's wrong to lie down at all. I'd made vows that were now broken, promises that were unfulfilled, but I had to wonder how wrong it had been for me to do so.

You can't help how you feel. And you can't help who you are. We are all born with faults, whether they be physical, mental or spiritual. We are all cast out into a world filled with both good and evil, with sadness and happiness, but mostly a world and life that has no directions.

We are born to survive and eventually die, and there's not always a *correct* path to travel.

Religions tell us they know the path, but what I always found funny was how those rules kept changing. Not the fundamentals; it'll always be wrong to murder, steal and hurt other people. But those aren't the only rules. No. Religion is far too complicated for that.

Perhaps the only way to bring the two halves of myself together was through faith rather than religion - faith that, although I was a fallen man, I could still be redeemed without need of hiding who I really am. Disguising it, hiding it behind a vow intended to be a sacrifice for my mistakes of the past, was not only a lie to myself, but a lie to God.

He knew what he created in me, and maybe he also knew that I would learn to control it. Perhaps it was His intent all along to put me on the path I now wander just so I could find Eve.

My darkness is what led me to Cassandra, and it was my fear of that darkness that forced me into the Church. If it hadn't existed at all, I wouldn't be here now to find and save a woman who was a true innocent in the world. That must be what they meant by God's perfect greatness: even the shadows he creates in the world have a purpose.

There was no reason I couldn't explore my shadow with a woman while also leading a congregation to the light. Celibate or not, I could still help the people in need, still fight for resources and funding when the town was suffering from loss. I could still use what's available within the Church to benefit those who need it most.

I could still be good.

With that thought in mind, I traced my finger down a line of marks I'd left down Eve's back. Except for the burn on her shoulder, every imperfection of her skin was the story of me. I hated that brand, an E walled in by the broad lines of a square, a reminder of who had created the perfection that lay before me. If I didn't know how horribly it would pain Eve, I would have cut the damn thing off already.

Her head stirred over her pillow in response to my touch, her eyes moving beneath her closed lids as her hair swept softly over the pillow.

Trailing my finger down farther, I traced the line of her ass, eventually settling my hand between her legs, hungry for another taste, another bite. The tip rested against the opening of her body, her hips moved in response.

Even sleeping, Eve was ready for anything I deigned to offer.

The sun hadn't quite breached the horizon outside and I had another hour or two before I would don the clerical collar. I was hard instantly at the thought.

Leaning over her, I allowed my breath to fan over the skin of one cheek, my finger pressing into her body as my teeth softly locked over the soft skin of her ass. She jumped in response, a tremor running through her core that made me smile.

Was it wrong of me that I didn't want to wake her before taking a taste? That I wanted her to open those pretty eyes and come to consciousness with my cock already inside her pushing her towards a release?

Creeping carefully over the bed to keep the mattress from dipping and rocking too much, I slipped my sweat pants down to my knees, my erection rock hard in front of me. I spread her legs apart and lifted her hips, taking care not to wake her where she lay sleeping on her belly.

I wouldn't mark her, wouldn't squeeze too tight with my fingers or bite down until it bruised. I just wanted to be inside her. I wanted her to wake up knowing I was the one who controlled her sin now, the one who held the power to cleanse it with pain's fire.

There was no doubt in my mind that the sin Eve believed she carried wasn't sin at all, it was just a craving she had for a sensation that drove adrenaline and endorphins through her body.

Pain is an ugly fact of life for most people, but for some, it is the only thing that makes them feel alive.

Eve moaned as I slowly pushed deeper inside, her hips moving in coordination with mine, even though her eyes were still closed. A smile pulled at her lips, and I knew she was with me at that moment, that she'd come to consciousness with the feeling of being connected to me in the most intimate of ways.

I rode that high for only a second before the truth slapped me in the face: She wasn't connected to me, she was connected to the man whose name was a prayer on her lips.

"Elijah," she breathed out, the reverence in her voice forcing my eyes closed. It was the sound of an answered prayer, the utter relief a person felt when they witnessed the divine for the first time. *His* name on *her* lips was the sound of a woman who didn't have to fight any longer simply because her lover - her reason for living - was close by.

His name.
Not mine.
The truth of it shredded me from the inside out.

And, yet, there I was, fucking her, taking every last bit of our combined pleasure and devouring it like I had every right to it.

I wondered if the day would come where she not only realized I wasn't my brother, but would also forgive me for taking advantage when she believed I was someone else.

I was taking what wasn't freely given to *me*, and I didn't give a damn about the consequences.

Slipping my hand down to massage her clit, I woke her fully. Her body pushed back against me wanting more - begging for it. Lifting her just a bit higher, I gave her what she asked for and watched as her fingers curled over the sheets beneath her, as her eyes flickered open and her lips parted on a sensual moan that drove my hips even faster.

Desperation overtook me, the need to know what she was feeling and thinking. Possessing her body would never be enough. I wanted every part of her - body, mind and soul. Anything less would never satisfy the greed I felt for her, would never subdue the sadist in me that wanted nothing more than to corner his prey.

Leaning over her, I wrapped my fingers around her neck, careful not to squeeze down on the bruises already blooming over her skin. Lifting her upper body from the bed, my chest was flat to her back, my mouth pressed teasingly against her ear. Eve's entire body went still, my cock still moving inside her.

No matter what I wanted to do, she would never resist.

"What are you thinking?" I whispered, my tone placid and tranquil to seduce the enthralled.

Soft moans crawled up the back of her throat. I pulled out of her until just the head remained inside, her hips pushing back, sounds of complaint floating sweetly across her lips.

A smile stretched my cheeks. "Not until you tell me, Eve." My voice lowered to a whisper, "Confess."

My hips moved just a bit, pushing in and pulling out. She whined for more. My fingers gripped over her throat just a touch tighter, my teeth bit down on the lobe of her ear. The breath rushed from her lungs.

"I need more," she whispered, "a - always need more. Pain cleanses sin."

My eyes closed in response to words spoken by the voice of an angel.

She was so screwed up in the head - so perfectly shaped and trained. I wasn't blind to that fact. I just didn't respect it. Which made me even more screwed up than her.

Pushing my hips forward, I slowly filled her, my finger exploring her clit. "Like that?"

She shook her head against the pillow. "More."

My brows drew together as my hand moved over her hip, my finger tracing the crack of her ass before stopping over the hole.

"There," she murmured, pure anticipation in her tone.

Breath rushed from my lungs. I vacillated for only a second, weighed the pleasure of the act versus how wrong it would be to take every part of her when she wasn't technically *mine*.

The potential for pleasure won the argument.

Slipping my cock from the wet heat between her legs I trailed up, finding and pressing against her ass. She moaned, the anticipation filtering through her as a full body shiver. Somehow, just that shiver made me impossibly harder than I'd been before.

I pushed the head in and her body went rigid, her fingers curling into the sheets until the bones beneath the skin of her hands were visible lines of tension. Using the slickness between her legs as lubrication, I did my best to prevent pain, but she reached back to grab my hand and pull it away.

My brows pulled together in question, her head turning just enough for her eyes to lock with mine with one clear message behind them: She wanted it to hurt.

In truth, so did I.

My hips thrust forward, pushing me in inch by inch as her mouth opened, her brow wrinkled and her fingers looked like they would shred the sheets trapped between them.

I didn't care how uncomfortable it was for her, not when it felt so fucking good on my end. She was almost too tight - almost.

The cry of pain that flew from her lips was the most seductive of music, the way her body constricted around me only to relax again was the fuel to my fire. Gripping my hands over her hips, my head fell forward until my chin touched my chest, my eyes closing as I thrust my hips burying myself completely.

I learned one of life's truths at that exact moment: Heaven wasn't a place above our heads beyond Earth and space, Heaven was located right here inside Eve's body.

It was becoming obvious that I wouldn't last long. My balls tightened with each stroke inside her. I was pushed closer and closer to climax.

The tip of my finger met her clit, and with two more strokes she came, her body becoming painfully tight, trembling as the sweetest music fell from her lips. My climax followed seconds after.

Waiting until I was soft, I stayed seated inside, my breath heavy and my forehead pressed to her upper back.

Several minutes passed before I could think clearly again.

Finally lifting my head, I spoke on a husky voice. "We both need a bath and you need to eat breakfast."

Pulling free, I playfully slapped her ass to get her moving. My brows shot up to see her hips push back instinctively, begging for more.

Dear God, what kind of devil have you sent me?

I wasn't sure I would survive if I gave her everything she wanted.

The bed shifted as I moved away. Eve grumbling in response to being pulled from the mattress.

Picking her up, I carried her to the shower.

It didn't take long to get us cleaned and fed. By the time I was stepping out of my bedroom and walking the hall toward the sanctuary door, I had a guilt-free smile stretching my lips while I fastened my clerical collar.

29

ELIJAH

To live is to suffer. To survive is to find some meaning in the suffering. - Friedrich Nietzsche

Eunice hadn't removed her veil by the time I walked into the women's dorm. Seated on a bench seat, surrounded by women tending to her wounds and offering her food and water, she wore one of the long navy blue dresses the female family members preferred.

As soon as I stepped foot in the room, Eunice's eyes darted to my face, the tension of fear weighing on her shoulders. Fight or flight was the alarm behind her stare, her instincts telling her to run as quickly as possible while her intellect told her to stay in place - to submit to the predator that was more powerful than her.

It was always the initial focused gaze - the terror and indecision to be found there - that forced my blood to pump harder.

I stopped within feet of her. "Are you ready?"

It was a struggle for her to strip her gaze from mine, but she eventually tore her focus from me to look at the women sitting to her left and right.

As if impeaching them for help, her expression fell when they all moved back, smiles adorning their faces because they knew what I offered this woman was a gift. They all offered the same gift to me when they had an opportunity, but I wasn't interested in those already besotted; I wanted the ones that were harder to pin down.

The last woman to whom it had been offered was still fulfilling her purpose, still demonstrating that she had not only seen God's power, but wanted a part of it for herself.

Without offered help, Eunice turned her eyes back to mine. Her throat worked to swallow the fear she felt. "For?" she asked on a shaky breath.

My smile didn't calm her. "We should take a walk and discuss your new life here amongst the family. I'm sure you'll appreciate what we have to offer once you understand that we are God's people."

Indecision wrinkled her brow. "A walk where?"

Resisting the urge to roll my eyes, to drag her from her seat for questioning me, I rolled my shoulders back instead. Why do people always have to ask so many questions? Why can't they simply trust that God knows what's best?

"Come, Eunice," I said, extending my hand to grab her and help her from her seat. "Enough with questions. It's time to prove your faith."

Her grip of my hand was hesitant at best, a tremor running through her delicate bones as I led her from the dorm into a large hallway. An exterior door stood at the end of the hall, thick metal once painted black, but now a sad grey with scrapes and dings from years of neglect and use. Once opened, the yard spread out before us, a chain link fence in the distance with one lonely tall gate.

Placing my hand on her shoulder, I didn't miss how she jumped in place. The poor girl's nerves were fried, but it didn't matter. When she learned the path God had chosen for her in this life, her nerves would be eased by her devotion.

"Beyond that gate is your salvation," I told her, my voice low and soothing, my hand strong where it still held her. "Are you ready for it?"

The wilting of her shoulders, the subtle downturn to the corners of her lips, the slight trembling of her arms told me she wasn't ready - would never be ready. But that made no difference to me. Every person had a purpose. Every person had a use. And every step they provided me toward what I ultimately wanted made them precious for as long as their purpose had yet to be fulfilled.

Even young Eunice.

The dogs couldn't have had better timing. Their angry growls and harsh barking echoed across the property grounds. But it was the high-pitched, agonized scream that emanated above their voices that caught Eunice's attention.

The older whore didn't last long against their sharp teeth and starved stomachs. Within minutes they could be heard being let loose on the property, approaching where we stood at full speed.

A smile stretched my lips. Leaning toward her, I brushed my lips along her jaw, sliding my warmth ever so slowly along her skin until my mouth met her ear.

"I would run if I were you. I can't be sure, but the dogs still sound hungry."

She pinned me in her wide-eyed stare, the sound of the dogs creeping ever closer while she made her decision. Would she face the woods as the sun set in the distance? Or would she face the bigger threat that approached on angry, fast paws?

Her head spun to look between both threats, and the woods won. It was too bad she didn't know the dogs would never have actually reached us. There were gates that remained closed that would have prevented them from leaving their portion of the yard.

Giving her a few minutes head start, I closed the gate behind me as I stepped into the shadow of the woods, my lips puckering on a soft whistle as I slipped through the trees on a casual stride, knowing well that I'd catch my prey regardless of how fast she could run.

30

JACOB

For the wages of sin is death… Romans 6:23

I spent a few hours in my office after leaving the rectory. Grateful for the quiet morning that led into a quiet afternoon, I spent my time speaking to the Diocese regarding issues affecting my town. As usual, their offer of assistance was paltry at best. Nobody cared about a town that had little to offer in tithes - a town that had been all but forgotten by the larger cities that sat hundreds of miles from its borders.

Praying had never done much good. Although, I wasn't sure I could blame God on that fact. Maybe it wasn't His fault for not listening. Perhaps it was mine for never having been very good at praying loud enough to be heard.

On that thought, I sat the pen I'd flipped through my fingers for over an hour onto the surface of the desk, my heart pained by the people who had next to nothing, but still had the decency to attend God's service dressed in their finest. To the resilient, having barely enough to survive was still a blessing to appreciate without question.

I couldn't help my anger on their behalf. They were members of a Church that could afford to help them all, but chose not to. Even then, and even though they were only scraping by, the people of the town gave what they could to the parish whenever they heard God's calling.

With that thought in mind, I darted a glance to the clock. Confessional hours started in less than three minutes and I had one hour reserved for the dark, foreboding box, and one for the reconciliation room.

Often, I sat alone in both, left to the company of my innermost thoughts, but I would still wait in case a parishioner was in need. Slipping out from behind my desk, I walked from my office to the sanctuary, my eyes widening to find Eve sitting in a front pew, her gaze turned up toward the stained glass windows designed with images of a cross and a dove.

Jewel tones bathed her face from the light pouring in from the windows, the dance of color across her skin almost as beautiful as the marks she wore from me.

Dressed in one of my plain t-shirts and a pair of sweatpants that were practically swallowing her small body, she sat in reverence and deep contemplation. I hated to disturb her, but I feared someone would walk in and find her.

In a larger parish, her presence wouldn't have been questioned, but everybody knew everybody in this town and a strange face was an oddity not easily ignored.

Laying my hand on her shoulder, I spoke softly. "Eve, I need you to return to the rectory."

She opened her eyes, tears shimmering within the soft green. "Will we ever go home, Elijah?"

The question caught me off guard - the name she used still driving a spike of anger and jealousy through the most sensitive parts of me. I should have corrected her, should have taken the time to explain a fact her battered mind would find impossible to comprehend, but I was too afraid of losing what I'd found in a woman who awakened me in ways I hadn't known in over twelve long years.

"We are home," I answered, sliding onto the bench beside her. "This is your new home."

I wasn't sure how I would continue to hide her, but I wasn't thinking clearly when it came to her. Even now, while bathed in the jewel toned light of the sun shining through the large windows, my body responded to this woman in ways unfitting for a priest.

Beyond that, my mind picked up on her submission to my will, on the manner in which she'd been warped and manipulated to be the perfect meal for a man with an appetite such as mine.

Silence fell between us, a heavy blanket stuffed with all the horrors of the past few days, by the question of right versus wrong, and by the uncertainty of my brother's purpose for everything he'd done and still planned to do.

"You're like two different people," she whispered, her sudden words catching me off guard for how observant they were. I would have explored further, pushed her to explain, but the large entrance door at our backs creaked open and stole away the time to question her.

Glancing back, I noticed the long red hair spilling down Annabelle's shoulders, the distraught look on her face as she darted a glance in my direction before making her way to the confessional. Knowing I was not inside, she still opened the door and climbed in, a silent plea to confess whatever evils she believed existed in her head.

"Eve," I whispered, hoping with everything I had that Annabelle hadn't noticed the strange face of the woman sitting next to me. "I need you to go back to the rectory for a few hours."

"Please," I added when she didn't immediately respond.

Rather than speaking, she simply nodded her head and cast me a strange look before pushing up to her feet. I waited until she was down the hall leading to the rectory door before turning my attention to the confessional.

Sucking in a deep breath, I realized there wasn't enough oxygen in the room to ease the panic I felt for what Annabelle would say. But I was a priest, regardless of the choices I'd made in the past few days, and I had a calling to help all of my parishioners no matter how uncomfortable is was for me.

With heavy steps, I walked to the confessional, opened the door and climbed inside the dark box that felt more like a coffin today than it ever had before. Sitting in the seat, I rested my head against the wall at my back and opened the small door that closed off the screen between the two compartments.

As soon as it was opened, I heard her small voice. "Forgive me, Father, for I have sinned. It has been three days since my last confession and I accuse myself of the following sins."

I wanted to skip the formality, wanted to bypass having to listen to whatever it was she had to say, but this was my cross to bear as much as hers. Although I hadn't been the one to use her body and cast her aside, in her mind, I was. I would take the weight if it helped ease the burden from her shoulders.

It was at least a minute that I listened to her breathing. "What do you wish to confess?" I finally asked.

Soft sobs echoed from the other side of the screen, her voice broken as she listed out her transgressions.

"I had sex with a man who was not my husband. It wasn't adultery, but fornication. Even though I know it's wrong, I have the desire to do it again."

My eyes closed as my hands slid over my thighs to grip down. We both knew what she believed she did with me, and I couldn't continue the formality any longer. "Annabelle, what happened can never happen again."

Another choked sob was her response. Waiting for her to speak was my own personal Hell, waiting to hear how her heart had been torn open by an evil within the world that had used her to get to me. She was innocent despite the choice she'd made - despite the lies she'd believed.

"I knew it was wrong, Father Hayle," she whispered just loud enough for me to hear. "I knew that I should have resisted. But I've had these feelings for you for a long time. I ruined you...and myself...and all I want, all I think about, is doing it again."

My teeth clenched so tightly that pain shot across my jaw.

Through her sniffling, she kept talking, kept telling me what she believed I'd done to her. "I need to unload this, from beginning to end and I'm sorry if it hurts you. I'm the devil. I used my femininity to lure you into temptation. I should never have told you how I felt."

That son of a bitch.

Suspicion filtered through me, cold ice meeting scorching flame. Jericho, in what little time he'd had with her, must have convinced her that she was the one to blame.

I knew it would kill me to hear the details, but I wanted to know exactly what he'd done. "Tell me from the beginning, Annabelle. Speak all of it so that God will hear you and offer forgiveness."

Another sob. Another sniffle.

"I can't live with myself. Not knowing what I've done and what I'd do it again if you let me. When I turned and saw you following me on the street, I thought you had something else to say about my confession. But when you touched me instead, when you pulled me behind those bushes so that we wouldn't be seen, I melted inside to feel your mouth on mine. I died inside when you moved my hand to feel how your body reacted to being near me. I knew it was wrong, Father, but that only made me want it more."

She paused, a keening sound crawling up her throat. "Oh, God, I still want it. I touch myself at night thinking about you, remembering what it felt like when you touched me for the first time."

Silence fell, only broken by the sound of her crying. "I'm touching myself now," she finally said.

Opening my eyes, I leaned sideways, my skin hot against the wood partition between us. "You must stop, Annabelle. You can't do that in God's house."

"Why does he make us this way?" she asked, her voice growing in strength. "Why does he design us so that it feels so good? Not initially, not when you first-"

Her voice cut off, only to return much softer. "Not when you first stuck it inside, but when you touched between us, when you showed me what my body could do. I learned from you, and now I touch that secret place just to feel it again and again. To remember. To pretend like it's your hand. Your finger. Your tongue."

A sharp inhalation of air sounded just before she said, "My finger is inside me now, but I wish it was you."

"Annabelle, stop. Right this second," I demanded.

"I'm sorry," she said, pleading with me to understand. "I can't help it. I've been opened, Father Hayle. And now it's all I want. What's wrong with me?"

I couldn't answer what was wrong with her because I was too busy wondering what was wrong with me. I had no interest in this girl. No desire to touch her in the ways she believed I had, but still, my body responded. The predator in me opened its eyes, begging to devour her innocence, hopeful that its will would be stronger than mine.

"What happened," I repeated, "will never happen again. You must resist those thoughts. You must stop defiling God's house by touching yourself now. You must remember what God wants from his children."

"I can't," she cried, "what don't you understand about that? I've tried, Father, but there is something inside me that wants you, will always want you. Please, Father Hayle. Tell me how to resist this."

The taste of bile crawled up my throat, the recognition that in every person there was a particular poison they found hard to resist. For some, it was sex. For others it was stealing. And for the rare few it was the desire to hurt and kill.

I'd often wondered if it wasn't some basic instinct we carried from a time long ago, a part of our nature that couldn't be corralled by religion, morality or the expectations of a controlled society.

310

"You must stop, Annabelle. You must remember that you have a scholarship, a future beyond this-"

"Why did you do this to me?" she screamed.

My heart was tearing into shreds, my hands clenching so hard over my thighs that I knew there would be bruises left behind.

The sobs came harder before I heard her shuffling around, her elbows and knees knocking against the wood.

"Annabelle, please, talk to me."

"I'm done talking," she whispered. "I'm sorry, Father Hayle. I already know I'm damned."

A metallic click drew my attention, but before I could react, before I could push up from my seat, throw my door open to get to hers, a gun blast burst through the sanctuary, the sound of a body slumping down as the weight of the gun hit the floor of the confessional.

31

ELIJAH

In reality, hope is the worst of all evils, because it prolongs man's suffering. – Friedrich Nietzsche

Run, little rabbit, run.

Soft laughter shook my shoulders as I strolled through the woods. The sun had set over an hour ago and the little scared woman I was chasing down was disoriented and tired.

Like the others, she'd chosen the well traveled path rather than wading through the areas of underbrush and bushes that prevented easy passage. Sadly, if she had chosen the road less traveled, she could have escaped my grasp, made it to the edges of the woods that spilled out onto the lonesome roads that would have led her back to town.

I shook my head at the humor of it. Too afraid of what could be crawling in those bushes, my prey always ran the direction I wanted them to go, always fell for the trap I had cleared out and set months before.

In the distance, I could hear the night animals scurrying about, their bellies empty and their mouths drooling in thought of what smaller creature they could overpower for their meal. I knew the feeling, my mouth was watering just the same.

I found Eunice crouching beneath a tree within walking distance of the cabin I kept specially prepared for ceremonies such as this. I liked to think of it as a transfer of power from the weak to the strong, as a transformation that pushed my mission forward as I laid each individual trap.

I was so close to ending this particular game, beginning a new one, that the anticipation was a fevered pulse just beneath the skin.

A twig snapped beneath my shoe and Eunice glanced up, fear and exhaustion battling for superiority behind her eyes.

"Are you done running?"

Her chest heaved with labored breath, her dress dirty where she'd fallen down several times after tripping over a random root or other obstacle. The relief she felt for no longer being alone in the woods was palpable.

"Y-you followed me?"

Squatting down, I grinned. "Did you think I'd leave you alone? I just wanted to see how strong your faith was. Considering how far you ran, I would say it's as strong as ever. Most people give up long before this point."

"Can we go back now?" she asked, a tremor in her words. "I don't like it out here."

I ran the tip of my finger down her jawline. "I have something a little more private in mind. It's closer, too. I know you must be tired."

She nodded her head and I nodded mine with her, smiling to see a spark of wary trust light her gaze. She hadn't eaten in days and now she'd just been run to ground. Her exhausted mind was a beautiful thing.

Offering her a hand, I helped her to her feet as I stood to my full height. We'd barely traveled a few steps before I slipped my arm around her waist to assist her over the rough terrain.

"Can I ask you something, Eunice?"

Her voice was as quiet as a mouse. "Yes."

"What made you decide to become a nun?"

She turned to look at me, almost tripping over a root in the process. I caught her weight easily before she fell.

"I don't know. I think because I wanted my life to have a higher purpose."

"You felt a calling?"

"Yeah. I did."

"And based on the calling you felt, you ended up here?" I paused, letting that thought sink in. "I guess the Lord works in mysterious ways, doesn't he?"

The cabin came in to view, the candles inside flickering through the windows. Richard was always quick when I sent him ahead to prepare the inside. "Here we are. A respite from the dark woods."

"I don't like this place," she insisted. "I just want to go home. Please," she begged, "please let me go home."

My hand locked over her hip, my mouth watering at the fear evident in her voice. "I'm sorry, Eunice. But you have a higher purpose. One I'll enjoy much more than you."

With one quick move, I opened the door to shove her inside, slamming it closed behind me as she ran to the other side of the cabin in an attempt to place distance between us.

Exhaustion overtook her before long.

314

"We can make this easy or difficult, Eunice," my lips pulled into a grin, "and since I prefer difficult to easy, I'm fine with either choice."

I stepped closer, she stepped back. The dance began.

"Stay away from me," she screamed, her eyes darting between the religious ornaments strewn throughout the room and me. It didn't take a genius to figure out what I intended, but still there was surprise in her eyes.

Canting my head to the side, I laughed softly. "Who will stop me? Who is powerful enough to keep you safe now that I have you here?"

Another step. "Will your God help you, Eunice? Will he come down from his mighty perch to rescue a woman bound to him alone?" My laughter grew louder. "You people really need to learn that there is nothing between you and the predators who take advantage of your delusions."

"I thought you were a devout man. I thought - what you said -" Her thoughts were scattering, her tongue unable to squeak out a full sentence as truth dawned on her in all its glorious light.

Eunice's back hit a wall as I moved closer, her body sliding down to its knees as I came within reach.

"Now isn't that a pretty sight? Did you want to wrap those gorgeous lips around my cock before I force it in your body?" A slight shrug of my shoulder. "Again, I'm fine either way."

Tears slipped from her eyes as I squatted down in front of her. I would say I pitied the poor creature, but then I'd just be lying. The fucking whore deserved what she was going to get. They all did.

"You know," I said, conversationally and without concern for what I divulged. Eunice, here, wouldn't have the ability to run and tell. "It amazes me to see how easily you all fall for the fairy tales and pretty lies told by generations. You deny yourselves the pleasures of this world because you believe, you actually *believe*, there is something waiting on the other side."

My hand struck out, locking her jaw in its grip. "Look at me when I'm talking to you."

Her gaze returned to mine.

"Thank you. Don't you know it's rude not to pay attention?"

"Please..."

Rolling my eyes, I released her face. "Please, please, please," I mocked with a dry, remorseless voice. "Stop your begging. It's pathetic."

"Let me explain this in a manner you might understand, *Sister*. You are a whore for the Almighty God, and my dear creature, in this house, I am that God. So you will do as you're told, or so help you, I'll show you my irrefutable power."

"Please," she wailed.

"You're boring me. Let's find another word to use, shall we?"

Her mouth opened and closed, her eyes working quickly to blink away her tears. Reaching out, I caught one on my finger and brought it to my mouth.

Her expression was horrified.

"Tastes sweet," I said on a laugh. "Make me another."

Oh, and how she did. So many tears were pouring and all I could do was wait out the storm, enjoy the terror and anticipate the enjoyment to come.

I tapped my palm against her cheek when it became obvious this woman wouldn't stop her crying. "That was a warning tap," I explained when she finally lifted her red rimmed eyes to mine. "The next one might sting a little."

Eunice froze. She opened her mouth to beg again, but I placed a finger over her lips and shook my head. "I'd be real careful what you say next. If I hear please, or stop, or any of those ridiculous words that waste our time, I'll make sure this hurts. The only thing I want to know is whether this will be difficult or easy. It's one word, Eunice. So pick one."

Slowly, I pulled my hand back, locking her stare with mine as she made up that pretty little scrambled mind of hers.

"Choose," I reminded her.

Her lip quivered. Her eyes blinked away a few more tears. Her body trembled where it kneeled on the floor. And finally - fucking finally - she opened her mouth to say, "Easy."

I sneered, but shrugged the disappointment away. "If you insist."

Pushing up to my feet, I offered my hand because I was nothing if not a gentleman. She was hesitant to take it, but eventually fell in line.

Giving her distance, I stepped back and jut my chin in her direction. "I think you know what to do with that dress."

More tears. More whimpering. But finally, she reached for the buttons that ran the length from her neck to her waist. One by one they slipped open, each one revealing more of the pale skin beneath, the side swells of her breasts and the smooth plane of her abdomen. How this woman had decided to give that

317

body up to God was beyond me. It was much too succulent to hide away beneath the tent of her habit.

Once the buttons were unclasped, she stopped, unsure what to do. I arched a brow in question. "I don't really need to explain what should happen now, do I?"

Those beautiful eyes narrowed in hatred. A low whistle blew from my mouth. "Now, that's an expression after my own heart." A grin stretched my lips. "Why don't you show me some teeth, too?"

Her expression fell.

"I'm waiting." I crooned. "The suspense is killing me."

If she wasn't careful, she'd die of dehydration with the amount of tears still spilling from her eyes. It wasn't *that* bad. I wasn't beating her or tearing into her flesh. I wasn't even screaming at her or anything of the sort. I'd given her a choice, hadn't I?

The dress slipped from her shoulders and I sat silently praising whatever God she wanted to believe existed.

"You, my lovely creature, are divine."

Pale skin stretched across, so pure and white, she resembled a porcelain doll. Her breasts were a decent handful, not too small, not to large. And even for a woman who had sworn herself off of sex, she kept her hair well trimmed, and her legs shaved as smooth as they were long.

"On the platform. Lie on your back and spread those beautiful legs apart."

"I - please -"

Cupping my ear with my hand, I teased, "What was that? I can't be sure, but it sounded like you just used a word I already told you was off limits."

My head angled to the platform where it sat in front of the fire. "I'll make it good, Eunice. I can promise you I have plenty of experience."

"You're a monster!"

"And you're a spoiled little brat who didn't think to check under her bed before tucking in at night, so do what the fuck I told you to do before I stop believing you really want this to be easy."

I had to hand it to her, when she got mad, she showed a level of strength I thought impossible for her.

Eunice didn't just walk to the table, she *marched* to it, her hands clenched at her sides and that perfectly round ass moving in ways that made me sway where I stood. Hopping up onto the platform, she leveled me with one more angry glare before lying back, lifting her feet to the edge of the platform and spreading her legs apart.

Halle-fucking-lujah.

Curious, I strode over and ran the tip of my finger between her legs. My brow arched again, my eyes studying the resolute expression on her face before I asked, "What's with the change, Eunice? Have you decided that you want this after all?"

"My God will see to your destruction. Do your worst, demon!"

A bark of laughter escaped my lips. "Oh, sweetheart, this is only the fun part. The worst comes later."

I dropped down before she could answer, my fingers parting the pink flesh between her legs before my tongue flicked out for a taste. Her legs trembled at the sides of my head, but she didn't kick out or cry, didn't do anything at all until I suckled on that sweet spot. The moan that crawled up her throat was music to my ears.

Dragging my tongue lower, I pushed it inside and kept a slow rhythm until the trembling in her legs became more pronounced. A wet musk blossomed against my lips, her body's reaction surprising considering how little I'd actually done. I knew this wouldn't push her to that edge so easily, and curious whether she was truly chaste or just pretending, I pulled my tongue away to slip a finger inside. My eyes closed to feel how tight she was.

"Oh, my dear girl, you are the real thing, aren't you? Truly a whore for the Almighty."

Standing to my full height I continued exploring that tight hole as I watched her face, studied the expression that flirted across her features as she closed her eyes.

"You may not have fucked a man in your life, but I suspect you let some little boy play with you before. Tell me the truth, Eunice. I'll keep your secrets."

Her hips bucked as my hand pulled away, her breasts swollen and large; the tips tight peaks just begging to be licked and bit, squeezed and nibbled.

Leaning over her, I brushed her breasts with my chest as I barely touched my lips to hers. Speaking against her mouth, I whispered, "Here, baby girl, taste how sweet you are." My mouth took control of hers, my brows rising up my forehead when she bit my tongue in response.

I always liked a woman who played rough.

Pulling away, I unbuckled my pants and ordered, "Get down off the platform, turn the fuck around, and bend over. You just turned me on."

Her expression still stern with rebellion, she did as she was told, her mouth moving to whisper a quiet prayer to a God I knew wouldn't help her.

Once my cock was free, I slipped it between her legs. Sliding the length along the dampened skin as I reached to play with her clit. Another moan escaped her lips, a remarkable sound that told me she was human beneath the veneer of the devout. They all were once they had to face their own bodily functions.

"I know you like it, Eunice. There's nothing wrong with that. Just let go to it, beautiful."

Her prayer grew louder, her rebellion making me lose all doubt that she was the perfect person for the purpose I had in mind for her.

Unable to take the cravings of my own body, I gripped my hands to her hips, positioned my cock at her entrance and said, "Pray harder, Eunice, let's see how long you can form words before I make your lungs cry out."

My cock slid inside her, the tight space a blessing to be had, and after crying out from the first time she'd felt a man's touch inside, she fought to pray again.

I laughed, my hips pausing as I absorbed the pleasure of wet heat, the slickness of two bodies combined in the most exquisite of sins. Fornication was the cherry placed atop the sundae created by the Devil himself.

My voice gritty with lust, I laughed and said, "Pray louder, Sister. Because I can promise you, your God isn't listening."

My hips pulled back and thrust in again, my head falling back as her voice broke over the words she spoke to her Lord.

I was talking to him myself as I thanked the Almighty for the treasure he'd bestowed upon me.

32

JACOB

In your anger do not sin. Do not let the sun go down while you are still angry, and do not give the devil a foothold.
Ephesians 4:26-27

Ten hours passed after Annabelle killed herself. Ten hours of the police stalking through the sanctuary taking their pictures, drawing their sketches and clearing the scene once the medical examiner had declared the young girl dead. It didn't take a medical examiner to make that official declaration. The evidence was enough with her brains scattered within the confessional and her blood a large puddle over the sanctuary floor.

They took the gun from the ground where it had fallen, took Annabelle's body away once it had been photographed to their liking, took everything that allowed them to declare that Annabelle had to have been mentally ill.

I knew she wasn't, knew the truth of what had led her to the moment of no return, but I lied to them anyway and claimed that she hadn't confessed a single word before lifting the gun to her head and pulling the trigger.

The police thanked me for my cooperation and left me standing in the sanctuary with nothing more to say.

Leaning against a pew, I stood facing the front doors now closed and locked until a cleaning crew could deal with the confessional. My heart could have stopped beating and it wouldn't have hurt as much as it did now. That poor girl had committed the unforgivable sin of taking her own life, and I began to doubt a faith that would hold her weakness against her.

Ripping the clerical collar from my neck, I held it in my hands staring down at a white strip of cloth that felt like a lie.

I was no better a man today than before making my vows - no stronger, no holier, and no smarter than I'd always been. The only truth about me that I could easily point to was that I was more of a sinner now that I was a priest than I had been as secular man.

I lied.
I fucked.
And I lied some more.
And until now, until watching a girl pushed to a decision that destroyed her, I hadn't felt guilty for any of it.

"Fuck..." I murmured beneath my breath. Staying in place with my face pressed into my hands, I was as lost today as I'd ever been, maybe even more so.

"Is it safe to come out now?"

Ripping my palms from my face, I turned to find Eve standing at the end of the hall leading into the sanctuary. She darted a gaze at the front doors and said, "I saw everybody leave."

Guilt flooded me again to look at her. Instead of immediately calling the cops after Annabelle's suicide, I ran to hide the evidence of my other crimes. I ran to ensure that my name couldn't be dragged in to the investigation regarding an innocent girl's demise.

It was then that I remembered the pictures.

Bolting from the sanctuary, I left Eve in the distance as I ran the halls toward my office. I didn't remember seeing a police officer walk this way, but I couldn't be certain. My door slammed against the wall as I threw it open, my hands shaking by the time I pulled open the drawer to find the photos still in place inside their white envelope. Relief swept over me as I fell into my chair, my head angling back as my eyes closed.

I needed to burn these damn photos before anybody found them. They were polaroids so I doubted there were duplicates, but that didn't mean Elijah hadn't taken more that he'd kept on him.

The stress I felt was eating me alive. And despite how wrong I knew it was, I pushed up from my chair in search of an outlet.

When Eve came into view, still standing at the end of the hall leading to the rectory, I crumpled the envelope and photos in my grip and marched in her direction.

"Elijah?" she asked, her eyes wide with concern.

I was on her before she knew what was coming. My fingers fisted in her hair, my lips rubbing along the line of her jaw, and before she could cry out from the pain of my touch, I growled, "I need you in my room, on my bed, without a stitch of clothing on."

33

ELIJAH

Fear is pain arising from the anticipation of evil - Aristotle

Buckling my pants, I wore a broad smile as I stepped out of the cabin. Eunice was still strapped down to the platform, tired and sated after I'd had my fun. She wouldn't admit it, but the sounds rolling off her lips told me just how much she'd enjoyed it. Several times during our trysts, the white veil she wore had slipped from her head. I forced her to set it back in place because I found that I liked it.

As soon as I stepped foot outside, Richard moved into the light from behind a tree. Soft laughter shook my shoulders. "Anxious for a piece of this one after letting the boys have a go at the older one?"

His eyes flicked to the cabin before returning to me. "I came to tell you about what just happened at the church."

My attention sharpened. "Don't tell me my brother killed Eve already. He always did play a touch too hard."

"He didn't kill Eve."

Interest arched my brow. "What happened?"

"The girl you fucked, the young virgin we have pictures of, she killed herself in the confessional."

My brows rose higher. "Tell me you're kidding."

"No, sir. She shot herself in the head right there in the box. I rushed out here to find you after one of the family came back from keeping an eye out. She said the cops were all over the parish, but they left within hours."

He paused, his eyes averted to the ground as his boot kicked at a twig. Lifting his gaze to mine, he asked, "Will it be a problem?"

I ran my hand through my hair before tilting my face toward the sky. A spattering of stars twinkled overhead, the dust that scattered out from the moon where it hung full. "No, it won't. In fact, it may help us out more than we realize." Straightening my neck, I smiled. "God is a gracious being."

"That he is," Richard laughed. He was the only man who knew my plan for what it was. And he wasn't like the rest of the family. A non-believer like me, he'd been instrumental in accumulating and acclimating the family to my cause. The family's remarkable faith in the Almighty was one of the main reasons they were so easily manipulated.

The family were a rowdy bunch, full of the spirit, but tired of the way the world was headed. They truly believed that the sinners had brought Hell upon us and that through my leadership they'd take back what they believed should have been theirs all along. They also didn't believe love would be the salvation that rode them all to Heaven's gates - they believed that could only be achieved through war.

None of it mattered to me much. I had one purpose, one single solitary task, and I wouldn't stop until that task had been completed.

"Tell you what, Richard. Eunice will be bored in the cabin all alone. Feel free to ease her suffering any way you like. Just do me a favor and ensure she stays alive. We'll need her to complete her purpose soon."

He cast a questioning glance. "But I thought -"

"I know what you thought. But don't you think it will be easier on us if she's able to walk? It will save us the heavy load."

Nodding, he strolled toward the cabin, stopping before he reached the door. "Was she pure like she claimed?"

"She was," I answered, "Which made it all the more sweet. It's hard to find a true virgin these days. You know how women are."

Laughter shook his broad shoulders. "Sluts, all of them."

"All but the family," I replied and winked.

I took a step to head back to the main building, but paused long enough to shout over my shoulder. "Hey, Richard, be sure not to tell her what's coming. It's more fun when you catch the demons off guard."

Richard laughed again and entered the cabin. Even from the distance I had walked by the time he took his piece, I could still hear the bitch screaming.

34

EVE

What comes out of a person defiles them. For it is from within, out of a person's heart, that evil thoughts come. Mark 7:20-21

Light always fades in part when the rush of his lightning touches me. The pain comforts and cleanses. The pleasure fills me until all I am is what he makes of me.

While apart, I'd struggled with the thought that I'd missed something in the past few days that I should have noticed. But then he returned, his body hard, his words demanding, his hands and tongue driving me to the sin I love to hate.

Tied to a bedpost, my arms were locked above my head, my body bent forward, my knees firm against the floor by his bed. My will to deny him was shredded by the promise of his breath across my skin, his words whispering the truth of my temptation, his hands driving out the pulsing need that was the chaos that muddled my thoughts every time he drew near.

My addiction to him is the sweetest of flavors.

Perhaps it was confusion that made me brazen, or sorrow that made me forget, but I'd questioned him when he forced me to his bedroom, I'd had a moment of weakness when I'd attempted to refuse his demands.

Demons are sneaky creatures. They crawl inside you when you're not paying attention and plant evil inside your head. They flay you open and rip out your heart, refilling the empty spaces with questions and doubt, needless panic and nagging whispers.

Even as his hands gripped my hips lifting me so he could drive out the wickedness inside me, I fought a battle against the endless thoughts that I'd been deceived by a man who promised to guide me.

My shoulders burned where they were pulled taut by my bindings, the ache a soft caress of fire down the sides of my body. His tongue was ice against the flame, his breath the steam that erupted when I'd driven him to the point of intoxication.

Filled by him, I moaned to relieve the pressure of his intrusion, the familiar spiral of lust building inside me until I knew that I'd burst all over again. He was always sensual and taunting, cruel and alluring, a man of two faces who plays with me like a forgotten toy rediscovered.

My body moved with his thrusts. My muscles clenched around him until all I knew was him. I bore the marks and bruises that spoke his name only, and I would wear them in this life and the life beyond. One day, I knew he'd destroy me, and I'd happily let go to the tempest storm - to the salvation that only he could deliver.

No matter how badly he hurt me, I would continue to beg for more.

"What have you done to me, Eve? What is it about you that makes it impossible for me to stop?"

His whispered words against my ear seduced me, the smell of his skin against mine a tantalizing perfume that drove me to the brink of insanity. I was a glutton, a junkie, a whore... I was a woman who'd become lost to the sting of his hand, the sharp bite of his teeth, and the sensual burn from the way he filled me.

Again. And again. And again.

I still *needed* more.

Pleasure exploded inside me. A momentary rush of relief that left me floating with the weightlessness of euphoria. Stars burst behind my eyes, God's promise shining down on me with the serenity of being hollow, with the ceaseless hope that sin would not rush back in to fill the empty spaces.

Almost as soon as he pulled away, I wanted him more, and I knew I'd lost my battle to the demons that plagued me, at least until he filled me again.

35

JACOB

The spirit clearly says that in later times some will abandon the faith and follow deceiving spirits and things taught by demons. Timothy 4:1

Three days had passed since Annabelle died. The confessional had been removed from the parish, a new dark box replacing it that was donated from a larger city. I'd stared at the striations in the cherry stained wood for over twenty minutes, my head leaned back against the wall, my hands folded in my lap while I waited for any person to feel the need to confess. I wished I could take pleasure in the momentary solitude, but more and more that cramped space felt like a coffin, the clerical collar I wore a noose that threatened to choke me with my own lies.

During the day, I still wore the smile of the parish priest, I still wandered the sanctuary waiting for the moment a parishioner needed me. I hadn't prepared the homily for Sunday Mass, and I hadn't been able to see beyond the darkness that continued to fill me.

Even as I waited, Eve was fresh on my mind. I'd left her bound to my bed, her body exposed, her mouth gagged and her legs spread. My last demand was that she remain in place, waiting until I found the time to play with her again.

The man I was before she walked into my life was gone, replaced with a shadow of who I wished I could have been. There was no hope inside me, no guilt, no emotion, no sorrow. There was only the driving need to take, to taunt, to find joy in the pain I delivered.

In that, Jericho had won. With very little effort, he'd stripped me of the humanity I'd embraced and believed could be whole again. He'd stripped away the cloak I once wore to reveal the darkness that had always been a whisper beneath the surface of my lies.

Left to my imagination inside a box that let in very little light, I thought of how Eve was displayed over my bed, my cock growing hard with anticipation, my hand working to free the button of my pants because there was no shame left anymore to warn me that my actions were wrong.

I had half a mind to drag Eve into the box, to bounce her over my lap rather than wrap my palm over the turgid flesh of a cock that only wanted to be sucked and fucked, licked and stroked, tasted while it worked to torment all the good little girls.

I was a monster, and as my hand stroked from the base to tip, as my fingers squeezed and my mouth opened on a pleasured moan, I allowed my eyes to close and witness the truth of what I'd become.

So close to the moment that my balls would tighten and my climax would cover my hand, I grit my teeth and stroked harder only to hear the door open on the other half of the confessional where I sat. It wasn't enough to know someone sat on the other side of the thin divider, not until a low voice rang through with accusation in its tone.

"I've come to talk to you, Father. Stop being a coward and open the damn screen."

My hand stopped, my climax balancing on that edge, but not providing the relief I sought.

"Mr. Prete," I answered, the hint of sex in my voice.

"Open the screen, Father. We need to talk."

The thought crossed my mind to be honest and tell him I was jacking off. To ask him to take a hike so I could finish myself off. *Sorry, Sir. But I can't help your daughter. I'm too much of a monster to save any souls.*

Shoving my cock back in my pants, I reached up to slam the small door open. "How can I help you?"

"Tell me what my daughter said to you before she died."

I turned to trace the shadow of his profile with my eyes. "She said she was damned."

Technically I shouldn't have said that much. I'd refused to tell the police because I was bound by the seal of confession.

"I know she was fucking someone, Father. I found her diary, but she didn't list a damn name. I need a name."

"A name won't bring her back," I offered, my tone without any hint of comfort or emotion.

Something slammed into the wood divider between us. I assumed it was his fist. "Tell me what my daughter said."

Annoyance filtered through me, sharp and scathing, it was a fire fueling the monster, the smoke choking out the man I'd been before Jericho returned to my life. Like a film I couldn't wash away, it festered and split me open, reaching in to infect every organ, every cell, every tendon until I was consumed within its rancid mouth. What it spit out was a toxin filled with turmoil and pain.

"Are you sure you want to know?" Although my words had been a question, the tone of my voice was edged with warning. I'd lost control, lost all sense of morality, lost everything with each passing day. The truth that I was helpless to save another, that, by design, I was a man who lived to deliver pain, left me open and exposed to the temptation of surrendering myself to the ministrations of my evil.

Whereas Eve was a pure soul clothed in the shell of her darkness, I was the wolf in sheep's clothing, the threat you didn't see until it was too late.

"I'm sure. Just tell me before I rip you out of there and force the words out of you."

Striking flint against stone, his demand had been the spark that ignited the bastard inside of me.

Clearing my throat, I ripped the clerical collar from my throat, dropping it to the floor while I told him what he insisted to know about his precious daughter.

"She was fucking someone, Mr. Prete. Annabelle told me that she enjoyed the feeling of a man's tongue on her cunt. That she wanted a cock shoved so far inside her that she could feel every inch of it pulsing with the need to cum. She wanted whoever it was to leave bite marks on her breasts, wanted his fingers driving her to orgasm, would have sucked off Satan himself as long as she had the opportunity to get off. Your daughter was a whore, Mr. Prete. She fingered herself while giving her confession, her small breathy voice broken up with how good it felt to touch herself. And then after she came, screaming with pleasure as she bounced over her hand, she took out a gun - one I assume she pulled from your unlocked collection - and blew out her brains with her fingers in her body and her come dripping down her leg.

"If you want a name, I can't give you one, but I'll leave you with the mental picture you just told me I was too much of a coward to give. I hope it's enough to lighten the weight from your shoulders. Maybe it's even enough to get you off tonight while you're riding your wife with thoughts of Annabelle in your head."

"You son of a bitch!" he bellowed through the thin wood. I could hear the door to his side slam open, watched the door to my side rattle as his fist banged against it time and time again. Red swam in my vision, a color I hadn't seen in many years, but demanded the violence be released against the man on the other side.

"Get out here and say that to my face, you piece of shit! How fucking dare you say those things about my daughter?"

Laughter shook my shoulders, the sound filtering out so that I knew he could hear it over the volume of his voice. "You asked. I answered. Now get the fuck out of my parish before I throw you out."

He sobbed on the other side of the door, his angry fists no longer a brutal force against the wood. A better man would have offered comforting words, but as I'd learned, as had been illustrated for me so fucking clearly, I wasn't a better man.

Tired of the charade, I opened the door and walked past the sobbing father now balled over himself on the sanctuary floor. I was done with this job, done with the parish, done with everything except for the woman tied to my bed, the one who waited patiently for days as I remembered who I was, remembered the darkness inside me that perfectly complemented her light, remembered the monster beneath the surface who could deliver the pain she'd been taught would be her salvation.

36

ELIJAH

*If we are not our brother's keeper, at least let us not be his
executioner*
– Marlon Brando

**It was time to set the carefully designed plans
into motion.** My spies were watching the parish night
and day, looking for the signs that it was time to turn
that small rural parish into a home for the family. No
we couldn't live there, but we could play. They would
construct their army for their God and I would use
every weapon I had at my disposal to fan the flames of
chaos.

My purpose was a higher calling, a message
written in blood, a truth revealed that the ghost of some
long dead Christ wasn't sitting above waiting for the
day he'd retake the world.

He was dead just like any other person who lived
and breathed on this planet. He was a memory that had
torn the world apart with the promise of something
better than the Hell we'd been born into, one by one.

My message wasn't one that could be ignored. It
was a lesson, a calling, a hand that ripped the veil of

lies from the faces of the supposedly *just* and revealed them all for who they really are.

Jacob had continuously asked me why when he confronted me several days before, and the answer I'd refused to give him was *why not?*

Did there really need to be a reason for the accumulation of power? Was there ever really a good explanation for the chaos that devoured the civilized?

Why couldn't people understand that sometimes *evil* occurs within the confines of a crowded world just because a sadist like me grew bored?

Strolling into the belly of the large room that sat front and center within the old building I called home, I caught sight of the team I'd assembled for the task.

Richard stood at the ready, his broad shoulders pulled back and his thick fingers wrapped around Eunice's thin bicep. Poor girl looked like she'd be ridden hard and put away wet, but that was to be expected. Richard was never gentle with his toys.

"Hello, Eunice," I cooed, my fingertip running along her jaw before I pressed my lips to her ear and whispered, "Would you like to go home now?"

Those beautiful eyes rounded with surprise, a slight tremor of her body belying the relief she wasn't sure she could trust. "Home?" she breathed out. "You're taking me home?"

A smile stretched my lips. "Of course. Unless, that is, you'd rather stay here? I've been told the accommodations were to your liking after a while."

Her eyes narrowed with hatred.

Laughter bubbled from my lungs. "Unfortunately, we won't be using a vehicle, so I hope you're up for a lengthy walk."

The three men escorting us on the journey laughed. They were familiar with the routes we took through the woods that cut through our town and to the parish. Over the past few months, we'd been overjoyed to find that large stretch of forest led us right to my brother's door and we've used the cover of trees to keep a watch on the parish.

Several of the family were able to sneak into the sanctuary on occasion to listen to Sunday Mass, to hear the rumors mixed in conversation by a town that was dying a slow death in the rural Appalachians due to changes in industry and the lack of concern for their lives by the bigger cities that had all but forgotten they existed at all.

Within three hours of walking, we were approaching the town. Poor Eunice looked like she would collapse from the exercise. Her body was broken down from lack of food combined with the rigorous demands of Richard's sensual tastes. It was a pity I'd only experienced her once, but I'd had more important matters to attend to over the past few days.

From what I'd seen during the several trips I'd made to the parish, Jacob had succumbed to what I knew existed inside him. He still played the part of a rural priest dedicated to his parish, but his efforts were feable at best.

Nobody came to him for comfort, and even the nuns left at the small convent down the street from the parish avoided it as much as possible. It would take time to rebuild the reputation he was slowly destroying, but that wasn't my concern.

Through windows, I'd caught sight of my greatest creation. Born into a life of beauty and temptation, Eve hadn't lost the hunger for pain I'd instilled in her. She

340

hadn't awakened to the truth that the man who ravaged her body wasn't the *husband* she believed she had. I'd be a liar to claim that the marks across her skin hadn't upset me.

Despite how I'd used her, despite how I'd planned to give her up for only a short time, I still craved the pure masochist inside her that I'd never found in another woman. Once she was mine again, I intended to delve into the abyss, promised myself that the next set of bruises would come from me.

Over a hill and through a thick stand of trees, the parish came into sight. Clouds obscured the brilliant sunlight that should have bathed the large fields surrounding the building. Lightning cracked in the distance and the responding thunder rolled above our heads like an inbound train.

Reaching the perimeter of the woods, I turned to Richard. His hand was still wrapped around Eunice's arm, but his eyes were tracking down her body like a hawk eyeing a scurrying rat. I'd have to find a new toy to keep him occupied once Eunice was gone.

"I'll go ahead and check in on the priest and Eve. I'd say it's about time to take back our wayward family member. Wouldn't you?"

Richard laughed, his eyes still locked to where Eunice's habit gave only a hint of the curves below. I knew he wanted to taste her treasure one last time, but he had a role to play in front of the other two men. The devout wouldn't fuck a woman who wasn't his wife, and Richard's wife was back at the compound anxiously awaiting his return.

"We'll stay here and out of view."

Staying within shadow, I skirted the edge of the forest where it rounded the fields. Several large oaks stood at the back of the parish near the rectory, providing ample cover for me to stay out of sight. Dressed in all black - clothes I'd stolen from Jacob's bedroom not too long ago - I dusted off the dirt from our walk and made my way to the buildings.

Not a soul was out and about. Not a single person who could confirm that Jacob had a twin brother. Creeping to the window, I angled my body enough to peek inside while staying out of view. My heart raced at the familiar sight.

Eve's body was in a particularly beautiful position over the bed, Jacob rocking his hips behind her. *Rocking* may have been a poor choice in words - what he was doing was much more violent, much more crazed as the entire bed shook with his thrusts.

Eve's arms were behind her, pushed forward towards her head and held in place by Jacob's right hand. It forced her head to tuck beneath her, her back to arch up and her hips to rise to the perfect height for Jacob's body. In that position, she would have been able to watch as he violated her like a man gone mad. The pain in her shoulders had to be unbearable, but I knew my precious girl was begging for it. She *always* begged.

My cock twitched at the thought of it.

Jacob's legs were between hers, spreading her out until he had full access to both her ass and cunt. His free hand was possessive over one of her tits, his mouth pressed to her back where it arched, most likely creating more of those blooming bruises and marks. Once he'd learned of the beast inside him, he'd always loved to mark what was his.

I hoped for a distraction, something that would pull him from my girl just long enough.

Getting comfortable, I waited and watched the show inside his bedroom. After a while, Jacob finished them both off. He dragged her to the bathroom for a shower, her expression sated and exhausted. Carrying her back to the bed, he tied her wrists to the top of the bedpost, forcing her to remain on her knees facing the wall.

Jacob dressed quickly, donning the costume of a devout priest. He left the room after eyeing Eve.

Stalking around the side, I peered toward the front of the parish, knowing full well Jacob had confessional hours today. Fortunately for me, a parishioner walked in.

Elderly and obviously frail, the woman used a cane to get around, her shoulders were withered forward, her hair a silver knot atop her head, and she carried a large leather-bound Bible beneath one arm. I only needed ten minutes to accomplish what had to be done, and I assumed that little woman might talk for much longer.

I gave her enough time to walk the distance to the confessional and start into whatever it was she needed forgiven before I rounded the back of the rectory and entered through an old, utility door.

Winding my way through the hall without worry of being caught, I turned the corner into Jacob's bedroom and my breath caught at the view.

Freshly scrubbed, Eve's skin glowed a faint pink over the alabaster. Dotted with marks, fresh and old, she breathed softly while staying in place, her cheek pressed to the post and her eyes closed. Exhaustion had wrapped its arms around her and forced her to sleep, her arms hanging limp above her head.

Crossing the room, I sat on the bed beside her, the mattress dipping with my weight.

"Jacob," she breathed out. She hadn't been asleep after all.

"Are we back to that again?" I asked.

Her breath caught, seconds ticking by before she finally whispered, "You told me to call you that."

My fingertips traced up her spine, my eyes watching her nipples shrink into tight buds. "Call me whatever you like for now."

I'd eventually correct Eve when I had her back, but for now, Jacob would do just fine. He didn't need to know I'd been back here, didn't need to know I was watching at all.

Fingers brushing the sides of her body I wrapped both palms possessively over the globes of her breasts. She moaned, so ready even after what my twin had already done to her this morning.

"Are you enjoying my attention? Enjoying the ways I've blessed your body with my own?"

Lips parted, she yanked on her bindings, her muscles pulling taut. I knew if I slipped my fingers between her legs, I'd find she was wet. Truly, she was a woman born for sex, for sin, for all the dark cravings that many people would fear if they had them. You have to live in shadow to understand it, had to be born to exist in the waning light to appreciate the beauty of nightmares and pain.

Although Eve believed she was a child of the light, she was something far darker, a creature attuned to the mystery of surrender, to the euphoria of a wicked kiss. She was prey to the fallen, a lover for the cruel, a queen within the ever crumbling kingdom that whispers of sorrow and pain.

She was everything I needed her to be. In her struggle between the dark and the light, Eve was my greatest creation.

My mouth was a teasing inch away from her ear, my hands a tantalizing promise of the agony I knew she craved. "What do you want from me right now?"

"Your touch."

Soft laughter shook my shoulders. "Will what I've given you ever be enough?"

Her head shook, her body trembling when my thumbs brushed the sensitive peaks of her breasts. "Never."

Heavy breath pushed her against my hands, the weight of her tits soft against my palms. Her mouth opened to relieve some of the anticipation building inside her. "I need more," she breathed out. "Please."

My eyes closed at the desperation in her tone.

Leaning over I pressed my mouth to her ear, my voice a soft whisper as my hand released her breast to trail down her abdomen and between her legs. " I could fuck you."

A hiss of air blew from her lips.

"I could hurt you in ways you've never imagined. I could steal the breath from your lungs and replace it with my own. I could make you bleed before I'm done."

"Please." It was a reverent prayer.

The cross I'd given her dangled between her breasts, the stone still in place above the secret compartment. "I need you to do something for me, my love. One last task before I can take you home to the family."

A slow rhythm, I pumped my fingers between her legs. "Will you do anything for me? Anything at all?"

A tear spilled down her cheek. "Anything."

"Open your eyes. I need to show you something."

Her lids peeled open to reveal the green beneath, the color shimmering with unshed tears. I held the cross up to gain her attention. "Did you know this has a secret?"

A small shake of her head.

Rotating the cross so she could see the small tab that would open the stone, I pulled it up to reveal the contents inside.

Her eyes stared transfixed. "What is it?"

"It's an herb," I explained, "one that will cleanse you thoroughly. I need you to take it, Eve, need you to swallow it down the next time we make love. But, I can't know you're doing it. I don't want to know because what it will do to your body will be a blessing for me. I'll see God inside you when it takes effect. I'll see the light that has always been shining behind your lovely eyes. It's a treat to be shared between you and me, but I need you to stay quiet and make it a surprise."

Pausing to give her time to soak in my instructions, I asked, "Can you do that?"

I sucked the lobe of her ear into my mouth, nibbled on the soft flesh as my hand continued tormenting her slick hole. Her muscles rippled and tensed and I knew she was so close.

"Yes," she answered. A moan slipped out, her eyes closing again. She once told me starlight burst behind the lids when her sin was driven out - that it was the most beautiful sight she'd ever seen.

"That's a good girl."

My hand pulled away from her body and she cried out in complaint. Shushing her, I flicked my tongue along the skin I'd just bitten.

"I'll leave you without the release this one time, just to make the next time I take you that much sweeter. Wait for me, Eve. I'll return to you soon."

37

JACOB

The soul that has conceived one wickedness can nurse no good thereafter
- Sophocles

If I stayed in the box much longer, my eyes were going to roll out of my head. Ms. McCormick could talk like no other person I'd known. She confessed every little violation she believed had somehow offended God: coveting her neighbor's flower garden, fantasizing about younger men, lying to a friend that she was out of sugar, while in truth, she hoarded it until her next Social Security check came in.

I wasn't sure why I even bothered.

"What should I do for penance, Father? I know I've been a sinner this past month."

Pinching the bridge of my nose, I clenched my eyes and refrained from telling her that her life was boring as fuck.

"Uh, three Hail Marys for the garden. Two for the young men. But I'm not sure God can forgive you for the sugar."

"What?" Her voice was grief stricken.

Another week and I could leave this place behind. I'd contacted an old friend - a guy I knew in college who had fetishes like me. He told me I was welcome to stay with him for a while, at least until I could get back on my feet.

Knowing I would take Eve and flee this place as soon as I settled out the last of my financial concerns was the only thing keeping me from losing my mind entirely.

"Yeah, I'm sorry. The garden isn't much of an issue because you didn't act on it, and the fantasies were also only in your mind. But the sugar? You actually turned down a friend in need. That's taking matters a step further. I'm sure God won't take that kindly."

She drew in a harsh breath and I laughed softly. Just because I was stuck in this hell for a few more days didn't mean I couldn't have fun.

"You might lose your precious Mittens," I said. "I'd keep an eye on her for the next few days just to ensure God doesn't take her in sacrifice."

"What? I've never heard of something like that. What can I do? I need to make amends."

"Yeah," I answered matter of factly, "it's a new rule they just figured out. Sin is tricky like that. I suggest you find another sacrifice before your kitty gets struck down. Maybe give up leadership of your knitting circle, or give Mrs. Banks the recipe to your prize-winning apple pie."

"Humph," she grumbled. "I'd rather give up Mittens than the pie."

"Well," I said, holding in my laughter. "That's why they call it a sacrifice."

"I'm not sure I can do that. Excuse my language, but Allison Banks is a bitch. She doesn't deserve the recipe."

"The pie recipe is your only hope, Ms. McCormick."

"I can't," she cried.

"Well, then you're going to hell," I answered, fighting to hold in the laughter. "I don't know what to tell you. Give up the pie recipe or face eternal damnation. It's your choice."

"Fine, Father. If you say so."

I grinned. "Go in peace."

Her door opened and shut, her steps slow and labored as she meandered her way out of the sanctuary. Within the silence I could hear the thud of her cane against the floor followed by the shuffle of her feet.

Thud. Shuffle. Shuffle. Thud.

I breathed out in relief when it was quiet again.

Stepping out of the confessional, I strolled to the front of the parish and peeked outside. No other parishioners were in need of God's pardon, so I made my way to the rectory. Eve, as usual, was right where I'd left her.

"Do you need to go to the bathroom again?"

She jumped at the sound of my voice.

"Yes," she finally answered, exhaustion implicit in her tone.

"You need sleep," I suggested as I pulled the ties that bound her hands over the post.

"No, please." Her eyes dragged up to mine. "I need you to finish me off."

Gripping her chin, I angled her face fully to mine. "You're insatiable. Do you know that?"

"I'll never get enough."

I had to hand it to Jericho, the man could warp a brain just right. My concern that it was wrong to take advantage had flown the coop several days ago. I didn't worry or wonder, didn't let myself get weighed down by the question of morality. The only thing I cared about was that she wasn't calling me Elijah anymore.

Smacking her bare ass, I angled my head toward the bathroom. "Go do what you need."

She crawled off the bed and disappeared into the small room. Closing the door behind her, she turned on the sink. It wasn't long before she came out.

A smile tipped the corner of my lip. "Come here."

Slowly, she closed the distance to the bed, her skin flush with color, her eyelids heavy with anticipation. I wondered what her personality had been before she was altered into a living doll that only lived for the cruel touch of a man.

"Lie over the bed, face down, ass out and spread your feet shoulder width apart on the floor."

She grinned.

My voice was dangerously low when I added, "Or, if you like, I'll let you suck me until I'm hard and take your ass like I know you love so much."

The grin tipped higher as she sank to her knees. Folding her hands together behind her back, she pushed out her breasts, her eyes closed and her head angled up as she waited.

Kneeling down beside her, I whispered into her ear, "Unfold your hands while you wrap those lips around me. I want you to play with your ass while you make me hard. You need to get both of us ready, love."

The shiver that coursed her body had my cock pressing against my pants. The blush that colored her

351

skin had my fingers clenching into fists. There was nothing she wouldn't let me do.

Stepping up, I unbuckled my belt, unbuttoned my pants and kicked them off my ankles. The belt buckle slapped heavy against the floor. Eve's eyes opened, her lips parting after I slid the head of my cock against the crease.

Still not fully hard, I pushed into the warmth of her mouth, my own hand working to stroke the base while her hips moved beneath her, those delicate fingers finding and exploring her ass. From my vantage point, I couldn't see the way she readied herself, but just knowing what she was doing had me hardening to full length as her lips slid over the surface of the skin.

Her moan was a vibration against my dick, her submission a balm that soothed the monster inside me. I didn't know what I would do to her if she ever rebelled, but I hoped a day would come where I found out.

Punishing her would be a game, a method of breaking her down again until she would gladly trade her life for just one more fuck.

"Stop," I growled out, my body coming to life so suddenly, I feared I'd come in her mouth before I fulfilled the promise I'd made to her. Breathless, my chest taut with a racing heart and labored lungs, I demanded, "Lie over the bed like I told you earlier. Wait for me with your hands tucked behind your back."

Eve pushed to her feet, her gait off center and stumbling as she made her way to the bed. The good little girl wanted it rough and she'd lost her balance just knowing it was coming.

Lying down, she took the position I'd demanded, her body patiently waiting, her back moving with heavy breath. She was still tight for as few times as I'd taken her ass. I only indulged her every so often, made it the sweet desert for all the full meals I'd made of her.

Moving behind her, I slowly slipped down to my knees, my hands brushing down the backs of her thighs until her cunt sat glistening and wet in front of my eyes. She trembled beneath my hands but didn't move or make a sound.

Opening my mouth, I blew against the slickened skin, my fingers tightening over the backs of her thighs when her hips moved just a touch. The moan that emanated from her throat when I ran just the tip of my tongue over her opening was making it difficult to keep going slow.

Pushing my tongue inside her body, I tasted the need that always poured out of her. My finger was still circling her clit as I stood to my full height. Dragging my hand up I used the slickness of her body to ready the tight hole of her ass.

"Tell me how it feels when I fuck you. I want to know every small detail. Confess for your Master."

With her cheeks pressed to the mattress, she clenched her eyes as my head pushed in. "It hurts, but feels good. I can't stand it. I need more. I'm so unclean. So unworthy."

Pulling out just a touch, I pushed inside deeper with my next thrust. Her words were garbled, her thoughts confused. Eve sounded like she was drugged, completely absorbed in the power of seduction.

"All the way. I want it all the way. Stop playing with me."

My lips kicked into a grin. Leaning down with only half my cock buried inside, I asked, "Do you want to fly free."

Her head nodded, her dark hair splayed over the white sheets of the bed. I indulged my adorable pet and wrapped a hand around her throat, squeezing until her lungs cut off, until her mouth opened to drag in air, but couldn't.

I shoved myself inside and her body tensed suddenly, my hand tightening even more as I began to thrust.

Men like me, we crave full control. It isn't enough to pretend a woman will bow to our every demand, isn't enough to believe that just because she fell to her knees, she's yours to do with as you please. We need to know that even the threat of death wouldn't stop her from surrendering to our dangerous desires.

Every so often, I let her take a breath. The mistakes of my past were still fresh in my mind. But that's the thing with this type of darkness, it creeps in and invades, slips over you like a caustic veil until you don't know anything but the pleasure of her body, the pleasure of her submission as you're riding her raw.

My climax was a burst of obsession, a driving need to dominate and control, a moment of temporary insanity that had my teeth clenched together, my fingers tight against her skin and my hips moving a heightened speed until she'd milked me dry of all my sin.

I didn't notice when her body went taut, but I did pay attention when it fell limp across my bed. Shaking her shoulders, I laughed at first thinking she was simply sated from the orgasm that had ravaged her body.

"Eve? Wake up. I'm not done with you yet."

A whisper of memory filtered through me, a night long ago that had chased me into the Church, that had left me with no choice than to swear myself off from sex for good.

"Eve?" I slapped her ass. She didn't react at all." "Eve!"

Rolling her over, I slapped at her cheeks before pressing my fingers against her pulse. There was nothing. Not a beat. Not a trickle of life. Nothing.

"Eve!" I bellowed, the world going black at the edges of my vision, panic setting in until I was lifting her fully from the bed. Her head fell back, her mouth opened and her eyes as blank as they were unseeing.

I dropped her and stepped back, my own pounding pulse a rush of thunder in my head.

"No," I breathed out. "I didn't. I haven't done it again."

Disbelief filled me, pain like I was being stabbed in the heart over and over until there was nothing left but mush. I couldn't suck in a decent breath, couldn't pull my eyes from the dead woman lying across my bed.

Slamming my hand down on her chest, I'd hit her so hard her body bounced over the mattress.

"Careful now, brother. I knew you were a monster, but I never figured you for one who beat on the dead."

My eyes lifted. Jericho leaned casually against the doorway, a smile across his face, his hands tucked casually in his pockets. Pinning me in his stare, he shook his head. "Guess I should have come sooner to pick up my property. Lord knows you can't be trusted."

Lunging forward, I had every intention to rip his head from his fucking shoulders, but I stopped short when he moved inside the room followed by two armed men.

"I wouldn't," he laughed. "Unless you'd like to join your toy."

My chest heaved as I stood naked, not giving a fuck that everything about me was plain to see for the men with their guns leveled at my chest.

"Did you do this?" I growled out. "What the fuck are you doing here?"

Jericho laughed. "I can't take the blame, Jacob. I wasn't the one who was just fucking her up the ass, but I guess that demon inside you wasn't quite done with his slaughter."

He paused, his eyes glistening with humor. "Then again, you always did play too rough."

Moving back, I snatched my pants from the floor, pulling them on quickly as I darted my gaze between Jericho and the two guns pointed in my direction.

"What will you do now, brother? You can't exactly call yourself a man of God while explaining to the police why there's a dead, horribly abused girl in your bed." He grinned. "What will the town say? Especially with your history."

Pulling on a t-shirt that I'd left draped on the post of my bed, I stood speechless. What would I do? How would I explain this?

My heart broke for the life I'd taken, and regardless of whether Jericho had a part in what happened with Eve, it was still my bedroom where her body would be found. I didn't know what the police would believe. I couldn't claim I was innocent of murder when I wasn't sure my hand around her throat hadn't been what killed her.

I wouldn't go to jail for this. I couldn't.

Death was a better option. Running became the only option.

"Is this what you wanted, you sick fuck? Was this what you've been driving me to the entire time?" My voice grew louder with every question. "Is this what you were hoping for when you drove this bitch to my door?"

He laughed, his head falling back before he straightened his gaze on me once again. "Ah, Jacob. I couldn't let you pretend any longer that you are a decent man. I'm your twin, remember. I can feel it when you're dying slowly on the inside."

"How the fuck did you get in here? How did you know?"

Rolling his eyes, he leaned against a wall. "Again with the endless questions. I'll ask my own: Haven't you figured out now that I've been watching you this entire time?"

Stepping closer, he folded his hands behind his back. "First that poor girl in the confessional, and now this? You have Satan living inside your parish, it seems. The death just doesn't stop coming."

My vision fogged over, the red driving me forward with violent hands, but the click of guns stopped me before I could reach my brother.

He grinned when I stared at him again. "I thought we already covered that threatening me was a bad idea. Really, Jacob. You should keep up."

There was nowhere I could turn at that point. Nothing I could do but escape the mess he'd made of my life - the mess I'd helped him carefully construct. Locked in place by anger, betrayal, disbelief and grief, I shook with the rage inside me that had no outlet.

357

"I tell you what, Jacob. Why don't you run along? Escape this town before the people find out about your particular tastes and I'll take care of my family member that you've killed. She'll get a good burial, and if you move quickly enough you won't be lowered into the ground beside her. I'd really hate to offend God by killing my twin. Even the Bible spells out how He feels about violence between brothers."

Moving close enough that I could feel the heat of his breath against my face, he said, "Just this once, though. If I see your face around here again, I can't make promises as to what my family will do to you."

His voice lowered so that only I could hear him. "I want you to live, brother. A long and miserable life knowing that the people you fuck have a tendency to turn up dead. What kind of monster does that make you?"

With that he stepped aside and his two men cleared the doorway while keeping their guns trained at my head.

I looked at Eve one last time before doing the only thing I could with so few options. My fingers clenched into fists, my nails cutting half moon circles into my skin. And after staring down at the evidence of the pure evil inside me, I grabbed the keys to my truck to run.

38

ELIJAH

There is a certain right by which we many deprive a man of life, but none by which we deprive him of death; this is mere cruelty
- Friedrich Nietzsche

Watching the dust kick up from the tires of my brother's truck, I laughed. Shoulders still shaking with my mirth, I crossed the room to sit on the bed next to Eve.

If Jacob hadn't panicked he would have noticed her pulse was still feather light, her nose drawing in enough air to add oxygen to her veins. I hadn't been sure it would work, wasn't positive he wouldn't see past the hoax that the beautiful woman had died, which was why I had to interrupt so quickly in order to refuse him the time to calm down.

"Is she..."

Eve's brother stood behind me, worry a wrinkle over his brow. "She's fine," I answered. "A little beat up. A little worse for the wear, but she's alive. God saw to it that we reached her in time and she will be rewarded for the part she played in helping our army."

359

Joshua's eyes lit with pride. "My sister was always strong."

Turning to him, I angled my chin toward the closet. "See what you can find for her to wear. We need to protect her modesty while taking her home. She should wake up within a few hours. We'll hide her in the woods until that time."

While he abided the request, Clemson lowered his gun, his hand gripping the stock with the butt of the rifle balanced on the floor. He reached up to brush the blond hair from his face, his brown eyes locked to mine. "What next, Elijah? What do you need me to do?"

"I want you to help Joshua carry his sister as far out as possible. The police will be swarming soon and we can't let them find her. Once she's able to walk again, you two head back to the compound. Richard and I will stay here to deal with Eunice and secure the parish."

He nodded as Joshua brought me clothes to use for Eve. After dressing her limp body, I planted a tender kiss on her chilled cheek. It was remarkable how well the mixture of herbs had worked. To any person not in their right mind, she appeared dead.

"Take care of her," I reminded her brother. "She is my wife, after all."

"Of course."

Lifting her in his arms, he carried her out with Clemson trailing behind them.

I gave the men a half hour to move deep into the woods before pushing up to my feet from the bed. Crossing the room, I pulled open a drawer to find a clerical collar. Lifting it from the confines of the dresser, I snapped it in place, my head shaking slightly at how easy the ruse had been.

There was only one task left to be accomplished.

While Joshua and Clemson headed left to backtrack into the woods, I turned right to where I knew Richard and Eunice were waiting. My stroll through the shadows of the yard hadn't taken too long, but I paused as I approached the location where I knew I would find them.

They weren't in easy view, and the noises filtering through the wind beneath the rumble of thunder told me Richard had taken that last taste while nobody was watching. I laughed at how the man was no better than a rabid dog.

First, I had to wait for Jacob to finish off Eve, and now I waited for Richard to finish off Eunice. I was starting to feel like a damn pimp minus the silver handled cane and flashy purple, velvet jacket.

Richard's breathing was rough and steadily building in speed. I didn't hear a sound out of Eunice, but I figured he was smart enough to cover her mouth or shove her face in the dirt. After a grunt filtered through the approaching storm, I figured he was done, but waited a minute or two for him to make himself decent.

Leaning my back against a tree, I called out, "Is it safe to approach?" Laughter bled into my voice.

His head poked around a tree and he smiled. "What's wrong? You growing squeamish?"

"Nope. Just wasn't in the mood to watch your ass bouncing. Bring her down here, will you?"

Flashing me a quick smile, he pulled Eunice from around the tree. Her expression was flat, her will to live gone. I guess it didn't take much for her to realize that God had stopped listening.

"You ready to go home, pretty girl? Because your maker is calling."

361

Tears sprang from her eyes. "Please," she begged.

I laughed. "There you go with that word again. Haven't you learned by now it doesn't do you a lick of good? Come on, sweetheart. You have to be smarter than that."

She finally looked up at me, her eyes rounding with surprise. "Father Hayle?" There was a note of hope in her voice I took pleasure in destroying.

"That's what everybody will believe in a few hours. It's too bad you won't be around to watch."

Jerking my head toward the parish, I barked out, "Let's go, Richard, let's get this chore over with."

Staying to the shadows wasn't hard, and we were fortunate for the storm blowing in. It kept the townsfolk inside the safety of their houses, far away from the parish where this last task would take place.

Breathing in the air thick with moisture and the electric buzz of lightning, I smiled like a lunatic. After today, my plans would be in place, the beginning of the end would have begun. Within a month's time, Hell on Earth would exist within a small, mountain town that the rest of the world had forgotten.

We made it inside the building just before the skies opened with pouring rain. Lightning flashed in the distance, its brilliance echoing through the large stained glass windows behind the pulpit.

"Where do you want her?" Richard asked, ignoring the way Eunice cried.

"Doesn't matter much to me," I glanced back and winked. "I've been in rectory all day, remember?"

Richard grinned. "This pew will do."

Shoving a large hand on the small woman's shoulder, he forced her into a seat. Not one to waste time, he reached behind his body to pull a hunting

362

knife from the sheath tucked into the waistband of his pants.

Eunice found what fight remained inside her when light flashed off the gleam of the large blade. Taking a place in front of her, but far enough that the spurt of arterial spray wouldn't touch my clothes, I locked my eyes to her face. It was too bad what fight she had left wasn't enough to get away from Richard.

"Any last words?"

Her red rimmed eyes looked up at me, pleading for me to step in and do something.

My lip twitched with humor. "Did you need me to give you Last Rites?"

"You're not a priest, you bastard!"

My grin tilted higher. "That's too bad, my dear, because you're no longer alive."

The knife slid easily across her throat, blood spurting from the artery as air gurgled up her trachea. Richard stepped back to avoid the puddle forming on the seat of the pew and the floor. The strong son of a bitch had damn near decapitated her.

Her head fell back and I could see the bones of her spine pushing out, the muscle beneath like meat shredded across the bone. It was too bad she had to die, Richard had thoroughly enjoyed her.

Once she was good and dead and her body no longer twitched against the seat, I lifted my eyes to the man that stood above her.

"You should make yourself scarce, Richard. The police will be here in an hour from when I call them. Take the woods back to the compound and keep an eye on Eve. Let the family know I'll be staying here for a while."

He nodded his head before slowly lumbering out of the sanctuary. I listened as the large door swung open and closed, the wind slamming it hard against the wood frame.

Biding my time, I took a tour of my kingdom, the parish that would be the center of our holy war. After an hour passed, I walked the halls of the small building. Once in Jacob's *former* office, I seated myself in his chair, kicked my feet up onto the surface of the desk and lifted the phone's receiver from its cradle.

My voice sounded terrified despite that fact that I didn't care.

"Hello, yes, this is Father Hayle at Our Lady of Serenity. You need to get down here fast. I found a body in the sanctuary."

It only took a half hour to hear sirens blazing down the road.

39

ELIJAH

(Two weeks later)

Men never do evil so completely and cheerfully as when they do it from religious conviction. – Blaise Pascal

The procession into Sunday Mass was a heavy hearted affair. The parishioners were weighed down by the crimes committed in their city, their faces angling this way and that to look upon the new members who had attended Mass for the first time today.

An air of distrust lingered like a thick cloud as the pomp and circumstance was carried out, as the hymns were sung and as the scripture verses were read. I watched from the pulpit, noticed how people had chosen seats to avoid being close to the confessional where Annabelle had blown herself away, or the center pew where Sister Eunice's body had been found.

Keeping my expression neutral, I cast a glance at Eve where she sat quietly off to the side of the church, her eyes gazing up at the stained glass windows behind me. Rather than the navy blue dresses the women normally wore, they dressed in ordinary outfits to blend in with the townsfolk.

The last scripture was read and it was time for the homily. I had the weight of their burdens fastened securely to my shoulders. It was my intent to ease their frustrations, to quiet the murmurs that God had forgotten them.

"Today's homily won't be my standard message. Not with the pain we've suffered recently. Not with the losses that have shocked our small town."

Lifting my gaze to the congregation I took a moment to make eye contact with the few people who stared ahead. Most had their heads bowed in contemplation.

"As you all know, we've experienced loss. Crimes have been committed that go against the will of God. We've been infected by evil, and I'm sure your hearts are as battered as mine."

Murmurs erupted across the sanctuary. Many nodded their heads in agreement, but a few men lifted their eyes that were narrowed in anger. They took pride in their town, in their homes, and the life they'd built here. They worried how they would protect their families from the tragedies that had befallen the parish.

They were ripe for the picking.

"I'd offer you kind platitudes if I felt that would ease your struggles, but as we all have seen, the tragedy grows worse despite our prayers. Evil has infected our world, and regardless of the devout lives we lead, regardless of our unshakeable faith in the power of the Almighty, that same evil has come upon us to take our young, to destroy our Sisters, to plague us while the demons laugh and carry on."

I paused and cleared my throat before lifting the volume of my voice higher. It echoed against the ceiling and walls with the spirit of my message.

"It would please my weary heart if, rather than offering an empty message and unanswered prayer, you will allow me to make a suggestion."

That got their attention. Not so much the women, but the men. They were desperate for any idea that would help them keep their families safe and make it possible to provide for the needs of their wives and children.

A smile tipped my lips as I stepped out from behind the pulpit and rounded the dark wood to lean against the front. Their silence was a heavy blanket stuffed full with anticipation. I let that silence punctuate my next statement.

Spoken clearly, my voice low and unhurried, I lifted my gaze to the congregation and said, "We need to take our town back."

The men made sounds of approval, their shoulders rolling back as their chests puffed out proudly. I saw the hope that lit their eyes and the glory they felt to hear a solution that, until now, had been denied to them.

"I want to introduce you all to the new people we've brought into the parish." Motioning with my hands, I directed the congregation's attention to my family members lining the side walls.

On cue they stepped closer, allowing the people of the town to see them fully, to witness the determination shining in their eyes.

"Like you, these people have suffered. They've seen their daughters dragged into sin, their sons lost to crime, their families destroyed by the demons that plague us all. And they're done with sitting idly by waiting for the salvation that Christ has promised us."

More murmurs erupted, the women now raising their eyes to look upon the others that were mirror images of them.

"The Bible said it clearly folks, the book told us what to expect at the end of times. It was said that the last days would be difficult times. That people would only love themselves and their money. That they would be boastful and proud. They would scoff at God and the children would disobey their parents like our beloved Annabelle."

A woman sniffled from the middle row, a man who had only looked at me with rage behind his eyes now easing his anger while putting an arm around his wife's shoulders. No doubt they were Annabelle's parents.

"It was said that people would reject God for the love of pleasure. That they would be puffed up and act like they were religious, but in truth they would reject the power that would make them godly."

A bark of humorless laughter flew from my lips. "Well, you know what I think about that? I think it's time we accept that power. I think it's time that we remember that we are God's people. And I think it's time we gather together to eradicate the sinners of this world, and we take back everything that has been stolen from us."

Pushing off from the pulpit, I walked to stand behind the altar.

My voice swelled with strength, the volume increasing until I was practically shouting. "I say that while taking the blood and body of Christ inside our bodies, that we remember who dwells inside us all and we use that strength to assemble God's army. I say we seek out the filthy demons that plague this world, and that we drag them back here to answer for their crimes! Our God is not a pushover. He's not a being that sits by and lets evil infect his world. He needs an army of those who believe in him to fight all the demons sent by Satan!"

Calming down, I breathed heavily, fighting the smile that pulled at my lips. My voice was far darker when I spoke my final lines. "If blood needs to be spilled, so be it. Because we, like the God that created us, the God that created us in HIS image, won't let our lives fall into the hands of the wicked!"

The men pushed to their feet, the women eventually standing beside them. They hollered and they whistled, they yelled and bellowed about how it was time. And as easy as it had been to create chaos in a rural, Appalachian town, I'd just convinced their people that violence was the only answer.

"This is just the beginning, folks. And by the end, the demons will have been run completely out of our town."

More shouts of approval, their hands coming together in applause of an answer they didn't know they were seeking.

A smile stretched my lips to see the fruits of my labors finally coming to fruition.

"I'll close the homily. We'll take Eucharist inside our bodies, and tomorrow we will assemble again to plan our holy war."

More applause boomed as I blessed the offering. And as they lined up to accept the body and blood of Christ, I looked into their gazes to see the insanity settling in.

Through their hands and numbers I would begin the chaos and slaughter.

Within an hour's time, those people returned to their homes, newfound pride the strength in their shoulders. The family left the parish to return to the compound save for one.

I stood by the pulpit and stared down at a woman who remained standing in the middle of the nave patiently awaiting my instructions.

Now that we were alone, I forced my voice into a soothing tone to talk to her.

"Have you missed me, my love?"

Eve's gaze traveled up to lock with mine, tears of happiness streaming down her cheeks. "Yes. I've missed you...and your sermons."

"I've missed you, too. I have one more matter to attend to before I can relieve you of the sin I know has built up inside you. I want you to run along to my room and wait for me on the bed."

Without question, she turned and disappeared down the long hallway that led to the rectory door.

Taking my time, I looked over the parish that would be the stage for my slaughter. I took in every pew, every corner, every relic and religious item. Satisfaction was the ember that sparked the flames of my scorching fire.

It would take time to acclimate the townspeople to violence, but it was fortunate that all I had was time.

Turning, I raised my gaze to the crucifix that hung over the stained glass windows and I raised my arms to my sides like the victor I was.

Laughter boomed from my chest and power flowed through me to know I'd succeeded. And with my eyes trained to the cross that in truth, had no meaning, I lifted my voice one final time.

Humor was the edge to my tone. My mirth a vibration through every word I spoke.

With a smile tilting my lips, I raised my arms even higher.

"Fuck off, God. This is my church now."

THE END

KEEP READING FOR A SNEAK PREVIEW OF BOOK TWO, FEAR THE WICKED.

SNEAK PREVIEW: FEAR THE WICKED

ELIJAH

It would take some finesse on my part to bend the morality of the citizens of the small town I'd inherited.

Every Sunday they showed up faithfully. And every Sunday I eased them into the violence I knew laid just beneath their skin. It was right there, an electric current waiting for the right outlet to be expressed. Time would pull them all into my mind, would set them on the path of salvation that the family had already begun to walk.

Most were readily pliant, others more difficult. My twin brother, Jacob, had done an impressive job losing the trust of his parishioners. During the week he went mad, he was rude to them, he'd distanced himself from them and he'd insulted them.

Especially the father of Annabelle Prete.

Just thinking about that poor girl had my shoulders shaking with soft laughter against the cheap, secretarial chair in Jacob's prior office.

Richard walked in and I tracked his short journey across the room, my eyes meeting his when he dropped his weight into a chair facing my desk. I pulled the clerical collar from my neck and threw it on the wood surface.

"How much longer, boss? The family is getting antsy."

"A few minutes at most. Eve is ready. The martyr that she is." More soft laughter was a vibration over my chest.

Grinning, Richard glanced over my shoulder toward the window at my back. "Joshua may have an issue with the example being made of his sister."

"Joshua knows," I explained, little concern in my voice for how the family members would react to the show.

Three months wasn't a long time in the grand scheme of things, but it was enough time to isolate the town. With the small farms and bevy of blue collar talents, it wasn't difficult to become a community without much need of outside assistance.

In response to my sermons, the citizens had slowly closed themselves off, had turned away from the televisions and internet, had burned whatever cultural items their children had acquired in an effort to blend in with the youth of the larger cities hundreds of miles outside our borders.

Isolation was key and to accomplish that, I'd spoken to the Diocese regarding the threat against the Mother and remaining Sisters at the convent following the discovery of Sister Joyce's body. There wasn't much left of her. It appeared she'd been abducted by the same psychopath that stole Eunice from the convent's doors, but rather than returning her to the Church, he must have left her to the wild animals along the lonely dirt road where she was discovered.

A smile had stretched my lips during that particular phone call, but fortunately they could only hear the feigned regret and sorrow in my voice.

The Diocese agreed that the remaining nuns should be removed to another convent far from our sleepy mountain, at least until the killer was caught. They'd left me in charge of the small congregation, alone and unsupervised, and then thanked me for the foresight to see to the nuns' safety.

Oh, yes, Father Hayle, you are so wise...

I'd laughed at the compliment. They were nothing but slack-jaws, all of them.

Richard's meaty hand ran through his brown hair. Shoulder length, it framed the parts of his face that his thick, long beard didn't hide. With broad shoulders and a rotund stomach bulging over the large buckle of his belt, Richard leaned back in his chair, kicked his legs out and crossed them at the ankles.

Unlike him, I was the sleek rural priest with black hair and blue eyes, shoulders as broad as Richards, but a stature standing a few inches taller. Built to seduce, my body was a weapon of deception as opposed to Richard's brute strength.

It was no surprise to me that the younger female parishioners - those girls that had come to an age where childhood was far behind - batted their eyes when I looked in their direction. In truth they were flirting with Jacob, not realizing I'd taken his place.

"Five minutes," Richard finally said, his voice as gruff as his appearance. "You should get in your robe and get out there." He paused, considering. "Not many people showed up from town."

"I didn't invite many," I explained as I pushed to my feet, grabbing my clerical collar to set it back in place. "And the cassock won't be necessary. This isn't Mass or anything formal, just a gathering of the family and the men from town that I think will be ready for this little treat. Once we have them convinced that it's normal, they'll help convince the other men. Once we have the men, we'll have the women, and once we have the women, we'll have the town." I winked at him. "Baby steps, Richard."

Nodding, he smiled and stood to walk with me into the hall, our booted steps against the ground heavy and in no hurry.

Turning the corner, we looked across the nave toward the sanctuary. Eve sat in a single, small chair to the left of the pulpit. Covered by a hooded black robe, she angled her head down so that you couldn't see her face.

Silent. Motionless. Both fearful and excited, Eve proved her worth to me every single day.

Anticipation was the tension across our shoulders.

"You think she'll scream?" Richard asked, a touch of humor in his question, his eyes darting between Eve and me.

My lips curled at the corners, desire crawling inside me as electric sparks beneath the skin.

"I know she will," I answered, "in both pain and perverse pleasure. And I can promise you, Richard, there is no other music like it."

375

2

EVE

But if I cast out demons by the Spirit of God, then the Kingdom of God has come upon you. Matthew 12:28

The ceremony would begin in a few minutes.

I listened to the people who gathered, felt compelled to peek out from beneath the hood just to know who would stand in attendance of the first *true* cleansing. But no matter how badly I wanted to know who would stand in witness, I kept my head bowed and out of sight, just as I'd been instructed.

Elijah warned me that it would hurt. Not as bad as the brand I wore on my shoulder, but more than what he did to me in bed. Yet, I didn't fear what was coming. Only because I knew that what would follow would be a release of pressure like I'd never known.

Wickedness is only relieved with pain. And pain is a balm to the sinner's soul. It flays you open, settles inside, and shreds you until there is nothing left.

You're meat, pulled open and tenderized while the pain whistles across you. But once you're clean, once every last ounce of the sin you carry is lifted and banished into the ether, you're free. A bird flying high.

A dolphin gliding through water. You are lost in a moment of pure bliss that is a comforting hug in the warm morning sun.

Only Elijah could give that to me.

Created. Molded. Shaped and formed I was what he wanted. I was what he alone knew existed inside me. But for all his power, all his wisdom and his strength, he was never able to remove the doubt I carried.

I loved him and feared him. Worshipped him and despised him. I couldn't live without him, even while knowing he would one day kill me.

The shuffling of feet quieted, the soft thud of bodies settling over the pews, and the sharp clatter of keys slapping against the wood from where the rings hung on the parishioners' belts.

Only one set of footsteps could be heard. Low and rhythmic, they approached the altar and pulpit, beats measured by a steady gait, the powerful and seductive walk of a predator.

"Good afternoon, gentlemen. I thank you for gathering together with me today."

Elijah's voice was a low hum across the room, a soothing melody in a rich tenor, a tone that was as soft as it was fierce. My heart sped at the sound of it.

"I'll start off this meeting with an explanation to those few who were invited. You'll notice there are no women or children in attendance, and the only people here tonight are the few men who I didn't doubt were ready to protect the serenity of their small town."

Grumbles of understanding and murmurs of approval were the harmony accompanying Elijah's words.

His manner of speaking was casual, a group of men discussing simple politics. There was no rush to the point, no emotions beyond the soothing laziness of a well-trained voice. I fell easily into the hypnotic lull of a peaceful summer afternoon just like the others.

Silence for only a moment. Broken when Elijah spoke again.

"I had a female parishioner approach me this week, gentlemen. She came to confess, came to speak in earnest about the sins she'd committed outside of town. I know this woman well, as do many of you. And it pains me to find that she's fallen for the Devil's seductive temptation."

He paused, his voice deepening. "She's possessed, it appears. Possessed by a demon that could infect your children...your wives."

More murmurs erupted, a few sharp inhalations of breath that exposed the shock felt by a few of the men in attendance.

"We owe it to this woman to help her. More than that, we owe it to ourselves to protect our families from the threat staring us in the face." Another drawn out pause before, "May I speak frankly, Mr. Prete?"

The man's response wasn't oral, but he must have given some indication that Elijah could go on.

"We haven't always seen eye to eye have we, Mr. Prete?"

Another silent answer.

"And I think most of the people in this room know why. But for those who don't, I'll state the facts of the situation as delicately as possible. Annabelle Prete was a good girl. She was a believer in the Almighty, a young woman with a bright future ahead of her. She

378

made her father proud and the town right along beside him. She was going somewhere."

I could hear Elijah pacing slowly to my right, his steps the only sound breaking apart the silence pregnant with trepidation and hesitant interest. It would have smothered me beneath its heavy weight if not for Elijah moving around.

"Annabelle is dead, and between what was said to me in her last confession and what was sent to me by an unknown person outside of town, I'm concerned that the spirit infecting the woman seated next to me was the same one that infected Annabelle."

His steps stopped.

"I won't show the pictures, but I can tell you they were indecent, immoral, and utterly shocking. They were porn, images of a young girl who didn't know she'd lost her way. Disturbing as they were, they only verified what the young woman said to me before she died. More disturbing than that was my behavior toward Mr. Prete following the death of his daughter. I was so full of righteous fury and intolerable regret following Annabelle's death that I'd forgotten the discussion I'd had with Mr. Prete. At least until he reminded me."

I remembered the girl's death, recalled that it changed Elijah in a way I couldn't understand. While I'd always feared the power inside him, I'd been shown a softness I never knew existed. The first few days in the parish, he'd tended to me with a gentle hand. Resisted me until I'd cried believing I'd been rejected.

When he resumed his attentions on me, the first few times had been a caress of healing hands and sensual teeth. But after that girl died, after he witnessed a woman lost to the demons that plagued her, his attentions on me had changed.

The pain was exquisite, yet agonizing. His fear that I'd be lost as well driving him to exhaustion as he worked his magic inside me, as he battled and fought the sin that filled me until I was practically screaming.

Elijah had changed from one man into another. I couldn't understand why that change frightened me. Perhaps I was coming to life for once in my life, or perhaps I was being dragged back into the veil of ignorance and doubt that had always consumed me.

"I want to apologize to you, Mr. Prete. For both my weakness and my cruelty. I'm sure having lost one of your daughters, you can understand the pain I was feeling."

Mr. Prete wasn't much of a talker and it drove me a little mad that I couldn't see what was happening in the room.

"I was unable to save that young woman from whatever sickness plagued her. I was unable to guide her away from whatever monster it was that stole her virtue and took pictures of the crime he committed against her - the pictures he thought necessary to send to me."

My breath caught. I knew what was coming. Elijah's voice grew in strength as he spoke his next words.

"I couldn't save Annabelle, but I can save this woman. However, I'll need a strong body around me, a group of men whose faith in the Lord is without doubt. I need prayers, gentlemen, while I exorcise the demon ensnaring this young woman. Can you offer that to me despite what you see? Can you bless me and this suffering child of God with your participation and understanding?"

The men in attendance spoke, each acknowledging that they would give Elijah whatever help he needed. Faceless voices in different pitches and tones, each one resolute in their agreement that my sin needed to be cleansed.

"We'll begin," Elijah announced. "Eve. Please walk to me."

My legs barely held me as I stood, but I managed to cross the distance between us, was able to remain on my feet at Elijah's side. I wondered if the pain would be excruciating.

"This may shock you, gentlemen, but I believe desperate times call for desperate measures. She has the demon of lust inside her. Its sharp claws are entangled in her heart, its razor sharp teeth embedded in her soul. It's stolen her virtue and sanity, her ability to think clearly in the face of temptation."

His hand touched my shoulder. I lifted my eyes to see the men sitting in attendance. My gaze stilled when it locked on the faces of my father and brother. There was no fighting the tears that fell.

"Eve," Elijah said, "We'll need you to confess before we can drive the demon from you." His voice softened. "Can you do that for me?"

I almost laughed. He'd never asked me that question before. Normally he demanded a confession out of me.

"Yes," I finally answered.

The fabric of the hood slid from my head as he removed it, the cloth sash tying the robe around my body loosened until the robe itself was pulled from my shoulders. When they witnessed my nudity, some

381

murmured in surprise while others stared at the parts of me that brought on my shame.

Fully exposed, I was the spectacle of a woman's deception.

"Calm down, gentlemen, I know this is uncomfortable. But if we are to help this woman we need to stand in witness of her shame and degradation. We need to believe in the Father who will lend us his strength in casting out the evil that holds her captive. We need to look upon her with the eye of pity rather than that of lust. It is just a naked body, one with a natural purpose that has been used to the Devil's advantage.

The hum of conversation grew quiet and I was directed to stand between two large posts, my face turned to the stained glass window, my arms bound above my head and to the sides of my body - cuffs attached to the posts that would secure me in place.

A shudder of doubt rolled through me, most likely the demon shaking beneath the knowledge that it would be expelled.

My head fell forward.

"Confess, Eve. Tell God your sins so that your penance will cleanse them from your body."

More murmurs of surprise erupted just before the strike of a whip cut into my back. The scream that burst out of me was unholy, my tears hot and steadily flowing as I forced myself to speak.

"I've had disgusting thoughts," I breathed out, trying and failing to add any strength to my voice. The burning line across my back felt like it seeped beneath my skin to set my lungs on fire. I couldn't draw in air, could barely think past the sting of purification. "Thoughts that no person should have."

Another strike and I screamed again, my throat torn by the sheer volume, my jaw aching from how wide I stretched my lips. My wrists shook in the cuffs that held them, my legs giving out until I couldn't find the ability to push to my feet again. Tears dropped to the floor beneath me, small, wet puddles of evidence that could be used against me. Those same tears soaked into my lips, the salt flavor of my agony coating my tongue.

Through sobs, I called out, "I've wanted immorality, craved sensuality, exposed my body and tempted men. I let one touch me. Let him press his naked body against mine." A terribly deep sob racked me. "He wasn't my husband."

The next strike of the whip cut through the cries of surprise and grunts of disapproval from the audience. Voices picked up, prayers being repeated as the men witnessed my shame. I wasn't sure my knees would hold me much longer.

Memory took me back to that night on the road, the night I'd willfully shown my body to a man who wasn't Elijah. For months I'd believed he'd forgiven me, but in a state of panic about my eternal soul, Elijah had remembered within the last few days, all because I'd confessed what happened that night had become a fantasy.

Not the man. Never him. Just the way he'd controlled me.

"I invited the man to look at me," I breathed out before the whip came down again. The snap of leather caused my body to jump. The burning strike against my skin driving the breath from my lungs. My voice cracked and splintered beneath the strain of pure torture.

Euphoria settled in as I hung limp from the cuffs that bound me, and I felt free once again, slickness evident between my thighs.

The whip stopped, its weight dropped to the floor at my feet.

Elijah stood silent for only a few seconds before turning to the audience and claiming, "Gentlemen, the purge of evil has begun."

3

JACOB

Darkness doesn't settle, it consumes.

Flames of burning onyx, smoke full of mortal dread. Talons that tear you limb from limb until you're only a shadow of what you once had been.

I know darkness, and darkness knows me. I'd stared into its eyes and breathed its noxious poison. I'd supped on the sensual torment of every girl who'd crossed my bed. They scream until the night is cut through by the violence in their voice, but they keep coming back, one by one, begging to do it again.

They weren't her, though - weren't Cassandra or Eve. Sure, they begged and cried like the other two, but not for me to keep going. They wanted me to stop. Fear overtook them, the pain unsettling, but I never listened, never cared, never fell for the pathetic pleas and moans.

They knew what they were walking into when they climbed into my bed.

My heart was absent after the loss of Eve, but I hadn't been knocked down by her death. I was brought to life. I was charged by vengeance and the patience of biding my time.

Because if the monster inside couldn't be glutted by the sadism in bed - if I could no longer grow hard over the trembling bodies of the weak and desirous, the temptresses who keep me enraptured - then that vengeance I needed would be the only escape, the only balm, the last wicked act that would console me.

It was only a matter of time...

If you are interested in reading additional books by Lily White or would like to know when new books are being released, Lily White can be found on:
Facebook, Instagram and
Twitter

Join the Mailing List!

If you are interested in receiving email updates regarding additional books by Lily White or would like to know when new books are announced or being released, join the mailing list via this link.
http://eepurl.com/Onoeb

Join the Facebook Fan Group!

If you are interested in receiving exclusive previews for upcoming novels, or to participate in giveaways, join the fan group for Lily White Books.
FAN GROUP LINK

Follow Lily on BookBub!

https://www.bookbub.com/profile/lily-white